T0247852

GRAVEYARD
OF
DEMONS

BAEN BOOKS by LARRY CORREIA

SAGA OF THE FORGOTTEN WARRIOR
Son of the Black Sword
House of Assassins
Destroyer of Worlds
Tower of Silence
Graveyard of Demons

THE GRIMNOIR CHRONICLES
Hard Magic
Spellbound
Warbound

MONSTER HUNTER INTERNATIONAL
Monster Hunter International
Monster Hunter Vendetta
Monster Hunter Alpha
The Monster Hunters (omnibus)
Monster Hunter Legion
Monster Hunter Nemesis
Monster Hunter Siege
Monster Hunter Guardian (with Sarah A. Hoyt)
Monster Hunter Bloodlines

The Monster Hunter Files (anthology edited with Bryan Thomas Schmidt)

MONSTER HUNTER MEMOIRS
Monster Hunter Memoirs: Grunge (with John Ringo)
Monster Hunter Memoirs: Sinners (with John Ringo)
Monster Hunter Memoirs: Saints (with John Ringo)
Monster Hunter Memoirs: Fever (with Jason Cordova)

THE NOIR ANTHOLOGIES (edited with Kacey Ezell)
Noir Fatale
No Game For Knights
Down These Mean Streets

THE AGE OF RAVENS (with Steve Diamond)
Servants of War

DEAD SIX (with Mike Kupari)
Dead Six
Swords of Exodus
Alliance of Shadows
Invisible Wars: The Collected Dead Six (omnibus)

Gun Runner (with John D. Brown)

STORY COLLECTIONS
Target Rich Environment
Target Rich Environment Volume 2

To purchase any of these titles in e-book form, please go to www.baen.com.

GRAVEYARD
OF
DEMONS

LARRY
CORREIA

A Baen Books Original

Baen Publishing Enterprises
P.O. Box 1403
Riverdale, NY 10471
www.baen.com

ISBN: 978-1-9821-9373-7

Cover art by Kurt Miller

First printing, November 2024

Distributed by Simon & Schuster
1230 Avenue of the Americas
New York, NY 10020

Library of Congress Cataloging-in-Publication Data

Names: Correia, Larry, author.
Title: Graveyard of demons / Larry Correia.
Description: Riverdale, NY : Baen Publishing Enterprises, 2024. | Series: Saga of the forgotten warrior series ; 5
Identifiers: LCCN 2024026489 (print) | LCCN 2024026490 (ebook) | ISBN 9781982193737 (hardcover) | ISBN 9781625799876 (ebook)
Subjects: LCGFT: Fantasy fiction. | Novels.
Classification: LCC PS3603.O7723 G73 2024 (print) | LCC PS3603.O7723 (ebook) | DDC 813/.6—dc23/eng/20240621
LC record available at https://lccn.loc.gov/2024026489
LC ebook record available at https://lccn.loc.gov/2024026490

Printed in the United States of America
10 9 8 7 6 5 4 3 2 1

To Jack Clemons

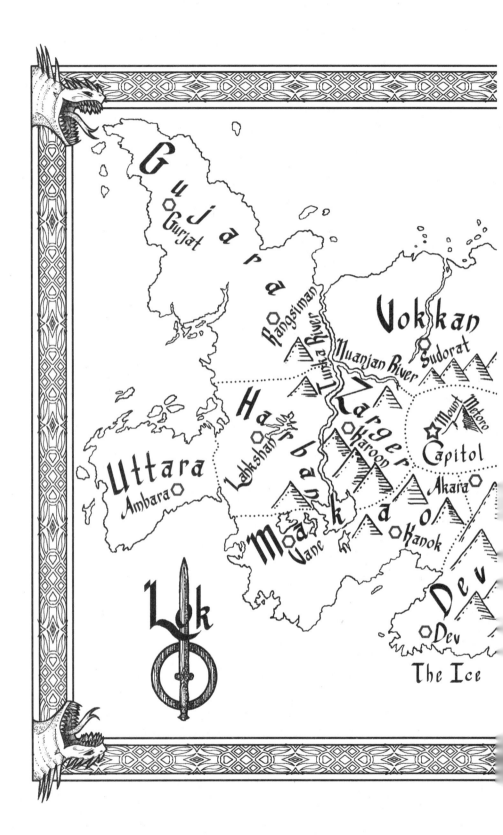

Goda

Vadal

Sarnobat

Vadal City

Marta Ban River

Red Lake

Apura

Warun

Thao

Somsak

Jharlang

Kharsawan

Neeramphorn

Guntur

Akara River

Nansakar River

akula

Akershan

The Hall of the
Protectors

Coast

Fortress

MaDharvo

Chapter 1

~~~~~~~~~

"Gather 'round, children, to hear the saga of Ashok Vadal, the Forgotten's holy warrior, who was chosen by the almighty gods and sent to save our kind from Law and demon alike!"

In the desert south of Akara, a group of casteless were clustered around a tiny campfire for warmth, eager to listen to the storyteller spin tales. They were mostly women and children, which meant their men had probably gone off to join the rebels. These scrawny, malnourished untouchables had clearly heard the elder's story many times before, yet still seemed to hang on his every word.

"Ashok's true name, his casteless name, was Fall, for he came from the north where there are giant trees that turn to gold and fall off when the seasons change. He was a casteless boy, tiny as some of you are now, and his obligation was to clean the floors of the first caste's mansions, scrubbing them stones till his hands bled and his fingernails fell off. In Great House Vadal he lived. They're the richest of the rich, where the whole men eat all they want and their endless river is clean and tastes like honey, except little Fall got none of that. He was poor, same as us, starving, living in a barracks shack over a pig wallow, working all day and getting bit by fleas all night. Let it be known Fall was a true casteless! No different than us!"

1

This particular audience understood that life of hardship well, for it was the only thing they'd ever known...at least until the horror of the Great Extermination had come along to make the harsh traditions of old seem merciful in comparison. Labor and hunger were preferable to mass murder.

"When the bearer of Vadal's magic black sword died it caused the whole men to fear, for the black swords are the strongest magic in the big wide world, and without that magic, great houses get crushed by the others! Like a bug!" The old man stomped the ground with his bare foot for emphasis. "The whole men of Vadal needed a new bearer so they could keep fighting their endless wars. Only black swords have a mind of their own. They only pick the bravest, the strongest, the most fearsome of all warriors. Vadal's best tried to pick up the sword, but they all failed, and when they did it punished them for it! Arms, legs, heads, sliced right off!"

"Serves them right!" shouted a listener, for the non-people loved the rare times their cruel masters suffered for their hubris.

"As the whole men died, poor little Fall worked his fingers to the bone scrubbing their blood from the mansion's floors. And they just kept coming. Hundreds, no thousands, of Vadal's mightiest got cut, for the sword was very unhappy. Then one night it was just Fall, doing his job, scrubbing that floor, and the terrifying black sword was there nearby." He lowered his voice to a theatrical whisper. "The sword called to him..."

Even though they knew what was coming next, the casteless waited, eager, to hear the result.

"And little Fall dared to pick it up..." The old man paused for a long time for dramatic effect. The littlest casteless held their breath. When the only sound was the crackling of the fire and the noise of the cold desert wind, he suddenly roared, *"The black sword let him!"*

The casteless cheered and hooted.

"That changed everything. They say we casteless are nothing. They spit on us and starve us and make us live in the mud and now they condemn us all to die, but on that night, that sacred night, a little casteless boy showed a great house he was better than them all! Better than their warriors! Better than the first caste! Fall was picked to be the bearer of a black sword, and bearers are mighty indeed!"

In that ecstatic moment, carried along by the story, the filthy youngsters were probably imagining themselves going from the life of hunger, fear, and rags they were used to, to one of power, wealth, and authority in an instant. A few of the little ones took up sticks from the store of firewood and began to swing them about like they were a terrifying black sword, because even the lowest of the low could still dream of something more.

"Oh, but the first caste couldn't bear it! A non-person with one of their precious magic swords? Such indignity! Such shame! They despise us and use us and sneer at us and work us to death, but they'd never ever share their power with our kind. They need us hungry and begging, not proud and armed, and this was more than twenty years ago, long before the Capitol decried we all needed to die. The Capitol has always been mean and evil, blaming us for all their problems, but it was a little kinder back then. Today, the Capitol is consumed by cruelty."

The children hissed and spit at the description of their hated betters. The little ones might not have understood the ways of the world yet, but they all knew that the first caste had condemned every casteless in the world to death. That was why they were here now, hiding in a canyon of rocks and sand, rather than the barracks they had always called home. Casteless quarters were places of disease and squalor, but at least they'd had a roof overhead.

The storyteller grinned at their rebellious spirit and continued his tale. "To keep Fall's triumph secret, the Great House Vadal wizard scrubbed Fall's mind clean as Fall did those mansion's floors. They took away his memory and used their magic to trick poor Fall into thinking he was and had always been a whole man. They named him Ashok Vadal, and pretended he was one of them all along. Unwitting Fall became Ashok, Protector of the Law, fearsome and terrifying, and for the next twenty years he did the Capitol's evil work, never knowing no better."

"They say Ashok's killed a thousand men!" one of the older children shouted.

"Yes," the storyteller affirmed. "Probably even more, because back then he didn't bother to count our kind. And not just men, but he's fought all manner of dark things in every corner of Lok, demons and ghosts and wizards and horrors that time's forgot. Ashok became the greatest killer the world had ever known. Fall cleaned blood. Ashok spilled it. Little did anyone realize that this servant of the Law wasn't a whole man at all, but one of us. Until one day, while fighting *two demons at once,* a defiant casteless broke the Law, took up a spear, and saved Protector Ashok's life! And deep down, seeing that courage from one of our kind reminded Fall who he *really* was. The wizard's spell began to break! Fall began to remember what had been *forgotten.*"

"Baba says the Forgotten has come back," whispered a little girl reverently.

The storyteller looked around the camp of refugees conspiratorially, as if they weren't already breaking the Law just by continuing to exist, and there might be masked Inquisitors hiding in the shadows, waiting to pounce at the mention of their illegal religion. The casteless could not know that there was one unseen listener to their story, who was secretly watching them from the bluffs above, but he was certainly no Inquisitor.

"Yes, child. Your baba speaks true. The forgotten gods have returned! Even as Ashok was deceived to fight against the very gods who had blessed him, those same gods sent a bolt from the heavens to anoint a warrior caste girl in the west, so that she could serve as their Voice. I'm told her name is Thera and the Forgotten speaks through her today. She's our prophet, and gives us the revelations that'll teach us how to free us from the tyranny of the Law. The gods also sent a priest to serve her—another casteless like us, but wiser than any of the judges—to teach our people the old ways again. He is called Keta."

"The Keeper of Names!"

"That's him, boy, and all the names of all of us casteless will surely get written in Keta's holy book, so that we may dwell in the Forgotten's paradise forever. It was Keta who taught Ashok his true name and who he really was. It was Keta who convinced him to join with the Voice. Together they gathered the Sons of the Black Sword—fierce warriors who love freedom and the gods more than the great houses they were born into—and together they went to war against the Law. Our hero's heart is pure, so once he knew the gods were real, Fall didn't hesitate to rise up and fight to save us!"

As Ashok listened, hidden in the darkness beyond the reach of their of firelight, the absurdity of that description of events made him shake his head. There was no purity in his heart, only a shard of black steel that should have killed him. The broad strokes of the tale may have been accurate, but his journey from

Law enforcer to Law breaker had been much more complicated than the old man made it out to be. It wasn't as if he'd woken up one morning and decided to forsake all he'd ever known to embrace wild rebellion. He'd been forced into it, bound by an unbreakable oath, and then it had been an exceedingly difficult path to follow, even for a man of his focus.

But as Keta had once told him, a simple people required simple legends.

"Remember, children, even as we hide in this wilderness, our gods watch over us. The great fire that recently split the sky apart was a sign of the gods' anger against the Capitol. The gods have called Ashok to smite our enemies on our behalf. He has fought entire armies by himself, legions of demons, and even other bearers and their black swords, and each time the Forgotten's Warrior has been victorious. Ashok has even been killed and come back to life!"

Several of the casteless—adult and child both—reflexively touched the tiny hook-shaped charms they wore on necklaces as the storyteller said that, and Ashok marveled at how fast a symbol that captured the imagination could spread across the world.

"As the gods will it, the Sons of the Black Sword will defeat the wicked Capitol, the Law will be thrown down, and we will be accepted, not as non-people, but as whole men, allowed to live free!"

Ashok was far from their camp, only able to eavesdrop because of the Heart of the Mountain aiding his senses. He had been leading Horse along the edge of a cliff when he had smelled their fire and, weary, had paused to rest. It was good that the dangerous beast had learned to instinctively tell when Ashok required him to remain silent. Usually Horse would have snorted and stomped his displeasure if they paused too long, and such an unexpected sound coming from the ledge above would probably have startled the refugees and caused them to flee across the desert, thinking the Great Extermination had finally caught up with them. The casteless were by nature skittish, and that behavior had been learned long before it had become the Law to kill them on sight.

One of the casteless mothers spoke. "You have big dreams, Guru, but right now we just want to live through the rest of winter. The warriors from Akara who killed our kin and burned our huts are searching the desert for us again."

"Don't be afraid. With Fall on our side, we will survive."

Ashok pondered on that prediction for a moment. With the seemingly insurmountable challenges and terrible threats arrayed before him, that was not a promise he could make to them. It would take a miracle to save them all.

He gently coaxed Horse away from the ledge, moving quietly so as to not frighten the casteless. They'd been through enough already.

Canda was full and bright tonight. The moonlight enabled him to keep traveling without danger of Horse stumbling and breaking a leg. The magnificent white stallion had been Ashok's only companion for the last month as he'd made the difficult journey across the cold southern reaches of Lok, from the mountains of Akershan to the high deserts of Akara. Through bitter winds, hail, and the occasional snowstorm. Now he would continue west toward the city of Kanok, because that was where the enigmatic Mother Dawn had told him he would find Thera.

Being imprisoned on the isle of Fortress had kept Ashok away from his duties for far too long. It was his obligation to keep Thera safe, and that responsibility had been neglected. If she was in danger now, it was his fault. He would destroy anyone who threatened the woman he loved, but in the meantime the uncertainty of not knowing what had happened to her gnawed at him. After his escape from Fortress he had returned to find their rebellion was in shambles and their hideout besieged. Keta was dead, killed in battle by another bearer. The location of the rest of the Sons of the Black Sword was unknown. Though surely if the rebellion's army was still intact, it was doubtful they would be with Thera in Kanok, for that city was the center of Great House Makao's power. In a direct confrontation against such an overwhelming number of troops, the Sons would certainly be destroyed.

Thera had rarely spoken to Ashok about that part of her life, but Kanok had been Thera's home during her miserable arranged marriage. It was doubtful she would have returned to that place willingly.

So Ashok continued west, into the unknown.

Chapter 2

The next morning, Ashok sensed demon in the air.

That was unlikely, for he was a long way from hell. It was true that demons would sometimes travel far inland, swimming up a river, but they were several days' journey from any water deep enough to conceal a demon.

Demonic flesh and bone were infused with magic, but Ashok had no gift for sensing the presence of magic, like his old sword master, Ratul, or the tracker Gutch. They had no smell. They rarely made a sound. Neither the black steel blade at his side, nor the shard buried in his heart, were sending him any sort of warning of impending danger yet.

Except a sea demon had a certain presence about them, a sort of dangerous energy that made the hairs on your neck stand up. That feeling of danger was on the desert wind. It reminded him too much of the ocean.

Before breaking camp, Ashok took his armor from Horse's pack and dressed for battle. Traveling in armor was uncomfortable, and might draw unwanted attention, but he had not survived this long by denying his instincts.

Ashok rode westward through a land of pale sand and flat red rocks. Settlements of any size were scarce in this rugged region and even rarer away the trade roads that he had been purposefully avoiding. He was a wanted criminal, but was weary of fighting warriors who were simply trying to fulfill their duty. He had killed enough honorable men already.

The bits of civilization he had come across in this part of the desert had been isolated worker-caste settlements. Armed with the stack of Capitol bank notes he had taken from the Cove, he was able to trade his money for their supplies. Ashok had never had much use or understanding of money, for that was the way of the worker caste, but he got by. The workers didn't care if he had the proper traveling papers or if he had an official reason to be in these lands. They only cared if his notes were real. And the workers would hold them up to the sun, squinting, to make sure the seal of the Capitol Bank wasn't some forgery. This was a far different manner of traveling across the continent from when he'd been a Protector and could simply claim whatever resources he required along the way. People didn't like having their property confiscated without compensation, but back then Ashok hadn't cared. He'd been a Protector. What was the discomfort of the lower castes when compared to preserving the sanctity of the Law?

As a criminal he could simply taken whatever he wanted from them. After all, that was what criminals did when the forces of the Law were absent. But Ashok would never lower himself to such barbarity. He had forsaken the Capitol, but he wasn't the villain they portrayed him to be. Even a man bereft of Law could maintain a code, and from what he'd seen since joining a rebellion, those without the Law were often far more honorable that the judges in the Capitol.

He spied a workers' settlement in the distance, consisting of perhaps a dozen small homes made from stacked stones, some conical buildings of unknown purpose, corrals for livestock, and coops for chickens. This discovery was fortunate, as his canteens were empty and he'd run out of rations two days ago. He'd let Horse drink all the water from the last seep they'd found. Forage was scarce here, and time spent hunting was time spent not finding Thera. His stomach ached and his limbs felt heavy.

Except Ashok wasn't fool enough to risk his mission over something as trivial as dehydration or hunger—he had once proven he could starve for a year and not die—so before approaching the settlement, he called upon the Heart of the Mountain to sharpen his senses in order to check for any potential threats.

First he strengthened his eyes. As the distant shapes became clear he was disappointed to see a single banner of the warrior caste flying there. It was a white flag with black mountains upon it. *Devakulans.* They were a stubborn, dour people, but produced hardy fighters who would surely be too prideful to let a criminal pass without a fight.

That was disappointing, as he would have to go around and remain hungry a bit longer. Horse would be angry at him, but Horse could graze on the desert scrub grass enough to live. Besides, Horse was always angry.

Then Ashok turned the Heart of the Mountain's magic from his eyes, toward his ears. As his vision returned to normal, his hearing became incredibly sensitive.

Screams of terror.

Switching back to the vision of a hawk and scanning the sands around the village, he noticed distant figures running for their lives from a misshapen black shadow.

Demon.

"Trespass," Ashok growled.

When a sea demon went on a rampage, it would range up and down a coastline for weeks at a time, killing until it ran out of things to kill, gorging itself on bodies until it needed to vomit them back up so that it could make room to eat more, and stopping only when its bloodlust was sated enough to return to hell, or it was killed. A violent response was mandatory, for their presence was an affront to the Law.

Except enforcing that Law was no longer Ashok's place.

Every warrior in that village was obligated to kill him on sight. The workers would be happy to take his bank notes, and then even happier to inform the Inquisition about his location afterward in order to collect a reward, conveniently leaving out the part where they'd aided a known criminal. These warriors had likely been the ones to put the local casteless to the sword and these workers had probably done nothing to stop them. Why should they? After all, they were only obeying the Law. Ashok owed them nothing. He was a Protector no more. Why should he risk his life for people who'd see his rebellion crushed, his friends murdered, and his woman executed for witchcraft?

That hesitation lasted less than the span of two steady heartbeats.

"Go, Horse!"

Horse didn't understand what was happening, but he always sensed when Ashok decided it was time to fight, and the eager beast never needed encouragement to run. Horse galloped toward the danger.

Warriors never used cavalry against demons, for no animal would willingly approach a sea demon, no matter how brave it was. Even war elephants panicked when they saw one of the soldiers of hell. Ashok suspected Horse might actually be the one animal in Lok confrontational enough to be the exception to that rule, but he couldn't risk losing control of his mount once Horse smelled what they were running toward. So a hundred yards from the edge of the village, Ashok leapt from the saddle and landed in the sand.

Keeping his sword sheathed, he sprinted toward the sounds of battle. Better to not let the demon comprehend the danger it faced until it was too late. Within the narrow tangle of homes there was only space sufficient for narrow footpaths. Fleeing workers crashed into him because their eyes were fixed on the danger behind them. Ashok shoved them aside and kept moving. He passed children who were crying for their mothers and panicking animals desperately trying to escape their pens. He heard a warrior bellowing orders, followed by the thud of steel against nearly impenetrable hide. That would be his target, and Ashok ran toward it as fast as he could.

There was an open area in the center of the homes. In the middle was a stone well. Across the sandy clearing were strewn the dead and dying, worker and warrior both. Arms and legs and heads had been ripped off. Torsos were missing big chunks from savage bites. Blood was dripping down the walls. All of this terrible brutality had occurred over the span of only a few minutes.

Such was the way of demons.

The stone wall of the home next to him came apart as a warrior was violently hurled through it. Through the cloud of swirling dust, Ashok spotted his foe. Demons came in all shapes and sizes. This one was shorter than the others he'd fought, barely a match to Ashok's imposing height, yet it was abnormally wide shouldered, with a chest big as an ox, stumpy legs solid as tree trunks, and thick arms that dangled nearly to the sand. Like all the others he'd fought, though, its hide was sleek and black.

The demon was turned away from him, occupied fighting six desperate warriors. Their thrusts bounced harmlessly off its skin. With an arm as long as their spear shafts, it swatted one of the warriors down, then lunged forward to stomp one wide, flat foot down on his helmet. The warrior's head popped like stepping on a grape.

Ashok drew his sword.

The demon turned his way. Like the others Ashok had encountered, this one had a featureless lump of a head, so broad its skull seemed to melt into its vast shoulders, almost as if it had no head at all. Demons possessed no eyes, yet they could still see somehow. It had a single wide line for a mouth, which slowly opened, far too wide, to reveal rows of black razor teeth.

The creature must have sensed the danger in his sword. Demon and black steel—two conflicting forces that could not exist in the same place. The presence of one meant the other had to be destroyed.

It stood perfectly still, studying Ashok for a moment, as the brave Devakulans continued to futilely stab it in the back. In addition to being unrelenting instruments of destruction, demons were also nearly immune to mortal weapons. Even with the finest steel, only the luckiest of hits from the strongest arm had any chance of piercing their incredibly tough hide...

None of that concerned Ashok. "Retreat, warriors," he ordered with the voice of a man used to being in command. "Get these people to safety. Leave this thing to me."

The sudden lull took the Devakulan warriors by surprise. They had no idea who the man in the mismatched armor was, to tell them what to do, nor did they understand why his presence had so fully captured the demon's attention that it had temporarily stopped slaughtering them, but Ashok hoped they would be smart enough to take advantage of the distraction he was providing to flee.

"I am Ashok Vadal, and I will deal with this soldier of hell."

Everyone in the world knew his name. The frightened warriors did as they were told, grabbed up their wounded brethren, and scurried away.

The demon remained standing there, unmoved. Ashok's name must not have been as well known beneath the ocean as it was on land. Thus, he would educate this creature before he killed it.

"I am the bearer of Angruvadal reborn." He held up the ancestor blade he had seized from Bharatas of Akershan to show the demon the method of its death. The length of black steel seemed to devour the sunlight, so dark it was like a slice had been cut out of the world. "Offense has been taken."

The demon started toward him, eager to fight.

Ashok met the creature armed with the combined instincts from forty generations of bearers of *two* ancestor blades.

One huge arm whistled through the air. The fist on the end would have hit like a war hammer... if he'd still been there. Ashok intercepted the arm with his blade as he ducked beneath. Green sparks flew from the demon hide. Ashok pulled through the cut. Milk-white blood splashed across the sand.

It was nearly impossible for even the finest steel to pierce a demon's hide, but Angruvadal was far sharper than normal steel. Black steel neither chipped nor dulled. It devoured. The demon's eyeless head-lump turned to examine the deep laceration in its forearm. Could demons be surprised? Ashok didn't know. If so, this one was.

"Years ago, in Gujara, I fought two of your kind at once. Even armed with Angruvadal, it was a difficult battle. I barely survived."

It attacked him again, so fast that no mortal man should have been able to dodge. Except Ashok stepped out of the way as that mighty fist flashed past his helmet, and with a flick of his wrist, he sliced the demon's other arm open.

"That Angruvadal shattered as I used it to slay a hybrid of man and demon."

The demon charged, trying to run him down. They were of similar height, but demons were so dense it easily doubled Ashok's weight. He whirled around the attack and thrust Angruvadal into the passing demon's back, piercing it deep.

He wrenched his blade free in a spray of white.

The demon *stumbled.*

Now it was fully aware that this was no normal foe.

They circled.

"A shard of that broken sword remains buried in my chest. It should have killed me. It did not. In the years since it has changed me. Strengthened me. It helped me to defeat *five* of you in the House of Assassins."

The demon wore no expression, so he didn't know if it was understanding his words or not. He was compelled to tell it anyway, not to boast to a thing he intended to slay, but it was Thera's belief that demons somehow spoke to each other, mind to mind. His message wasn't for this demon, but for all the rest who might be listening.

"I am far more than I was before. Now that I have retrieved my sword, one of your kind is *nothing* to me."

Ashok went on the offense, thrusting for its chest. The demon darted to the side, incredibly fast, but Ashok still pierced it. Then immediately he shifted back to block its counterattack with Angruvadal's edge. It was like chopping wood by holding up an ax and letting someone swing a log at you.

Ashok stepped aside, unharmed.

The demon's severed hand hit the sand and lay there, fingers twitching.

"This particular demon will die here now, but it is my hope the rest of you will somehow witness this death and understand."

With both long arms suddenly crippled, the demon made one last desperate push, ducking forward, its snapping jaws aimed for Ashok's face. Strengthening his arms with the Heart of the Mountain, he intercepted it with a terrible downward slash, slicing through the demon's open mouth, and across its broad chest, hard enough to split ribs. Even with an ancestor blade and superhuman strength, only a perfect cut could wound a demon so deep. Ashok sidestepped the beast as it passed and struck it again, low in the back. Angruvadal cleaved through the base of its spine.

"Let it be known, trespass will not be tolerated."

The demon lurched to the side, and crashed into a poor worker's house, breaking through the walls, and collapsing the entire thing down around it. It disappeared in a pile of falling rocks, clay shingles, and obscuring dust.

Ashok took a deep breath, and waited, listening for other threats.

Animals and people were crying, but it was from the residue of fear, not the fresh terror of witnessing or experiencing violence as it unfolded. Ashok had a trained ear for such distinctions. It appeared this particular demon had been raiding alone.

In a testament to the courage of the Devakulan warrior caste, after their wounded had been carried to safety, four men rushed back into the village center, ready to fight once more. They'd returned to their obligation despite facing certain death, just to buy more time for the villagers to escape. Ashok respected that.

"Where is it?" one of them gasped. "Where'd it go?"

He pointed toward the broken house. "Beneath there. Dying."

They were clearly too stunned to believe him. But then the rubble shifted, and all the wide-eyed warriors turned their spears that direction.

Surprisingly, the demon wasn't dead yet, proving that the soldiers of hell were incredibly resilient. The debris fell away as the wounded creature struggled free. Ashok was ready to continue their battle, only the thing appeared to be done for. Mortally wounded, it dragged itself slowly across the sand, stubby legs limp and unresponsive, leaving a wide white trail behind as its strange white blood gushed out into the sand.

It was trying to escape . . . but they had to be miles away from the nearest stream big enough to conceal a demon. Ashok followed the crippled thing, curious as to where it thought it would be able to hide from his wrath?

The demon was crawling toward the well.

That couldn't be.

Ashok gestured toward the circle of stones with his sword. "Did this demon come from down there?"

"It did, sir," one of the warriors answered. "Crawled up outta nowhere sudden like and started ripping into people. We had no warning. No warning at all."

A splintered bucket and frayed rope were still lying on the ground. The small roof had been broken, probably as the thick beast had levered itself free. The well's opening was barely bigger around than the demon. Ashok could scarcely imagine the reaction of the poor workers who had been drawing their water when this thing had come scrambling up out of the dark. Their shock had probably not lasted for long.

The demon got its one remaining hand onto the stones and began pulling itself up. It would fall into the depths, to hide and heal, and eventually return to kill again. That, Ashok would not allow, so he closed swiftly, raised Angruvadal, and cleanly smote off the top of the demon's skull. The body flopped over as the contents of its head spilled out.

He walked to the edge and looked down. The well was deep

and dark, and even his unnatural eyes couldn't make out what was at the bottom. In all his experience, and in his Protector training, he had never heard of a demon coming up a well before. Rivers, yes. But the deep waters drawn from the ground itself? Never. He picked up a stone and dropped it in. There was a long pause before the distant splash.

"How far down did they dig this?" he demanded.

The warriors were still catching their breath and staring in awe at the dead thing that had torn through their unit as if it had been nothing. The eldest among them was barely more than a boy, and he had to shake himself from a stupor to answer Ashok's question. "I got no idea, sir."

Ashok wasn't in his chain of command. In fact, he was a wanted criminal. However, he had just killed a demon in front of them, so the warriors reflexively applied the honorific.

"That well's been here since my grandfather patrolled this desert," said another warrior. "Always been good to drink, but it got tasting odd just this last week."

"What do you mean, 'odd'?"

"Salty. Foul. We'd no idea it was because there was a demon living at the bottom! Wonder how long it was hiding down there?"

These poor warriors were too simple to grasp how dire this development was. They had no comprehension of the ancient world that existed below this one, of the massive tunnel system that stretched beneath the isle of Fortress and all the mainland, or that parts of it had been broken into and flooded by the sea.

"I must speak to your commanding officer immediately."

"It swatted our havildar's head off and it flew out into the desert somewhere."

"One of your senior nayaks, then."

The brave survivors looked at each other. One shrugged. They were amazed that they were still alive. In such a chaotic situation it was difficult to keep track of everyone else.

"I think that's part of Nayak Nadim over there." When that warrior finally noticed the unnatural nature of the sword in Ashok's hand—a blade so dark it seemed to devour the sunlight around it—it must have brought to recollection the words Ashok had announced upon his arrival. "You . . . You're really the Black Heart?"

"I am," the most infamous criminal in the world told them. "Will this be an issue?"

"But you're dead. Killed at the hands of Devedas!"

His brother had certainly tried, and would have succeeded, if the shard of Angruvadal hadn't had more use for him and kept him alive as his body had floated across the icy sea. "I have returned. This sword and that dead demon should prove to you I speak the truth. Do you intend to try and capture me, then?"

They may have still been in shock from facing a demon, but thankfully none of them were foolish enough to challenge the man who had just defeated the creature that had easily slaughtered all of their comrades. A legend had just dispatched a demon. What were four tired warriors supposed to do about that?

"You saved our lives. We were good as dead."

"Then offense has been ... postponed," Ashok suggested.

The warriors collectively breathed a sigh of relief. When they were all in agreement of truce, Ashok sheathed Angruvadal. There was no need to clean the demon blood from it first because such impurities never managed to cling to black steel. His mismatched armor, on the other hand, had been splattered with the vile white liquid.

"You must send word to the Protector Order. Tell them of this attack, and my warning that demons may be burrowing under our very feet, using tunnels the ancients built beneath Lok and the ocean. If demons have broken in and flooded some of those, turning them into arteries of the sea, they will be able to travel inland with impunity. Nowhere will be safe."

"We'll ride for Akara as soon as we can," one declared.

"There are Protectors there?"

"Yes, sir. Searching for the rebels who ..." Then that poor warrior trailed off as he must have realized exactly who he was speaking with.

"Rebels who did what?"

The warriors shared a nervous glance, as if they'd just survived a sea demon, only to draw the fury of another, even more dangerous killer. One of them swallowed hard, before managing to spit out, "The Sons of the Black Sword collapsed part of the Capitol aqueduct, then defeated our army that chased them into the Sanjit Ravine."

"Really?" Ashok had known that Thera had led the Sons out of the Cove on some kind of secret mission, but he'd not expected an attack so audacious. "The Sons actually destroyed one of the great works of Lok?"

"They did. A span of it is ruined. The first have commanded it be repaired, but that could take years."

The Capitol had to be furious at mere rebels stealing their water. The first caste didn't like to be reminded that they, too, were vulnerable. The Sons had certainly been busy while he had been gone! "Where are they now?"

The warrior seemed confused how the man he'd been told was leading the rebels didn't know where those rebels were. "Uh... That's why our paltan was patrolling. They vanished into the desert with their murderous Fortress rods. We were told they've got to be wintering somewhere in the borderlands."

Ashok had just come from the southeast, and the snow had made that route extremely difficult. Surely he would have seen sign of the Sons' passage. Westward into Makao would be nearly impassable until the spring thaw. Going north would have taken them closer to the Capitol and the might of the Law. If what this warrior was saying was accurate, Ashok had allies hidden somewhere in the region.

"We'll gladly stop looking for your friends," a different soldier added helpfully.

"That would be wise. Warning your Thakoor and the Protector Order of this demon incursion is more important. You have no time to chase rebels or murder helpless casteless when such an important message needs to be delivered. No one will question your honor over abandoning your obligation, when a more pressing one arises." Ashok waited to make sure they all nodded in agreement. *Good.* It took incredible courage to fight a demon. Even though he might have to kill them tomorrow, he was glad his timely intervention had saved them today. Ending such honorable lives would sadden him, but that was the nature of rebellion.

Chapter 3

Somewhere on the road between the Tower of Silence and the Capitol, Grand Inquisitor Omand Vokkan smoked his pipe and watched a corpse pile burn.

No stranger to having heretics put to the torch, Omand had recognized the smell of burning human flesh a long time before his carriage had drawn near. When his guards had notified him about the bonfire, he had ordered them to stop and find out what was going on here. They had investigated and then reported that the bodies upon the fire were merely casteless non-people, and thus of no importance whatsoever.

Yet he had decided to get out of his carriage anyway. Omand was a very important man, with many important things to do, but Inquisitors were by nature curious.

Of course his presence had caused a great deal of consternation among the local authorities, as anyone rational feared drawing the displeasure of someone as powerful as the Grand Inquisitor, but Omand had assured them that he did not intend to meddle in their affairs, he was merely passing through on other business, and this was as fine a place as any to rest the horses for a time. These Law-abiding men had absolutely nothing to worry about from the Grand Inquisitor.

Nobody ever believed him when he told them that, and Omand liked it that way.

He had told his guards to leave him be for a time, so that he might enjoy a moment of desert solitude, to relax from the ride and ponder the nature of things, while he watched the bodies char and twist and crumble.

Omand had been informed those thrown on the bonfire were wretched untouchables, being disposed of as the Law now required. Except it struck him as odd that there would still be any casteless left to kill this close to the Capitol, so many months after the Great Extermination had been passed. It wasn't as if there had been very many wretched non-people in a city of such wealth and prestige to begin with. The Capitol was a marvel of lofty palaces, sprawling markets, and gigantic government buildings designed to showcase the might and splendor of the Orders housed within, yet even the mighty needed someone to do the filthy unseen chores which kept a city livable, like maintaining the sewers or hauling off the corpses. Those casteless had been the first to go, put to the sword within minutes of the Great Extermination going into effect, as everyone had rushed to annihilate the lowest of the low to curry favor from the highest of the high.

Omand held no special hatred for the non-people. He cared about them as much as he did anyone else...as in, not at all. Arranging their genocide had been nothing personal. It had simply been something that had been necessary to satisfy the deal he had made with a sea demon. Only a few people today understood that the casteless were the descendants of ancient Ramrowan, the first king. But the demons knew, and even a thousand years after Ramrowan's death the demons still despised him. The demon had wanted that bloodline destroyed, and in exchange, it had promised to show Omand the secret location of the ultimate treasure that he'd devoted his life toward claiming.

So Omand had conspired with a demon to kill millions of untouchables, and then through subterfuge, blackmail, and manipulations both subtle and overt, Omand had gotten his Great Extermination. There had been corpse fires like this across all of Lok. Or the casteless had been hacked with blades, starved, or hurled into the sea. The method hadn't mattered, only that they all die. The number who had perished so far was unknowable. Since they weren't actual people, the accounting for them was rather lax.

Some houses had been more vigorous in enacting the Great Extermination than others. No great house liked their casteless, but for some of them, their economies were dependent on that source of cheap and abundant labor, like agrarian Uttara or the miners of Thao, so they had been slow in their response, only grudgingly committing to mass murder. Other great houses, like Makao or Vokkan—who had very little use for their non-people— had been gleeful to finally have the opportunity to eradicate their vermin. They probably would have done so generations ago, but at the time the Law had prevented such slaughter and required every house to maintain a population of casteless within their borders. Only with the passage of the Great Extermination had those houses been eager to drown their lands in casteless blood. The wealthiest of all the houses—Vadal—had disregarded the Great Extermination order entirely, for reasons that Omand's spies were still unsure of. Omand suspected that rebuke was simply Harta Vadal trying to annoy him.

Thus, it had been a most lopsided genocide so far.

The whole thing was also completely unnecessary now, since merely starting the Great Extermination had been enough to trick the demon into revealing to Omand its secrets. Now that demon was dead, its body harvested for parts, and a large expedition of Omand's Inquisitors were busy excavating the site the demon had shown him in the jungles of Gujara. So far the expedition had found enough to confirm that this time it was the real source, and not another demon trick like the scourge that had been unleased in Vadal.

Soon, very soon, Omand would go and claim his treasure.

So the Great Extermination had fulfilled its true purpose. Omand could try to stop it now, but a fire so great, once started, could not be easily contained. It would simply have to burn itself out. Millions more would die, but that was a small price to pay for Omand's immortality.

A sharp wind blew across the sand. There was a bite to it.

Someone stopped a polite distance away and waited to be noticed. Omand saw that it was his loyal assistant Taraba, who had—as usual—anticipated his master's curiosity and found out exactly what was going on here for him. He had removed his golden mask so he could smoke his pipe, but Taraba was one of the few who Omand allowed to see his true face. Not that the mask of flesh he'd been born with gave away any more secrets than his official mask made of gold.

"You may approach, Taraba. Tell me what you learned."

"These casteless were the ones who carried the city's trash to the burn pits in the desert. They should've been killed months ago, but their worker-caste overseer was softhearted, and more fond of his animals than he was loyal to the Law. After the Great Extermination passed, the overseer hid these casteless on one of his nearby properties. When one of his family found out, they promptly informed on him to the Inquisition. This is the result."

"How prosaic." For a moment, Omand had thought there might be something more to this, but alas, such disobedience was an all-too-common thing. "The worker?"

Taraba inclined his head toward the fire. "Already on the pile."

"The informer?"

"Compensated handsomely in bank notes and a promotion in status."

Omand nodded. "As is proper. People are the same as dogs. They must be trained to be obedient. Punish wickedness. Reward devotion. Do both publicly so the rest will learn."

"Of course, sir."

They were quiet for a time as Omand watched the flames flicker. Taraba knew to remain silent, patiently awaiting the needs of his master. Taraba was a good servant, so loyal he had once disguised himself as a casteless to assassinate the Chief Judge with a Fortress rod on the steps of the Chamber of Argument upon Omand's command . . . but Taraba's greatest use was as a listener who allowed Omand to talk out whatever was troubling him, without having to worry about betrayal.

"Did you confirm the message from Great House Akershan?"

"We're still awaiting word from our other spies there, but if the rumor about their sword isn't true, the Akershani army still seems to believe it is. Their Thakoor has made no public statement yet."

The message had been so outlandish that Omand had hesitated to believe it. Not only had it claimed that Ashok Vadal was still alive, but that he had defeated Akershan's bearer in single combat and claimed their ancestor blade as his own. Now Ashok was holding the sword hostage, and Akershan had to spare its rebels and casteless or else Ashok would break another precious ancestor blade. And who would dare doubt him? Ashok had already broken one of the irreplaceable things.

Omand had already used his magic to check that no one else was watching them except the skulls in the fire, so spoke freely. "In turning Ashok Vadal into a criminal, I envisioned a wonderful tool of destabilization and disruption. He was a good Protector, but he has been an *outstanding* rebel. Ashok has far outperformed the use I imagined I'd wring from him. Yet, his use to me is over. Now he vexes me by not dying when it is convenient for me. I believe I may have created a monster, Taraba."

"Harta Vadal's mother and their house wizards created that monster. You were smart enough to see the opportunity Ashok represented."

"It *was* rather ingenious of me," Omand agreed.

"Indeed, sir. Yet when word spreads that Ashok still lives now, it may damage Raja Devedas' reputation. Part of his reputation is based upon being the one who defeated rebel Ashok once and for all."

Taraba was astute. To overthrow the judges and take over the Capitol, Omand's puppet king had required a legend sufficient to unite all the houses and castes behind him. Defeating the infamous murderer Ashok had been Devedas' crowning achievement, near literally. Omand had not been quite ready to move against the judges, but when the pillar of fire had struck Vadal for all the world to see, he had capitalized on the judge's fear. In that moment of crises they had longed for a strong leader, respected by all, and Omand had been happy to provide them with Devedas.

"The Capitol is under my thumb. I have replaced their truth with one of my own construction. The troublesome have been removed or negated. The few who dare to say the Inquisition goes too far are shouted down. Who will question the need for firm leadership, while beams of scalding fire shoot from the sky, and the rebels have stolen away the very water they drink?"

"Another brilliant move to allow such a thing, sir."

"It was." Though Omand recalled that letting the rebels have that victory had been Taraba's suggestion. "I marvel that after inflicting so much uncertainty and dread upon this people, even after presenting them a perfect villain, a madman armed with a black sword leading mobs of bloodthirsty savage casteless to massacre their brothers and sisters of the First, it was seeing their

gardens wilt and flowers die as they rationed their drinking water
that finally sealed their fear enough to let me do whatever I want.
Comfort is such a mundane thing to sacrifice a society for, but
such is life ... We now have a king again in all but title, and that
king is *mostly* under my control. Devedas is too prideful to be a
proper puppet, but that great pride of his keeps him predictable,
and thus manageable. As long as Devedas makes the first caste
feel safe, he will retain their favor. I'd hate to lose that."

"You have invested too much effort into constructing this
king, to create a new one now."

"Correct, Taraba." Perhaps the boy was too clever for his own
good? Perhaps a test was in order. Omand smoked his pipe and
mulled over his troubles. "I think we should send everyone we
have available to find and kill Ashok. Preferably quietly."

"I can arrange that, sir."

"I'm not just speaking of Inquisitors, but activate every hidden
witch hunter, hire every illegal wizard and all the survivors of
the House of Assassins, bribe every cutthroat if you must—spare
no expense, the deed must be done. The black heart is a variable
I can no longer account for. His use to me has passed. Ashok
Vadal must die."

"I will see to it at once." Taraba began walking away.

"Wait ..."

Omand hesitated because the hour of his triumph was at
hand. Decades of planning, preparation, and study were near
fruition. Ashok was only one man. The forgotten gods may have
been a myth, but their power had been very real. If they were
not true gods, then they had still been godlike in their abilities. In the old world, before the rain of demons, the ancients
had controlled incredible magics, altering matter on command
and bending reality on a whim. They had created new forms of
life, and even overcome death itself. Those ancients had fallen
before the demons, but they had understood that eventually the
world would be ready for their heir, and they had prepared an
inheritance accordingly. Seizing that inheritance had become
Omand's life work. He could not jeopardize it now, while it was
so tantalizingly close.

Omand took a long draw from his pipe.

"Amend that order, Taraba. Recruit that dark cadre, but do
not send them against Ashok. Instead I will give you that secret

army to use as you see fit, for you will be going to the north without me."

Taraba hesitated. "Sir?"

"Priorities, Taraba. Priorities. It will take a careful hand to push Devedas in the correct direction. His familiarity with war is also his weakness. He has seen so much combat, he has no glory left to gain from it, and thus no hunger for bloodshed. Our plans require bloodshed. I suspect Devedas will try to forge some manner of peace with Harta Vadal. They are the only house strong enough to threaten my hold on the Capitol, thus Vadal must be crushed. Do whatever it takes to ensure our Raja and his Army of Many Houses is manipulated into waging war against Vadal. You know who the players are and what they value the most. Do whatever you must to achieve our goals there. See to it I get my war."

Taraba's mask covered his face, but the surprise was apparent in his voice. "I am incredibly honored by your trust, but—"

"I know, I know. This is such an important endeavor that normally I would oversee the operation myself, but I must focus upon more important matters. Once I am satisfied that there is no one left in the Capitol to rise up against us—and a war in the north will see to that—I will journey to Gujara, to personally monitor the expedition there."

His assistant was obviously confused, as even Omand's closest conspirators didn't know about that part of Omand's plan. They thought that they were *merely* overthrowing the government and putting themselves in charge. What was the point of taking control of the Capitol, only to abandon it? Taraba was a good Inquisitor, but he lacked the vision to grasp what was really at stake. Omand didn't just intend to rule all of Lok. He intended to do so *forever*.

"Do not fret, Taraba, this experience will prepare you to assume my title of Grand Inquisitor once I retire to be our new king's only *advisor*. In the meantime, I will remain in contact with you via demon bone. I understand you want to ask why this expedition in the jungle is so important, but alas, you should not. Do not offend me by trying."

"As you wish." Taraba bowed. He seemed intimidated, yet confident in his abilities. It was a good balance. The boy would do fine. He was cunning, murderous, and imaginative, and Omand had just told him there were no limits. It would be interesting to see what the boy could accomplish when taken off the leash. "Thank you for this responsibility. I will gather my killers and leave for Vadal immediately."

"Excellent. Motivate them by coin, demon, or duty, I don't care, as long as you do not fail me." Omand gave him a fatherly smile, not that he was actually capable of feeling any such prideful emotions. Taraba would do what he was told, which was why he would be a perfect replacement for a man who never intended to give up any real power. "Go and tell my driver to prepare my carriage." The casteless had been so thin, the fire was already running out of fuel. "I'm almost done here."

Alone once more, Omand contemplated his next move in the great game. It was odd. So many decades had been spent guiding events to this point, and now everything was happening all at once. There was an old Uttaran saying that seemed fitting: *Things move slowly, until they don't. Nothing changes, until everything does.*

Yet Omand remained troubled, and that was not a feeling he was used to. As he smoked his fine Vadal tobacco and watched the last flesh char into ash, he realized it wasn't the unpredictable actions of dangerous men like Ashok or Devedas that were bothering him, nor even his impending apotheosis... He was troubled by the last words of his demon prisoner. It wasn't sufficient to label the torturous mind screams of a demon as *words,* but that description would have to do. The creature had been so overjoyed upon believing the lie that the entire bloodline of Ramrowan had been wiped out, that it had gladly shown Omand where the source of all magic had crashed into the world. Its attitude had been *let Omand enjoy the power of the gods, because what did that matter now?*

Omand was always honest with himself. Only weak men deceived themselves into believing comforting things that were untrue. Great men dealt in cold reality. What was truly distressing him was that final message the tricky demon had managed to send by magic to its brethren beneath the sea:

It is time.

Time for what? Omand didn't know, and it was his place to know everything. He had believed the demon's motivation had been simple revenge, annihilating the bloodline of the man responsible for driving them into the ocean so long ago. It had been a logical assumption, for a demon's capacity for hate was incomprehensible, and demons never forget. Alas, he suspected there was something more. What made the weak and powerless non-people so important to the mighty demons? What had he missed?

It is time.

No matter. Whatever it was would be a small price to pay, for when Omand ruled, he would do so not as Lok's king, but as its god.

Chapter 4

High on a bluff overlooking the freezing desert, Ashok sat atop Horse, marveling at the destruction the Sons of the Black Sword had wrought.

A section of the Capitol aqueduct had collapsed. The water must have kept running for a long time before word had reached the source to divert the flow, because it had turned a rocky valley into a lake, and that new softness of the ground had caused mudslides that had made other sections of the great structure shift and crack. Ashok was no architect, but to his untrained eye, he guessed that a few hundred yards of the massive stonework would have to be replaced. Maybe more if the shifting had caused damage inside its hidden channels.

Only a few months had passed since the attack, but thousands of workers and craftsmen had been gathered and were now busy repairing the damage. There was a tent city below him, and that camp was guarded by a great number of warriors, prepared in case the Sons of the Black Sword somehow returned to finish the job. It appeared there were even a great number of casteless drafted to labor among them. Even though the casteless had all been condemned to death, that wouldn't stop the Law from pressing them into service first and wringing every last bit of use out of them. First they'd be used to fix the Capitol's water supply, and *then* the forces of the Law would go back to murdering them. The Law was pragmatic like that.

This spectacle was not what had brought Ashok here, however, and he quickly returned to his mission before being spotted by any guards.

Mother Dawn had told him that Thera would need him in Kanok. Soon he would reach the first of the mountain passes that would take him down into Makao lands, but those passes would probably still be choked with snow and impassable to any regular man. He would have to abandon Horse and continue on foot, trusting in the Heart of the Mountain to keep him alive.

Along the way he hoped to retrace the path of the Sons of the Black Sword, hoping that perhaps he might find some clue as to their whereabouts. Last he had heard, Thera had been with the Sons. Just because the mysterious Mother Dawn had told him one thing, that did not make it true. Mother Dawn seemed to be able to predict the future, had appeared to the faithful wearing many different faces, and seemingly had the ability to travel across great distances in the blink of an eye, but none of that rendered her infallible. The fanatics considered her a heavenly messenger. Ashok knew she was *something* more than human, but not what. Thus far Mother Dawn had consistently aided the rebels, but he didn't know if that loyalty would continue, or if she would ultimately betray them to further her own enigmatic goals.

Ashok also hoped to find the Sons because he had been named their *general*. It was an archaic title from the time before the Age of Law, but it meant it was his responsibility to lead them. As far as Ashok was concerned, he was a leader in name only, as he did not consider himself a proper officer. Ashok was a figurehead, with no understanding of how to be a normal soldier, because he had never been a normal anything. Officers led, but following Ashok into battle was a certain way for mortal warriors to get themselves hurt, for Ashok ranged across the battlefield to wherever he could do the most harm, always fighting with unmatchable savagery. When regular warriors tried to keep up with Ashok Vadal, they died.

The Sons had been in much better hands when cunning Jagdish had commanded them. A consummate warrior, Jagdish had been an exemplar of his caste: honorable, effective, and never spending the lives of his men foolishly. Though apparently, judging by the ruin of one of the Capitol's greatest works, the subsequent defeat of a great house army, and their clean escape afterward, Jagdish had taught the Sons well! The results of this attack were astounding. No band of criminals had ever struck against the Capitol so blatantly before and survived. His officers had drastically exceeded all of Ashok's expectations from when he had chosen them. Ashok may not have been a good commander himself, but apparently he had an eye for talent.

Oh, what an odd journey his life had taken, that Ashok could now feel pride in how good he was at inspiring rebellion.

As Ashok rode through the narrow valleys where the Sons' running battle had taken place, he searched for signs of his army. It was too dry to snow much here, so the sandy ground was mostly visible. Everything of value—every dropped weapon, bit of broken armor, strap, or buckle—had already been scavenged, but there were still clues about what had taken place. The obvious being the unnatural stacks of stone, left in memorial by the families of local warriors on the spots where the bodies of their sons and husbands had been collected, as was a Devakulan tradition. There were a great many of those funeral piles. The Sons had fought well.

There were other indications of battle as well, including scorch marks on the rocks left by Fortress powder bombs, and lead smears from where the gunner's bullets had ricocheted off stone. The sheer number of those bullet scars baffled Ashok, for his rebellion had possessed sixty rods in total when he had last seen them in Garo. The sheer quantity of these marks seemed far too numerous for so few weapons, unless the Devakulans had sat here all afternoon and let Gupta's gunners pour volley after volley into them.

Ashok reached the end of a deep canyon that appeared to be a dead end. Here was where the Sons had stopped to make their final stand . . . yet they had prevailed and escaped so cleanly that it was as if the desert itself had simply swallowed them. There were no more clues to point him in the right direction. Wind had long since obliterated any tracks that might have remained, otherwise the warrior caste would have chased down the Sons already.

He had not known what he'd hoped to find here. Perhaps some sign only he could read, left behind to tell him exactly where Thera was to be found safe. *What foolishness.* Ashok cursed himself for wasting time on this diversion and turned back toward Makao.

A short time later he heard someone approaching on horseback. From the sound echoing on the canyon walls, it was a single rider, moving quickly. Being spotted now would not do. He had managed to avoid warrior patrols so far, but surely word of his encounter with the demon in the desert would spread, and the forces of the Law would be on the lookout for him once more. Ashok coaxed Horse under a shadowy overhang, where they could hide and wait for the other rider to pass by.

Ashok heard the rapid clomp of hooves slow to a walk. The other rider stopped a mere twenty yards away and the rider dismounted with a great deal of grunting and muttering about the discomfort and the miserable cold, which got the response of displeased snorting from what sounded to be a very large horse.

"I know you're out there!" The rider's voice was so loud in the cold air that it must have startled him, because when he continued it was at a much more conspiratorial volume. "I was in the work camp when you rode by. You've got so damned much potent black steel magic on you that your passage is about as subtle as a Vadal hurricane, and there's only one piece of black steel I've ever come across that feels like that peculiar shard stuck in your heart, Ashok Vadal."

He recognized that voice, but it couldn't be. "Gutch?" The last time Ashok had seen the illegal magic smuggler had been on the far end of the continent, and he had been on his way northward from the swamps of Bhadjangal with Jagdish, carrying a fortune in demon bone packed onto a train of mules.

"I've been following the lingering magic trail all morning, and frankly, my ass is too sore to continue at this reckless pace...so please have mercy upon your humble servant Gutch and show yourself, General, so we can get out of this rocky maze before a thousand vengeful Devakulans arrive to murder us."

Ashok rode out into the open, and sure enough, sitting upon a gigantic steed was the ponderous bulk of the worker Gutch.

"I did not expect to see you here."

"I didn't expect to be here either!" Gutch grinned, appearing to be genuinely relieved, when he saw that it really was Ashok he'd been chasing. The enterprising criminal was larger than ever, considerably plumper than when they'd been subsisting on roots and lizard meat in a swamp. Back then they'd all been dressed in rags. Now Gutch wore a fine coat made from the fur of a white southern bear, with a golden sash across it that suggested he was a very wealthy merchant. "Oh, thank goodness. For a moment I was worried I'd come across some other random bearer, and I was going to have to explain how this was all one great big misunderstanding! There's only a handful of your kind in the whole world but that'd be just my luck now, wouldn't it?"

Gutch led Ashok across the desert.

They had ridden swiftly from the canyon lands, as Gutch had been eager to put some distance between them and the aqueduct camp's multitude of guards. Rumor among the worker caste there was that there were Inquisitors hidden among their number, monitoring the repairs in order to catch saboteurs. Gutch didn't know if that was true, but it was better not to risk an encounter with the masks.

Once they were several miles from the camp, Gutch slowed his mount to a walk through the sagebrush, and Ashok drew alongside so he could question the criminal.

"Do you know where Thera is?"

"Sorry, I don't. She was separated from the Sons during the battle and not been seen since."

Ashok could not feel fear like a normal man, but his stomach could still tie itself in a knot of worry for someone else. "Her safety was the Sons' responsibility."

"Yeah, how dare they?" Gutch said sarcastically. "The way I hear it, they followed *her* plan, when she insisted on leading them into battle *herself*, to poke the Capitol in the eye like no one has ever done before. Then they managed to survive while being scattered and hunted. It was the smart one from Kharsawan, Eklavya, who took your woman's orders and figured out how to collapse the aqueduct. The boy is clever. He would've become a master in some kind of trade if he'd been lucky enough to be born in the worker caste, that's for sure! But that ploy used up most of their powder. And then Ongud the horseman was who managed to get them through the canyons in one piece despite being out-numbered ten to one. That bunch'a slothful ingrates, achieving the impossible against insane odds. And they still should've died, if me and my boys hadn't come along to save them."

Gutch was right. Ashok's anger was misplaced. Thera's safety was his obligation. Not the Sons'. "Saltwater."

"I'm sure your woman is fine, Ashok. She's a crafty one. Don't worry. If the Capitol had caught her, they'd be bragging about stamping out another false prophet. If they'd caught the ringleader of the rebels who took away their water, they'd be crowing about it to any who'd listen. They haven't, so they don't," the big man assured him, before turning in the saddle to look at Ashok, as if still trying to believe his eyes. "I truly thought you were dead."

"I *was* dead for a time."

"Ah..." Gutch grimaced when Ashok didn't elaborate on that pronouncement. "You were never a man to dwell too long on pleasantries, like 'Nice to see you my old friend and associate, Gutch. Thank you for saving my army of religious fanatics from certain doom and hiding them from the Law all this winter, at your great personal expense.'"

"The Sons of the Black Sword are safe?"

"Most of them, yes. Thanks entirely to me. You're welcome."

The criminal had always been full of surprises. While Ashok was motivated by a sense of duty, Gutch was motivated by profit. It was as foreign a philosophy to Ashok as the religious mantras of the monks of Fortress, but somehow, it seemed Gutch usually managed to do the right thing by his friends.

"Your efforts are appreciated." Ashok gave Gutch a deep nod of respect. It was as close to a proper bow as could be done from the saddle, but even that seemed to surprise Gutch, as Ashok was not known for showing such considerations. "Can you take me to them?"

"That's where we're headed now. They've been hiding out at one of my many properties. This particular place is far from any trade roads, with no nosy neighbors to inform on us, and enough roofs over their heads that even a wizard pretending to be a bird won't notice that many extra bodies. In the rare event that a warrior patrol happens by, I've got secret passages aplenty. Rebels hide easier than contraband."

"You are doing illegal business here?"

Gutch roared with laughter that was loud enough to startle Horse, who was bred for chaos and combat. "Sheltering a rebel army is the least illegal thing I'm doing there! I can't wait to show you what I've been up to."

Ashok had never understood the nuances of worker-caste rank, but Gutch was wearing the insignia of someone with extremely high status, and that haughty station was reinforced by the many diamonds and rubies encrusting his golden rings and chains, and the fact he sat upon the biggest Zarger warhorse Ashok had ever seen. Such a fine animal would be quite the prize, so muscular even fearsome Horse did not sneer at this one in contempt.

"Why are you disguised as a wealthy man?"

"Disguise? What disguise? My good Ashok, I'll have you know I've been rather busy since you were declared dead. I'm a leader of industry now, respected in every great house I do business, which is nearly all of them, and even in the golden halls of the Capitol itself, where the bankers need to use wheelbarrows to cart about the notes I have amassed to my name…which, said name is, and has always been, Vinod of Guntur, should anyone of an inquisitorial bent ask about me."

"If we see any Inquisitors I will simply kill them."

"That works too. How are you even here? The whole world thinks you're dead, defeated in a duel by Lord Protector Devedas. They held parades in the Capitol celebrating his great victory before they appointed him Raja."

"What is…Raja?"

"Some new office, I think it is like a great commander of sorts." Gutch waved one hand dismissively. "You know how the first caste is with their offices and titles. This one's special, though. He's got an army made up of warriors from every house. All the printers' presses across the land were commanded to make copies of this announcement to post for all to see. They cut a whole forest worth of paper to make so many flyers announcing the promotion of Devedas to this mighty new station that I can't believe you've not seen one yet."

So his brother would make himself king after all? This did not surprise him, for Devedas was a man of incredible will. Though it did pain Ashok that the infamy of his name had surely helped propel Devedas along his path of illegal ambition.

"Devedas cut my throat and I was hurled into the sea. Only the shard of Angruvadal was not done with me yet so it sustained me. Lingering near death, I remained in prison for a time."

"You'd have thought the Law would have crowed about having you captive!"

"They obey a different Law in Fortress."

"Fortress? But nobody goes..." Gutch tilted to his head, thinking that surely Ashok was joking, but Ashok did not *joke*. "Nobody's been to Fortress and lived to tell the tale."

"I escaped their prison, defeated a wrathful god in an abandoned city beneath the sea, then burned the island's ruler and hurled him from a tower. I think I may be their king now. It is a very confusing place."

Gutch stared at him, mouth agape, for if this was anyone other than Ashok telling such a mad tale, he certainly would have called him a liar. "Well, you've been busy! Yet here you are now, and if my keenly honed smuggler sense isn't irreparably broken, that's *another* ancestor blade at your side."

"It is. I took Akershan's from them."

"Oceans, man! There's only like a dozen of the things in the entire world. How many do you need? Wait. So does that mean the Law knows you're alive? Never mind. I'll get you to my estate, and you can take your men and be on your way while everyone else still thinks you're dead. As soon as the Law realizes you're still kicking they'll be ransacking the countryside looking for you again."

"After I defeated Bharatas and claimed this sword, I announced to the army of Akershan that I still lived."

"Why would you do that?"

"It was an attempt to protect the casteless. I warned the warriors that if their extermination continued, I would be displeased, and would not return their sword."

"You're certainly not one to take advantage of anonymity. Well, at least we're a long way from the Akershani border. The Law will never suspect you were in these lands, so my operation will remain unexamined and safe."

"I killed a demon just east of here yesterday. There were several witnesses."

Gutch sighed. "I swear every time you speak, my life grows more complicated...Wait. A demon near here? How'd it walk so far from a river? That would've taken forever to cross the desert. I haven't sensed even a whiff of living demon magic in forever."

Being able to sense the presence of magic was an exceedingly rare gift, and why Gutch had become an accomplished smuggler in the illicit trade of demon parts, but even a bloodhound could not follow a scent if it was buried deep enough. "This demon traveled here underground."

"Well, I certainly hope they don't make a habit of that!"

Several hours later, they reached Gutch's *estate*, which consisted of a cluster of workshops, cabins, and a stable above a canyon which was filled with a warren of scaffolding, ladders, and pulleys to bring up buckets of some kind of ore. The place looked dusty and poor. Dozens of rough men were moving across the wooden walkways between pits and mineshafts, carrying tools, and doing various worker things Ashok had no understanding of. Though he had seldom bothered to learn what their purpose was, Ashok had seen hundreds of busy places like this scattered across Lok.

"This does not look like a criminal enterprise."

"Then I've done well, if it passes even the suspicious eye of a Protector."

"Do not call me that." Ashok had been forced to kill many of his former brothers now, and they had all been good men. Better men than him. Ashok would not claim an honor that was not his. "I am no longer a Protector of the Law."

"Alright, former Protector, then. Regardless, I've done my job, for if the Law realized what I've got going on here—and in many other places like this—the Inquisition would choke on their own masks and the judges would soil their robes! This is an audacious endeavor, even by my rather high standards." Then Gutch eyed him nervously. "In fact, experience has taught me that despite your current legal status you retain enough of an ingrained dislike for certain criminal behaviors, that I'm a bit worried you're gonna forget our previous associations—and dare I say camaraderie—that you'll reflexively lop my head off when you see what we're up to here."

Since last they'd met, Ashok had spent a very long time shackled and starving in the dark, with nothing else to do but contemplate the multitude of terrible things he had done in defense of a Law that was built on a foundation of corruption and lies. Memories of the past had gnawed on him more than the dungeon's rats. The structure of perfect obedience built into his mind by the wizard Kule had crumbled worse than the Capitol's aqueduct.

"I decide my own Law now, Gutch."

"Ah, then I shall not worry about you suddenly decapitating me, then!"

"I did not promise that."

"I'll take what I can get."

They were spotted by the workers and a shout went up, *"The master returns."* Servants promptly ran out to take their mounts. Ashok had to give Horse a comforting pat on the head to assure him this was fine, because otherwise it was his nature to bite strangers. Gutch would probably say that Ashok and Horse were similar in temperament like that.

Gutch dismounted and told one of his men, "Find the leaders of our honored guests. Tell them I have a wonderful surprise for them, and to meet us inside the factory." After that worker rushed off, Gutch gestured for Ashok to follow him down a cobblestone path. "I'll show you around, then we'll have a hearty supper. We may dwell in a forsaken stinking hole of a desert, but I make sure my people eat well."

Whatever it was Gutch was excited to show him must have been very interesting for a man of such profound appetites to postpone a meal after such a long journey. The two of them walked to a humble structure. Ashok might not understand worker-caste things, but surely this rough desert barn they were heading toward could hardly be called a factory. It was big, but decaying, and had lost many boards and shingles to the wind. The workers at the entrance appeared to be stacking boxes, but they stopped their act when they saw who it was and greeted Gutch warmly—he was either a kind master or paid them very well—and then stepped aside. From the blades Ashok noticed were stashed nearby, these weren't laborers. They were guards.

Inside the barn, Ashok realized that the appearance had been deceiving, for this was truly a factory as much as any of the smoking monstrosities the worker caste had built in cities like Neeramphorn or Vadal City. There were dozens of laborers toiling. A great coal fire was burning in the back of the barn, and molten metal was being poured into forms. Ashok marveled how the workers moving those flaming things about with metal tongs were so heedless of the sparks that they worked barefoot. Women and children were sitting on the floor, using files to shape small metal parts, placing those parts in bowls, and then pushing the bowls down the line to the next worker for more attention.

Gutch had to shout to be heard over the noise. "The illicit nature of this endeavor makes it hard to have a centralized location that can make everything, but I simplified the plans so even the dumbest fish-eater can assemble the parts once they get them. We send them out disguised as other products. Here? We make barrels and the lockwork parts. I've only got a couple places that can handle work that fine. Nearest place carving wood for stocks is across the border in Zarger, and I've recently taken over another logging camp in Kharsawan to get production up, but worse comes to worst, your rebels can fashion a handle out of a sturdy stick."

Ashok understood no point to any of what Gutch was saying, except the big worker was brimming with genuine excitement, for Gutch was as gifted at industry as Ashok was at combat.

"I bought up all the sulfur left in Shabdakosh. The nearest powder gets made over near Karoon, where they've got caves with millions of bats in them, then near Guntur or Ambara where they're not too far from giant cliffs that seabirds have been shitting on for generations, and it's all ready to mine. Nasty business that, but I pay them well."

He recalled the words of Thera, explaining to him the nature of the illegal alchemy she'd practiced. "You speak of Fortress powder?"

"Indeed I do, and your Sons of the Black Sword should be glad they're not wintering at one of my properties that makes that nasty stuff instead of this one. It turns out there's some complications to making powder in such big quantities. We had a vat of it explode for no reason in the wilds of Sarnobat and flatten half a village. Now *that* was quite the economic setback!"

With growing dread, Ashok was beginning to understand the true scope and nature of Gutch's operation. No wonder he had been worried Ashok would cut his head off, for this was one of the greatest crimes imaginable. Fortress magic was banned. Anyone caught with any of it was to be immediately executed on the spot.

Ashok, Protector of the Law, would have immediately slaughtered everyone here and then burned the place to the ground. Ashok the rebel could only steady himself and then ask, "You're manufacturing Fortress rods and alchemy on the mainland?"

"Obviously." Gutch went over to a big crate of ore and gestured for a few of his workers to come help. "Move this aside, please, so I may continue giving my tour to our most esteemed visitor."

With a great deal of grunting and heaving the workers moved the heavy box, which had been strategically placed to cover a well-concealed hidden door. No casual inspector would have bothered. Gutch unlocked the secret door with a key attached to one of his golden chains and opened it with a flourish for Ashok to see what was on the other side.

"These are all complete and stashed for a rainy day, like when your Sons of the Black Sword were in sudden need of rescuing by me and my boys. Though thankfully it didn't actually rain because that makes the powder very unreliable."

Behind the door was an old mining pit, and it was filled with Fortress rods. At least a hundred of them. Perhaps more. Ashok walked inside to examine them more closely. These were not like the ones that Ratul had gotten from the isle of Fortress, which had gone to arm Gupta's gunners. Ashok did not care for those things, but those had obviously been crafted with great painstaking pride. That skill made sense after Ashok had met Sachin Chatterjee, master of the Weapons Guild of Fortress, and seen how seriously the foreigners took their duty to defend their island. In comparison to those, Gutch's rods were blocky, simple things. The rods from Fortress may have been untraditional and without honor, but they were still proper weapons built with all the care that art entailed. The guns of Lok looked more like rough farm tools, designed to be churned out as quickly as possible.

"How many of these have you made?"

"Over the last year, it's hard to say exactly because of how spread out we have to be, and it's not like criminal enterprises keep meticulous yet incriminating records...but thousands."

"*Thousands?*"

"Come on, Ashok! Considering the legal challenges, distance, and time involved, that's a rather impressive achievement. A forge master smith of lesser talent would still be overwhelmed by the magnitude of this challenge, but not industrious Gutch!"

Gutch misunderstood his tone. Ashok was not scoffing at the amount for being insufficient, but rather because he was stunned by the audacity of it. A mere sixty rods in the hands of his rebellion had routed a great house army and felled an entire unit of Protectors.

This changed everything.

"Well, perhaps almost a thousand, by the end of this month

that is, and that's spread out across all of Lok, but as you can see there's a great many more coming. I'm not sure how many of the early batches made it to their final destination without getting intercepted by the Law. I'm still conquering the logistical challenges there, but I can assure you that many of my fine products have been promptly distributed to the rebellious non-people as per Mother Dawn's instructions."

Ashok should not have been surprised. "This is her doing?"

"It was her suggestion and financial backing. You know how meddlesome those bankers are when it comes to money—though the schematics she supplied me were admittedly top rate, but this endeavor is my doing. Without my expertise she'd still be making a handful a year, and most of those would be promptly seized. It takes a man of vision to accomplish so much in so little time! Before my legal troubles I was rather respected in Vadal City for a reason you know, and Vadal City is the greatest city in the world. Fools say it's the Capitol, but the Capitol only makes Law, while Vadal City makes everything else, and I was the best forge master smith they've ever seen."

A banker . . . Of course, to Gutch, Mother Dawn had appeared as the wealthiest example of his caste. She always looked like whatever she needed to in order to be trusted by whomever she was trying to sway. To the warriors, she was warrior caste. To the workers, a fellow worker. Oddly enough, for Ashok, she'd been casteless.

Whatever she really was, Mother Dawn had unleashed chaos into the Law-abiding world. Ashok had mostly gotten over his reflexive disgust for Fortress rods, and now he recognized them merely as the tools they were. As a prideful swordsman he had no love of something that could make anyone with a few days of training the match of a warrior who had fought his entire life, yet if enough of these deadly things were concentrated in the hands of the casteless, exterminating them would become nearly impossible.

Gutch waited, hesitant and anxious, as Ashok stood there looking at the illegal weapons, his expression inscrutable. Finally, the smith asked, "Well? What do you think?"

"You still have your head."

"And for that I'm exceedingly grateful!" Gutch grinned. "So you approve?"

Honestly, Ashok was torn. He had vowed to save the casteless, but he couldn't predict the repercussions of a change this great. No one could. He doubted even the gods and their prophecies knew what would happen if the lowest of the low were suddenly capable of besting the warrior caste in battle. And once they did, what loyalty would they have toward a Law that had just condemned them all to death? What respect would anyone have for a government that would make such a terrible pronouncement and then fail to complete it? Man and demon both were abandoning their traditions. The world was changing too rapidly, old ways were dying, being replaced by the unknown new, and such uncertainty left him uneasy.

"This will either save us or damn us all, Gutch. I know not which."

"Huh . . ." The big worker thought that over for a moment. "Not the answer I was hoping for, but I'll take it."

"Ashok lives!" someone shouted from inside the factory. "Praise the gods!"

Ashok turned back to see who was yelling illegal religion and saw a young man dressed in humble worker's garb. Then he realized it was Eklavya, warrior of Kharsawan, and it was good to see he was still alive, for he was one of the best among the Sons. When they had met, Eklavya had been a humble, low-status warrior of Kharsawan, and a secret believer in the old gods his entire life. He had proven himself in battle against man and demon and become one of the leaders amongst their gang of defiant rebels.

Eklavya rushed into the secret room as if he couldn't believe his eyes, and reached out to touch Ashok's arm, apparently to confirm this was no illusion. "Can it be?" And once he understood Ashok was flesh and blood, he snatched his hand away, so as to not give offense.

"At ease, Risalder. It is I."

"Forgive me, General." Eklavya quickly bowed. "My senses were overcome."

"Rise, Eklavya. Having learned what the Sons accomplished while I was away, it is I who owes you respect."

The warrior got up, and quickly wiped his suddenly damp eyes with the back of his hand, because warriors of some houses did not like to display their emotions before witnesses—Kharsawan among them—even if that emotion was genuine relief. "I knew you'd be back for us."

"It took longer than I liked. What's the status of the Sons?"

Eklavya immediately snapped to, because he was an officer first, religious fanatic a distant second. "There's a handful still recuperating from their injuries who won't be able to travel for a time, but we've kept most of your men alive, in good health and good spirits. All your chosen officers survived, and we've been busy. Our numbers have grown substantially as we've gathered more secret faithful recruits from the armies of Devakula, Makao, Zarger, and even distant Harban."

"These were also told where to find you by Mother Dawn, I assume?"

"Don't look at me. I didn't tell her they were here," Gutch said defensively. "I've not seen her since she gave me her investment money."

"The recruits mostly come from her, General, but some just got curious and hopeful enough after the aqueduct fell to come looking for us, and our scouts picked them up and brought them in."

"Have you been checking for spies?"

"Of course. If there's a mask among them, I'll take responsibility and fall on my sword. You've got a hundred and eighty more proper warriors since last we met. We've been integrating them best as we can while staying out of sight. Plus we've trained more rebel workers and casteless to use Gutch's guns, and Gupta's gunners have more than tripled in number from what you had in Garo. Say the word and the Sons are ready to fight anyone."

He had no doubt they'd willingly fight the whole world if he asked. "Well done, Eklavya." That report was far better than expected. If they were a proper army, Ashok would have recommended they all receive commendations. "Have you word from Thera?"

Eklavya cringed as Ashok dashed his hopes. "I was praying the prophet was with you. We've not seen her since the aqueduct fell. After the main body of the Sons escaped into the canyons, we sent scouts everywhere. We found her bodyguard, Murugan, slain, but Thera was missing, along with the priest, Javed."

That news saddened Ashok, for Murugan Thao had been a good lad. "Did Murugan die well?"

"It looks like he fought several witch hunters, crippled one, and took another with him over a cliff," said a woman who had entered the secret room behind Eklavya. Young and petite of stature, she'd been so quiet that Ashok had barely noticed her presence before. "Murugan must have been very brave."

Ashok suspected that was true, as Murugan had been devoted in his duties and utterly loyal to Thera. The boy had understood how rare it was for one of his caste to get a second chance at redeeming his honor and done the most with it. "How do you know they were witch hunters?"

"From the amount of magic they had on them. Though I couldn't sense it until they were close and then it was too late."

The girl claimed she could sense magic, which was an exceedingly rare gift. Ashok looked to Gutch, who nodded. "She's not as keen at it as I am, but she speaks true."

The girl looked vaguely familiar to Ashok. "Who are you?"

"I am Laxmi, stolen from Gujara, once a slave in Lost House Charsadda, then servant of Thera. Now I'm the lone wizard among the Sons of the Black Sword."

She was barely recognizable as one of the mentally broken slaves they'd freed from the House of Assassins, and then led from the swamps. It was heartening to see the vile spell used to make Sikasso's magically gifted slaves mindless and docile be so thoroughly defeated.

"The rest of the freed slaves used their abilities to help defend the Cove. They fought well. Their minds were greatly improved from before, but when I left they still spoke as if they were in a fog. You seem fine."

Laxmi flashed him a brilliant smile. "It's good to be back. Knowing the pattern, my brothers and sisters will recover too."

"She's been a gift from the gods, sir," Eklavya testified with obvious pride in their wizard. "We wouldn't have survived the canyons without her."

Ashok could not help but be suspicious. "Wizards are rare and valuable. You could find status and comfort anywhere you wished inside the Law. You choose to stay with the Sons on your own free will?"

"These are my people now, General Ashok. I owe you and Thera my life."

"There is nothing owed to me. I am sure Thera would say the same. You are no longer a slave. Do as you will."

Yet there was clearly no question in her heart. "Then I will continue to serve."

A once-broken slave had healed and found her place. Even though it felt as if the entire world was spiraling into chaos, that small moment pleased dour Ashok. Life goes on.

"You honor the Sons of the Black Sword. Welcome." That was all the time he would allow himself to dwell on frivolous things, for there was work to do. "I come from the Cove with dire news. Eklavya, gather the rest of the officers so that I can brief them. Then prepare the men to march. We will leave in the morning."

"Our destination, General?"

"I'm going to the city of Kanok. The Sons of the Black Sword will follow as best they can. That is where we will find Thera."

Chapter 5

〰〰〰

This wasn't the first time Thera Vane had been held as a hostage.
Such a fate really wasn't that odd in Lok, where high-status people
were often used as bargaining chips to be traded between houses.
Border raiders would capture enemy warriors, vital workers, and
sometimes even members of the first caste, to ransom them back
to their families. The Law went into excruciating detail about
how each class was allowed to be treated in captivity, and great
would be the suffering of any house that willfully violated those
protocols.

Unfortunately for the criminals—like Thera—there was no
punishment for the captors if they harmed prisoners who existed
outside the rules. The Law offered no shelter for those who rebelled
against it. Her captors could have tortured or raped or flogged
her naked back and made her walk barefoot across the desert,
then killed her when they grew bored, and the Law wouldn't care
in the least. Her captors had clearly wanted to do all that, and
worse, because they were led by a phontho who despised her with
a deep and personal hatred—her former husband, Dhaval—but
luckily for Thera, and this was the part which still baffled her, it
had been a different traitorous murderer who had protected her
while she'd been in captivity. By some nonsensical twist of fate,
she'd been spared from Dhaval's unhinged cruelty only because

a lying, backstabbing, two-faced, false priest, who'd pretended to be a friend even while he'd been secretly spying on her for the Inquisition, had intervened to keep her safe.

It was Witch Hunter Javed Zarger who had placed his body between her and the vengeful warriors of Makao. At great personal risk—for there were no witnesses in the desert—Javed had saved her from their wrath by declaring that she was the property of the Inquisition, in possession of a strange magic that the Inquisitors needed to study, and that if so much as a hair upon her head was plucked unnecessarily it would draw the incalculable ire of Grand Inquisitor Omand himself.

Though Dhaval was a petty, bitter man, luckily for her, he was also a coward, so he had backed down when Javed had warned him that even if every Inquisitor who had been transporting Thera to the Capitol had been murdered to the last man and their bodies buried deep in the sand, Omand would still find out, because eventually Omand found out *everything*. There was no figure more frightening in the minds of the Law-abiding than the Grand Inquisitor, as many believed his secret minions lurked in every shadow, read every letter, and eavesdropped on every conversation.

However, keeping Thera alive and unharmed was the only compromise they'd reached. When Javed had demanded she be given back to the Inquisitors to be delivered to the Tower of Silence, Dhaval had refused, because according to the Law, within the borders of his own lands the Thakoor of a great house could overrule the Grand Inquisitor's wishes. Dhaval might not be able to torment and kill Thera, but his master certainly could, and even mighty Omand couldn't stop that. Kanok was a long way from the Capitol.

Also, Thera suspected that Dhaval had been intrigued by the idea of her getting a rigged trial followed by a public execution. He'd enjoy a spectacle where her family name was smeared while his was redeemed, far more than simply torturing her to death, then leaving her body in the desert to be eaten by birds. Dhaval had waited years for retribution against his former wife. What were a few more months?

The man could certainly hold a grudge.

So Thera lay upon a bed of moldy straw in a cell in the dungeons beneath the great house in Kanok and pondered her fate. When the Thakoor returned to his home, he would most certainly pronounce her a traitor to Makao and have her hung...

or the Inquisition would find some way to reclaim her, then she'd be taken to the Tower of Silence to be dissected as they tried to figure out how to rip the Voice's unique magic from her head. There seemed to be no third option where she didn't die horribly. The Voice could probably save her if it felt like it, but it was an unreliable, fickle thing, the aid of which could never be counted upon. It would manifest when it felt like it, or not at all.

A child of Vane never quit, but some nights when it was particularly cold in the dungeon, as she was curled up and shivering, she'd had thoughts about killing herself in order to deprive both camps the satisfaction of using her. That wasn't quitting, she reasoned. That was just spite. Except each morning as the sun rose through the tiny windows of her cell, she'd push those vulnerable thoughts aside, and go back to plotting her escape.

She woke up from a dream, not remembering what it was about exactly, but it had been a foolish, hopeful dream, because in it Ashok had been alive and coming to save her again. It was a young girl's dream, not fit for a woman who had been abused by life. But maybe she was allowed some girlish hope, as Ashok had saved her before. If he was alive, he would find a way back to her. But realistically, he was probably dead, as she would be soon.

It was very dark in her cell. The windows were merely narrow slits, more to allow for a small bit of ventilation than light. She heard something moving across the straw and her first thought was that it was the rats again, except this sounded bigger. Had Javed's threats worn off, and one of the guards decided to have a bit of fun with her? Thera slowly moved her hand to the rock she'd pried from the wall and hidden beneath the straw just in case. A misshapen rock wasn't a proper weapon, but it had a good enough point to it that she was fairly sure she could crack a hole in a skull with it if motivated enough.

And Thera was *very* motivated.

There was a whisper. "Be calm, prophet. It is I, Javed."

That motivated her even more.

She swung the rock for where she thought the whisper had come from, but the witch hunter must have been expecting her to attack. He blocked her arm, then a gloved hand was slammed over her mouth and she was roughly shoved down. When she tried to bring the rock back around, Javed planted one knee on her wrist and pinned it.

"Quiet, I beg you. I've come to help, not to harm you."

Thera kept struggling but Javed was far stronger than he looked, and it was said witch hunters were as well trained for violence as any warrior. She was more angry than afraid. If this was the end, better to get it over with.

"Please, listen to what I have to say, Thera. I'm trying to free you."

That was surely a lie, but she quit thrashing. It wasn't working anyway, and maybe if she got him talking she could catch him unaware and find another angle to kill him.

Javed slowly removed his hand from her mouth, but his weight kept her pinned against the straw. "This restraint is for your own safety until you hear me out." The guards rarely patrolled the dungeon halls this late at night, but Javed kept his voice low just in case. "Don't be a fool. You kill me, the Makao kill you. You shouldn't be trying to hurt the only reason you're still alive."

"You're the only reason I was captured in the first place, treacherous scum."

She couldn't see his face in the dark, but she heard him sigh in resignation. "That's true, and I'll regret what I've done for the rest of my days."

That made no sense. "Spare me your lies."

"I'm telling you the truth. I must atone for what I have done. Let me make this right. It was my obligation to infiltrate your rebellion."

"Oh, you did a right fine job of that, murderer."

"That's right. More murders than I can count. Probably more than even you can imagine. And none of them troubled me in the least until I was exposed to the corrupting influence of that damnable Keta, and all his talk of fate and consequences. And now all those dead *haunt me.* I was better off before I ever heard Keta's words, because I was blessed by ignorance, but with wisdom I become a man condemned. I served the Law when I should have been serving the gods. On the road to the Capitol they told me this themselves."

What? The way he said that was terrifying in the dark. This was not the calm fake priest or the calculating witch hunter she'd dealt with before. Javed spoke with the fervor of a fanatic, and this really didn't feel like another act.

"The gods told you? You mean when you collapsed with sun stroke."

"My delirium wasn't caused by the sun, but by a being nearly as bright as the sun. It wasn't heat that felled me, but guilt, because she told me I must fix what I've broken." Slowly, almost gently, Javed took his weight off of her and backed away. "That's why I've protected you from Dhaval all this time and why I'm going to get you out of here. I've spent every waking minute that I've not been politicking to keep you alive or plotting your escape, writing down every sermon Keta ever gave, every lesson he or Ratul ever taught, and every pronouncement of the Voice, so that someday the rest of the faithful might read them and learn . . . all in the hopes that'll be sufficient apology for these ghosts to *stop tormenting me.*"

He delivered that last part through gritted teeth.

The two of them sat there in the dark, one of them desperate, the other baffled.

"Is this some new Inquisition trick, Javed? Free me from this dungeon so that your masked friends can steal me from the Makao and carry me off to the Capitol so your real master can pick apart my brains panning for gold? Better to kill me now and save us the journey. Sikasso and his wizards couldn't find a way to claim the Voice. I doubt Omand will either."

"Don't be so sure. Omand is a far greater wizard than anyone from the House of Assassins. He is probably the most powerful wizard in the world. You have no idea how dangerous he truly is. But no, this is no trick." Javed slowly shifted away, probably in a vain attempt to appear less threatening, except now the master deceiver was an intimidating black shadow crouched a few feet away. "I no longer answer to Omand. Now I truly serve the gods . . . and you."

"I've heard that one before." Thera sat up and rubbed the feeling back into her bruised arm. "The man who pretended to be a believer once again claims to believe again. No chance."

"I was lying then. This time I'm telling the truth."

"You killed Toramana's boys. While you captured me, your friends killed Murugan." She grew furious just thinking about that again, watching helplessly while her noble bodyguard threw himself off a cliff trying to save her. "You deserve to die."

"I do. And I'll happily slash my wrists once I've done as the gods have commanded and I've righted my wrongs. All I can do is hope that I accomplish enough to appease them before I die, so when they decide what to do with my spirit I'm not condemned for eternity."

The Law declared there was no life after death, just an endless nothing, but most of her rebels believed differently, and carrying on beyond death seemed to be the fanatic's favorite part about Keta's made-up religion, promising an endless paradise for the faithful, another chance at life for everyone else, and eternal torment for the vile. There was no way Javed really believed that nonsense now. "Brave illegal talk, fake priest, but I'm not buying it."

"Then don't. You don't have to trust me. Just be ready to run when I give you the opportunity. I'm working on a plan to get you out of the city. You'll have more chances to escape outside these walls than you will avoiding their entire warrior caste inside."

Javed's words were worth saltwater, but that much was true. She'd once cut a deal with the wizard Kabir to escape a similar situation and he'd ended up with his throat cut for it by his fellow conspirators... She'd be overjoyed if Javed met the same fate as Kabir. "What's this plan of yours?"

"The Thakoor has been called away to the west, due to war breaking out against Harban. You're safe until he returns to pass judgment over you. That gives us some time. I'm gathering other Inquisitors to break you free, in the idea that we're reclaiming our Order's rightful prize. What is the anger of Great House Makao compared to the favor of the Grand Inquisitor? Only once we're safely away from the city, I'll turn on my brothers, kill them, and free you."

"Oh, you're good at that, aren't you? Getting people to trust you, then stabbing them in the back."

Javed was quiet for a long time. "Yes. I'm extremely good at it. You have no idea. Then when the Inquisitors are dead you can return to your people."

"And I'll imagine you'll want to come along, to finish what you've started."

"That'll be entirely up to you." The shadow moved, and something solid landed in the straw next to her. "Careful, it's very sharp."

She reached out and found a tiny knife. "They're less useful when they're dull."

"That's true of people too. You have proven yourself to be a razor. Hide that blade well, prophet. When the time comes, after I've got you out safely, if you still want to plant that steel in my heart as payment for all the terrible things I've done against the children of the gods, so be it. You have my word I'll not try to stop you."

Then the shadow was simply gone.

Witch hunters knew magic. Javed had stepped outside the real world, and would reappear elsewhere nearby, with the guards being none the wiser. Thera recognized that spell, as the Assassins had tried to teach its pattern to her, and the Voice had once used it to save her from a charging demon.

Thera sat there, wide awake, wondering how she'd gotten herself into this mess. She'd been searching for an option other than execution, dissection, or suicide, and now she had one. She doubted trusting Javed was much better than getting hung or having her brains scooped out, but at least it was something.

Shivering, Thera kept the dagger close as she tried to go back to sleep, and she cursed herself for not asking for a blanket.

In the morning, Thera's only confirmation that Javed's visit hadn't been a dream was the little knife and her bruised arm. She tore off a strip of her ragged clothing and used that to hide the knife beneath one sleeve. Then she went about checking her cell for weaknesses for what seemed like the thousandth time since she'd arrived. As usual, the Forgotten hadn't seen fit to deliver her any miracles, like loose bricks around the windows, or a guard forgetful enough to leave the door unlocked.

If the Forgotten wasn't so stingy with his miracles, she wouldn't mind part of him living inside her head. Her unwelcome tenant rarely helped, and even if it did bother to show her another perfect magical pattern for her to use again, she had no demon parts to fuel it.

The sudden rap of a club against the wooden door made her flinch.

"Wake up, prisoner. You got esteemed visitors."

The heavy door creaked open and two brawny warriors entered, truncheons in hand. Guarding prisoners was a low status, no chance for glory, position, but these men took their obligation seriously, always worked in pairs, and never gave her any opportunity to run. The first day she'd been here their havildar had whispered to her that he didn't give a damn about her former husband's grievances, but he'd heard rumors she practiced witchcraft, and he'd told his boys that if they suspected she was trying to use any foul magic on any of them, to beat her to death on the spot, Inquisitors' wishes be damned.

So Thera had kept on her best behavior with the guards. She remained sitting, in the hopes that she'd look less threatening that way. Not that posture would make a lick of difference to a real wizard.

The guards were followed by a female official dressed in the black-and-yellow robes of a Makao junior arbiter, who promptly announced, "Presenting Phontho Dhaval of the Kanok garrison, and Witch Hunter Javed of the Order of Inquisition."

"So much for 'esteemed,'" she muttered.

The dumber guard reflexively snorted a bit at that, but then his partner looked at him and shook his head, as if to say *Shut your damned fool mouth,* and the dumb one promptly did.

Dhaval entered, wearing an ostentatious uniform with far too many medals pinned on it. There was no way such a weasel had rightfully earned so many commendations in battle. Even his eye patch had a ruby on it, like an unblinking red eye. The city folk of Kanok had always struck her as a vapid, showy bunch, completely opposed to the straightforward yet effective warriors of Vane. It had annoyed her father to no end that this house of fops had conquered theirs generations ago.

Dhaval scowled at the dismal, grungy, dark surroundings, and then looked down at Thera, with even more disgust than he had for the flea-infested dungeon.

The feeling was mutual.

"Husband."

"Bitch."

"My greatest regret in life is that I didn't manage to cut out both of your eyes."

Dhaval's hands curled into fists, and he took a step toward her, but Javed had entered the room behind him and warned from behind his golden mask, "Calm yourself, Phontho. We aren't here to rehash the unfortunate nature of how poorly your arranged marriage worked out."

"You'll get yours." Then Dhaval turned back to Javed. "She's very lucky that her freakish nature makes her interesting to our illustrious Grand Inquisitor. It would amuse me to see her picked apart like a surgeon's practice corpse."

"Then end your crusade and turn the prisoner back over to my custody, and I can promise she'll suffer far more at the Tower of Silence than anything you could possibly do to her here."

"Tempting," Dhaval lied.

And Javed surely knew he was lying, because Dhaval was far too prideful to let logic get in the way of his revenge. "The Inquisition is very competent at the art of inflicting pain. Perhaps someday you will step over a line, and will have the opportunity to experience our skill firsthand."

Dhaval feigned offense. "Unlikely, for I'm a Law-abiding man, as demonstrated by my patience here today."

"Get on with it," Javed snapped at the arbiter.

"Of course, Witch Hunter."

Thera gave him a polite nod, because regardless of rank and status, only fools—like Dhaval—annoyed Inquisitors on purpose. "As specified by the Law for a case of this nature, before we waste our Thakoor's precious time with a hearing, the accused must be given a chance to confess."

Thera's eyes narrowed. *What game is this?* She glanced toward Javed, who was either scheming to get her back to the Capitol as a prize, or he was secretly a converted fanatic on a mission from the gods. His mask was the monstrous face of the Law, and it revealed nothing.

"I've not got anything to confess to."

Dhaval gave her a mocking laugh. "You've secretly engaged in illegal witchcraft since childhood, spewing false prophecies to the gullible warriors of Vassal House Vane to inspire them toward rebellion. Then you were married into Great House Makao in order to spy and conspire against us, and when the treasonous uprising of Vane against their rightful masters was insufficient lawbreaking to suit you, you went on to lead a rebellion of caste-less maniacs as their false prophet, going so far as to destroy one of the great works of the Capitol."

Thera sneered. "Oh, you mean *that...*"

"I believe the charges have been sufficiently listed before the accused by Phontho Dhaval," the arbiter stated. "Do you confess to these things, prisoner?"

Thera couldn't help that defiance was her nature. "I grant Dhaval nothing but my scorn."

"So be it." The arbiter seemed annoyed that she'd been dragged here. "The opportunity for confession has passed. We will proceed. Testimony will be presented before Thakoor Venketesh Makao and then he will pronounce his judgment upon her."

"If your Thakoor is a man of judgment, he'll say my greatest crime was that I slashed Dhaval across the eyes instead of his throat. If my aim had been better I could've spared all of us from his endless whining."

"I assume the accused is aware of the penalties for crimes of this magnitude—"

"Some rather gruesome form of execution, I imagine."

"Of course. Thakoor Makao does not tolerate criminality in our fine lands. Hanging, burning, or beheading are the traditional methods of punishment for rebels here."

"I'm hoping for all three," Dhaval said.

"Not if he grants my petition to have Thera returned to Inquisition custody where she belongs," Javed interjected.

Which merely meant a longer, more excruciating form of execution, while the Grand Inquisitor's wizards ripped the Voice from her head...unless Javed had been telling the truth for once in his miserable life and intended to help her escape. She wasn't going to get her hopes up.

"Is this pointless exercise in petty torment done yet?" Thera gestured around her tiny cell. "As you can see I'm rather busy."

"Tell her the best part," Dhaval suggested. "I want to see her squirm."

Thera grew suspicious, for Dhaval seemed genuinely delighted, and his malicious nature meant he was only truly happy while he was being cruel. "Don't leave me in suspense."

"The honored Phontho Dhaval has requested our Thakoor's judgment, not just upon you, a single rebel, but upon your family line, alleging that crimes of such magnitude as you have committed would not have been possible without the approval and support of your family. If Vassal House Vane is judged guilty of hiding a child's illegal witchcraft, their name will be stricken from the records, removed from the protection of the Law forever, and their people—whoever the Thakoor decides to spare at least—and all their property will be subsumed fully into Great House Makao."

"*What?*" That was absurd. "My family had nothing to do with this!"

"On the contrary, they rebelled because of your false prophecies," Dhaval said. "You've doomed not just yourself, but everyone who shares your traitorous name."

Thera was aghast. This made no sense. "My father, Andaman

Vane, was the only one naïve and hopeful enough to believe the Voice, and Protector Ratul killed him for it years ago. Your house already blamed the last foolish war you started with Harban on Vane. They were punished. I'm already forsaken. My family has had nothing to do with me ever since."

"I am not your judge. Save your excuses for the Thakoor. The accusation has already been made," the arbiter declared. "The technicalities have been satisfied. I am finished and tire of this stench."

"Thank you, Arbiter." Dhaval gave her a respectful bow. "Guard, escort our high-status guest back upstairs and see to it she is offered refreshment."

Thera waited until those two had left and her cell was slightly less cramped. "Using me to destroy Vane? What're you really after?"

Dhaval seemed almost gleeful to explain himself. "Vane was a troublesome and disobedient vassal to our Thakoor's father, which makes him more likely to rule my way. Allies of mine desire their land. Other garrisons will divide up Vane's warriors—the ones who are smart enough to give up their names, at least. The rest will be named criminals and hunted down as if they were casteless. Mostly . . . personally . . . I want your name extinguished just because you were always so damned proud of where you came from, so I want to take that away from you. Then you can die knowing that you hurt them one final time."

Thera hated this smug toad so very much that she was tempted to draw the knife Javed had given her and lunge for Dhaval. With the element of surprise on her side she could probably mortally wound him before the remaining guard slammed her against the wall hard enough to shatter every bone in her body.

But no . . . finding a way to survive this would spite him more than death.

It was hard to believe that all those years ago, briefly, ever so briefly, she had deceived herself into thinking her arranged marriage to this man might not be such a bad thing. Oh, what a fool she had been. "You always were more politician than warrior, Dhaval."

"You always failed to understand they're really the same thing, Thera."

"Keep telling yourself that. I've heard Makao has gone to war against its old enemy Harban once more, and yet here you are, safely behind the tall walls of Kanok, so very far from the fighting."

"Someone needs to be here for your trial and shaming." Dhaval made a big show of shivering at the chill. "It's so cold down here. I think I will return to the warm bed of my new wife now."

"Oh, you've managed to not murder this one yet?"

The remaining guard looked at the floor as she said that. The regular warriors probably knew about what had happened to the others, because rumors flew quickly in Kanok. The whole city probably suspected what manner of man Dhaval really was, and when Dhaval saw that low-status warrior's reaction to her words, his remaining eye narrowed with fury. It was a good thing the deadly witch hunter was there, because that insinuation probably would've gotten her killed otherwise.

Dhaval sneered at her but left without another word.

Javed just looked down at her and shook his head. If he'd spoken true about his fanatical conversion last night, he gave no indication of it now. Witch hunters were the greatest actors in the world, and behind that leering mask he might as well have been a stone statue for all the emotion he revealed.

But then Javed told the guard, "The phontho speaks some wisdom. Fetch some warm blankets for this prisoner. And see to it she's being properly fed and given clean water. If she falls ill before her trial, the Inquisition will hold your unit responsible."

That threat clearly terrified the guard. Dhaval may have been a devious worm who had somehow gained far too much authority, but an Inquisitor was an Inquisitor. Warriors could weather the occasional bad commander. Inquisitors represented the careful malice of the Law itself.

"It'll be done, Witch Hunter."

Once they were all gone, Thera wondered if more warmth and food had been meant as a small mercy, or was that small kindness merely an attempt to keep their magical curiosity alive? It was impossible to know for sure. Then her thoughts turned to the plight of her birth house. Vane were proud warriors, who surely had no use for a criminal like her. They had no loyalty to her, nor her to them. She had her own people now, criminals and fanatics.

Only Dhaval had been right about her pride, and she hated him for it. Thera was a warrior daughter of Vane, and though they surely hated her now, they were still her people. It tore her heart out that she might be their doom.

Chapter 6

As a proper warrior and Law-abiding man, Jagdish didn't believe in gods... but he did believe in luck, or fate as he'd call it on those grim and unfortunate days where everything went wrong. And days like that were far too common for a soldier.

Part of him could understand how the religious fanatics he'd known had begun believing in gods, who all had their peculiar thoughts and feelings and godly opinions and a deep and abiding desire to screw with mankind, because over the years, Jagdish had often found himself thinking of fate that same exact way. Fate was a she—Jagdish didn't know why, fate just was—and she was usually out to get him. Just as Keta had preached about his precious Forgotten like he was some kind of relatable being who just happened to be all-knowing and all-powerful and live in the sky, soldiers also tended to think of fate like she was a living thing... and Jagdish had come to know her well!

Now, a lazy warrior blamed everything on fate, even when it wasn't her doing. If your sword rusted in its scabbard, that was because you failed to properly clean and maintain your equipment, not the malign will of the universe out to get you. That was stupidity or laziness, not fate. As an officer, it was Jagdish's obligation to beat that kind of dimwitted behavior out of his men.

Yet deep down every warrior knew that sometimes you could

do everything right, and things would still go wrong. If you were going on a march on a beautiful day, don't be surprised when the storm clouds come rolling in. Or if you were counting on your fresh rations being delivered on time, you could expect that wagon to lose a wheel. Ropes break. Horses throw shoes. Junior nayaks do dumb things. These were immutable facts of warrior caste life.

Beyond those inconveniences and annoyances, fate could also be a fickle and murderous thing. In battle good men died because they'd looked right instead of left, or up instead of down, and just as easily the opposite direction too.. Every warrior understood you could do everything right and die in humiliation, while you could do everything wrong and survive and, if you were born of status, probably get some commendations along the way.

Smart warriors never counted on luck to carry them through. They trained hard, used their heads, and made their own luck. Except when the horn sounded and the steel flew, no matter how solid the soldier, they hoped for all the luck they could get. Before battle, every warrior *wished* that fate would be on his side that day. When death loomed, it caused a man to examine his life, and what he'd done up until that moment, right and wrong, and a great many promises were made that if they made it through that day, they'd try to do more right and less wrong. A fanatic might even call such a thing *prayer* but that was foolish religious talk that could get a man crosswise with the Law.

Regardless, whether it was the overt rituals of the Sons of the Black Sword asking their imaginary gods for help, or his loyal-to-the-Law Vadal troops making promises to the endless nothing that if they lived through the day they'd try to be better men tomorrow, every warrior hoped fate would be on his side in battle.

She usually wasn't, but that was just the nature of soldiering.

But on that bright morning in the edge of the woods overlooking a vast hay field on the border between Vadal and Sarnobat, Jagdish knew that fate didn't always have to be a stone-hearted hag, spreading misery, failure, and bad fortune. For today, fate had delivered an unwitting army of Sarnobat right into Jagdish's hands, and he intended to crush them.

"I know that banner. That's the symbol of Daula Memon dar Sarnobat. Of all the phonthos they could send against me, I'd hoped it would be him." Jagdish lowered his spyglass. "This wolf tends to stray too far from the rest of his pack. Daula is too eager. He's jumped his lines. They're overextended."

"Just as you predicted he would, Phontho," his bodyguard Zaheer observed. "Good guess."

Jagdish had done his best to learn everything he could about all of his potential opponents. He had looked up the official records of all their raids and battles—then promptly discounted those stuffy and impersonal accounts—spoken with every warrior under his command who'd ever fought against Sarnobat, interrogated prisoners from the house of the wolf, and even sent spies across the border to sit in the humblest taverns to listen to what the lower ranks praised or complained about their leaders and units. Taking all that intelligence, filtered through his own hard-won experience, Jagdish had created a picture in his mind about the real nature of his enemies.

"Daula is a fine raider, but a bad campaigner. Give him a few hundred men and point him in the direction of whatever it is you need burned, and it'll be on fire soon enough. Give him a few thousand men and a supply chain to worry about and his impatience will outrun his sense." Jagdish inclined his head toward his most senior officer. "Do you agree with my assessment, Roik?"

Old Kutty had been promoted and demoted so many times over his long career that it took him a moment to realize that he was the roik in question. "Yeah, I do. Look at how these fools ride in the open, with half their forces still on the other side of the river. Not a care in the world. He smells blood and easy victory, because even with only half his force present he still outnumbers us."

Kutty's demotions hadn't been for being a bad soldier, but for having strong opinions about the decisions of his superiors. Jagdish didn't see that as a negative, as he himself despised suckups and yes-men. Any coward could place blame after that fact. Poking holes in your superior's plans before things turned bad took courage. If Jagdish was wrong, he'd rather his counselors tell him that *before* the dying started.

"What would you do with them, then?"

"Same as you, I imagine, Jagdish. Two against one is better than four against one. This is our best chance. Let's smash these bastards."

"Good." Jagdish had already sent one paltan ahead to make

contact and then immediately turn tail and flee. When a rabbit runs, a wolf gives chase. In his eagerness, Daula Memon had let his horsemen outrun his infantry. With the last great army of Sarnobat split in two, the lead element was riding straight into Jagdish's trap. "Make sure Phontho Gotama knows our foe took the bait, and to cut off their reinforcements at the Mara bridge."

"I'm on my way." Kutty immediately rode off.

Jagdish wasn't too worried about Gotama's army being where it needed to be at the right time. His soon-to-be father-in-law was a sly one, but Jagdish would leave nothing else to fate if he could help it.

Surveying the upcoming battlefield, he saw that the terrain was relatively flat, just gentle levees through the fields so the workers could flood irrigate in sections. The enemy was rushing into an area with little cover. The ground was dry and firm. There weren't too many gopher holes to trip up his horses. The air was cool. The sun was shining, and high enough it wouldn't blind his archers. There were wolves of Sarnobat invading his homeland. It was a marvelous day to make war.

Jagdish turned his horse, so he could get a good look at the rest of his command staff waiting in the shade of the trees. Some seemed eager, others nervous, but they were trying not to let it show. That was good. The men needed their leaders to act certain. Jagdish was nervous too, but he wasn't about to let any of these boys see his hands shake. None of his officers were new to this bloody business. Every man under his command had been handpicked because he could fight. Jagdish's army had no political obligations among its leadership. He'd despised useless officers back when he'd been a lowly nayak, so he'd been damned if he'd have any of those parasites serve under him once he'd been promoted to the prestigious rank of phontho.

"I want fourth and seventh paltans to ride for the southern creek. Second and fifth, take the hilltop to the east. That's the direction Daula will try to break through once he realizes they're encircled." Jagdish made those sudden changes based upon his gut instinct in the moment. If he were wrong, men would die for it. That was just the nature of things. "Questions?"

"What of us wizards?" Mukunda asked.

Jagdish was unused to having battle wizards under his command, but this one was an experienced campaigner, and not nearly as annoying and entitled as the other magically gifted sorts Jagdish had dealt with over the years. Mukunda must have spent too many years obligated to serve around regular warriors, because he had none of that regular wizard haughtiness about him, and seemed as ready to fight as any warrior. Regardless, Jagdish didn't trust wizards. Even the good ones had a reputation for being more destructive than selective, and those were his men out there.

"Unless Sarnobat's ancestor blade is on the field, you wizards will hold back. Save that demon bone for tomorrow, because today belongs to the warrior caste."

"And if their bearer does show his face?" Risalder Joshi brought up what all the officers were nervous about.

"It isn't his face I'm worried about, boys." They all laughed at that, because nobody in their right mind looked forward to fighting against a magical sword that could thresh armies like wheat. "If their bearer is here, I want Mukunda and his men to light that bastard on fire or drop a boulder on him from the sky or whatever it is they do."

"We'll set the boulder on fire and then throw it at him," the battle wizard quipped.

"Good. I didn't carry half a ton of demon bone all the way from Bhadjangal to Vadal just for you wizards to wear it as decoration."

"It's true you supplied us with so much magic we're the envy of every other house"—Mukunda gestured at the necklace of shining black demon teeth he wore over his armor—"but you must admit, it also looks really good on me."

The warriors laughed. Jagdish loved how his people could find mirth even in the moments when bloody chaos loomed. Too much tension would rob men of their effectiveness.

"Is there anything else? Speak up now or hold it until the battle is through."

There was nothing. These warriors knew what they were about. As phontho, Jagdish gave them the broad strokes, then it would be up to each of them to direct their paltans as events unfolded around them. Only a foolish commander believed he could still control things once swords crossed. Good commanders lead. Bad ones meddle.

"Alright, boys. It's time to skin the wolf."

The risalders returned to their paltans. Runners were sent. Banners were waved in the appropriate patterns. A thousand Vadal warriors began moving from where they'd been hiding in the forest. Jagdish pulled his pocket watch out and made a note of the time. Surely the Historians would want to record the pivotal number that would mark such a decisive blow in the house war against Sarnobat... Or, really, Jagdish had already done everything he could and he found some small measure of comfort in keeping his hands busy playing with the tiny mechanical device. There were two stars on his turban now, but right then he was as nervous as the day he'd presented himself at his first assignment as a low-status child of the warrior caste... though hopefully he concealed those nerves much better now.

Ten minutes after Jagdish had given his commands, his entire army was on the move. His chosen officers were as efficient as the gears in his watch. He had built this army from nothing, starting with the castoffs no other units had wanted, including men who had been as thoroughly dishonored as he himself had once been, and he had given them another chance to bring glory to their names. Most of them had seized that opportunity, they'd achieved victory after victory, and now all of Vadal spoke of his army with respect and admiration.

Jagdish had gone from prisoner to phontho, from looming execution to highest promotion. He had been both enemy and friend to the most dangerous man in the world and had fought his way across the continent and back, slaying demons and wizards along the way, all to redeem his name. He had been a loyal husband, a good father, and had done his absolute best to truly live up to the ideals of his caste.

Fate might not be thwarted often, but she seemed to have a soft spot for those who gave their all.

Chapter 7

The battle of Mara Fields began.

Hidden within the tree line, Jagdish watched as his officers flawlessly executed his plan. Daula's horsemen were cut off from their infantry before they even realized Vadal had an entire army on the field. Jagdish's heart was filled with pride as he watched the paltans he'd organized, led by officers he had trained, move into place, and that pride changed to worry, because he knew the face of every single Vadal soldier who was about to die today.

This was the worst part for Jagdish, because there was little he could do for now but watch. This part was not a static battle of orderly ranks. This was chaotic maneuvers between two swift forces on horseback, with dozens of clashes and retreats between them. A phontho who tried to manage his paltans now would only make things worse. He had to trust his boys. Even if Jagdish saw an angle that could be exploited, by the time he got that signal to the officers up close it would be too late for them to take advantage of it. He knew from experience it was hard to hear a signal horn over the sound of thundering hooves as your blood was pumping and your ears were thudding back and forth inside a steel helmet.

Arrows crossed the sky. Men and horses died screaming. The Sarnobat forces discovered too late that they had cavalry moving all around them. If they survived, Daula would surely have his scouts flogged, but it wasn't their fault. Jagdish had enlisted locals, warriors who had grown up here, and used their knowledge to take advantage of the terrain, hiding his men in locations the enemy scouts wouldn't think to look.

The forces of Vadal were in armor of blue-gray, and bronze. The enemy wore blacks and browns and whites, the same as the pelts of the wolf packs that constantly haunted Sarnobat lands. Blood bloomed red on both sets of colors.

"Spyglass." Jagdish stuck out his hand to one of his bodyguards, who promptly smacked the valuable brass-and-glass tube against Jagdish's palm. He put the tube to his eye in order to search for his true goal.

"No sign of their ancestor blade yet," said the wizard Mukunda. "You'd feel it?"

"Maybe. I don't have that particular gift, but it's said the swords have got a terrible presence about them when they're used in anger."

"That they do," Jagdish agreed, having watched Ashok duel many a fool who had tried to claim Angruvadal from him. As he recalled the many warriors who'd been killed or disfigured trying to take that precious sword for themselves, and how his current orders were to try the same thing with Sarnobat's ancestor blade, Jagdish muttered quietly to himself again, "That they do."

It was as if the spyglass brought the battle six times closer, and that made Jagdish jealous that he didn't have eyes like a Protector, which could just observe distant things like this whenever they felt like it.

Daula Memon dar Sarnobat was proving to be a cunning foe. It didn't take him long to grasp that his horsemen outnumbered the Vadal attacking them and counter. Sarnobat spread this half of their army apart farther, sending paltans west and south to fight back against Jagdish's harriers.

Time seemed to slow as Jagdish watched with agonizing anticipation. His precious watch was in his pocket, but he didn't need to check it to know exactly how much time was passing, for he could count every pounding heartbeat in his chest. This part required patience, for he needed Sarnobat even more split and vulnerable. It wasn't just enough to win—Jagdish wanted to win decisively. He waited a few hundred steady beats for the enemy to be fully committed to their counterattack before ordering, "Send in our infantry."

"Spears up! Spears up!" Roik Kutty bellowed, and he had lungs on him like a town crier. That shout was repeated by other officers crouched and waiting ahead of them. Armored infantrymen rose from their hiding places in the fields, hundreds of them, sprouting like a deadly crop. They immediately formed up into their proper ranks, shoulder to shoulder. "Let's water these fields with Sarnobat blood! Ahead quick march!"

"Have the archers follow."

"Bows up! Bows up!"

The rest of Jagdish's army began moving toward the Sarnobat forces. Even walking through tripping plants and across uneven levees, the spearmen maintained their formation. Expected, since they'd been drilled on this sort of thing thousands of times, beneath burning sun or freezing rain, until it had become part of their basic nature, no different from taking a leisurely stroll with several hundred of your closest friends. Too many officers who'd earned their rank by birth forgot that formations weren't about looking pretty to impress the first caste during parades. Formations were vital, for no matter how tough an individual warrior was, on his own he could be surrounded, overwhelmed, and defeated. An army without organization was a mob. It went against man's natural inclinations to fight as a team. Undisciplined, untrained, and left to their own devices, one man could still be incredibly savage, but watching groups of such fight was little better than seeing the monkeys of the northwestern jungles battle over food. Put them shoulder to shoulder, united, and men became a terrifying killing force. There would always be reasons for war, but the warrior caste brought order and effectiveness to the bloody endeavor.

Jagdish watched the enemy, waiting to gauge their reaction once they understood they were surrounded. They were the red-hot steel on an anvil, and the hammer was coming. Daula's banner dipped and waved. Horns blew. The enemy phontho must have seen their doom marching toward them, for he was trying to call back his cavalry, only it was too late. One brave risalder on the enemy side spotted Jagdish's infantry and moved his men to intercept, probably hoping to slow them, to buy the main body some time. Arrows flew, but Jagdish's infantry was prepared for that and held up their round shields, each man protecting both himself and the brother to his left. Arrowheads bounced off steel instead of piercing flesh. Not a single man broke formation. As Jagdish had spent the last year constantly barking at them, *discipline wins battles.*

The infantry kept marching on.

Jagdish saw an opportunity open. "Turn, turn," he urged his distant risalders, not that they could hear him from hundreds of yards away, but fate must have carried his wishful words over to them on the wind—or far more likely Risalder Joshi was a clever lad and had seen the same thing Jagdish had—because his paltan suddenly shifted to the right and launched themselves forward at a run. The brave Sarnobat horsemen who'd tried to stall for time were now pinched between Joshi's infantry and Fourth paltan coming up from the south on horseback. It was a glorious thing, seeing officers he'd taught rise to their full brilliant potential.

The three groups collided. Trapped between thrusting spears and a sudden hail of arrows from the horse archers, many Sarnobat warriors fell. Bodies were tossed from rearing horses. Horses were impaled on spears. Joshi's men were relentless, methodical, moving as one, continually stabbing. Those who tried to flee were swiftly run down, slashed by saber, pierced by arrow, or trampled beneath furious hooves. Fifty of Sarnobat's finest were wiped from existence, just like that.

And the rest of the enemy saw it happen.

"Push, lads. Break their spirit," Jagdish whispered, and it took all of his will to stay where he was and not ride into the fray to help his boys. Except that wasn't his place anymore. He was a commander. There were probably a hundred men out there who could swing a sword nearly as well as he could, but there was only one among them who was obligated to lead. But oh, how difficult that ugly fact was for a warrior proud as Jagdish to accept!

"The wolf's faltering," Kutty said. "I think we have them."

"It's not over until Daula surrenders," Jagdish cautioned. "But now that he knows he's trapped, maybe I should ride over there and see if he'll face me alone in a duel. He might accept to save face and what's left of his army. Stopping now would spare lives on both sides."

Kutty stared at him incredulously. "At times I forget that you're still young for your rank and possess the iron sack of a demon hunter, because that nayak-style, wishful-thinking foolishness is the dumbest idea I've heard in quite a while. Daula's equally likely to have his archers stick arrows in your face ... sir."

Jagdish laughed. "Allow your commander his dreams, Kutty. It hurts me to watch from the shade and do nothing."

"Me too, but don't forget it's our jobs to get the youngsters ready to fight. Us veterans have already had our chance for glory, and you've claimed more than your share."

That he had. "You're right ... but if I see a gap out there in need of filling, danger be damned, I'm joining in."

"And that's why the men love you, Jagdish."

A messenger rode along the tree line shouting, "Phontho Jagdish! Phontho Jagdish!" Warriors pointed him in the right direction.

"Over here!"

It was one of Gotama's men, and from the froth on his horse, he'd been riding hard. He snapped a salute when he spotted the starred turban that marked Jagdish's rank. "The army of Gotama has caught the enemy on the other side of the river trying to push through. We've got them pinned on the banks with our archers above killing them as they try to ford across. They're in disarray."

Jagdish grinned, for he'd had faith in that wily old fox. Gotama was as sharp a commander as his daughter was a courtier. "That's excellent news." But from the stricken look on the messenger's face, he knew there was something else. "What?"

"There's one among them we think might be the bearer of their black sword."

"Have you seen this weapon?" Mukunda snapped.

"Some of the men are saying they did. All we know for sure is one among the Sarnobat fought as a demon, carving his way through several of us. We killed his horses and most of his men. The rest dove off the bank and waded across to this side of the river just a few minutes ago. We lost sight of them after that."

"If it is the bearer, he could be trying to reach his imperiled commander," Kutty suggested. "We're winning, but a black sword could still turn this fight in Sarnobat's favor."

"Where are they?" Jagdish demanded. "And how many?"

"They crossed by Ban Sagar Pond. Ten, maybe twelve of them survived."

Jagdish looked to one of his bodyguards, Zaheer, who had been stationed here before, and thus knew this part of the border well. "That's not far, Jagdish. If they're on foot we can intercept them."

Excited, the wizard Mukunda turned in his saddle to shout at the other four wizards who were waiting to unleash their mayhem. "This is it! We will claim this magic for the glory of Vadal!"

There was nothing else Jagdish could do as a commander now, but perhaps there was something he could still do as a swordsman. Only the most desperate of fools would challenge a bearer for a chance to take up an ancestor blade, and Jagdish was no fool, but orders were orders. Harta Vadal had commanded Jagdish to push this illegal war in the hopes it would draw out Sarnobat's ancestor blade, so Vadal could take it. Even if Mukunda's wizards struck down the bearer from a distance, someone from Vadal would still have to try and pick up that blade to claim it for their house, and any it found unworthy, it would force them to cut themselves. And there was no such thing as a shallow wound when it came to black steel. Jagdish would order no man to take such a risk, for what kind of commander would he be, if he would not volunteer himself first for such a test?

Also, not that he would ever say such a thing in front of his warriors, to this day Jagdish still wondered what would have happened if he had tried to claim Angruvadal from Ashok back when he'd had the chance . . . Honestly, he probably would've died poorly in that duel, but surely Sarnobat's bearer could be no Ashok!

Old Kutty must have understood what Jagdish was thinking and known there'd be no swaying him from it. "I can handle things from here for now, Phontho, but please do return quickly. I'd rather not be the one getting blamed if things go wrong."

Jagdish ordered his bodyguard to show him the way.

This was no bearer.

The lead Sarnobat warrior was fearsome looking indeed, but having seen the real thing in action, disappointed Jagdish knew that was no ancestor blade in his hand. The steel was darkened, but it was from some manner of protective coating, probably of oil and soot. Only someone who'd never seen the eye-searing blackness of a true ancestor blade would mistake this mere metal weapon for one of those terrifying things.

The enemy were at least a dozen in number, pushing through the tall reeds along the riverbank, trying to make their way toward the sounds of battle in the distance.

Ancestor blade or not, Mukunda had been unleashed, and he didn't hesitate to use his magic to cover all those men in fire. The reeds ignited and burst in the sudden magical heat. Warriors screamed as fur, cloth, and hair burned. Those who panicked died flailing. The smarter ones threw themselves into the mud or back into the river shallows. "Burn, Sarnobat dogs! Burn!"

"Save your demon, Mukunda. There's no ancestor blade here." Jagdish waited until the eager wizards indicated that they understood and would stay here and not do anything ridiculous—he had little faith in wizards' tricks and even less in their judgment— then he and his bodyguards continued riding toward the now scorched and scattered enemy. The ground was soft along the banks and their steeds began to stumble, so Jagdish ordered his men to dismount. They drew their blades and walked forward, lingering just long enough to let most of the flames die down first. No use in getting their uniforms singed.

The Sarnobat warriors came out of the mud swinging, but they'd been badly rattled by the wizards' attack. Jagdish's personal guard were all superb combatants, and they rushed ahead to protect their master. Though the two groups were nearly even in number, the way the Sarnobat raiders had been staggered meant that each of the enemy ended up throwing themselves individually against two or three of Jagdish's men. Even if they'd been equals in capability, it wouldn't have mattered the way his Vadal soldiers worked together. As one intercepted an attack, his brothers would flank, stabbing and slashing, and another man of Sarnobat would fall. A kidney was pierced. The tendons of a leg were severed. A skull was smashed open by a mace.

By the time the enemy leader with the darkened sword came splashing his way back from the river, roaring at his men to fall back toward him, it was already too late. This skirmish had been won before it had even really started.

"Surrender and live or fight and die," Jagdish said. "Decide quickly. I've got a battle to see to."

All but one of the survivors dropped their weapons and raised their empty hands. Only the lead raider kept on climbing up the bank, cursing his men as cowards. He was extremely tall, corded with muscle, covered in scars, and he still had his sword in hand. There was no indication there was any quit in this one. Jagish could respect that.

"Fight me, Vadal!"

Command obligation be damned, Jagdish's blood was up. "Secure these prisoners and then back off, lads. This one's mine."

Reluctantly, his bodyguards did as they were told. It wasn't that they didn't have confidence in their phontho's abilities, for Jagdish had beaten every single one of them in their sparring sessions, but if their charge died under their watch, it would bring great shame to their names. Jagdish understood that worry well, having once lost a Thakoor himself, but he'd come here to fight a duel, and he wasn't leaving without one.

When the big raider saw Jagdish standing there waiting for him, he pushed his way through the smoking reeds and roared, "Fight me, coward!"

Jagdish lifted his sword in response. "What else do you think I'm intending to do here, imbecile?"

That wasn't the proper legal challenge to begin a duel, but it would have to do.

The raider came at him without hesitation in what looked like a careless manic charge. Jagdish prepared to sidestep and send him to the great nothing. Only the raider slid to a stop a few feet away, and feinted, before thrusting for the chest. Jagdish narrowly avoided that, then barely managed to block the follow-up swing. The shock of the impact told Jagdish that this man was extremely strong. With a flick of the wrist Jagdish slashed for the eyes, but the raider slipped back and ducked away.

The next thrust came from below, remarkably swift. Jagdish parried the soot-darkened sword away and moved back, appraising his foe with new eyes. This warrior had the appearance of a brute, but his sword form was excellent. "Seems I've got an actual challenge for once."

"The last one you'll ever face, Vadal swine."

The raider leapt at him, stabbing for Jagdish's stomach. He caught the enemy's blade with his own and shoved it aside at the last instant, then swung around low, trying to clip him in the side, except his foe was far too fast and managed to dance away. Jagdish kept after him, constantly striking, pushing the raider back, hoping to trip him up along the soft mud of the bank, but the Sarnobat raider was as clever as he was fast, and rather than slipping, he used his momentum to slide to the side before jumping back onto firm ground and soft grass.

Twenty feet from where they'd begun, they parted and circled as a cloud of biting flies rose up around them.

"You're very good."

"You're no slouch yourself, for dung-eating Vadal trash, but you really should've had your wizard cook me when he had the chance. I'm more than a match for you."

The raider sounded so confident that Jagdish was worried one of his bodyguards might grow worried for him and preemptively put an arrow into the man. "This is my fight, Zaheer!" Jagdish didn't risk looking back their way even for a heartbeat, but he'd just have to trust upon their honor not to interfere.

The raider shifted his stance, changing the angle of his waiting blade slightly. Something about that simple movement reminded Jagdish of his time spent sparring against Ashok Vadal in Cold Stream Prison.

"I recognize that form."

"Doubtful," the cocky raider snapped. "It's a rare school, fiercer than anything taught in your pampered house."

"It's the traditional style of Vassal House Memon, learned by a sword master named Ratul, who taught it to Ashok Vadal, who showed me how to defeat it." Jagdish changed his stance to mirror his opponent's. "I will demonstrate."

The raider blinked several times, confused, then frowned. "Wait—"

Except by the time that word was uttered Jagdish's attack had already been launched. He went high and slashed downward, bypassing the raider's guard. Sadly, he clipped the bands of armor atop the shoulder instead of the flesh of the neck as he'd hoped. That powerful blow made the raider stumble, and Jagdish relentlessly followed, striking high again, then low, and each time he was met and countered, Jagdish rapidly struck again.

Somehow the raider survived that onslaught uncut, and they parted, both of them breathing hard, but neither was bleeding. Yet.

"Stay your hand, Vadal. We must talk."

"Oh, now you want to surrender? I'll not be barked at by a wolf of Sarnobat about mercy. You bastards once tried to burn my house down while my daughter was inside it. Die with some dignity, man."

"That's exactly what I'm trying to do! You know of Keeper Ratul?"

"Keeper?" The only *Keeper* Jagdish had met was Keta. The rebellion's priest had called himself the Keeper of Names. "That's a title from a criminal's church, but *Protector* Ratul taught the man who taught me."

"You mean Ashok? So you claim to have met the Forgotten's holy warrior?"

Another fanatic's title. "Met him? Ashok and I rode together in the Sons of the Black Sword." It was rare that he bragged about his association with the most hated man in Vadal among his own people, but that time was still a matter of great pride for Jagdish, for they had accomplished the impossible together. "Ashok Vadal was my friend."

"Cursed whore of fish stink, *you're* the one I'm supposed to find? Hell's oceans piss in my eyes! The gods have sent me to save the life of a *Vadal* man?" The raider tossed his sword on the ground, then spread his arms so that Jagish could easily stab him in the heart if he wanted to. "Forgotten, just slay me now and spare me this shame!"

"Have you lost your damned mind?"

"No, but apparently the gods have!"

Jagdish was very glad there were no Inquisitors among them because that kind of illegal religious talk had complicated his life before. Why did fate see fit to keep introducing him to secret fanatics? The last time he'd ended up leading a paltan of them. "What're you going on about?"

When neither Jagdish nor the gods saw fit to strike him down, the mad warrior sighed, as if resigned to his fate. "Mother Dawn commanded me to cross this river, because I'd find the man I'm supposed to defend with my life on the other side today. I'd know him because he was an ally of Ashok and the Keeper of Names. The sacred heavenly messenger never warned me that the man I'm supposed to save would be a Vadal pig-dog!" He shook his fist at the sky. "Why must the gods test my faith?"

Many of the Sons of the Black Sword had spoken of their encounters with Mother Dawn, and how that strange woman had gathered them together and sent them to join with the rebels.

Very much doubting this was some clever trick for the warrior to distract and murder him, Jagdish glanced back at his body-guards to make sure they weren't close enough to hear what he was about to say. Since the enemy had clearly thrown down his sword and given up, Zaheer and the others were approaching. They were good lads: Jagdish didn't want to implicate them in any illegal religious zealotry. So he closed with the warrior, shoved him to his knees, and placed his sword against his throat, before whispering, "Mother Dawn sent you for *me*?"

"Unfortunately. The gods are cruel and my life must be a joke to them, or they must enjoy watching me suffer. She told me that my new master would be a great warrior, but not a believer. Except the gods needed me to keep him alive because he still has a part to play in fulfilling their will. So I rushed here fast as I could, thinking I'd be saving some great warrior of Sarnobat, perhaps even Phontho Daula himself, not"—he looked at Jagdish, disgusted—"*this*."

"Oceans." Jagdish was tempted to just slit the religious fanatic's throat to spare him this complication, but he had too much respect for the Sons he'd commanded who'd believed this same kind of nonsense about mysterious women dispensing prophecies to do so. "Not this again."

"Also, I'm supposed to tell you that a black sword isn't the answer to your problems. Only aiding the gods' chosen will do that." The madman looked up at him defiantly, then thumped his fist against his chest. "I am Najmul Memon dar Sarnobat, master of every weapon, the fiercest combatant among all the wolves for ten years, secret worshipper of the Forgotten for five, and by the gods' holy will I pledge my life to you...whatever your name is."

"Jagdish."

"Then I will serve Jagdish!"

"Great." His men and the wizards were close enough to hear the conversation now, and the last thing Jagdish needed was any of them reporting this religious nonsense back to an Inquisitor. So Jagdish slammed the pommel of his sword against Najmul's head, laying the fanatic out cold in the dirt.

Zaheer joined him. "I honestly thought he had you there, Phontho, then it was as if he just gave up. Want me to kill him for you?"

"No. Tie him up and put him with the other prisoners to be ransomed." Then Jagdish recalled Keta's tendency to tell wild tales of gods and heroes to stir up a mob wherever they'd gone. He certainly didn't want someone reminding everyone of his previous brushes with forbidden religiosity. "On second thought, have him chained and isolated. I want to interrogate him myself."

Chapter 8

A few nights later, Jagdish sat in a hot bath to let his sore muscles soak, trying his best to not fall asleep and drown. There was no form of fatigue greater than the kind felt after days of battle. It was as if one's body was a rag that just kept soaking up excitement and terror, and that rag got wrung out over and over again. It was the most profound kind of exhaustion that could be experienced.

After most of his battles he'd been lucky if there had been a water bucket to scrub some of the blood and filth off his face and hands, some moldy naan to eat, and a place to throw his bedroll on the hard ground to sleep. Being able to ride back to an estate, where grooms cared for his horse, armorers maintained his equipment, and cooks prepared him a fine meal, before he went to sleep in a real bed, was far nicer than being a regular soldier. The old saying really was true: a phontho's bathhouse was a palace compared to a nayak's barracks.

Only Jagdish wasn't the sort to forget where he came from, and tomorrow he'd be back among the men, leading from the front like a real warrior should. But for now, his battle was won...so he'd sit and soak and ache and worry about nothing.

The curtain was thrown open so suddenly that he reflexively reached for the sheathed sword that was resting next to the tub.

"The hero has returned from winning glorious victory for Vadal!"

"Lady Shakti!" Jagdish relaxed when he realized it wasn't a Sarnobat assassin sent to murder him—but only a bit, for though their marriage had been arranged, the official ceremony hadn't been performed yet. Being accused of stealing the virtue of a high-status woman could get a man killed just as easily as a battle. He did his best to cover his nakedness with his hands. "You can't be here."

Shakti was a beautiful young woman, but did not care much for propriety or tradition, so she waved one lovely hand dismissively. "Don't worry, Jagdish. I've got a fine excuse to be visiting your border estate: I'm on official business delivering a message of congratulations from the eastern command to their triumphant phontho." She held up a letter with a blue-wax seal and waved it at him. "See?"

"Do you often deliver letters our caste's commanders while they're in the bath?"

"No, this is a rare treat. Only your bodyguard knows, and Zaheer doesn't strike me as the gossipy sort. My bodyguards are waiting downstairs, and they've seen me visit you in more inappropriate places than this. There will be no scandal."

His betrothed had a tendency to only see things from a political perspective, which was simultaneously a gift and a curse. "I'm not worried about rumors, Shakti. There's been far worse things spread around about me than being a womanizer, but I really don't want your father to take offense."

She openly scoffed at that. "Oh, father's dueling years are far behind him."

"Gotama's still got some damned good duelists in his army he could order to serve as his proxy."

Like everything else about her, Shakti's laugh was pretty. "You fought the scourge and stood beneath the pillar of fire together. My father loves you like a son, and he's happy enough to finally find someone to marry off his most troublesome daughter to that he'd overlook far worse indiscretions than this."

Jagdish grinned. "Is that an invitation for further and worse indiscretions, then?"

She remained a polite distance away...well, polite by Shakti's standards. She really shouldn't have been in the same building without a chaperone, let alone in this kind of compromising situation. "Don't get ahead of yourself, warrior. As the old worker saying goes, nobody pays for a goat if they are already getting free cheese."

"Workers can be very wise."

"Exactly. We have a marriage arrangement to honor. I'd hate to upset the arbiters who worked so hard on it."

They both knew that was a lie. She'd drawn the contract up herself, and then coerced an arbiter into putting his stamp on it. Theirs was an odd arrangement. She had sabotaged every previous attempt by their house to arrange a marriage for her and decided on Jagdish instead. It was rare a woman of her high status picked out her own husband, and rarer still that one this astute would choose a man burdened with such a perilous future.

"I would never dream of upsetting the delicate sensibilities of the first caste."

"That's my Jagdish. A gentleman and a war hero."

"I'm no hero, just a soldier fulfilling my obligation, same as any of my men..." He groaned as he leaned back in the tub, as his body was covered in bruises. He'd not been very good at staying away from danger as a proper phontho should, but what kind of warrior wasn't tempted to join a good fight? "I'll admit this has been a fine week for the armies of Great House Vadal. So, after this victory, do you think Thakoor Harta is more or less likely to blame his illegal war entirely on me?"

"That's a good question. You blackened Sarnobat's eye and, between you and my father, captured over a thousand prisoners for us to ransom back. We both know Harta's true goal is to get us a new ancestor blade, which sadly Sarnobat has been wise enough to hold back and not risk." She picked a robe off a hook on the wall and threw it at Jagdish. "Cover yourself, before you endanger my virtue, knave."

He caught the robe and hid his nakedness as best as he could as he climbed out of the water. They were both of the warrior caste, which was by its very nature pragmatic in its sensibilities—that couldn't be avoided when most of their caste grew up with very little privacy in the humble barracks of their various military districts—but it really was the polite thing to do. Shakti had been spared such indignities in her youth, because she had been born into a high-status officer family. Jagdish had blundered into this opulence through sheer stubbornness.

"I've been trying my damnedest to annoy Sarnobat into sending their bearer to fight, but they've not bitten yet. For a moment I thought I had him, but that one just turned out to be a lunatic." Jagdish had nearly forgotten about Najmul, who was currently chained to a wall. He'd have to figure out what to do with that one eventually.

"If you win enough victories, Sarnobat will have no choice." She gave Jagdish an appraising look as he dried off, and he hoped that meant she was pleased that the warrior she'd picked to be her husband by his reputation alone had also turned out to be a rather fit and handsome man, but then Shakti quickly returned to her true passion, politicking. "In normal times this would be a fine strategy, as their first caste would grow tired of the embarrassment of suffering an endless string of defeats and demand greater action from their warrior caste. Their bearer would have no choice but to fight, or else his entire house would lose face. It would be a race between their pride and the Capitol's greed. Because once the Capitol grew tired enough of the cost of the war and its interruption of trade and taxes, they'd dispatch the Protectors under the guise of enforcing the Law, to execute those guilty of starting it."

"Which is when Harta will give the Protectors me."

"Of course. Protectors always have to execute *somebody*. It's what they do. House war is illegal, but Protectors can't go around punishing Thakoors. They're too important and executing them brings too many complications. That's unseemly. Harta will need a high-ranking commander to blame."

"He already despises me. Convenient."

"Indeed," Shakti agreed, which didn't help. "You also have a reputation for ambition, and a dangerous carelessness toward obeying the exact specifications of the Law, so the judges will have no problem believing you are at fault. After tales of your accomplishments grew into legend, your promotion rallied the troops, but simultaneously gave Harta someone perfect to blame for a war he intended to start anyway. Regardless of the outcome, Harta gets something he wants. I simply marvel at his foresight. Our Thakoor is truly brilliant at this."

Jagdish had to chuckle at the absurdity of his situation. "I'm not fond of the part where I'm hanged for his crimes, but other than that I suppose he's done well by our house."

"If a lesser man were running Vadal, after losing our sword

and dignity as suddenly as we did, we'd already be occupied by all our neighbors and they'd be carving up our power, as we begged for the Capitol to save us."

"Fair..." Jagdish would just have to take her word for it. By background and training he was a common soldier, unused to the courtly machinations of phontho-status warriors. "You said 'in normal times'—I assume what makes things different now is the challenge presented by Devedas. Last I heard, the Capitol's new Army of Many Houses remains camped near Red Lake, supposedly offering aid for a crisis that's already passed."

"They're still there, and no one in the Vadal City courts believes the Capitol's claims that Devedas was sent here to fight the scourge."

Jagdish shuddered as he remembered the horror of that day, as endless waves of tiny demons shredded everything in their path. It had been the most terrifying moment of his life, being helpless before such a threat. "The scourge makes for a convenient excuse, but even if mighty Devedas and his great Capitol army had arrived immediately, they would've just been more fodder for that demonic plague. There was no stopping those things by regular means."

Shakti hadn't been there, but she'd heard both Jagdish and Gotama tell the tale many times. "Father said ten thousand spearmen wouldn't have even slowed them down. The pillar of fire saved us, but it's unfortunate that it was so big it could be seen all the way in the Capitol."

"Trust me, it was even more impressive standing directly under it." Jagdish went to a side table, retrieved a bottle, pulled the cork, and poured them both a glass of wine. A phontho's wine was a quality drink and he got as much as he asked for. As a risalder he'd been lucky to get a ticket for a watery ration of beer. Even if Harta intended to sacrifice him to the Protectors, Jagdish would at least live well until then!

"Regardless, Jagdish, my understanding is that fiery display was so shocking that it frightened the judges. It was the catalyst for factions within the Capitol to make moves to seize more power for themselves. I believe this is what has sent this new Raja—as they're calling Devedas now—to Vadal's doorstep."

Jagdish went over and offered her the glass of wine. "Do you think this will turn out for good or ill?"

"A mystery. Vadal politics I know well. The Capitol is an unfamiliar country to me. But there's something strange going on there—rumors of mass arrests, out-of-control Inquisitors, and judges who are absent or oddly silent about such tyranny. I fear there's a darkness growing in the desert." Their fingers touched when she took her glass of wine, and she lingered for just a bit too long before moving her hand away.

Luck had been on Jagdish's side for his first arranged marriage. Even though marrying a disgraced warrior to a woman of the worker caste had been meant as an insult, he'd quickly come to love Pakpa with all his heart. He still missed her every single day. Though he suspected Pakpa would approve of him marrying Shakti—especially since Shakti was so good with their daughter, Pari—their flirtations still made Jagdish feel as if he was being unfaithful to his first wife. Even though logically a man couldn't be married to a ghost, and the Law-abiding didn't believe in ghosts anyway... It was what it was.

Jagdish sighed. "The seasons pass too slowly."

"Our wedding date is set. Spring is nearly upon us."

In Vadal, spring brought the monsoons, and mud made it logistically difficult to conduct war. Especially in the eastern borderlands, where in the months of Chaitra and Vaisakha they'd sometimes get flash floods sufficient to drown an elephant. Thus spring was the most appropriate time for a commander to take time away from his duties, so that was when they would be wed.

The delay had been necessary, for there was no way to handle an event of this magnitude and complexity quickly. If it had been up to him, they'd have just had an arbiter make the pronouncement on behalf of the Law and then get on with life. But, Jagdish's newfound status and the historical greatness of Shakti's family demanded an appropriately large celebration, with feasts and dancing for hundreds of guests, over several days of celebration. Since he'd had a campaign to run, Jagdish had paid very little attention to her plans, which was just as well, because he wouldn't know what to do anyway, and Shakti had a rather specific vision.

"So, did you invite Harta to the wedding?"

"I sent him an invitation, yes."

Jagdish nearly spit out his wine. "What? You're serious."

"Of course I invited him, silly. It's a good thing you've got me to think of these things for you now! The people believe you're Harta's chosen hero, the one he secretly sent in pursuit of the Black Heart. My father is an important man and you're currently the most famous warrior in Vadal. To not invite our Thakoor would be seen as disrespectful. Harta will acknowledge our invitation, otherwise it would be seen as an insult to our entire caste, but don't worry, he'll certainly have some important duties calling him elsewhere and be unable to attend. No offense is given. Everyone is happy. Our family gains prestige."

"Will this extra prestige make it harder for the Protectors to execute me later?"

"Probably not. Harta would just declare that decision was out of his hands, but a personal connection between the two of you would make the event seem far more tragic and make your supporters sympathetic to him. As I've often said, Harta is very good at making the best out of any outcome."

Shakti truly was a political animal. "It sounds like you should have married Harta."

Now it was her turn to smirk. "He's not my type. I prefer a challenge. Someone that conniving doesn't need someone like me." Shakti poked him in the chest. "*You*—my honest and honorable warrior who always tries to do the right thing—*really* need someone like me. I'll help you maneuver through these courtly obstacles, and after you are made head of the warrior caste for all of Great House Vadal, we will look back at this time and laugh."

Jagdish snorted. "You are a baffling woman."

"Besides, Harta was already taken. I'm joking, Jagdish. I would have sabotaged that arrangement proposal like I did all of the other offers I've received. I picked you for a reason. Everything in life isn't merely a transaction or competition. I have a touch of a romantic streak too. What woman doesn't desire a bit of adventure?"

Chapter 9

‑‑‑‑‑‑‑‑‑‑‑

Radamantha Nems dar Harban was sick to death of adventure.

Her comfortable life as a Senior Archivist at the prestigious Capitol Library had been turned on its head. She'd gone from being a respectable librarian, to unwilling criminal conspirator, to fugitive, to bearer of some manner of ancient black steel device, to hostage, back to fugitive, and now once more she was a hostage again. Not that Great House Vadal would label her as such. Oh no. The Vadal were far too polite for that. She was no *hostage.* She was an *honored guest,* who had come to an equitable arrangement with their Thakoor, wherein she couldn't leave until she had employed her scholarly wisdom to decipher the messages written upon the artifact of black steel she'd *delivered* to them. If by delivered, they meant confiscated.

That device was the Asura's Mirror, a menacing and destructive thing that had somehow called down a mighty pillar of flame from the sky to obliterate a vast swarm of locust-like demons. That event had severely damaged the mirror, yet somehow it remained capable of displaying words in the language of the ancients upon its cracked surface. In exchange for her translating these words and using them to find a promised treasure hidden somewhere in Vadal, Thakoor Harta had promised to repay her by not participating in the Great Extermination as the Capitol had ordered. Find the ancient's treasure: This simple task was all Rada needed to do to keep a great house from murdering all their untouchables, which was a most heinous thing that was apparently happening everywhere else in Lok... and it was partly her fault.

But she was no *hostage.* Harta's warriors, who accompanied her wherever she went and watched her every move, were simply there for her protection. That was despite the fact that Rada already possessed her own bodyguard in the fearsome form of Protector of the Law Karno Uttara, who had been dispatched to watch over her by her beloved Lord Protector Devedas.

In retrospect, she could hardly be considered a hostage when she could wander about mostly free, with someone as terrifying as Karno by her side. For if Blunt Karno had decided they needed to leave Vadal, they simply would, and he'd certainly use that terrifying war hammer of his on whomever tried to stop them. The Vadal warriors might have orders to try and contain Karno's wrath, but everyone seemed aware that would be rather messy, and thus best avoided. So it was all very polite.

Since the Asura's Mirror had recently burned miles of Vadal countryside, and everyone with any sense was rightfully terrified of the cryptic device, her Vadal escort probably had orders to immediately hack her to bits if it appeared she was doing anything suspicious or dangerous, like attempting to call down more heavenly fire—an act she had repeatedly assured them was impossible since said fire had come from the smaller of their two moons, Upagraha, and that had been the last arrow in its quiver. The mirror had told her so itself.

However, Rada didn't know if anybody actually believed her.

Regardless, she had made an agreement—her translation and guidance in exchange for the lives of Vadal's casteless—and honor demanded she fill her part of that bargain. Only then could she return to Devedas with her conscience clean, having made the most of the opportunities she'd been given to atone for her previous mistakes. Despite knowing that she had only played a small part in causing the Great Extermination—and had in fact been a victim of the real villains behind that scheme—Rada still blamed herself. This murderous new addition to the Law had been based on dishonest scholarship on which she had signed off. She had been threatened and coerced into doing it, but an Archivist's reports must be factual above all else. Normally, when one of them signed off on something fraudulent it caused a scandal. The one and only time in her life that Rada had ever turned in an incomplete report, it had resulted in genocide.

Rada didn't even know any non-people, but the fact that something with her name on it had caused so much pointless death and misery haunted her.

Sadly, today her conscience wasn't the only thing haunting her.

Access denied.

"Curse this stubborn mirror!"

Rada was one of the few people in Lok who could read the ancient's language, but it wasn't the meanings of the multitude of ever-changing words that appeared on the mirror's surface that vexed her, but rather the artifact's obstinate nature in only showing her what it felt like.

"Give me your war hammer so that I may beat this stubborn device with it."

Protector Karno raised an eyebrow at his charge's words, for Rada wasn't given to angry outbursts. "What now?"

"According to the mirror, there's supposed to be some manner of black steel stored in this tomb." Frustrated, Rada gestured at the damaged stone slab before her, which was empty of treasure. There were alcoves in the walls, but those were filled with urns containing nothing but ashes. She was a Librarian, not a Historian. Her obligation was books, not rocks. "Not *was* stored here either, but the device speaks as if it still is. Yet when I ask to be shown where exactly this artifact is hidden, the Asura denies me."

Karno merely grunted, as if to say, *Such is life.*

There wasn't much to explore inside this ancient tomb either. It wasn't very large, and the Inquisition had long since smashed every carving that they'd decided might hold some religious significance, which from the scarred walls and broken bits on the floor had been nearly everything.

This particular tomb was carved into the rock beneath the oldest part of Vadal City. On this spot had once stood some kind of monument left over from the Age of Kings, but it had been torn down over five hundred years previously and replaced with a cluster of government buildings. It was fortunate the Vadal had left the foundation and the tunnel leading down to this tomb untouched.

It was crowded in here. The air was stuffy and Rada didn't like being a hundred feet beneath the ground. Their group consisted of

Rada and Karno, a wizard of Great House Vadal, and four warriors, carrying lanterns and looking rather uncomfortable at disturbing any of the urns that held the ashes of their house's founders. It was against the Law to believe in an afterlife, but Rada had found that the lower castes were still instinctively predisposed against giving offense to the dead.

Who was she to judge such superstitions? The strange Asura creature that lived inside the mirror occasionally spoke directly into her mind. What were unquiet spirits compared to a being like that?

"Your reading of the mirror must be mistaken, then," the wizard Saksham suggested.

"I've gone over every character with painstaking scholarship. There is no mistake in my translation this time."

"That's what you claimed last time."

Rada hated being second-guessed by a man who'd gained his status simply by being born lucky enough to have the rare gift of being able to work magic. "This is the oldest city in Lok, and now it is arguably the largest. There are whole districts of it that have been rebuilt ten times over. A great deal has been lost. Yet, despite those challenges, I'm certain this is the location now."

"Yet there's nothing here but the ashes of the dead. The mirror has a crack through it. Perhaps that has corrupted the words somehow."

"This isn't water spilled on a page to smudge the ink, wizard."

"What is it, then?" Saksham demanded.

Rada was uncomfortable telling anyone that the knowledge contained in the mirror wasn't merely long-ago recorded words, but something far more complicated ... and seemingly alive. The stress of keeping her safe beneath a pillar of fire so hot it had melted the rocks around them *had* put a crack in the mirror, but it had not shattered. Everything she'd ever read about black steel artifacts suggested that when they were through, they came apart in the most spectacular manner, leaving behind nothing but fragments.

Rada knew the Asura that lived inside was damaged, not dead. It had not spoken to her recently, but she could feel it.

"Study is a process, wizard. Learning takes time."

Saksham scoffed at her. "I have learned to harness the power buried in demon flesh to bend fire and wind to my will, and you speak to me as if *reading* is difficult?"

Luthra, a charming young warrior of the Personal Guard, was the leader of the soldiers who'd been sent to watch over her. Wise beyond his years, he sensed the tension between Rada and the prideful wizard and tried to calm the hurt feelings. "I know our search has been frustrating, but it's obvious the Inquisition purged this place of illegal imagery long ago. It's possible they found the black steel back then and took it with them."

"Stealing the property of our house is a bold accusation to make against a Capitol Order. Especially one as vindictive as the Inquisition," Saksham snapped. "Mind your tongue, warrior."

"I'm only making an observation, not an accusation..." Luthra lifted the hood of his lantern so they could get a bit more light into the corners of the cramped tomb, but it revealed nothing but more dust and debris. "Besides, there's no Inquisitors here. It seems our Thakoor neglected to notify the masks that anyone was going down here."

"A fortunate oversight," Karno mused.

"Lucky us." Luthra had already killed one Inquisitor over an issue of mistaken identity, so he had even more reason to want to avoid that particular Order than most warriors. He had repeatedly demonstrated that he would put honor over blind obedience to the Law. If Harta ever found out how his guard had helped her, Luthra would surely end up demoted or dead. So Rada rather liked Luthra.

The wizard clearly did not. "Be silent, warrior. I hear enough excuses from her as it is. More likely, the Inquisition stole nothing, because there was never anything down here to steal to begin with. The librarian is wasting our time."

Though she'd met very few wizards in her life, thus far every last one of them had seemed to possess that same sneering condescension for those they saw as inferior, which was damned near everyone. Being able to work magic was a rare gift. Scarcity made them valuable, and that value made them prideful. A couple of years ago, Rada would probably have remained silent in the face of such slander, but frankly, she'd grown weary of her caste's constant snide pettiness.

"I will accept no disrespect about my integrity from the likes of you, wizard. I'm a Senior Archivist of the Capitol Library, a respected expert in my obligation, and if you were half as literate in the ancient language as you've deceived your Thakoor into thinking you are, you wouldn't need me here at all."

"How dare you question my word!"

Rada held the broken mirror out toward the wizard. "Here. Show me how easy it is."

"Keep in mind it ate the arm off the last man presumptuous enough to try," Karno stated.

Saksham kept his hands at his side. Rada had suspected he wouldn't dare touch the incredibly deadly thing. Black steel artifacts were notorious for their vengeful nature.

"As I expected, Saksham, I'm more educated than you are, *and* the mirror has clearly chosen me to be its bearer, so leave me be so that I may concentrate."

He scowled and folded his arms. "My orders are to never take my eyes off of you, lest you abscond with what rightfully belongs to our house—or worse, use that thing to call down destruction onto our heads once more."

"Then you can do so with your mouth *shut*." Rada turned away and muttered, "Damnable know-it-all wizards."

One of the warriors snorted but managed to stifle his laughter just in time. Saksham glared at him but was too distracted to take offense.

She went back to the mirror. By touching the cracked surface with her bare fingertips she could move the words about, only they were still flashing denial. In truth, Rada shared the wizard's frustrations. In a moment of terror and chaos, with only an invisible wall holding back a swarm of vicious little demons and their stabbing razor legs, the mirror had inadvertently given up some of its secrets, including briefly showing her a map where some other weapons had been left behind by the ancients to be used against the demons when all other options had been exhausted. It had refused to show her that map again, and it was only due to her perfect recollection, combined with combing through Great House Vadal's records—many of which were incomplete or damaged—that had led her to this place.

Sadly, in a city this vast and old there were a multitude of catacombs, tunnels, and chambers beneath it. This wasn't the first dusty old place they had explored, and every other one of their expeditions had left them nothing to show for their efforts. Perhaps she was being too rude to the wizard after all.

"Forgive me, Saksham. I'm aware of your frustration. I really do believe this is the place this time."

"My house is currently threatened on three sides. You will have my forgiveness when you deliver what you have promised to my Thakoor."

Rada sighed. "Very well."

She didn't need to put up with this. Devadas had sent her off to keep her safe while he worked to expose the conspirators. Only now everyone in Lok had heard about how he had returned to the Capitol, triumphant. She no longer needed to hide. Devedas was even in the south of Vadal now, bearing some unique new title, leading an army made up of soldiers from many houses. There was nothing stopping her from returning to her lover...

Except her word.

She knew there was a weapon here, and not just by research and memory, but by instinct, for the Asura was acting evasively, like there was something here and she wasn't supposed to have it. The entire time she had been trying to fulfill her bargain with Harta, the strange being within the mirror had remained elusive, allowing her to read some things while spitefully denying others. There seemed to be no logic why some of its books were open while others remained locked to her. Yet even with Rada's limited access, the knowledge she had gathered was shocking, and quite certainly illegal. Enough so that she didn't dare speak of it to anyone, including Karno. Who, despite being her friend, was also an unflinching Protector of the Law. And the Law had no patience for religious nonsense.

"Luthra, hand me your lantern, please."

The warrior did so, and Rada used that light to better examine the destruction left by the foul Inquisitors. It saddened her that in their haste to scrub anything that might reference the old gods or their teachings, they'd destroyed so much other precious knowledge along the way. Their effort to defend man from the tyranny of a prior age had simply led them into a new form of tyranny. Little did the people of Lok realize how much had been stolen from them. They lived in an age of darkness and were too ignorant to realize it.

The closer light revealed one of the few remaining marks, which caused Rada to grin. "I knew it!" At the time those Inquisitors had done their work, this symbol wouldn't have been seen as religious at all, but rather representative of an office within the newly formed Law, so it had been spared from their wrath.

"Look at this one, Karno. Do you recognize it?"

The big man didn't bother to get closer, and instead used that Protector trick of his to focus his eyes in such a way that it allowed him to see things far better at various distances than a regular man could. It was a skill that Rada was wildly jealous of, as her vision was notoriously terrible, and her eyes required the aid of special glass lenses in order to read. The particularly fine set of glasses currently perched on her nose right now had been given to her as a gift by Harta.

Karno frowned, as he clearly knew that sign. "What's that doing here?"

"What is it?" Luthra asked.

"It's an old mark the Protectors place on our holdings. It's tradition that design is used on the armor issued by my Order. I'd show you if I still had mine." Then Karno looked around at the many urns, as the realization set in that these might have been some of his predecessors. "Are all these ashes from Protectors of the Law, then?"

"According to the records I found in Harta's library, most likely. Though this dates back to before your Order was named the Protectors of the Law. In those days they were still called the Protectors of Mankind. Either way, this was a tomb for heroes. It's always been Vadal tradition to cremate their dead, with the high status kept in places of remembrance, while the lower caste's ashes are just poured onto the wind."

"And the low status, they burn whatever percentage of the body the family can afford to cremate and then toss the remainder in the river," Luthra said. "But what's this got to do with our treasure?"

"Within the mirror, this symbol is repeatedly used for all things defensive in nature. The Protectors were one aspect of the ancient's defenses. Before the Protectors served the Law, they answered to their gods."

Karno frowned as she said that. He was her friend, but he would certainly not abide that kind of slander against his beloved Order. She'd be safer insulting his mother.

"I mean that figuratively, of course. Gods aren't real! Obviously. But the men who founded your Order had different beliefs before the Age of Law. Many of our oldest traditions share a common origin in those times of madness. That's why the Inquisition had to destroy so much that was here before, to stamp that out. Your Order was originally commanded by that same first king all the people thought had been sent to rule by their gods. This king was named Ramrowan. It is written that this King Ramrowan recruited the mightiest warriors from every tribe, and then granted them special abilities which made them more powerful than regular men could ever aspire to be. Their obligation was to protect everyone who couldn't defend themselves, regardless of their rank or status. It was only later than this Order's mission was changed to serving the Law rather than the people."

It was rare that Karno let much emotion show, but it was clear her tale angered him, for his entire life had been devoted to an Order that was supposedly unchanging and above corruption. "I believe none of that."

"It's possible the Historians might have been wrong or biased." Rada went back to the wall before saying anything else that might give offense, because she sincerely doubted her scholarly predecessors were that fallible. "Either way, this promised ancient weapon and your Protectors share the same symbol according to the mirror. It must be hidden here somewhere. It's probably behind the stone or buried under our feet."

"Then we will tear this place apart." Saksham rubbed his hands together in eager anticipation as he told one of the warriors, "Obligate a crew of workers and have them start digging immediately. In the meantime, we can dump out all these urns and sift through the ashes."

Karno glanced around at the remains, undisturbed for a thousand years, and growled, "The hell you will."

Even as important as a wizard was, nobody wanted to cross a Protector of the Law. Saksham took an unconscious step back. "I meant no offense, Protector. But what Law does my command break? These are Vadal lands. If this ancient place was, in fact, once a holding of your Order, it clearly is no longer. There's no legal reason we can't do as we wish with our own property."

The wizard was legally correct, but for once, Karno seemed to be motivated by emotion rather than Law. Rada could tell that defiling this place was—for whatever reason—a line he would not cross. "Give the librarian time to figure out this puzzle."

"She's had enough time. If she says the promised weapon is hidden somewhere within this tomb, we must not delay. Harta

Vadal is the ultimate judge of the Law here, and I am his appointed representative. I have spoken. Why do you protest this action, Protector?"

"These ashes were my brothers."

"So? What does the Law care about that?"

Karno had no proper answer to give, for a perfect servant of the Law couldn't come out and say that *legal* and *right* weren't the same thing. It was obvious the idea of dishonoring those who'd come before disgusted Karno, and Saksham would happily destroy even more of his house's history in a moment of eager greed, but the Law didn't worry about that sort of thing, so Karno wasn't supposed to either.

"I will take your glowering silence for assent, then." Saksham barked at the warriors, "Fetch some workers."

Luthra nervously looked toward Karno before acting. Wizards could throw their weight around, but no mortal warrior wanted to risk drawing a Protector's ire. The big man just stood there, scowling.

"Karno, please," Rada begged. "I've made a promise to Harta. These men are dead. Vadal's casteless are still alive, but not for long if I can't fulfill it."

The Law said the untouchables had to die. Pleading for their lives shouldn't have swayed the Protector... yet it did. Dead Protectors and living non-people were equally useless in the eyes of the Law. She didn't know if Karno cared about the fate of the casteless, or if he was simply trying to help her assuage her guilt, but whatever the reason, he relented.

"Very well... but before you ruin more of your own heritage, as this was once a Protector holding, let me try one of our secret rites. I will require a moment of privacy."

"Not a chance," Saksham spat.

Karno blinked slowly, then showed absolutely no emotion as he told the wizard, "Rada has an agreement with your house. I do not. I am aiding her. You, I would gladly kill without a care."

The Protector said that so flatly and directly it took a moment for it to sink in that it had been a threat. The wizard blanched. "You dare challenge Great House Vadal?"

"No. Just you."

"Karno..." Luthra tried to keep his voice steady and calming. "There's no need for anyone to start a duel here. We could move the urns outside first, and then bring them back when the workers are done."

"Disturb this tomb and you will have my offense. Or you can go upstairs and wait until I am done."

There wasn't much space in the tomb and Karno's bulk took up a good percentage of it. There was no doubt he could inflict terrible violence upon all the warriors if so moved. It became very tense in the tiny room. Karno had been unfailingly polite to the Vadal for their entire stay, but that didn't mean he wouldn't hesitate to crush their skulls.

"Come, Saksham. Let's give the Protector his space," Luthra suggested nervously. "If there are black steel treasures here, it isn't like our honorable guests are going to sneak them out in their pockets." Even though it was a violation of protocol to put his hands on a man of such higher status, Luthra took the wizard by the arm and guided him back toward the winding stone stairwell that had led them down here. "We will return in a bit."

The other Vadal warriors appeared glad to retreat.

Once she was certain they were sufficiently far away, Rada hissed, "Have you gone mad? Are you trying to get us killed?"

"No." Karno brushed past her as he went to the wall.

"You can't go picking fights with Vadal wizards when the Law's not on your side!"

"There's a feeling about this tomb that reminds me of a different place, far from here. I must check something. Look away, Rada."

"You don't trust me either, Karno?"

"I trust you more than anyone other than my brother Protectors, which is why I know you will honor my request."

That was high praise coming from the likes of Karno. "Alright. Fine." Rada turned her back in order to let him do whatever mysterious Protector business it was he needed to attend to. It irritated her ever-curious nature, but she'd not expect him to betray the secrets of his Order any more than she would reveal the secrets of the Library to an outsider.

She heard Karno roughly brushing dust from the wall with his hands, as if searching for something. He whispered a few words under his breath. She knew how to read the ancient language, not pronounce it, but she suspected Karno was speaking in the old tongue.

Suddenly the entire wall next to her moved.

A seam appeared as tons of ancient stone moved aside with barely a sound. Rada gawked at the impossibility of it, for to move such a weight the people on the surface should have felt the rumble and heard the grinding, but there was almost no noise or shaking to it at all. She'd read of such ancient engineering marvels, as there were a few examples in the Capitol still, but she had never heard of one as smooth as this.

Rada lifted Luthra's lantern to reveal that there was another room on the other side, equal in size to the tomb. Just as the modern Vadal felt the need to carve beautiful images into every-thing they touched, their ancestors must have been the same, because it was truly astounding. Floor to ceiling, every surface was covered in wonderous designs: images of man and beast and what had to be gods, and battles in the heavens and pillars of flames shooting down from a circlet of moons that no longer existed to burn endless legions of demons, and thousands upon thousands of words carved into the stone to explain every story there. Best of all, these carvings had never been touched by Inquisition picks and chisels. There was so much to learn!

Yet before Rada could try to read any of it, she realized that in the middle of the secret room there was something profoundly *odd.*

The thing was black as the Asura's mirror, but oblong, around two feet wide and a foot tall. It seemed to hungrily suck in the light of her lantern in a way that hurt to look at. Then it pulsed. A pause. Then it moved again. Repeating the cycle. As if it was slowly beating . . . like a heart.

Karno gasped, and that sound made Rada jump. Because even when faced by witch hunters or demonic plagues, Rada had never Karno make such a noise of surprise. His all-too-human reaction was rather unnerving. Karno did something with his hands again, tapped the wall while saying a different word in the old tongue, and the stone closed as swiftly and quietly as it had opened.

The strange door's movement barely even unsettled the dust. Once the battered wall settled back into place, Rada could almost trick herself into believing that she'd imagined the whole thing.

Her mind was reeling. Nobody truly understood black steel. Not even wizards. Even tiny fragments of the stuff held an incredible amount of magical power, while whole artifacts were capable of astounding feats. The thing in the secret room was comparatively gigantic compared to a sword or the mirror...and that was no fragment.

"We must go."

"What was *that*?"

"I cannot tell you. You must trust me. Tell them you were wrong about this place. Tell them there is nothing here."

"But Karno, I gave my word! That's the only thing saving Vadal's casteless from extinction. If I don't give Harta what I promised soon—"

He laid one gigantic hand gently on her shoulder and stared into her eyes, pleading. "I would not ask you to abandon them, only to delay for now. Do this for me. I must seek wisdom, for what we've seen here is beyond my understanding."

Rada had never read about anything like this black-steel artifact before in all of the Capitol Library. Who in the world could possibly know of such a thing? "Seek wisdom how?"

"Devedas will know what to do."

Chapter 10

Two of the most powerful men in the world sat in a tent, negotiating the fate of millions.

There were forty men in the vast command tent, twenty from each side—commanders, courtly men, their assorted functionaries, and a handful of bodyguards who had agreed to meet in the gentle hill country south of Vadal City. As a show of good faith, both of them had only brought along a token escort of a thousand soldiers. Both sides had far more they could send for if offense was taken.

The meeting had started as such things usually did, with the arbiters and diplomats making announcements and sharing niceties, speaking on behalf of their Raja or Thakoor. When the benevolent Capitol had learned of the demonic scourge and the great fiery destruction in the north, they had dispatched the Raja's army to aid Vadal in its time of need. *"Ever Law-abiding Vadal thanks the Capitol for its concern, but the problem has already been corrected and the Raja's army is no longer necessary and should return home."* So on and so forth. Escalating back and forth. Now they were to the point where the Capitol's eyes needed to see this destruction for itself to confirm the threat was really gone, Vadal taking offense at this insinuation that it was unable to attend to its own internal security, and the Capitol insisting that this scourge was not just a danger to Vadal, but all of Lok, and thus the jurisdiction of the Raja.

For nearly an hour, Raja Devedas marveled at the endless lies and distortions the first caste vomited up without hesitation or shame. So many words, to say so little that was objectively true. They danced around difficult realities, unable to speak plainly. It reminded Devedas why he hated his birth caste, and was further proof why Lok needed one king to rule with a strong hand.

The entire time, Harta and Devedas said nothing. Harta let his arbiters speak on his behalf, and Devedas allowed Omand's pets, who had been placed among his entourage, to make their demands, all while the only two men who ultimately mattered studied each other.

"The Raja has yet to speak," Harta suddenly said, cutting off one of his own arbiters. "Does he have his own voice? For all I've heard thus far are the wishes and platitudes of the Grand Inquisitor."

Did Harta think he was weak? Did he wrongly believe that Devedas was simply another of Omand's pawns?

"I have much to say, but I would speak with the Thakoor, man to man. The rest of you should wait outside." The high-status men on both sides immediately balked at that, but Devedas silenced his by saying, "Begone."

Harta smiled at this development. Apparently, he had been as bored by the first caste's nattering as Devedas had been. "I'll gladly forgo the rest of these chirping birds, but you have me at a disadvantage, Raja Devedas, for you are a formidable man, a legendary duelist and combatant, while I am but a humble orator. To maintain my confidence, I shall keep my bodyguards here."

Devedas nodded in understanding. "Of course."

"I will take no offense if you choose to do the same."

"I don't need any bodyguards for this." That wasn't bravado. Just simple fact.

"Of course. The rest of you may leave."

The functionaries did as they were told. Omand's spies—and he was certain to have many—wouldn't like getting thrown out of the tent, but Devedas didn't care. Their master spider was back in his Capitol web, cementing their new authority. Devedas was his own man, with his own goals, and a crisis to attend to.

Raja Devedas had dealt with Thakoor Harta Vadal before,

but only at a distance. When Devedas had been obligated as Lord Protector, Harta had already been Vadal's Chief Judge and representative in the Capitol. He'd had nothing but hatred for the man, since Harta was allegedly one of those responsible for the lie that was Ashok. Harta's powerful connections had made him untouchable, even to the Lord Protector. For the crime of creating Ashok and deceiving the Law, Harta deserved to die.

But now was not the time for bloody revenge, and personal vendettas needed to be set aside in order to further his grand ambitions. Devedas had his own conspiracies to tend to, and Harta was one of the last obstacles standing in the way of his becoming king.

Now it was just Devedas on one side of the tent, and Harta and a handful of very proficient-looking warriors in fine armor of blue and bronze on the other... as well as a single, elderly wizard, who had never been introduced. If that old man was still present his magic must be formidable indeed. Devedas wasn't worried this would turn violent because Harta's reputation was that of a statesman, and he wouldn't jeopardize that to strike down someone as famous as Devedas in such an uncouth manner.

Besides, the golden armor Devedas wore had been crafted to add gravitas to the new office of Raja, but he had insisted that it be as functional as it was awe-inspiring. If Harta was foolish enough to try him, Devedas would happily fill his tent with Vadal blood.

"Though I am very good at the games of our caste, sometimes I tire of them. Now we may speak plainly," Harta said as he adjusted the pillows he sat upon. "You, and your army, are not needed here."

Most of Vadal's warrior caste were already occupied dealing with Vokkan incursions to the west and a war against Sarnobat to the east. Vadal already had two fronts to contend with. One it had asked for, a second it had not. They could not withstand a third.

"The Capitol disagrees."

"The Capitol, or Omand Vokkan?"

Devedas was tempted to say that everyone knew they were one and the same now, but he refrained. "My army will remain encamped outside Apura until I decide the crisis is over. The scourge and the pillar of fire struck Vadal but threaten all of Lok. I have been appointed Lok's singular representative. This is my obligation."

"Thus this new title you bear... *Raja*." Harta rolled the word around in his mouth as if it had a foul taste. "In a moment of fear, how quickly my fellows were to give up their power for a promise of safety."

"The judges are rational men. In the name of expediency, they simply delegated all their emergency authority to me, Thakoor."

"Which requires your emergency to never end." Harta didn't even try to hide his disgust. "My spies have told me about what's going on in the Capitol right now. Men of status are being labeled as dissidents and traitors, imprisoned, or tortured upon the Dome... or the Tower of Silence, as Omand so haughtily changed its name. Judges cower in their estates like common criminals while the Chamber of Argument sits empty and quiet, as none dare speak out against Omand's campaign of terror."

"I am not Omand."

"But you *are* his man. He willed your position into being, and then provided legendary hero Devedas, his honor above reproach with loyalty to no house, as the inevitable choice to fill it. Omand plays a dangerous game. The great houses will not stand for this. In time, they will restore the judges to their rightful place."

"'Rightful'?" Devedas' laugh was genuine. "What foolishness."

"Do you insult me, Raja?"

"It's our traditions which insult us all. For two decades I traveled to every corner of the continent, enforcing the Law. I've been to every great house and most of the vassals. I've dealt with every caste, from the mightiest of judges to the filthiest degenerate fish-eater, and I've taken more lives than I can count. What all this taught me is that there's no *rightful place* but what one takes. The men currently in charge, those who benefit from the way things are, they talk of the sanctified Law, while breaking it constantly for their own benefit. They held power so long they came to believe they deserved it forever, simply for existing. I am the cost of their complacency."

Harta had wished for them to speak frankly, but he had clearly not expected this level of honesty. "You brag of treason."

"Treason? No. *Effectiveness*. Where the judges would squabble and play their little games from the comfort of their palaces, the Raja will act and do what must be done. I won't accept lectures on morality from one of the conspirators who tricked a stray dog into believing it was a Protector in a vain attempt to save his house's ancestor blade."

That caused Harta to glance at his warriors, because apparently that old family secret wasn't even known to his closest guardians.

However, Harta didn't bother to gauge the wizard's reaction to the accusation, which told Devedas much.

The Vadal wizard was a tiny, frail man, wearing black robes decorated with owl feathers. His eyes were milky and he had to be nearly blind.

"This charge doesn't seem to surprise you, wizard. You must be Kule. I didn't recognize you. I was only a boy when I saw you deliver Ashok to the Hall."

The frail old man nodded as his name was revealed. His voice creaked. "My Thakoor has asked me to return from my retirement, due to recent events."

"You erased a casteless and built a fearless servant of the Law in its place. You are the one who made Ashok what he is."

Kule chuckled. "Cruel circumstances created Ashok. I will admit to no crimes."

Ashok had been his closest friend, and yet Devedas didn't know how much of that construction had been real, and how much had been the fabrication of this wizard. Somehow that felt like the greatest betrayal of all.

"I wonder... The spells you used to shape Ashok's mind—were there flaws built into your foundation, or did your construction erode over time?"

Kule pondered on that. "I would never commit such a terrible crime, but any wizard who did such a heinous thing would certainly never expect a creature with its fear removed to survive long for it to matter. Ashok should have expired long before the pattern began to fray... but life is full of surprises."

"Enough," Harta ordered his prideful wizard, and Kule bowed his head in apology. "You never made these wild accusations against my house when you were appointed Lord Protector, nor is Ashok's deception why you've led an army to my door now. You have been remarkably forthright with me, so I will cut to the chase. I know why you're here, Devedas. The scourge—which, let us remember, was released by the Inquisition—and the resulting destruction was all the excuse Omand needed to seize great power for himself. Vadal is the only house strong enough to stand against him on its own. If I don't bow to this new government of his, other houses will follow our example and refuse to as well. But if mighty Vadal is brought down, then the rest of the houses will tremble and kiss Omand's feet. I'm just trying to decide if you are Omand's equal...

or his slave. Do I speak to a Raja, or a mere messenger for his true master?"

"You speak to the man who will rule all of Lok. Be thankful I'm in a merciful mood."

"Omand wants me dead and my house in ruins. What do *you* want, Devedas?"

"A righteous justice and a ruler wise enough to dispense it."

Harta blinked. "I thought we were past the flowery lies of the courtiers."

"You judges have spoken in nonsense and poetry for so long that when a man who understands the true purpose of the Law tells the truth, it baffles you. I swear, the judges are as fallen as the fish-eaters and the Capitol is as unclean as the ocean. I will correct their errors and stop their excesses. The Chamber of Argument will become secondary and subservient to the Raja as I provide that righteous justice."

"You'd force us into a new Age of Kings."

"We never really left. We merely replaced one singular vision with hundreds of corrupt, petty, bickering, divergent ones. Great House Vadal can either support me in restoring that rule, or Vadal can be destroyed. It's that simple."

"Simple, eh?" Harta stroked his beard thoughtfully, but his face gave away nothing. "I've seen what Omand has been working toward all these years. You'd have all the great houses become vassals to the Capitol. For what?"

"The great houses already answer to the Capitol in all the ways that matter. You rule only as long as a committee says you can. You mint your own coins, but the Capitol controls the central bank notes you all use to trade. Their Orders tell your industries what they are allowed to make, and then tax you for it. They tell your scholars what they are allowed to learn. They tell you how much magic your wizards are allowed to have. They tell you when and how you can make war on your enemies. And when you cross enough lines to get a sufficient number of judges to vote against you, they send my Protectors to execute your commanders in punishment. No, Harta, you're already vassal houses. Vadal has just been the best at using this broken system to its advantage, so you've abided your servitude. Only we both know with the way things are going, Vadal's supremacy isn't going to last."

"Vadal is stronger than you can imagine."

"So was Dev, until it wasn't."

"Ah, yes. There it is." Harta gave him a cruel smile. "I know your history, Devedas. We are alike in some ways. Sons of the first, heirs to a great house, our fathers both bore ancestor blades. Only my father, the great Bhadramunda Vadal, died honorably—only to have his sword be taken up by scum—while your father's sword shattered and he took his own life in disgrace. Your house was conquered while mine grew stronger. I was obligated to serve in the chamber, while you were given to the Protectors. If our fortunes had been a bit different, perhaps you'd be the Thakoor, and I'd be the madman telling him of my plans for overthrowing the Law in order to crown myself king."

Perhaps Harta was right, for Devedas's birthright had been stolen from him. The difference between them was that Devedas was strong enough to forge for himself a new one.

"The judges have already lost, Harta. Their time is done. You're fortunate I'm the one who will take that crown, rather than one of the empty shells Omand would have installed otherwise. Those sheltered creatures of the Capitol would have no understanding of the costs of subjugating all the great houses. That is a degree of bloodshed and terror that I'm trying to avoid, for I have seen more war than anyone else alive... Perhaps one other man was my equal—and I killed him."

"Good riddance to the Black Heart," the Thakoor agreed, but then he leaned forward on his cushions, a courtly predator stalking its vulnerable prey. "You speak of costs. That's because we both know your mighty Capitol army is barely unified, made up of warriors obligated from different houses who all hate each other, temporarily forced together by the whim of a Capitol whose will those warriors suspect will falter when it matters most. How much would it cost you to fight me?"

"Don't forget, Harta, I'm also on unfriendly ground, with long and vulnerable supply lines which must run through other houses I can't rely on. Oh yes, I'm very aware of my challenges. Which is why we're talking now rather than butchering each other."

"My army could defeat yours."

"Likely true, but I don't need to *win*. Merely weaken you enough that it will allow your neighbors have their way with your house. My Army of Many Houses could hurt you enough that Vadal would never recover."

"Even if Vokkan or Sarnobat burned all of Vadal to the ground afterward, you would forever be Devedas the Defeated, and no one would support your mad ambitions after that. We would both lose."

Devedas smiled. "Yes. That sounds unfortunate, doesn't it?"

Harta considered this for a long time. Devedas was clearly not at all what he had been expecting. This was no puffed-up warrior, thinking glory could carry the day, but a pragmatic realist, willing to destroy them both in pursuit of his goals.

"You know the way in which we both lose, Raja, but is there a way both of us can win? If you would be as wise a ruler as you claim, then demonstrate it to me now. I would consider your proposal, but you must meet my terms."

"Name them."

"The Raja can have the Capitol and its Orders. Do with them as you see fit. Replace a hundred judges' votes with your singular decision if you feel like it. Yet, the great houses *must* retain their autonomy. Leave us to do what we will over our own lands. Let us settle our feuds, manage our trade, and govern our people, free of the Capitol's chains... or test us, for if Vadal were to prevail against your army, even briefly, it would send a message to the rest of the houses that the Raja's threats are empty. Then you will have replaced the judges with nothing but chaos, as every house would then battle to claim whatever scraps it could. That righteous justice you seek would be destroyed in flames of division. But make us partners rather than servants, and you will have the great houses' respect."

Omand would never agree to such a thing, for he despised the great houses' ability to push back against the Capitol, but the thought of thwarting the Grand Inquisitor in this way pleased Devedas. Omand was a sinister manipulator with an insatiable appetite for power. Their agreement had benefited them both so far, but Devedas would need his own allies for the future.

"I'm sure we could work out an arrangement like that."

"We will let our courtiers debate the little things. That's what those lesser members of the first are for. For now, if my terms are acceptable to you, then I could see Vadal supporting your claim to rule the Capitol."

Harta was too good at this. It was impossible to tell when the best speaker in Lok was lying or not. His opponent was shrewd, but not suicidal. Was Harta buying time, hoping the situation would change somehow? Or was he astute enough to realize Vadal was trapped?

Time would tell.

"Then we will part today with a new understanding, Thakoor. We're both reasonable men, who want what's best for our people."

"Agreed. Let us bring our staff back in and let them argue over the details of how a *free* Vadal could best support our new Raja."

Omand would be furious. So be it. A real king did not require his advisor's approval. With a tentative peace brokered, Devedas turned to a matter of the heart. "There's one other issue, a personal one, and your resolving it would be a sign of our new friendship."

"Name it, Raja."

It was dangerous to ask, because merely mentioning her name demonstrated her importance to him, but Devedas had to know the truth. "I've been informed that Senior Archivist Radamantha Nems dar Harban is a hostage within Great House Vadal."

Harta paused before responding, as if trying to decide why someone like her mattered to someone like him. "Radamantha has been a guest of mine. In fact, she has been serving as one of my scholarly advisors. Inquisition witch hunters tried to illegally haul her off. My guards stopped them."

That was doubtlessly true, and once more confirmed that Omand was never to be trusted. Devedas tried not to let his anger show, because Harta might think it was directed at him, rather than the Capitol's spider. "She is well?"

"She is in my care, of course she's well. Rada even has one of your Protectors watching over her at all times. A gigantic beast of a man named Karno."

"One of my best." When Devedas had charged Karno with keeping Rada safe, he'd never imagined that he would hide her in the home of one of his enemies. Karno was far too honest to ever be made aware of Devedas' schemes, so Karno couldn't possibly have known his Lord Protector would end up at odds with Great House Vadal.

"Rada possesses a quick mind and a remarkably charitable heart by the standards of our caste. I have enjoyed our walks and discussions in my garden. May I ask how you know her?"

"I'm merely a friend of her family," Devedas lied about the

woman he intended to be his future queen. "Before I left the Capitol I assured her father I'd find her and return her safely to the Library. I would like for you to turn her over to me."

"And I would like for your army to move their camp from the north side of Red Lake to the south while we work out the details of our new arrangement."

If they did go to war, that was valuable ground to give up, but it was a small price to pay to get back the woman he loved. "An equitable trade, but we'll wait where we are until she arrives, though, to spare her from having to travel that much farther."

Harta chuckled, then he surprised his guards by getting off his cushions and walking over to Devedas. In the northern lands, it was tradition to bow to equals and superiors. In the south, agreements were sealed by the clasping of arms. Apparently Harta was familiar with the icy southern ways, as he extended his hand.

"There will not be peace in the north as long as Vokkan and Sarnobat press us, but let there at least be peace between the Raja and Great House Vadal."

Devedas stood and shook the hand of one of the men conniving enough to have unleashed Ashok Vadal on the unsuspecting world.

Chapter 11

―――∿∿∿∿―――

"I swear I will make things right!"

Senior Witch Hunter Javed's own shout startled him from his nightmare. He was breathing hard and drenched in sweat, the words of the terrifying Mother of Dawn still echoing in his ears.

Begin by saving our Voice.

As his heart slowed to the point it didn't feel as if it was about to burst, Javed was glad that he had been given a private room within the Makao palace so that nobody would hear him shout incriminating things in his sleep.

Sunlight was coming through the window. He didn't know what time it was, as he no longer slept like a rational man. His time was spent plotting and scheming, and in every spare minute when there were no witnesses around he wrote down the words of the Voice and the Keeper of Names as best as he could remember them. Every prophecy. Every sermon. Every lesson. Even the casual discussions they'd had as Keta had pondered philosophy and Javed had pretended to care. Every little thing he could rack his guilty mind to recall, he'd recorded, working feverishly throughout the nights, all in the hopes that none of those precious words would be lost. It was as if a fire of inspiration had descended upon him from the gods themselves, and it had burned away his ability to sleep. Only when he was totally spent would he collapse into an exhausted stupor to be tormented by nightmares.

Irrationally terrified that he'd been found out somehow, Javed got out of bed and went to the small writing desk. There were numerous nubs of burned down candles and empty glass pens scattered everywhere, but all the pages that contained illegal incriminating religion—and there were hundreds of those now—had been hidden beneath a board he'd pulled up from the floor, which now had one leg of the desk set atop it.

Shoving the desk aside, Javed lifted up the board, and saw that his scriptures were still safe...for now.

Javed stumbled back to his bed, sat, and put his face into his hands, still weary beyond comprehension. Getting caught with such illegal religion was a death sentence, but who was he to argue with the will of the gods? He'd tried to save so much over the last month, the prophecies of the Voice, the teachings of Ratul, and the sermons of Keta, yet none of that would matter if he couldn't save Thera herself. Writing down all the prophecies had convinced him once more just how incredibly important the Voice was for the gods' great plan. For if she was not present at the final battle, all would be lost.

There was a knock on his door.

Javed quickly composed himself. If he was witch hunter enough to convincingly play the fanatic, then he could be the fanatic enough to convincingly play the witch hunter. He threw on a robe, put on his most basic silk Inquisitor's mask, then opened the door.

The mask had been unnecessary, because it was his fellow witch hunter, Nikunja. "Did you just wake up, Javed? You're a mess. It's the middle of the afternoon."

Javed glanced up and down the hall, but Nikunja was alone. "I'm not feeling well. It's this damned climate." He gestured for his comrade to enter, and then shut the door behind him and pulled his mask down, as there should be no need to hide his true face among his brothers. "How do people live in a place so cold and damp? The perpetual chill is tiresome."

"Spare me your tales of suffering, desert born. I'm from the northern jungles. How do you think I feel about this frozen wasteland?" Nikunja also discarded his mask. He was a good witch hunter—not nearly as accomplished as Javed, but utterly devoted to their Order and sharp in his observations. He noted the state of the writing desk. "Composing a letter?"

"Trying to," Javed lied smoothly. "I was hoping to find some leverage with members of the first caste in this backwater house to help pressure their Thakoor into giving us back our rightful prize."

"Can I see what you came up with?"

"Sadly, no. After wasting my time writing, I realized the mere act of asking made our Order sound weak, so I burned the letters."

Nikunja nodded. "That's wise. The Grand Inquisitor has already stated his offense and sent his demands to the Makao. What weight could we add to that which the illustrious Omand Vokkan could not?"

"That was my eventual conclusion, but the waiting infuriates me. Dhaval is an annoying, entitled twit. Thakoor Venketesh would be a fool to risk angering Omand just to appease one imbecilic phontho. Especially now." They had only heard rumors of what was going on in the Capitol, but the word among the local Inquisitors was that their Order had been granted much greater leniency in pursuing those suspected of disloyal illegal behavior, especially among men of wealth and status. Powerful and connected individuals had been arrested recently in the Capitol for all manner of crimes. Their Order had never been allowed to be this aggressive before. Everyone had already feared them before. How much more powerful would they be now?

"I'm just sad we're stuck here, when we could be in Capitol terrifying judges!" Nikunja laughed. "Can you imagine?"

"Don't worry, brother. When we deliver an unknown kind of magic to the Tower of Silence, we'll be welcomed as heroes and rewarded handsomely."

"You certainly will, Javed. You near single-handedly beheaded the fiercest rebellion the Inquisition has seen in generations."

Javed inwardly winced at that reminder of his terrible sins. If it hadn't been for him, Thera would be safely back in the Cove, leading her people with the revealed wisdom of the gods, instead of rotting in the dungeons beneath this palace. "That's the truth. I've earned my reward. Now what brings you to the mansion?"

Lacking Javed's status, Nikunja had been quartered in one of the Inquisitors' holdings in Kanok. He probably thought Javed had asked to stay in the Thakoor's estate for the luxury, but really it was so that he could be closer to where Thera was being held. The Makao were less likely to try and hurt her if they knew a vengeful witch hunter might show up at any time.

"I bring good news, Javed. Our waiting will soon be over."

"What do you mean?"

"They're traveling in secret to avoid Harban spies, but word among the locals is that the Thakoor will be returning to the city tonight. We'll have our judgment sooner than expected."

Tonight? This news took Javed by surprise so badly, that for a moment his face slipped, showing his true emotions to Nikunja. He cursed himself for not keeping his mask on.

"What's wrong, brother? Whichever way the Thakoor decides, Omand knows it's not our fault, and we can finally get out of this miserable place. I never thought I'd miss the scalding sands around the Capitol, but they're preferable to this land of fog and mold."

If Thera was given back to the Inquisition tonight, he wasn't sufficiently prepared to neutralize Nikunja and the rest of the escort they were sure to have without great risk to her. And if the Thakoor ordered Thera's execution, he'd have to break her out immediately and then try to sneak her out of the city much sooner than expected. Using the rebel ciphers Keta had taught him, he'd been trying to make contact with the secret faithful in the area to obtain their aid, but thus far he'd gotten no response. He needed more time.

"It's just that I worked too hard, hiding among fish-eating trash and cutthroat rebels, to be robbed of my glory now. That witch is my prize, and I intend to deliver her to the Grand Inquisitor personally."

"Such an investment. I've never had the opportunity to engage in a cover so deep," Nikunja said wistfully. "Assignments such as yours are legend in our Order. Only our most trusted can be placed in such a situation, drinking from the enemy's cup, becoming confidant and friend to the criminals, until"—he crashed his fist into his palm—"our trap is sprung!"

"I'm sure you'll get your chance someday." Javed pulled out the stool and sat at the desk. "Such an assignment's not what you imagine it to be, though. There's a toll paid, in body and mind, the longer you play at being something you're not."

"I imagine, and they tell us this in training, but oceans,

brother, you became their *priest*! Of such deception, I stand in awe. They must have trusted you as their own flesh and blood."

Why was the younger witch hunter bringing that up now? Javed waved his hand dismissively. "I merely told the rebels what they wanted to hear, and they loved me for it. It is easy to charm simpletons."

"I was taught there's always a danger in assignments such as yours that the witch hunter might eventually lose himself, and forget which face is his real one. That when playing the fanatic, there is the danger you may truly become one. If you repeat the enemy's lies enough, you might even start to believe them."

Javed was consumed with a feeling of sick dread. Where was Nikunja going with this? "Luckily these rebels believe in religious nonsense no sane man could ever stomach."

"This is, what, your fourth, fifth time hiding among fanatics?"

"Something like that. I am very good at what I do."

"You've practically spent more time being a criminal than an Inquisitor!" Nikunja casually walked to the side of the room, as if he was searching for something. "Is that why you've been leaving coded messages for the rebel underground here in Kanok? Nostalgia?"

And too late, Javed realized that Nikunja had just placed his body between him and where he'd left his sword and demon bones. While Nikunja had entered with a sword sheathed at his side and surely had a piece of magic hidden upon his body.

"Who told you such fantasies?"

"It was an understandable mistake for you to make. It's been a long time since you worked in these lands. You wouldn't know that one of those criminals you reached out to had turned informer now. He gave you up for a pitiful amount of notes."

Javed had to think fast. "So what if I tried to find some rebels? I'm one of Omand's chosen. Don't presume you know the extent of my assignments. You speak of how well I tricked the criminals all those years, do you think our Grand Inquisitor would waste such an investment? The religious fanatics know of Javed the rice merchant who became their hero then priest. Why wouldn't I use their trust to try and get them to reveal more of their conspirators while I'm trapped here, bored, with nothing better to do?"

"That sounds logical," Nikunja agreed, but his manner had gone from envious to malicious in the blink of an eye. "Too bad for you, we already queried the Tower via demon bone, and they had no knowledge of any such additional assignments."

"That's why I'm better at this than you, Nikunja. I show initiative."

"Spare me your righteous act, Javed. I'm no fish-eating dope you can confound with clever words. The Tower's confirmation was when we really started spying on you. Why have you been skulking about, and what have you been writing all night, every night?" Pointedly, Nikunja glanced at the boards under Javed's feet. "What is it you've hidden beneath this floor?"

Written upon those papers was Javed's doom.

"What're you accusing me of?" he demanded, trying his best to hide his growing fear. "Choose your words carefully."

"I accuse you of nothing, brother. I'm merely the distraction while the Makao house wizards moved into position to restrain you."

There was movement behind him as two figures stepped out of the dark space that existed just outside of reality, to appear inside his room. As Javed glanced over his shoulder to see that the wizards already had their swords drawn, inwardly he cursed himself for being such a fool. Of course they'd been prepared for violence. They wouldn't underestimate a witch hunter of his reputation.

"You're making a terrible mistake, Nikunja. Omand will have you flogged for this."

"You'll just have to sort that out atop the Tower of Silence with our superiors. I'm but the messenger. Though you might be tempted to lunge for your bag of demon to try some manner of escape, while we've been speaking warriors of the Makao Personal Guard have been surrounding this room. They didn't react well to the suggestion that someone staying under their Thakoor's roof might be consorting with rebels who've been plotting to assassinate their beloved leader. I'd suggest surrendering peacefully, as the Makao are not a patient people."

"That we are not, Witch Hunter," warned one of the wizards. "This one will be bound and questioned while our lord is here, and then your Order can do whatever you wish with him. That is the agreement."

"You should be thankful I brokered such a deal on behalf of the Order," Nikunja added for Javed's benefit. "The Makao wanted to simply kill you, but I insisted you *might* have a good reason for what you've been up to. If you're lying, then I'll get a promotion for catching you. If your excuses are true, then Omand will be pleased by my thoroughness and your resourcefulness, and no harm will come from this misunderstanding."

Only once they read what was hidden beneath the floor, there would be no talking his way out of this. "I understand, Nikunja, and no offense has been taken. It's good you are being so careful. Our Order must be on constant guard against corrupting influences. I will submit, and then we can sort this out back in the Capitol." He slowly stood and held up his open hands, showing that he had no magic upon him.

"Good. You know how this works."

Indeed, he did. Which was why he kicked the stool, launching it at the other witch hunter, then hurled himself back into the nearest wizard. That one's sword narrowly missed piercing his back as he crushed the man against the wall. Grabbing hold of the wizard's sword arm, Javed rolled him over his hip, slamming him against the floor.

The other wizard stepped forward, lifting his blade to strike, but Javed didn't even try to defend himself, as he was too focused on snatching from the fallen wizard's sash a dangling chunk of demon bone.

They'd expected him to try for his own magic supply, not steal theirs.

Javed focused on the pattern to step *outside* and the sword whistled harmlessly through the air where his body had just been. Without hesitation he leapt through the wall of the guest quarters, passing through as if it were made of mist temporarily entering the dark place just outside of regular matter..

The Makao wizards must have expected him to have some demon already in hand, and been prepared for such a trick, as another one of them was already waiting there in the place between, his magic ready.

The pattern was broken and Javed was hurled violently back into the real world, dropping into the hall behind the guest quarters... surrounded by warriors in the black-and-yellow armor of Great House Makao's elite guards. They hadn't been prepared for the man they'd been sent to capture appearing suddenly in their midst, but that surprise would only last for a moment.

Javed called upon the tiger pattern, to change form and run, but the tiny piece of demon bone he'd seized had already been depleted and crumbled to dust in his hand. He threw that dust into the nearest warrior's eyes, then shoved him into the others.

Before he could rush past them, a warrior caught Javed's robe, pulled hard, and slung him back against the wall so hard a rib cracked. Pain shot through this torso like a bolt of lightning. He kicked that warrior in the hip and managed to stab another one in the throat with his fingertips.

When a gauntlet struck him behind the ear, Javed stumbled, and that was all it took for three more warriors to immediately lay into him with fist and boot. He was struck repeatedly in the head and neck. Someone kicked him in the kidney. He went down, but caught himself, only to have a descending heel crush the bones of his left hand and grind them into the floor. They hit him over and over. There were so many rapid agonies being inflicted upon him, his mind couldn't keep up.

They beat him down, until he fell on his face, then the warriors continued to stomp him senseless a bit longer for good measure.

"That'll do."

The world was spinning so rapidly Javed could barely lift his head. When he tried to talk, blood splattered against the fine rug. "To the ocean with you, Nikunja."

The other witch hunter was standing in the doorway, thumbing through the precious pages the gods had inspired Javed to write. "I can't believe this. This is all religion. It's the ramblings of a deranged fanatic."

Javed coughed, and that somehow hurt even more than the beating. "Those are the words of the gods."

"Omand will want to see this."

"The whole world will see them. They will remember what has been forgotten. You can't stop it."

Disgusted, one of the wizards spat. "Take this madman to the dungeon and chain him!"

With a warrior on each arm, Javed was dragged down the stairs to be imprisoned next to the prophet he had already failed once before.

Chapter 12

Thera heard a terrible commotion coming down the hall. From the warriors' shouting, they had a new prisoner who was putting up quite the struggle. There was thrashing, yelling, and the sound of a body being hurled to the floor. One of the guards yelped. "He bit me!"

There were several meaty thuds from clubs striking muscle and a roar of pain, but those fierce blows must have finally subdued their prisoner, because the next thing Thera heard was the grunting of several guards dragging someone past her door. They went into the next cell, and there was the jangle of chains as shackles were locked. Thera was glad she'd at least managed to avoid that particular indignity.

"That ought to hold him." That guard hocked his throat and spit, probably onto the new prisoner's face. Then that heavy door closed and locked, and the guards walked away, laughing.

She'd not had a neighbor before.

Like every other big city in Lok, Kanok had a real prison. These dungeons beneath the great house itself were an antiquated leftover from an earlier time when this place had been the entire seat of governance, rather than just the home of their Thakoor. Nowadays, it appeared these cells were only used to hold the most peculiar cases that required their leader's personal judgment.

Curious, Thera waited until she was certain the guards were truly gone, then went over to that wall and spoke. "Hello?" The stones were thick and well fitted, but hopefully that other cell had a design similar to hers, and he'd be able to hear her through the narrow window slits. "Are you still alive in there?"

The poor fellow must have gotten worked over, because the moan he let out when he tried to respond reminded Thera of the worst beatings she'd ever taken and then some. She imagined he was waiting for the fire in his chest to die off enough he could fill his lungs to whisper.

"I'm sorry, Thera . . . they found out."

Oceans. It was Javed.

Was this some kind of elaborate Inquisition trick? He'd been trying to convince her of his miraculous conversion in the desert. Was this a continuation of that ruse? Or in the incredibly slim chance he'd been telling her the truth, had her tiny hope of escape just been dashed?

"I've failed you and the gods." Javed was slurring his words like a man concussed, but witch hunters were good fakers, especially this one. "I swear I tried to save you."

"I'll start to believe that only if we go to the gallows at the same time, and I still won't be convinced until I see your rope snap tight." There was another noise from the hall. "Quiet. Someone's coming."

It was several men, and they stopped at her door, not Javed's. She moved back to the far corner and went to her knees on the straw, feigning obedience. There was a jangle of keys in the lock. The door opened, and in stepped wretched Dhaval, who was grinning from ear to ear.

The sick realization sank in that the one thing that had been preventing her abuse and murder at her former husband's villainous hands was now in the next cell, in chains. The knife Javed had smuggled her was hidden in the straw beneath her knee. If Dhaval tried anything, she vowed the last thing she'd ever do was stick it in his remaining eye.

"Did you hear the news, Thera?"

She decided to play ignorant. "What news?"

"It's been discovered that your protector is a traitor."

"*My* protector is Ashok Vadal, who is a better man than you in *every* way."

Dhaval licked his teeth. "So the witch was the great criminal's whore. How unsurprising. But no, I speak of Inquisitor Javed. He was caught consorting with rebels."

"That's his job, isn't it? Witch hunters, lying deceivers, pretending to be loyal friends, til they stab you in the back." She hoped Javed heard every word of that.

"It turns out he's a secret fanatic. Just like you were, hiding your evil in my own house, bringing shame to my family and name when you were exposed." Dhaval stood there, hate-filled and haughty, yet tantalizingly just outside of knifing range. He was dishonorable scum and a murderer of women, but his high-status upbringing had provided him with the finest sword trainers, so Thera knew he was skilled. He was also far bigger and stronger than she was and there were guards waiting in the hall. The last time she'd managed to slash him had been before her palms had been crippled and burned, so her hands were clumsy in comparison now. Her only hope to kill him was surprise.

She wouldn't waste it. "Then come over here and do what you intend to do to me. Get it over with already."

"You've got no idea how long I've dreamed of choking the life out of you while staring into your eyes as you go into the endless nothing," he said wistfully.

"Then get on with it, coward."

"Oh, how I want that, so very much. You can't comprehend what it was like for me—the rumors, the glances, as our caste whispered behind my back about how I'd been played the fool enough to be married to a traitor, rebel, and witch!" Dhaval made a big show of balling his hands into fists and shaking against the powerful temptation, but he didn't get any closer. "Great was my offense. Terrible was my indignity!"

"Yet you still managed to get promoted a few ranks somehow. You were always good at kissing up while spitting down."

The truth stung, and Dhaval's gloating mask slipped just a bit, to show the raw anger beneath. He was a kicked dog with a long memory. "However much I'd like to break you of your smug ways, I'll not sabotage the moment of my name's redemption. Our young Thakoor has returned early. Tomorrow evening he'll hear my petition before the entire court of Great House Makao and all the notables of Kanok. This is lucky for you, because if I'd had to wait the rest of the winter for him to arrive, I don't think I could resist the urge to hurt you for that long."

Her trial was *tomorrow*? "I imagine you'll cry the victim, and claim to be a hapless dupe, unfortunate enough to have his arranged marriage have been to a disloyal spy."

"Because that's the truth! You chose to do illegal magic in secret. You chose to help your vassal house rebel against their rightful masters!"

Dhaval had always had a gift for provoking her to anger. "That's your craven version of the truth. I didn't *choose* the Voice. I was a little girl who got her skull shattered by a bolt thrown down from the sky! I had no say in the matter."

"Listen to your madness. How can our Thakoor not recognize that I resisted the evil seduction of your false religion, which has turned thousands toward rebellion. Your lies are so compelling they even corrupt mighty witch hunters, though they're the very Order that's supposed to guard us from such things. Despite your trickery, I, Dhaval, remained true to the Law!"

If she was going to get executed tomorrow, she might as well goad Dhaval into attacking her now. She was dead either way, so better to take him with her. Keta kept telling her there was an afterlife. *Let's find out.*

"You're an impotent dolt with a habit of murdering his wives when he flies into a drunken rage. The real problem with the Law, Dhaval, is scum like you hiding behind it! A Law that only applies to the poor is no Law at all! I never asked to be the Voice of illegal gods, but you're damned right I rebelled against your wretched house, and if I could I'd help my father do it all over again, only this time I'd make sure it stuck. Your army is soft, and your officers unfit to lick the lowliest nayak of Vane's shit-encrusted boots! I bet you got that phontho's star for massacring casteless because you're too scared to have ever faced a real foe. You're an insult to your caste, and I curse you, before the gods and the Law and the demons and whoever else is listening, that you'll die, dishonored and despised, like the craven rat you are!"

As she delivered that tirade even the guards peeked around the open door, curious to see what would happen next.

Dhaval's fury was apparent, but her former husband must have learned some restraint since she'd last seen him and he'd hurled her into the ocean. Now his anger burned cold and calculating, rather than the flash of mad fire she'd been used to before. "You and the fanatic Inquisitor will have a chance to plead your case, but know that it will be futile. Thakoor Venketesh's decision is a forgone conclusion. After he condemns you to death, he'll disband your vassal house to cut out any potential rot, and I will profit *greatly* from the end of Vane. I've borne the indignity that you brought my family this long. I can wait one more day for my reward...for tomorrow you will die. Sleep well, Thera Vane."

He walked out of the cell. The guards locked the door behind him, leaving Thera to stew in her hate.

Javed coughed, and it trailed off into an agonized wheeze. His ribs were really broken. Even a witch hunter wasn't that good an actor. She *almost* felt pity for him.

"Don't worry, prophet. The gods will find a way to deliver us."

The gods rarely delivered anything but misery. The Voice had stepped in to save her life before, but only when it felt like it.

"I hope you choke to death on your own blood, Javed."

"You should pray to the gods for their help. They'll heed their servant."

Little did the false priest realize that she had been praying every single day that she'd been in this damned place, trying to bargain with the unseeing and uncaring gods, like the time she'd put her own life in danger in the Cove to force them into showing her how to cure a plague. Only now that her life was in danger once more, this time they'd remained silent. Deep down she was terrified that the revelation about how to harm the Capitol by stealing their water was the last thing they'd needed her for.

"I'm afraid the gods have no more use of me. Now they'll throw me away."

Javed was silent for a long time, then he spoke with great conviction, as if trying to soothe her, even though he was the one in agony. "There are still prophecies unfulfilled. You can't die yet."

"Why not?"

"The Voice must be at the final battle or all of humanity will perish. I have faith in the gods...and you."

Well, at least someone here still did. "When I get condemned tomorrow, my final request will be for them to hang you first, so I can at least have the satisfaction of watching you die before I do."

Chapter 13

Crossing the mountains had been brutal, but not impossible like it would have been in the bitter freezing month of Magha. The Heart had sustained Ashok and kept his fingers and toes from being consumed by frostbite, and even then he'd nearly fallen many times. It had been a miserable journey across the pass, but no struggle would keep him from finding his woman. Once on the other side, it was all downhill to Kanok.

It appeared spring was coming early this year. In the south of Lok, the warmer seasons were for fighting and winter was for surviving. If Keta had still been alive, surely he would have blamed this fortunate turn in the weather on the gods, and such an early thaw was them blessing Ashok so that he could reach their beloved prophet. That was foolishness, for if the gods could truly make the sun shine brighter or the clouds part sooner, then they could just as easily free Thera themselves, rather than forcing Ashok to climb up ice walls that would send any normal man plummeting to his doom. Keta would claim such efforts were necessary as a show of devotion toward fulfilling the gods' commands, and whatever the faithful could not accomplish, the gods would surely make up the difference.

Ashok found it odd that he passed so much time on his

arduous journey having a philosophical argument with a dead man, but such was the nature of lonely travel. He had left the Sons to dig their way through the pass and proceeded by himself. He alone possessed the physical might necessary to scale these treacherous frozen slopes. Even the Sons who hailed from mountainous regions, who climbed their home peaks to show their courage, knew they would die if they attempted to follow him. Some of them were still prideful enough to try until Ashok ordered them not to.

He traveled light, with only the warm clothing he wore, a few meager supplies, and his sword. The better to run. The better to avoid checkpoint-manning warriors who would demand to see traveling papers he did not have. He continued day and night, stopping for a few hours at a time only when he absolutely had to sleep. He passed many villages but stopped at none. When he ran out of rations, he killed an elk with a thrown rock, and ate his supper over a campfire made with the reliable fire starter given to him by Collector Moyo Kapoor.

The southern slope was an endless vista of brown grass and white drifts. In the distance, too far even for Ashok's magical eyes to see, lay the ocean. Perhaps it was the relative closeness of their greatest city to the deadly sea that made the Makao so brittle. He had known many Protectors who'd come from this house, and most of them seemed to be perpetually in search of offense to take, especially against anyone hailing from the richer houses of the north. Makao was the strongest of the southern houses, but that was nothing compared to the wealth of Vadal. Ashok's fellow acolytes had assumed—even though they were all equally miserable in the Order's training program—that his northern life had been so much easier than theirs. A silly assumption, considering his life had been a wizard's fabrication and hadn't even been real at all.

Ashok saw several patrols. The Makao warriors seemed agitated and had deployed in great numbers. The Sons had warned him that Harban and Makao were feuding once again, apparently having forgotten the bloody lessons that Ashok and the Protectors had dispensed the last time he was here. Despite this looming threat of house war, Ashok was able to avoid the warrior caste's attention all the way to his destination.

Kanok was the most populous city of the Ice Coast. Unlike the sprawling Vadal City, Kanok was a long but narrow strip between the mountains and the ocean. Their districts stretched from east to west because the workers had to stop building north when the hills got too steep, and south when they got close enough to see the ocean. The higher a family's status, the higher they lived on the slope; the lesser of station, the closer they were placed toward the sea. No whole man was willing to live beyond the point where solid ground turned to perpetual mud, for just beyond that wet boundary lay hell. Those southern marshes were where the whole men had forced their casteless to dwell. Thousands of non-people had lived there in vast casteless quarters of huts built upon stilts over the muck. Kanok's untouchables were like a fence made of flesh, serving as a distraction and early warning for when a demon occasionally wandered this far inland.

When he sharpened his eyes, Ashok could see that all that remained of Kanok's casteless quarters now was ruin and ashes. That massive casteless population that had once dwelt here was all gone, either murdered or driven off, because the Makao had embraced the Great Extermination. How many frozen refugee corpses had he unknowingly passed along the way because they'd died and then been buried in the snow?

A terrible anger grew in Ashok's heart, colder than the winter air.

Only the oldest parts of Kanok were walled, so Ashok was able to enter the outskirts without challenge or being asked to present his traveling papers. The streets were busy with workers going about their business. Despite rumors of looming war, or perhaps because of it, the markets were bustling with trade. No one paid him any mind. His long winter coat marked him as a humble worker of unremarkable status, but mostly he wore it to hide his sword.

This particular city had always irritated him. The Makao were as Law-abiding as any other great house, but to him it had felt as though they only accepted their place with grudging animosity. They were not openly defiant or rebellious. It was more that they pined to be something they were not . . . Devedas had explained it to him once, that the other southern houses accepted that their life was hard, their lands poor, their winters long, and they adapted accordingly. They didn't try to deny their circumstances. Except the elite of Makao liked to pretend they were no different from Vadal or Vokkan, who through their fortune and circumstances dominated every trend, whether it be in culture, art, or even warfare. But Makao rarely created anything of its own. It merely copied what others had already done, and those copies always seemed pale and inferior in comparison.

Perhaps his former brother was right about the Makao. It was a challenge for Ashok to understand people at all, but he could see how foolish it was for this house to copy the flamboyant, immodest, and impractical fashions of the Capitol in this land of biting cold, while their fine Vokkan-designed carriages struggled along their roads filled with ice and slush and mud, to eat Vadal-style dishes that he could tell by smell alone were sadly bereft of all the potent spices his birth house took for granted.

Mother Dawn had told him Kanok was where he would find Thera, but he didn't know where, and it was a very big place. The wizard Laxmi believed that Murugan had been killed by witch hunters. If that was the case, Thera might be their prisoner. But why would Inquisitors bring Thera here instead of their Dome? Or she could simply be in hiding among the criminals. That's how she had gotten along before they had ever met. But if so, why flee all the way here, far from the Sons of the Black Sword who had vowed to serve her? Thera had once lived in this city, but those had been unhappy years for her. She had no love for the great house that she'd been married into, so it was doubtful she was here willingly.

Ashok needed information but didn't know where to seek it. Back when he'd been a Protector he could simply demand answers from anyone he met and expect their compliance. Threatening random strangers here would merely result in his having to fight every warrior in Kanok, and that was a pointless distraction if they couldn't lead him to his woman.

So he wandered the streets for a time. There were public boards with notices pinned upon them, with announcements from the various Orders and worker organizations, advertisements, and various proclamations of Law. Most of Kanok's citizens couldn't read but it would be the legal responsibility of those who could to inform the others of what was written there. Sadly, he found no mention of a false prophet or rebel leader on any of the notices, but at each board he stopped at, there was the same mass-printed notice celebrating the appointment of Lord Protector Devedas to a mighty new office of the Capitol. Those notices recounted how all should know and respect Raja Devedas because of his triumph over the infamous Black-Hearted Ashok in a duel...

This lie annoyed him. Devedas had not *triumphed*. On the contrary, the only reason he still lived was because Angruvadal had gone so far as to stop Ashok's heart to keep him from crushing Devedas' skull. He couldn't comprehend why the shard would want Devedas to continue pursuing his illegal ambitions to take over the government, but it had. But oh, to see the disappointment on Devedas' face when he found out Ashok still lived would be quite the thing.

Using some of the rebellion's bank notes, he purchased curried noodles from a street vendor, and ate among the workers, sharpening his hearing so he could listen to their rumormongering. The Heart of the Mountain enabled him to listen in on even distant conversations, yet their talk was mostly vapid worker things: complaints about bosses and taxes and how their backs hurt or their wives were cruel. The workers knew they were at war with Harban, but not why or what it meant, only that they expected more or less work or profit from it, depending on what it was they made. Ashok wasted an hour this way, but none of them were foolish enough to speak about rebellious witches, even if they had known of Thera.

The workers were of no use, so Ashok walked to the nearest warrior's district and repeated the process. His false insignia marked him as the wrong caste, but there was much intermingling in this city, so it was doubtful anyone would care about his status. However, this area was more dangerous because a keen-eyed warrior might note his scars and demeanor and recognize that Ashok was no mere worker. He wasn't some actor who could disguise his true nature from another experienced combatant, and in a time of war, the warrior caste would be extra suspicious of strangers. So Ashok had purchased a big straw hat to keep low over his face and then had spent his time sitting alone in the darkest corners of the various establishments he visited. In each place he would order a single cup, and then take his time drinking it while he used the Heart of the Mountain to listen. The Makao preferred a flavorful foaming rice beer, which Ashok had to admit was preferable to the puddle water he'd been drinking to make it this far.

As time passed, Ashok grew increasingly frustrated. He would give this method of investigation until sundown, and if that didn't work he would try something more direct. He wasn't sure what that would entail yet, but he had a vow, a vengeful sword, and many targets to choose from.

"You look tired, Sanjay."

That warrior stifled a yawn. "Phontho Dhaval's making a stink again."

Dhaval had been Thera's husband's name. Ashok had been skimming a dozen conversations simultaneously, but now he focused on only that one. The two warriors were sitting at a table in the far corner. They wore the rank of lowly nayaks and an insignia of black and yellow that Ashok did not recognize.

"We had to get everything inspection-ready last night. The Thakoor returned to the great house unexpectedly."

"Really? I thought Venketesh was away in the west, inspecting the border garrisons to make sure they're ready to repel Harban invaders."

"He was. Our Thakoor's been hungry for a proper war since his father lost the last one." The nayak looked around conspiratorially before telling his friend, "Only there's been some falling out with the masks and Phontho Dhaval that he has to sort out here at home first. Word is, he's not happy."

"Of course it's always Dhaval causing problems, that one-eyed prick. I don't know why Thakoor Venketesh puts up with that fop, living inside the great house grounds likes he's a firster."

"Because Dhaval's from the most powerful family in our caste now, is why. They've got notes, land, and troops. If it were the likes of me or you pissing off Inquisitors like Dhaval has, Venketesh would have us sewn into a sack filled with rocks and thrown into the sea."

"What're the masks mad about now?"

"Those bastards are always mad, but they're arguing over who gets to execute some important prisoner or something. Dhaval demanded a public judgment tonight. Not my problem. I'm off duty. Some other poor saps are manning the mansion's gates now to let in the important guests wanting to watch a spectacle."

Ashok stood and walked quickly from the tavern. In the street, he looked toward the north, far up the slope, to where the walls of the old city towered over the newer estates. It was near sundown. He would need to hurry.

Nearby, a girl was holding a bucket beneath one of the many hand pumps that supplied Kanok's drinking water. A look of sudden revulsion crossed her face. "Ugh. It's gone bad."

An old woman cupped her hand beneath the still-trickling pipe, then placed it to her lips, and promptly spit it out. "It's turned to saltwater!"

Ashok began to run.

Chapter 14

Thera had to hand it to Dhaval. Somehow he'd actually gotten smarter since they'd been together. At first she'd been thankful when some house slaves had brought her buckets of warm soapy water and a rag so that she could wash herself. She had even assumed it was just so the stench of captivity didn't upset their first caste's delicate sensibilities with her stinking up the place during her show trial. But when she saw what fresh clothing had been left for her to change into, she realized that Dhaval was being clever. For she would appear in chains before the Thakoor, not as a filthy prisoner, but rather wearing fine silks dyed in the maroon of Vassal House Vane. The tan sash marked her as being born Vane's warrior caste, and the bastard had even taken the time to have someone embroider the symbol of her father's old command on it.

Dhaval wasn't going to merely parade her out as someone who could be easily dismissed as just another wild-eyed religious fanatic spouting off false prophecies, but rather as a symbol of a conquered vassal with a history of violent rebellion. She wouldn't be just another criminal, but rather the daughter of the legendary war leader Andaman Vane. Her house didn't love her. They had married off their embarrassing sickly girl who'd spent years of her childhood comatose, and surely they'd disavowed her completely after her father's failed rebellion, but Dhaval was still going to use her very existence as a weapon against his political enemies.

Dhaval had been born into the wrong caste because that was the sort of vile political machinations the first lived for.

As the slaves had stripped her, Thera had asked if she could keep her old clothing instead, but they had orders to take those bloodstained rags to the furnace immediately. Though it would surely upset Dhaval's careful plans, she was too proud to appear before the court naked. So she'd have to wear the colors of her old house, and that was that.

As they violently scrubbed the dungeon filth from her until her skin was red and raw, Thera was just thankful that she'd hidden Javed's knife beneath the straw. While the slaves were distracted, she smoothly palmed it, and hid the blade beneath her sash. As they combed and decorated her hair—for the Makao did nothing without frilly, pointless, ornamentation—she thought about how best to make use of her weapon. She was under no illusions she would live through this, but if she had just one moment to run steel across Dhaval's neck, then she could die content. Planning gave her something to think about, which beat pointless worrying.

Javed had begged her to pray for help, and she had, but as usual, the gods hadn't responded. The useless bastards. They'd once shown her how to make a molten spear sufficient to pierce the heart of an ancient demon king, but the cost of that magic had been high, leaving the palms of her hands badly burned. Now her hands retained but a fraction of the great dexterity she'd once had. She suspected the gods had intervened simply because back then, they still had need of their Voice.

She was in danger once again, but she was done begging. If they needed her alive, they'd send a miracle to save her. And if they were done with her, so be it.

Maybe, just maybe, Keta and Ratul had been right about all that afterlife business... there was more than a great nothing beyond death. Rather, there would be a land for the faithful, free of suffering. And oddly enough, if that was the case, Thera found herself hoping that she might find Ashok there. For when she looked back on her odd and troubled life, the happiest she'd ever been had been in the arms of that man. Even though their lives had been constantly threatened with danger, that was where she had felt the safest. The gods may have been cruel bastards, but at least they had given her the chance to fall in love with Ashok Vadal.

That was an unexpected realization, but it was true.

Ashok was probably dead, and she would join him soon.

Calm, Thera went to her trial.

Chapter 15

The central hall of Great House Makao was a vast space with great curling staircases in every corner. The ceiling was easily thirty feet high, with a central dome made of colored glass and carved wood. Ostentatious decoration and gaudy tapestries hung from every wall. In the pleasant months they'd have used flowers, but in the winter, fabric had to suffice.

Thera was escorted into that opulent chamber with her wrists chained together and a warrior at each elbow. These weren't the low status-warriors who'd been guarding her either, but rather the Thakoor's personal guard, elite handpicked warriors who represented the finest of Great House Makao's armies. Thera did her best to look weak and unthreatening next to them. Which wasn't difficult, because both of them looked like they could easily break her in half if they felt like it. She was tall for a woman, but these muscular warriors towered over her, and a Thakoor's elite were never picked just for being pretty. Only skilled and decorated combatants were tasked with protecting a man of such importance. Their presence was going to make it very difficult for her inflict a fatal wound on her former husband.

The hall was filled with hundreds of high-status people who were currently bunched up into groups full of conversation and loud laughter. Their fashion was bright, colorful, and complicated.

The mood was festive. This was no trial. It was a party! If there had been a band, they could have held a ball immediately after pronouncing the manner of her death. There were even tables laden with many kinds of food for the first-caste sheep to graze upon. Since she'd been subsisting on gruel and stale naan those delicious smells made her mouth water.

A herald was announcing the arrival of each guest and listing off their rank, status, and notable achievements. Thera got no announcement as she was marched to the side and roughly seated upon a simple wooden chair. She was a curiosity, not a guest. Even so, the arrival of the evening's oddity was still noticed, and many of the conversations tapered off as eyes shifted her way. *There is the savage rebel. The false prophet. The practitioner of illegal witchcraft. I wonder how she'll be executed.*

Thera met each gaze in turn, unflinching, and it brought her some measure of satisfaction when each of them looked away first. For a people who didn't believe in religion, the first caste were still afraid of curses. Let them think she was a witch. *Good.* She hoped she'd give them nightmares.

A moment later, the elite of Kanok had a second criminal to gawk upon as Javed was brought in. He too had been cleaned up to be presentable, dressed in Inquisition black, but he'd been stripped of his mask and the face that revealed was a mess of cuts and bruises. Javed walked in with a limp and each time he put pressure on his right side he winced at the pain of what had to be broken ribs. While Thera was being watched by two guards, Javed had been assigned four. Of course, they assumed a witch hunter was more dangerous than a false prophet. High-status Makao women tended to be pretty but weak, flighty things, helpless and soft, so of course they would assume the same thing about her. Hopefully that prejudice would grant her a bit more time to stab Dhaval when she got her chance.

Javed was shoved into the chair next to her. Seeing his injuries up close, it was clear this was no act. This beating hadn't been a trick to deceive her. Even wrapped in a bandage she could tell that the bones of one hand had been smashed. She doubted even a witch hunter was dedicated enough to their deceit that they'd let warriors injure them this badly, just to fool her.

"You were telling the truth," she whispered.

"I lied to you before. Everything I've said since has been the truth. Just as I'll tell the truth before Thakoor Venketesh, and the gods will convince him to set us free."

"You really are a fanatic then, aren't you?"

"Call me whatever you want, prophet. But in the desert I was shown the error of my ways. I am truly sorry."

"Sorry won't save your miserable life, traitor. Or mine. I'm here because of you."

Javed tried to blink sudden emotion from blackened eyes that were nearly swollen shut. He failed and a tear rolled down one bruised cheek. "I know."

The guards took up positions around their chairs to keep the curious away. Gradually, the fine people tired of staring at them like they were animals in the Capitol zoo and went back to their business of gossiping and meddling and all those other dishonorable things first casters did. She noticed Dhaval strutting about among them, wearing ribbons and medals upon his uniform that she was certain he'd never actually earned. Smiling, bowing and scraping, Dhaval was surely making alliances, cutting deals, and apparently having the time of his life. He was so preoccupied with his unctuous dealings he barely even noticed the presence of his former wife, and when he briefly glanced her way, it was with sneering contempt.

She would need him to get closer...

The court herald had a voice that surely could be heard all the way to the seashore: "Presenting our illustrious and honorable leader of Great House Makao, son of wise Urktesh, Master of the Seven Hills, the Hawk of the South, Thakoor Venketesh Makao. Great and prosperous has been the second year of his rule. Long may he reign."

The room fell quiet. A gangly, thin boy walked out onto the balcony overlooking the central hall and lifted one bejeweled hand in greeting to his adoring people. He couldn't have been more than fourteen years old. Even wearing a giant turban covered in rubies and golden thread, he looked tiny compared to the warriors flanking him. Thera hadn't realized the Thakoor was so young. When she'd been here last, Urktesh had still ruled, and Dhaval had been of rank insufficient to attend any function where she would have actually met the Thakoor or any of his heirs.

Despite his youth, Venketesh was clearly used to these sorts of gatherings, and had no problem taking immediate control of the room. He spoke like one who was used to being listened to.

"Greetings, my children. I have just recently returned from the west, where I inspected our most decorated garrisons and found them to be acceptable. It brings me great joy to announce that the incursions of the Harban swine are being swiftly dealt with, and they will soon be punished for their insolence. My father's dream of our renewed dominance in the west lives once more."

Every member of the first caste politely clapped at that vague announcement, though Thera noticed the members of the warrior caste exchanging nervous glances. The last time those two great houses had squared off in a real war it had resulted in the Protectors putting a stop to the whole thing rather violently.

"I am eager to finish the campaign my father started all those years ago, but I am told there is a matter of grave criminality requiring my attention first." Venketesh snapped his fingers, and two men rushed out from behind a curtain carrying a huge, cushioned chair. They placed it near their Thakoor, so that he could sit above Thera and Javed in judgment. Venketesh waved those servants away, adjusted his robes, and sat down. "Let's get to it, then, before I grow bored of these tedious matters. Arbiters, you may begin."

The same woman who had visited Thera in the dungeon stepped from the crowd. "Yes, my Thakoor. Below you are two criminals accused of the most heinous crimes of treason against Great House Makao as well as rebellion against the Law as a whole."

"Two criminals?" Venketesh seemed mildly amused by this development. "I was told there was but one very special criminal tonight. A wildwoman of Vane, prone to witchcraft and stabbing my officers in the eye."

The first caste openly laughed at that. Thera caught a glimpse of Dhaval, teeth gritted against that unexpected sleight. Perhaps he wasn't as beloved in this noble crowd as he imagined himself to be. *The fool.*

"Who is the second criminal?"

"Inquisition Witch Hunter Javed Zarger."

"One of the Inquisition elite?" Now the young Thakoor seemed intrigued, and he leaned forward on his mighty chair to better study the accused. "It isn't often one sees a witch hunter in chains!"

"Javed is accused of following and promoting Thera Vane's false prophecies. He was found in possession of illegal religion—texts written in his own hand—and conspiring with rebels to help his false prophet escape our custody."

"Perhaps the Inquisitor was on a secret mission to seek out enemies of the Law, as that Order tends to do. My father once told me to think of the Inquisition's hunters as snakes who wear the fur of rodents in order to slither about mouse holes as if they belong there." Venketesh was a youth, but he was clearly educated about the insidious nature of the Capitol's most dangerous Order, because Thera found that description a fair one. "Does the Inquisition have an official statement on this matter?"

A man wearing a mask representing the savage face of the Law stepped from the crowd. "I am Senior Witch Hunter Nikunja Gujara." From a leather pouch at his side, he removed a stack of papers and held them up for all to see. It was a meaningless gesture, since nobody was close enough to examine the papers for themselves, and who among these grass-eaters was going to question an Inquisitor? "I have the evidence of Javed's illegal religion here. Thus my Order offers no defense for him. He is forsaken by us. Do with him as you will."

It turned out Venketesh had more spine than Thera had expected. "I would do as I would anyway, Inquisitor. I don't require your permission to do anything in my own lands, for I'm the ultimate judge of the Law here. It would behoove you to remember that."

Chastised, Nikunja bowed deeply in apology. "Thank you for the reminder, Thakoor Makao. Please forgive my poor choice of words."

"Your offense was minor and already forgotten." Venketesh dismissed the witch hunter as if he were no more important than the house slaves who'd carried out his comfy chair. "Everyone has heard of the wild rebellion in Akershan lands, and the mad destruction caused by this criminal's false prophecies, but even the vilest scum is still allowed to present their defense in Makao lands, for we are a just people. If the Inquisition offers no defense for their man, and I see no representatives of Vassal House Vane stepping forward to speak on behalf of their woman, who will plead for them?"

Javed suddenly stood up. "I will."

All the guards around them reached for their swords, thinking that this might be some kind of witch hunter trick, but Venketesh lazily lifted one hand signaling for them to refrain from killing anyone quite yet.

"A lowly criminal is not worthy to speak directly to our Thakoor!" the arbiter shouted.

"I obey a higher law than yours," Javed responded.

Oceans, Thera swore to herself, because the way this was going she'd get tortured *then* executed.

Venketesh gave them a cruel smile. "This brazenness amuses me. I will allow him to speak."

The guards slowly relaxed and stepped back to give Javed a bit of room.

"State your defense, forsaken Inquisitor."

It was obvious that even straightening his back was an agony for him, but Javed stood tall, and managed to speak with defiant authority. "I was dispatched by Grand Inquisitor Omand to spy upon this rebellion, acting the part of a humble rice merchant and secret believer in the old ways, to ingratiate myself to their leaders. To become indispensable to them. My orders were to aid their prophet in her mission of rebellion. This was all part of Omand's secret plot to use the brutal reputation of Ashok Vadal to destabilize the Law so that Omand could overthrow the judges and take control of the Capitol."

There were cries of shock and outrage from the audience, as the Thakoor incredulously asked, "You claim the Grand Inquisitor did *what?*"

Nikunja stepped from the crowd once more. "I would advise against listening to this mad fanatic's outlandish tales—"

"Silence. The Inquisition has covered itself in enough glory for one day."

"But Thakoor, letting Javed slander a righteous Capitol Order so publicly is a mistake and—"

Venketesh frowned. "Damodar."

"Yes, my Thakoor?" asked a grizzled white-haired warrior who was standing at the young leader's right hand.

"If that mask interrupts me one more time, I want you to go down there and use our house's ancestor blade to decapitate him."

"Understood, my Thakoor." Damodar placed one hand on the black hilt of his sheathed sword. "It will be done."

So Great House Makao's bearer was here as well... Thera idly wondered if that was how she'd be executed, guts exploded on the end of a black-steel blade.

Nikunja prudently held his tongue and stepped back. No

matter how powerful the Inquisition was, they were a long way from the Capitol, and nobody dared cross a Thakoor in his own house. Venketesh might have been bored when this trial had begun, but he was fascinated now, leaning so far forward on the edge of his chair that he seemed poised to topple over the railing. "Continue your story, forsaken."

"Grand Inquisitor Omand was plotting against the judges and the great houses to seize control of the Capitol, in order to install a king." This wild accusation caused a great deal of consternation among the assembled members of the first. There were gasps of outrage or shock, and many of them began to whisper to each other. "My small part in this plot was to help guide the rebels in a manner that their destructive criminality would be the most useful for Omand's purposes. I was chosen for this assignment because I was the best among my Order. However, during my time hidden among the rebels I learned the truth. That this woman"—Javed's chains clanked as he gestured toward her—"Thera Vane, really does speak with the blessing and authority of the old gods."

Venketesh laughed uproariously. The crowd followed his example. Even the hard-as-nails-looking old bearer cracked a smile at that outlandish claim.

"Don't make the same mistakes I made! The gods will not be mocked!" Despite Javed's passion, the crowd continued to roar in amusement "You've seen the signs. Surely you saw the mighty pillar of fire that cut the sky in two. The Forgotten is real. I have seen him with my own eyes and heard him with my own ears. The gods manifest their will through Thera, providing us with prophecy and knowledge. I testify that the Forgotten has returned and his chosen walk among us!"

"Enough, enough." As the Thakoor wiped the moisture from his eye, the laughter tapered off. "Brilliant. Such conviction! You are very brave. Insane, but brave."

"The reverse is true, Thakoor Makao. I am rational, but I was a coward. For even as I was racked with guilt for all the terrible things I'd done, I still denied the truth, and helped my Order capture this prophet. Afterward, in the desert, the gods sent a shining messenger to condemn me for my crimes. Mother Dawn appeared to me in her many-armed form and commanded that my penance is to repair the damage I have done. I tried to destroy the truth, so to atone I must spread the truth to all who will listen. What has been forgotten will be remembered. Just as the gods showed me the error of my ways, I promise they will show you yours."

"There is no error in my ways, fanatic. I'm a Thakoor. Everything I do is correct by the act of my doing it. Though this has been amusing, I've heard enough superstitious nonsense for one evening. I will pronounce my ruling now."

"The gods' rule is greater than your Law!"

The audience gasped at that, but Venketesh theatrically turned his head side to side, as if searching for that alleged higher power. "You claim that, yet I see no illegal gods here. Since I'm the one with a vault full of bank notes, an army at my command, a mighty bearer by my side, and the lineage that declares me to be the rightful master of this house, my ruling is sufficient to have you killed. Sit him down now."

As the warriors roughly shoved Javed back into his seat, Thera had never before wished so hard for the Voice to appear in all its terrifying splendor to shout into everyone's minds some vague yet thunderous pronouncement as it had done so many times before...but as usual, the gods didn't give a fish about what she wanted.

"My Thakoor, may I beg an indulgence?" Dhaval walked out to where he could be seen from the balcony. "Your loyal officer has a small request before you pronounce your wise and final judgment."

"Are you going to ask for mercy upon your former wife?"

Dhaval snorted. "Of course not."

"I didn't think so. Nobody has ever accused you of being merciful. Speak your request, Phontho."

"I believe Vassal House Vane is directly responsible for these troubles. They concealed Thera Vane's witchcraft. Her father was the same man whose untimely rebellion sabotaged your father's righteous war against Harban, betraying us right at the hour of our ultimate victory. For their complicity I have sent a petition to your arbiters proposing the dissolution and assimilation of Vane."

"I have read it."

"And?"

Venketesh frowned at that prompting. "I will consider it."

Despite his age, the boy seemed cunning, quick-witted, and

perhaps—most dangerous of all—curious. He may have been inexperienced, but the sly nature of the first caste obviously ran thick in his blood.

Thera hated diplomacy but running a rebellion had made her decent at it. She had to at least try and help her former family. "May I speak?"

Luckily, Venketesh didn't take offense at a second criminal addressing him so boldly. "I doubt it will be half as amusing as what your Inquisitor friend just said, but I am intrigued. Proceed, witch."

Thera stood, and she did so slowly, mostly because she was worried about the unsecured knife slipping from her sash and clattering at her feet. Luckily the blade stayed where it was supposed to.

"Vane has no loyalty or love for me. There are hundreds of witnesses who saw that I was struck down by a bolt from the heavens as a child."

"This tale is widely known," Venketesh agreed.

"Vane concealed nothing from you, because that's all they knew about it. They only saw the impact, not the aftermath. They demoted my father because he cared for his injured daughter more than his garrison. When I recovered instead of dying as expected, my house was happy to be rid of me, and quickly married me off to a pathetic, cowardly dog."

Dhaval began to shout a response to that offense, but the Thakoor silenced him with an annoyed glance. "You had your chance, Phontho. Let her finish her story."

"Vane denied my father's rebellion, and me along with him. Then Dhaval threw me in the ocean, where I barely escaped being killed by a demon. Since I was cast out of my old house I have never returned since. I hold no love for them now, and they, none for me. I've had no contact with them since. Vassal House Vane has had nothing to do with me, or the rebellion I have led, or any of the other great list of crimes I'm charged with. The only reason my former house is implicated today is the greed of one honorless officer, seeking to profit off the destruction of innocent parties. Hang me, but please, I beg you, noble Thakoor, leave my old family out of it."

Dhaval was seething with rage, and for a moment she hoped that he would rush over to strike her, so that she could stick him, but even he wasn't stupid enough to push his luck with all those personal guard standing around her.

"If you have no love for them, why do you still defend them now?"

She wasn't really sure. "Habit, I suppose."

"I find that plausible," Venketesh said, which was actually surprising. "My advisors have told me your rebellion has made a *habit* out of defending any they deem to be innocent and down-trodden. Even the worthless non-people. My eyes in Akershan have said you took those there beneath your wing, even going to war against the mighty Protectors to try and save casteless con-demned by the Great Extermination... and somehow you won."

"That is true."

"You make no excuse for those crimes?"

Thera weighed her words carefully. "I don't think doing the right thing should be a crime. The casteless did nothing to deserve such slaughter."

"The judges disagree. And unlike Akershan, Makao is a Law-abiding house. There's no rebellion here sufficient to resist the Law, and the Great Extermination became Law the day after a fish-eater assassinated the Chief Judge. Unlike other great houses which dithered and were afraid, Makao's casteless have been thoroughly destroyed. I'm assured whatever remnant that's left in my lands are hiding in the wilderness and will be dealt with as they are found."

Bragging about so much senseless murder disgusted her, and though she was about to die, at least she did so knowing that she'd saved those within her reach. "You sound so proud, Thakoor."

He shrugged. "I'd rather have used those resources fighting Harban, but in this house we honor the Law and meet its demands. Returning to Dhaval's petition, you defend Vane's innocence, but not your own?"

"I don't deny I fought against the Law, but I did it with Vane's condemnation, not their help. I'll not be silent while a miserable excuse for a warrior uses my dishonor to punish the innocent so he can profit."

Some of the witnesses nodded at the logic of that. It was a truth so obvious that even a criminal could state it and be believed. Dhaval looked angry enough that Thera thought a vein might burst in his head, which delighted her.

Venketesh leaned back in his chair and thoughtfully stroked a chin that couldn't even grow hair on it yet. "Your protest is noted, witch. I've heard enough from you and your frothing-at-the-mouth Inquisitor. Does anyone else have any further testimony to submit before I make my decision?"

"I do."

That had come from directly overhead, where no one should have been. Everyone in the room looked up toward the dome of the ceiling to see a dark figure standing in an alcove, high above them. The man stepped into space and dropped, hurtling toward the marble floor. Even though a fall from that height should have shattered bones, he landed in a crouch, as if the distance meant nothing to him.

The personal guard reacted immediately. Swords were drawn. Bodies stepped between their leader and this new threat. Archers rushed to the edge of the balcony and readied their bows. House wizards grabbed hold of bits of demon tied to their clothing and prepared their magical patterns.

The new arrival slowly rose to his full, imposing height, and surveyed the room and all the dozens of men who were ready to try and take his life, and frowned, as if unimpressed. He was dressed in a drab worker's coat, but everyone there immediately understood this was no mere worker. Something truly dangerous was in their midst. A tiger had leapt into a pen of sheep.

Thera gasped. Because, sure enough, it was *him*.

"Ashok!"

Chapter 16

Ashok Vadal stood in the middle of the vast hall, completely surrounded, but utterly unafraid. Where a normal man would hold his fear, Ashok had only a righteous anger, and now it burned hot as a forge. He would show them the light of that fire.

They had all heard Thera cry his name, and the mob began to whisper. *Could it be? He's supposed to be dead! Is the Black Heart really among us?*

Thera was behind him. The Thakoor of Great House Makao was seated above him. All around were warriors and wizards, ready to kill with steel or magic. No one dared move. The hall fell silent except for the creaking energy of drawn bows.

"Everyone be still. There will be no bloodshed here until I say so," the child Thakoor ordered, and it was a marvel that his forces listened. He appeared but a callow boy, yet spoke with words of iron. "Hello, trespasser. To fall so far and not cripple yourself, you're clearly some manner of wizard. She calls you Ashok, but everyone knows the infamous criminal Ashok Vadal is dead, slain at the hands of Raja Devedas. Considering how eagerly the Capitol commanded us to print notices of that triumph and post them everywhere, that had better be true or I wasted a great deal of expensive ink and paper. So before I have you killed, tell us who you really are and why you have dared interrupt my court."

"I am Ashok Vadal, come to testify on Thera's behalf, either by word..." He let his coat hang open, so that they could see his sheathed blade. "Or by sword."

The first caste reacted with terror or revulsion, for Ashok's name was legend among their kind.

The boy scoffed. "You're not the Black Heart." He addressed one of the archers standing ready upon the balcony. "You, end this nuisance."

That archer released.

Ashok drew Angruvadal and split the speeding arrow in half.

"Impressive trick!" declared the boy Thakoor before he grasped the true nature of the sword that had appeared in Ashok's hand, so black it seared any eye that lingered on it too long. "Is that...?"

"That's a real ancestor blade, my lord," confirmed the old warrior beside the Thakoor.

Every warrior in the hall took an unconscious step back. A woman screamed. Someone else shouted, "Ashok's come to kill us all!" Some of the first caste who were closest to the doors fled, but most of them didn't have the sense to bolt, and they stood there, transfixed.

Now that Ashok had confirmed his identity and truly had their attention, he shouted, "Hear me, House Makao, for I am Ashok Vadal. I have come to take back what is mine!" He turned toward where Thera was seated, only to discover that one of the warriors there had wrapped his arm around her shoulders and had a dagger pressed against her neck. That one met his gaze. The soldier was obviously terrified, but there was no doubt if Ashok got any closer, he would end Thera's life. A sword was placed against the back of the other prisoner, and his face was so battered and swollen that it took Ashok a moment to realize that it was the priest, Javed.

"Remain calm," the Thakoor ordered, mostly for the benefit of his mewling first caste. They were trembling with fear. His warriors remained ready to fight, so they were made of sterner stuff. Apparently too, was their leader, for the boy didn't seem to have any cower in him. "Ashok Vadal may be among us, yet he is still outnumbered and outmatched. He said he came to testify. The Law and traditions of our house allow that. Deliver your last words, then, criminal."

"Thera is why I live. If she is dead, my entire purpose turns to revenge. If you kill her, I will slay every last one of you. Your entire house, your entire line, will be dust."

The Thakoor appeared stunned by the audacity of such a threat. "How dare you speak to me as if—"

"*Silence!*" Ashok roared. "I was not finished stating my terms. If you allow harm to come to my woman, I will kill any warrior who raises his blade in a vain attempt to save you, then I will put every last member of the first caste of Great House Makao to the sword—man, woman, and child. Not just those who dwell beneath the roof of this mansion, but in every province you hold and in every Order and embassy of the Capitol. I will do to you what you did to the casteless, but *more*. Some of them have escaped the Great Extermination. None of you would escape my wrath."

"You cannot defeat the bearer of our ancestor blade!" a lady of the first caste shrieked.

"Send your bearer against me then. Akershan did..." Ashok lifted his black-steel blade overhead so all could see. "Behold the result. Summon your bearer, so that I may claim another sword."

"I'm already here."

It was the old warrior at the Thakoor's side, at least twenty years Ashok's senior, with long hair gone white. Except age was not the primary decider when fighting a man imbued with the combat experience of generations of bearers. That warrior slowly drew his sword, and Ashok saw it was truly black steel, and like Angruvadal, hungrily absorbing the light from the lanterns flickering along the walls.

"Good. Then I can have one for each hand. Call for your wizards as well. Send your entire army against me. I will visit violence upon them the likes of which you can scarcely imagine, for my only remaining purpose will be to annihilate your house."

The hall was dead quiet. The arbiters and judges were terrified. The eyes of the personal guard of Great House Makao lingered, frightened, on the new Angruvadal, because they all knew that if their leader put pride over sense, that sword would be taking their lives shortly.

"Or...let Thera go, and we will leave here in peace. Take those forces you would waste against me and use them instead to prepare for the greater threat that is already at your door."

The young Thakoor sat upon his throne, fuming at the terrible insult of having a rebel break into his home, but since he'd not barked out the order for his men to charge the legendary foe armed with one of the most destructive magics in the world, clearly he was not a fool.

"Those are your terms, then, criminal?"

"Those are my terms, Thakoor Makao."

"This is madness!" a warrior wearing an eyepatch shouted. "The traitorous witch must die."

"Are you Dhaval?" Ashok asked.

It was almost as if the warrior had not expected his noise-making to have any consequences, since he flinched when Ashok called him out. But then he took a hesitant step forward. "I am Phontho Dhaval of the Kanok Garrison!"

Ashok nodded slowly. "I hold no special animosity toward the rest of these men. Their lives I would end quickly. *You* have offended my woman. Your death will hurt."

Dhaval took a halting step away from Ashok, then desperately turned back to his leader. "Do not listen to him, Thakoor! When it's known you can be cowed by a rebel's taunts, the entire world will think we're weak!"

Their leader snapped, "You state the obvious, Dhaval. If only you'd had the sense to handle your sordid family business in private, rather than bring this nightmare into *my home,* I wouldn't have to make such a choice at all. This entire issue is your fault."

When uttered by a Thakoor, such public words were condemnation resulting in ruined names, resignation, banishment, or execution. At best, Dhaval's stiff-necked pride had delivered to Great House Makao embarrassment, and at worst, Ashok drowning the place in blood. Regardless of how the Thakoor decided to proceed, Dhaval was doomed.

Only Dhaval was too furious or stupid to realize it. "What's done is done! I have brought this traitor here for punishment. Her guilt is obvious. Condemn her and be finished with the matter." Dhaval scoffed at Ashok. "Let the criminal make his threats. Our warrior caste will easily deal with this menace."

Many of the Personal Guard looked toward Dhaval, incredulous at that claim. Only the bravest warriors would be appointed to such a prestigious position, but ancestor blades cut down courageous or cowardly the same. This was not a commander who spent his men's lives wisely.

It seemed Ashok cared more about them dying pointlessly

than their officer did. "Today they call me Ashok, breaker of swords. Be wise, Thakoor, so that tomorrow they do not call me Ashok, breaker of houses."

The boy was clearly weighing the costs. "Damodar..."

Without hesitation, the bearer responded, "Do you wish me to duel him, my lord?"

"You are my most trusted advisor. Should I?"

The old man had been sizing up Ashok the entire time, and Ashok returned that courtesy. This was a proud warrior, but also a wise one. He was unafraid—accepting of death the way all great swordsmen must be—and confident, but not overly so. Before they even crossed swords, he must have recognized that Ashok was more than his physical match. Not just from age, but that Ashok had to possess some form of magic beyond just bearing an ancestor blade to be able to effortlessly fall so far without injury. The rest of the world was ignorant about the powers bestowed by the Protector's Heart of the Mountain, and no one—not even Ashok—truly understood how much the black steel shard embedded in his chest had changed his body as well. It had sustained him through famine and ice, and even brought him back from the realm of death. It would carry him through this duel as well.

Ashok looked the other bearer in the eyes in the hopes that he would see the truth there... that Ashok Vadal had survived injuries and abuse that would have obliterated anyone else in the world, for he was more than a bearer, more than a Protector... Ashok was simply *more*.

Damodar understood.

"I would advise against single combat with this man, Thakoor Venketesh."

"And against you and all the warriors assembled here?"

"We would win, but the cost would be *far* greater than what you expect."

"You're certain?"

Damodar possessed the combined instincts of every man who had used his sword before him, and none of them had ever faced a foe like Ashok. Perhaps the oldest ghosts in his sword might have known one similarly capable once, but that had been mighty Ramrowan himself, a name that was as forgotten now as the names of their gods.

"I am certain."

Ashok nodded to his foe. *Respect.*

"An unfortunate situation then, because foolhardy Dhaval isn't entirely wrong. A leader who fails to punish criminals *will* be seen as weak," the boy Thakoor mused. "You spoke of a greater threat already at my door, Black Heart. What threatens my city? Other than you, of course."

As he had in the desert, Ashok could sense a deadly presence gathering in the air. Only this felt thicker. There was an ominous weight this time. "Demons are near."

"This is a trick, Thakoor," said one of the officers. "My garrison mans the sixteen watch towers between here and the shoreline. Demonic raiders would have been seen, and the alarm raised, long before any demon reached Kanok."

"These will come not from the sea, but from beneath your feet."

That same warrior scoffed. "Demons don't burrow like gophers."

"They are using tunnels dug by the ancients, flooded into underground rivers. Heed my warning, or do not. They are coming for you either way." Ashok turned back to the Thakoor. "We are out of time. Release Thera now and we will leave, or condemn her, and I will destroy this house so utterly there will be nothing left for the demons except your corpses to feast on."

Thakoor Venketesh was quiet for a long time, glaring at Ashok with hatred and contempt, but he made no rash pronouncement. He was wiser than his years suggested, but Ashok knew no one of his status could survive the indignity of letting such infamous rebels defy him in his own hall. Especially not in front of so many illustrious witnesses. The Law said every man had his place. It was an oft-repeated slogan, but it really was the way of things. Even a Thakoor couldn't escape that burden. Ashok knew what the inevitable verdict would be and prepared to act accordingly.

He took in every threat and angle. He looked back toward Thera and the guard who still had his knife at her throat. She was twenty feet away. A distance that would be difficult even for Ashok to cover before the warrior could react to his Thakoor's command and cut her throat. He'd save the priest if he could, but Thera's life came first.

Thera's eyes met his, and surprisingly enough, in that terrible moment, she gave him a sad little smile.

"I am glad to see you too," Ashok said quietly.

Thakoor Venketesh stood and placed his hands on the marble rail, the better to grimly survey the assembled members of the first, the workers wealthy enough to attend his court, and the warriors and wizards he was about to send to their deaths. Damodar also must have known what was coming and began walking toward the nearest spiral staircase to make his way down. The bearer knew he was Makao's best chance to prevent a bloodbath, so he would engage Ashok quickly, even though his instincts were surely warning him such an action would cost him his life. Duty came first. Such was the nature of all bearers, otherwise their sword never would have picked them to begin with.

"I've made my decision." Venketesh was somber, for he knew even in victory, what would come next would be a bleak day for his house. Much like bearers and their swords, Thakoors were doomed to do what they must on behalf of their people. "Thera Vane, Javed Zarger, and Ashok Vadal... have offended the Law. Kill them. Kill them *now*."

An archer let fly.

Ashok snatched that arrow from the air and spun to hurl it at the guard holding Thera. But that warrior had already lost his blade and was clutching at the deep gash Thera had inflicted on his wrist with a knife that had seemingly appeared from out of nowhere. So Ashok adjusted slightly and flung that arrow at the warrior about to run Javed through with his sword. With normal human strength a thrown arrow would flop about uselessly in the air. Driven by Ashok's arm, that arrow pierced the warrior's eye socket and burst out the back of his skull.

All the warriors charged.

Before they could get there, Ashok was suddenly engulfed in a terrible heat as a wizard turned demon bone into fire. His coat burst into flames.

Ashok whipped the burning garment off and threw it over the head of the nearest warrior. Entangled, that one began flailing about, until Ashok kicked him in the ribs hard enough to throw him back into two of his comrades.

More arrows flew. Ashok knew where every one of them was without sight, and simply moved his body out of the way or struck them aside with Angruvadal. An unlucky warrior behind him caught a broadhead in the throat. To the witnesses, Ashok moved faster than their eyes could track, or their minds comprehend.

Then the armored Personal Guard were upon him. Even clad in gold-painted plate and black mail, that hardened steel did *nothing* against Angruvadal.

With a brutal downward cut, Ashok split a warrior's chest in half. He moved past a thrust and sliced the top of the next warrior's head off, helmet and all. He collided with the next, shouldering him back into a marble wall hard enough to break his spine, then caught a descending sword, turned it aside, and struck that one in the hip. Angruvadal bit deep and the pelvis shattered.

These warriors were very skilled. Against any other opponent, they surely would have prevailed. Except he was undying Ashok, armed with mighty Angruvadal reborn, and they were not.

Instinct warned him of an incoming sword, and Ashok parried it aside. He stabbed that warrior in the lung, shoved him back into another, and pierced that one through the heart. Ribs burst and blood boiled until Ashok kicked both bodies off his sword and turned to meet the next challenge. He ducked beneath a slash and effortlessly severed a leg, caught a blow with Angruvadal's guard, twisted into it, and cut that warrior open from sternum to belt. As that one fell, Ashok pushed past to brutally stomp on the neck of one of the men he'd previously set on fire, who'd been rolling about on the floor trying to put himself out.

In the span of a few heartbeats, half the warriors who'd come at him were dying or dead. More were on their way, but so much brutality, all dispensed by one single foe, so quickly, caused even the most hardened among them to pause. The hall had been painted with pumping blood. Warriors were screaming in agony. The first caste were screaming in terror. Men and women were trampled as the crowd tried to escape out the doors.

"I warned you what I would do!" Ashok shouted at their fleeing backs.

Except there would be no need to destroy this house if he could get Thera out alive. That was the price of his vengeance. He had not specified the price of mere offense. This violence would suffice.

Ashok rushed to Thera. With complete trust, she held out her shackled wrists toward him, and Ashok struck quickly. Angruvadal easily split the links of the chain. More arrows flew, and ghostly instinct told Ashok to turn back to strike them from the air. "We must go."

The hall was a chaotic mess of panicking first caste trying to escape and desperate warriors searching for their targets. Ashok beheaded a guard, then kicked that bouncing head and helmet into another warrior's feet, causing him to stumble. He struck that one in the arm, and Angruvadal sheared through metal, flesh, and bone, to leave the arm hanging limp and squirting.

"Which way?" Thera shouted.

"I do not know this place." He had scaled the outer wall and snuck in along the roof. Picking a direction, he ran, but more guards appeared from around that corner. At this rate he'd have to cut his way through every warrior in the city to get out.

So be it.

A paltan worth of black-and-yellow-clad enemies were rushing into the hall. There were too many of them. Javed had picked up a dropped sword, and even with his wrists bound, and one hand bandaged, he fought them with incredible ferocity...In fact, he seemed far too skilled for one whose obligation had been rice merchant, but Ashok had no time to dwell on that.

A warrior thrust a spear at Thera's back. Ashok sheared through the wood and then clipped the spearman in the throat. As he spun away, that arterial spray coated his brothers' golden armor red and got in their eyes. Ashok slashed at one of the blinded warriors, but before Angruvadal could kill again, it was intercepted by another black steel sword.

When the two ancestor blades crossed, the entire room shuddered. An ominous tone resonated in the ear. Everyone except for the two bearers flinched and cringed at the noise, for it was a visceral, dangerous sound—seldom ever heard in the history of Lok—battles between bearers were rare events.

History books were written about such things.

Bearer Damodar stood ready, black sword raised to a high defensive position. "Stand back, warriors. The Black Heart is mine."

Ashok grabbed Thera by the sleeve and shoved her into an alcove behind him, placing his body between her and his foe. The only way she could be reached was through him, but he shouted at Javed. "Stay by her side. Kill anyone who gets past me."

Damodar waited to make sure the warriors had heard and understood his command. Satisfied they were moving away, he addressed Ashok. "I am Damodar Makao." He spun his sword around so Ashok could see what he was up against. Great House

Makao's ancestral blade was a wider blade, with a short one-handed grip and flared pommel. "Behold deadly Maktalvar."

Ashok gestured toward the bloody puddles between them. "My introduction has already been made."

"Indeed it has." His opponent eyed Ashok's sword. "I was told you had broken Angruvadal. It appears—like yourself—that tales of its demise were exaggerated."

"The tales were true. We both died, only to be reborn since."

Damodar wasn't there to converse. He had merely been buying time long enough for the warriors to drag their injured out of the way. As soon as they were clear, the bearers' battle commenced.

Despite knowing he was outmatched, Damodar went right at him. There was no reluctance. No testing or prodding. Forty generations of instinct must have told Damodar that his only hope was unrelenting ferocity.

Their swords clashed. With each impact the world seemed to flex and bend around the competing pieces of black steel. Nearby windows and discarded wineglasses shattered from the tone. As Ashok and Damodar locked guards, they were eye to eye, only inches apart, sliding across the bloody floor. When Ashok glanced down, it was interesting to see that that the energy of the crossed blades was forcing the blood away, as if the droplets were being rolled by a great wind.

They broke apart. Each of them immediately striking, countering, and trying again. Back and forth they danced through the blood, continually slashing and blocking with blades that could only be damaged by dishonor. Every second brought a new attack, a new response, and a new chance to die.

Blades parted, they circled. Driven by the impulses of ghosts and a lifetime of training, Damodar's technique was flawless. This was surely the finest swordsman Ashok had ever faced other than Ratul or Devedas. One of them had the powers of the Heart of the Mountain and the Shard of Angruvadal, while the other did not. Damodar did not understand what it was he lacked in comparison, nor apparently, did any of Maktalvar's previous bearers, but they all sensed the inevitable.

Ashok lunged and thrust. Damodar dodged aside and slashed for Ashok's legs. The parry created a black steel echo that shook the hall. The vibration made his teeth hurt. Ashok's attacks sped up. Damodar's began to slow. They clashed again, swords crossed down, the blades cutting effortless patterns through the marble below. Calling upon the Heart, Ashok drastically increased the strength of his arms, forcing Damodar's hands lower. Instinct and skill could not save him from being off-balance and in a bad position.

"You will lose now," Ashok stated.

They both knew it was true.

"Then I will do so with dignity." The old man was breathing hard, as his muscles strained against Ashok's unnatural strength. "From here, you can strike me before I cut you, but I *will* cut you. Hopefully that will be enough for the rest of these boys to make up the difference."

Maktalvar had chosen its bearer well.

The floor beneath them shook. Cracks spread across the stone, before it began to buckle and rise between them, as if a bubble was forming in the mansion's floor.

"What witchcraft is this?" Damodar demanded.

"It is not my doing."

Across the hall, members of the first caste screamed as a big section of floor suddenly collapsed beneath their feet. A dozen of Makao's elite plummeted from sight. Long black arms reached up out of the darkness, the fingers webbed, ending in terrible pointed claws. Bodies were impaled and violently yanked out of sight.

The demons had arrived.

The soldiers of hell must have been digging beneath Kanok for weeks in preparation, but Ashok had always been taught demons were drawn to the scent of blood, and he had spilled so much, so quickly, that the pull must have been irresistible enough to draw them out. Or perhaps the clash of black steel magic had driven them into a frenzy. Regardless of what had brought them to the surface, death was among them now.

Demons seemed to be coming from everywhere. Their numbers were incomprehensible. This did *not* happen this far inland. The warriors who weren't overwhelmed with fear struck back but were immediately thrown aside as if they were nothing. There were more terrified cries from the side, as a thick, eight-foot-tall demon waddled out from behind a colorful curtain, grabbed a woman costumed in peacock feathers, and shoved her into its jaws. The demon shook her like a dog killing a rat.

"I warned you."

Damodar was wide eyed, and with sword still trapped, he risked a glance back toward his Thakoor, but the boy wasn't visible behind all the warriors who were rushing to their master's defense. Makao's bearer was needed, but if he tried to break free, Ashok would take his head.

"I beg you, Ashok, grant me a truce for now?"

If Ashok simply killed Damodar, that would be one less deadly threat in the future, but it wouldn't be *right*. "Live to defend your house, bearer." Ashok released trapped Maktalvar, and then slid along the bulging floor toward Thera.

Damodar immediately ran toward the nearest demon, roared, and slashed it across the belly. The vicious black blade spilled white guts across the floor.

Thera was still in the alcove, armed with nothing but a little knife, obviously shocked by the sudden appearance of the sea demons, but the forces of Makao were even more surprised than she was, so she recognized the opportunity. "We've got to get out of here!"

"This way." Ashok took her by the hand and pulled her toward a curtain that didn't reek of demons, but then he saw that Javed had been swept from his feet by the heaving floor. Ashok lost sight of him as too many running bodies got in the way. "I must save the priest."

"Leave him. Javed's a traitor."

Ashok trusted her. She could explain later if they lived. The two of them rushed across the hall, colliding with panicking guests, servants, and slaves. No more warriors tried to stop them. They had more important matters to deal with than criminals. Nothing focused the attention quite like demons.

No warrior...except one.

"This evil is your doing, witch!"

Ashok heard the thrum of a string released, and though his bearer instinct usually only warned him of dangers to himself, he reflexively swung Angruvadal to block the speeding bolt that had been aimed at Thera's back.

It had been launched by Thera's former husband.

Even surrounded by rampaging demons, Ashok would make the time to kill *that* one.

Only he didn't need to, because Thera did it herself.

As it was one of the proudest traditions of Vane, Thera had

spent hundreds, if not thousands, of hours of her life throwing all manner of knives and spikes at a variety of targets. She'd been extremely good at it once, but wielding the gods' molten spear in the graveyard of demons had left her hands so badly scarred that she'd lost that beloved skill.

Yet in that moment of pure reflex, even thrown by damaged hands, her blade flew true.

Dhaval stared at Thera, remaining eye wide in disbelief, as he reached for his chest only to find that the knife she'd flicked at him had slipped right between his ribs. It had gone so deep that he couldn't even grasp enough of the slippery handle to pluck it out of his heart.

"I've still got it," she said.

Blood gushed out over his many medals and dripped down the ribbons. Dhaval dropped the bow he'd taken from a guard, took a few halting steps, went to his knees, and then fell on his face.

A rampaging demon stomped on Dhaval's head, bursting his skull.

Ashok and Thera ducked beneath a curtain and ran down a hall. Someone had begun ringing an alarm bell. Such a sound would have made all the difference if the demons had been seen coming out of the ocean, but the warning wouldn't help near as much as the forces of hell materialized beneath their very feet.

The courtyard was in pandemonium. Long ago the Makao had built a huge statue in the form of a hawk here. The towering structure was leaning to one side now, as something truly massive had shifted the ground beneath it. The basin of water around the statue drained as the soil heaved open beneath it. The hawk statue toppled. One stone wing snapped off when it struck the ground.

More terrible creatures came crawling out from beneath it, obsidian hides covered in dirt, and they immediately began tearing apart every living thing they could find.

The demons just kept coming.

This was no raid. This was an invading army.

Chapter 17

The stones collapsed beneath Javed's feet. Sliding wildly toward the darkness below, he managed to catch one meager handhold on a broken edge and stop his descent. Warriors and courtiers tumbled past, screaming. With the stone crumbling beneath his grasp, he hung there, but with wrists chained together and one hand broken, was unable to find a way up. Fingers slipped. Javed fell.

Plummeting into the dark, his body hit with a splash rather than a thud. Immediately he came up thrashing. He was back in the dungeons that had been his recent home, but the mansion's lower levels had become flooded somehow. There was almost no light, but stinking, filthy water was everywhere. There were men and women all around him, terrified and struggling, trying to stand in rushing water that was already chest deep.

The water frothed and turned red as unseen demons pulled them down.

All Javed could hear was screaming and begging and the snapping of bone and tearing of flesh. Smooth black shapes rose around him to fight over the bodies. Human limbs were torn off. Stone, dust, and people continued to fall as more foundation walls collapsed into the still spreading watery hole. It was chaos and death and horror beyond even what the mind of a witch hunter could withstand.

Ratul had told Keta of a realm called Naraka—a hell other than the ocean—a place of torment and punishment for the wicked dead. In that awful moment, Javed knew this had to be Naraka and Mother Dawn must have condemned him here for his sins.

"I've vowed to continue your work, Forgotten. Spare me so I can!"

An eyeless dome of a head came out of the water right in front of him, and slowly split open, revealing pointed obsidian teeth. The demon prepared to feed.

Except the gods provided their faithful servant a miracle.

Another man tumbled down the collapsing floor to crash right into that demon's face. It reflexively ripped into him with tooth and claw, biting down and throwing his body side to side, so hard that the snapping of bones was audible even over the screaming. In that terrible instant, Javed recognized the golden sash of a Makao court wizard. With shackled hands he grabbed the wizard's sash and held on.

"Help me! Help me!" The dying wizard's fingernails scratched long bloody furrows into Javed's arms. It was hard to tell in the bad light, but this was probably one of the same wizards who'd helped capture him. Now he was reduced to begging a fanatic for help. Even if Javed had wanted to, there was nothing to be done for this man. Javed intended to save himself, and with this wizard the gods had delivered him a potential way out.

Grasping about desperately, Javed found a single piece of bone jangling from that sash and snatched it away. As the crying wizard was dragged beneath the surface, Javed formed the magical pattern in his mind and stepped outside of reality.

He had traveled the pitch blackness of the place between many times, but for the first time ever, Javed saw lights there. It was as if he were surrounded by millions of tiny stars swirling about in complex patterns. Except that light was made of demons; the magic that infused their tissues seemed to float like dust motes in a beam of sunlight all about him. It was strangely quiet and beautiful compared to the savagery of Naraka.

Now possessing a body made of matter with the consistency of fog, Javed willed the steel of his shackles to fall through his wrists, then lifted himself upward and away from the hole, to step back into the real world crouched atop solid marble floor that wasn't yet collapsing into the dungeons.

Javed was back in the hall, body whole once more, but drenched in seawater and blood. The gods had delivered him from the foulest depths of hell, but only to the bloody nightmare one level above it. He saw at least four or five demons rampaging about the great hall, but it was difficult to count because they were leaping about so fast, and destroying lanterns as they went, plunging the hall into ever-increasing darkness. Warriors were being hurled through the air to be smashed against walls with bone-shattering force. People were dying by the score.

Then it was revealed why the gods had seen fit to spare his miserable life, for Javed spotted Witch Hunter Nikunja running up the stairs, still carrying the pouch that contained all of the sacred pages upon which he'd scribed the teachings of Keta and Ratul and the sacred prophecies of the Voice.

The words of the gods must be preserved.

Javed rushed toward the nearest spiral staircase in pursuit of his former brother, but there was a demon near the base. It was eight feet of sleek black death, mobbed by desperate warriors. There was no way past.

The surviving Personal Guard had retreated from the unstable floor up to the balcony in an attempt to defend their Thakoor. Violent magic was unleashed as wizards struck at the approaching demons. Fire rolled off their impenetrable black hide without so much as scorching it. Bursts of invisible force that could hurl a strong man down barely even budged the creatures. More warriors were rushing in from every entrance, but it was clear this battle was already lost. For every launched arrow or thrusted spear that managed to stick into a demon's flesh, fifty others bounced off. Dozens of swords and spiked maces struck against the demons, but it seemed very few managed to do any damage at all.

Only one weapon there seemed to be effective, as the bearer Damodar wielded Maktalvar with deadly precision. Yet even black steel couldn't wound a demon with every blow, and Damodar's uniform had been torn open and he had bloody claw marks across his chest. The senior warrior was staggering, but he fought with such ferocity that even the hosts of hell seemed hesitant to approach the fury of that magic sword.

As Damodar held back one massive demon, the Personal Guard behind him escorted their leader to someplace more secure. Nikunja was heading toward the Thakoor's group, probably assuming his office and status would earn him a spot in whatever more fortified place within the great house they were falling back to.

That would not do.

Javed checked the bone in his hand and found there was a small measure of magic left inside, barely enough to fuel a pattern for a brief time at best, but it would have to do. For just a moment, weakness gnawed at him, and he thought about using that precious magic to flee this doomed place, to run from the demons and escape into the city, but he cursed himself for that thought. Instead Javed willed the matter of his body to flow into the powerful tiger pattern. A searing darkness engulfed him and then a mighty cat erupted out the other side.

With incredible speed, Javed bounded toward the demon at the base of the stairs. He leapt, striking the creature in the head, but even his magical claws couldn't pierce demon hide. Instead, with an explosive burst of power, Javed shoved off its shoulders, launching his body toward the balcony high above. The tiger form cleared the railing, landed on the marble, and slid. He struggled to find purchase with all fours as he spied Nikunja, then scrambled after his former brother.

The tiger form pounced onto the witch hunter's back, taking him down hard, and whether the instinct was in the tiger pattern itself, or just his own human viciousness, Javed immediately bit him on the neck, savagely tearing and breaking the spine. Nikunja died so quickly he'd probably thought he'd been felled by a demon.

With magic spent and hot blood streaming down his face, Javed returned to human form. He rolled off his former brother's twitching body, the tiny fragment of demon bone crumbled to dust. Nikunja's pouch was there, but it had spilled open on impact, and the sheaf of papers had been spread across the balcony.

"No!" Hundreds of pages had been scattered. Fleeing members of the first left bloody sandal prints on the precious papers as they ran for their lives. Pages blew over the edge to flutter down to the waters of Naraka. It was futile, but Javed began snatching up whatever papers he could. The teachings had to be saved!

Demons were scaling the balcony. The big one he'd jumped off of had killed enough warriors that it could begin walking up the stairs unimpeded. Somehow, the demons must have understood that the boy the warriors were trying so hard to protect was the human most in need of destroying. There was a demon on each side of the Thakoor's dwindling knot of defenders. Trapped and desperate, cut off from their escape route, the Makao Personal Guard were making their final stand on the balcony.

Damodar ran a demon through with Maktalvar, but the bearer was clearly exhausted, robes damp with sweat and limbs trembling. When he kicked that dying beast off the end of his sword, the next demon struck him with a wild swing. That fist hit hard as a war hammer, and the bearer was flung down with bone shattering force.

The black steel blade was lost from Damodar's grasp and went sliding across the floor, through the pages of scripture, and stopped... only inches from Javed's outstretched hand.

The black sword was right there. Tantalizingly close.

There were demons all around. Warriors were dying. He would be next. His work was lost. His prophet had cursed him. There was no escape.

Javed knew that if he picked up that blade, and it found him unworthy, the demons wouldn't need to kill him, because the sword would make him do it to himself. When someone unworthy tried to wield an ancestor blade, it would cut them. The more unworthy, the greater the offense it took, the greater the wound. Javed knew he was evil, a murderer and deceiver. He had to be the most unworthy man alive.

Were the gods testing him?

So be it.

Javed picked up Maktalvar.

It stung his palm, sudden as a Zarger scorpion, so painful that he might have reflexively dropped it... if it would have let him.

The sword saw him, knew him, knew everything about him, everything he had ever done, good and bad, just and unjust, weighed it all, and found him wanting. It judged him as harshly as Mother Dawn in her many-armed form. This was not for him. This was not his duty. This was not his place within the grand plan. This one had been claimed for a different work. This one belonged to the Unassailable.

He was unworthy.

Yet for now, he would have to do.

Javed remained there, on his knees, sword in hand, as a thousand conflicting memories that weren't his collided in his mind. His body was battered. His muscles torn. Bones in his chest and hand were broken. Maktalvar took all that into account and adjusted accordingly. Past battles against man, demon, and other beings he couldn't begin to understand flashed by as the sword took in the situation and directed him how best to proceed.

What happened next was a blur.

Javed leapt up and ran toward the demon that had felled Damodar. It was only the size of a man, yet still possessed incomprehensible strength. The sword knew this shape of demon was swift and deadly, but with its attention fixed on the wall of shields and spears that had formed around the Thakoor, it was vulnerable, and it never saw him coming.

The first cut split its leg behind the knee. When the demon instinctively tried to backhand its attacker, Javed had already slid beneath it on his knees, and rose in a draw cut, opening the demon from hip to armpit. He hit it again, and again, anticipating each of the demon's strikes before they came. It stumbled, and Javed immediately placed an overhand strike into the top of its head. A long sliver of skull snapped free and white blood sprayed out. That demon fell.

All witch hunters were trained swordsmen, but Javed had never dreamed of such skill. That had been a purity of movement beyond comprehension. The sword took potential and turned it into action.

A wordless warning came for him to slip to the left. He did.

Nikunja's body flew through the space he'd just been standing, thrown so hard it was as if the corpse had been launched from a Kharsawani catapult. The dead witch hunter hit the guards' shields with enough energy to knock half a dozen warriors from their feet.

Javed turned to see the huge demon that had been ascending the stairs had arrived. A terrible fury swept through him when he saw the monster's gigantic bloody feet carelessly stepping on his precious scriptures.

This demon was truly massive, towering over the humans, and the sword warned him a single blow from one of those mighty fists would shatter every bone in its bearer's body. The demon lumbered forward, arms lifting. The sword told him when to move, and how, so the demon's first blow cracked marble instead of his skull. The response was so automatic, Javed wasn't sure if it was him, or Maktalvar, or they were temporarily the same thing, countering. He struck the retreating wrist, but green sparks flew from the impact, as even black steel struggled to cut demons sometimes.

The creature bent its long body at the waist, going to all fours, to bound about like one of the muscular apes of the Gujaran peninsula, swatting at its enemies. All Javed could do was try to stay alive as the great demon tried to crush him. Many warriors died as they attacked the beast, but they were mere distractions to be swatted away, as the demon concentrated on destroying the one thing here strong enough to slay it. Sword points were driven into the demon's armored skin to no avail. Men died horribly. If it hadn't been for the brave sacrifice of the Personal Guard, Javed would've been killed several times over.

With most of his men dead or broken, Thakoor Venketesh crawled toward the corner, helpless. He'd lost his bejeweled turban and his fine robes had been soaked in the blood of his loyal servants. He looked like the frightened boy he still was.

There were only a handful of warriors left on the balcony. With one too-long arm, the demon swept two of them over the rail to drop screaming into the expanding flood below.

The sword saw a slim chance, and Javed did his best to execute its will. Ducking beneath the arm, he feinted for its center. He was too overextended for Maktalvar to penetrate, but he only required the demon to believe it was, for this sword knew demons *very well*.

By reflex, the demon tried to bite him.

Maktalvar drove itself right between the snapping jaws and upward into the monster's brain. With a twist of the wrist, Javed turned the edge and drew it out the side of the demon's head. Skin that was nearly invincible from one side parted easily when sliced from the other. A gallon of white blood spilled as the contents of the demon's skull hit the marble with the sound of a wet mop falling. He jumped back as the great beast toppled where he'd been standing.

While the sword analyzed the battlefield and searched for more threats, Javed stood there, overwhelmed and breathing hard. There were demons below, but none were close enough to strike. The rest of the demons were heading into the courtyard, chasing after those who had run into the city.

It was then that Javed realized the handful of remaining warriors had protectively placed their bodies between him and their Thakoor. Each of them was staring at the black sword in Javed's good hand. They'd fought with him against the demons, probably not having time to understand who he was until that awful moment of comprehension. They understood now. Surely they had to believe this religious madman was about to kill their master.

Why shouldn't I?

The boy had condemned him and the Voice. Venketesh had laughed at the truth. The casteless of this land had been annihilated or driven off. This was an enemy of the gods. The Thakoor deserved to die.

Javed took one step that way, but stopped, for the terrified face of Great House Makao's leader suddenly reminded him of some different boys who Javed had murdered in order to complete his mission for Grand Inquisitor Omand. Parth and Rawal had been innocents silenced in the name of his obligation ... He'd killed children for his Order and his own ambitions.

He would not kill children for his gods.

"You must flee. There are more demons below. They're collapsing the great house from beneath its foundations. Hurry."

"*You* saved us?" Thakoor Venketesh was staring at Maktalvar in wounded disbelief, as if seeing his family's sword in the hands of a criminal was the greatest betrayal of all. "The sword let *you* wield it? It can only choose the greatest and noblest among us!"

"He's a criminal," said one of the guards. "And a fanatic. He ... he's not even of our house!"

Damodar was still alive, though barely. The old bearer lay on his back, gasping. "I am done. Maktalvar has chosen." He coughed up blood. "You must respect its wishes."

The Thakoor rushed to Damodar's side. "Rest, dear friend," he said as tears streamed down his cheeks.

Javed had always been detached from emotions. He was able to fake them convincingly, but it was as if everyone else was speaking a language he couldn't really understand. It had taken a god to teach him how to feel guilt. Now this moment made his heart ache in a different way. He wanted to hate the Makao, not pity them.

"The testimony I presented was the truth, Thakoor. The

Forgotten has returned. The sword must know this to be true. Now you have Maktalvar's testimony as well."

"But...but...that means..." The boy's mansion wasn't the only thing crumbling around him. "This can't be!"

"The forsaken witch hunter is our bearer now?" asked a very confused warrior.

"I am neither witch hunter, nor bearer." Javed looked at the ancient weapon in his hand, then shook his head, and bent down to gently place Maktalvar on the floor next to the dying Damodar. Then he stepped back. The whispering of ghosts abruptly stopped. "The sword isn't mine. The gods called me to be their priest instead. I'm already the Keeper of Names. That is my obligation."

The warriors just stared at the sword. Refusing such an honor was incomprehensible to them. No one had ever willingly given up an ancestor blade before.

Javed turned and began limping away.

The Personal Guard helped their young leader up and began leading him toward safety, but suddenly Venketesh shoved them away and shouted, "Wait, priest! Name your reward. My honor demands it. For slaying these demons, saving my life, and returning our sword, anything within Great House Makao is yours. Name it!"

At best, he hoped to save a few of the sacred pages before this palace fell down or another demon ate him. His body was racked with agony, and even though he'd only held the ancestor blade for a moment, the sudden silence left him feeling hollow and weak. The wisdom of Keta and Ratul was scattered, or blood-soaked and illegible, and Javed despaired that he'd survive long enough to write it all down again.

But then something on the wall caught his eye. It was one of the multitude of printed notices that had been distributed by legal mandate, announcing the appointment of Devedas to the new office of Raja, and it was as if the gods themselves told him exactly what to do.

"I claim your house's printing press."

Chapter 18

〜〜〜〜〜

Alarm bells rang throughout Kanok. Word of the demons moved fast as a wildfire, causing panic among the people. Once the workers saw their illustrious first caste running for their lives, bloodied and terrified, trampling each other in an attempt to escape the old city, all doubt was removed.

Demons are among us!

Thera and Ashok had gotten to the lower district before the narrow streets had become hopelessly crowded as thousands surged outside. They were trying to understand what was going on, or then running for their lives once they heard. In the presence of demons, all sense was lost. The fleeing mobs collided with the hundreds of warriors who'd been summoned to their master's mansion to fight. From the horrified screams echoing through the streets, demons had appeared in other parts of the city as well. The chaos spread.

Thera had to take hold of Ashok's arm and tug him toward a tiny alley, away from the many crashing bodies. Unlike Ashok, she couldn't sprint so far without tiring. Her exercise had been limited to pacing about a tiny cell for months, but even at the strongest she'd ever been, keeping up with Ashok was impossible. The muscles of her legs hurt, her heart was hammering, and her lungs burned. The Voice granted her mad prophecies. It certainly didn't help her run like a deer, like whatever it was the Protectors had put in Ashok's blood.

"Are you alright?" he asked, not even short of breath. "Have you been injured?"

Thera had to put her hands on her knees as she gasped. "Give me a...moment." Inhaling all that cold air made her cough uncontrollably.

Seeing that she was merely overcome with exertion, and no longer concerned that she was about to die, Ashok went to the corner, looked both ways, and did that odd concentration trick of his that made it so he could see farther and hear better. How he was able to do that was one of the secrets he'd vowed to never reveal, and this was a man who kept his vows. His presence here tonight was undeniable proof of that.

She didn't need Protector ears to know that things were bad out there. Never before had she heard an entire city be consumed with fear. Thera had to clear her throat and spit. It felt as if her heart might burst and her legs had gone to water, but at least she could breathe again. "I thought you were dead."

"I was for a time." Satisfied there were no demons about to eat them, he came back to her. "I sense there are more of the creatures ahead of us. The main body attacked the mansion, but others broke into the sewers and storm drains to cover more ground. If I fall, you must continue east, along the trade road to the mountain pass between here and Akara. On the other side is where you will find the Sons of the Black Sword waiting."

"I missed you too, Ashok."

Surprisingly, he gave her a smile. Then he took her hand, pulled her close to him, and kissed her with a passion that she'd not known Ashok was capable of. The two of them remained locked in a long embrace as the city was torn apart around them.

When their lips parted, Ashok looked her in the eyes. "The memory of you kept me alive through times too dark for me to describe."

"You'll have plenty of time to tell me about it once we get out of here."

"We must go now. There are too many demons. This city cannot hold."

It took a moment for that incomprehensible idea to sink in. Great House Makao wasn't her enemy. One boy had ordered their deaths, and one of their phonthos had been an evil bastard, but the multitude who lived here had done her no wrong. "Can we do anything to help them?"

Ashok shook his head. "I'm more powerful now than when you last saw me, but against so many, at best I could only stop a fraction of them, and I would have to abandon you to do even that."

Thera couldn't imagine how Ashok could be any stronger, since he'd already been the strongest man she'd ever met, but if he said it, then it must be true. "Then leave me and save whoever you can. I'll find my own way out."

"You need to survive to lead your people, not die to in a futile effort to save those who condemned you."

She'd gotten enough of her breath back to try and feign confidence. "You're sworn to obey me. I could order you to help them."

"You could, but it would be the death of us both." Ashok took her hand and pulled her back toward the street. "Come on."

Terrified people were scrambling in every direction. With demons appearing in their midst, nobody knew which way was safe. Workers were shouting for their families. A small child who'd been separated from her mother began to wail. Seeing that tore at Thera's heart, but there wasn't anything she could do. Life had been easier back when she hadn't let herself give a damn about anyone else. She'd despised this city and everything about it when she'd lived here, but she'd still weep for its dead. Her hatred of this place had been because of Dhaval, and at least he was dead now.

It was if Ashok read her mind. "That was an excellent throw of the knife back in the hall."

That had been a far more satisfying conclusion to her marriage than merely having some arbiter stamp papers of divorcement. "I may have bad hands now, but I've still got good instincts."

There was smoke in the air. Something must have caught fire. In a city so packed with wooden buildings, fire was always a danger. It would be far worse when everyone who was obligated to the fire brigades were too busy running away from demons to fight the fires. They made it a few more blocks east, and the smoke kept growing thicker. Kanok was built on one long slope, but at least Ashok wasn't leading her uphill. After so long in her tiny cell, if he'd tried to make her run uphill now, she'd have to swallow her pride and ask him to carry her.

Neither of them knew their way around this part of the city, and it was too crowded to run, so they were trapped walking with the shuffling crowd. As they entered what appeared to be a poor worker district, the mob ahead of them suddenly broke apart as workers flailed and panicked, trying to get away from whatever it was they'd just seen. A woman covered in blood stumbled out of a market stall, screaming incoherently. It took Thera a moment to realize that one of the worker's arms was missing, and she was so incoherent with fear that she didn't even seem to realize the limb was gone yet.

A demon ducked beneath the awning and followed her into the street.

The creature was a pitch-black, twisted nightmare, seven feet tall and thin as a scarecrow, with fingers long and pointed as a hayfork. The workers lost their minds, crushing each other in their desperate attempt to get away from the terrifying thing.

Drawing his sword, Ashok bellowed, "Make way!" When they didn't move fast enough, Ashok shoved workers aside so he could get at the demon.

A fat man collided with Thera and knocked her down. From her position on the ground, all she could see between the pumping legs and slapping sandals was Ashok and the demon's lower halves. Without hesitation, Ashok rushed the creature. Its spindly legs danced back, but white blood splashed across the cobblestones regardless. Then some frightened fool tripped over her, and Thera could see nothing but colorful robes in her face.

Narrowly avoiding being kicked in the head, Thera shoved the fat man off her and fought her way upright, to see that the demon had leapt back onto the wall of a building, and was scaling its way up the bricks, fast as a spider, trying to escape Ashok's onslaught...only to have Ashok grab it by the ankle and yank it back down. Terrible was his wrath.

Thera ran to the wounded lady. Blood was pumping from her stump, but she was obliviously screaming at Ashok, "It bit me arm off! Kill it! *Kill it!*"

Ashok was happy to oblige the request. Angruvadal rose and fell, over and over, as he hacked that skinny demon to pieces.

Thera took off the woman's sash, looped it around her arm, and pulled as hard as she could. The woman shrieked in pain,

"What're you doing?" Then she saw that her arm was missing and she started to thrash, which made the whole process worse.

"Hold still. I'm trying to save your life." Thera tied a knot, but it wasn't tight enough. Then she spied a mallet that had been dropped on the ground, so she snatched it up, shoved the handle through the sash, and turned that for extra leverage until the blood went from squirting to merely dripping. The woman cried and wailed the whole time, but at least she quit struggling. "You there, merchant!" Thera shouted at the worker who'd fallen over her. "Yes, you! Come here. Hold this tight and help her out of here."

Luckily the worker obeyed, as that caste tended to do when bossed about by someone they assumed to be their superior. Perhaps it had been a good thing that Dhaval had dressed her in the fine robes of vassal house leadership after all.

Ashok reappeared, splattered in demon blood, and extended one hand to pull Thera up. "Come. There are more nearby."

"Did you kill it?" the now delirious woman asked.

"Yes."

"Good. Bastard ate me arm."

Thera and Ashok left the workers of Kanok to their fate.

Sadly, now they *had* to run uphill.

Chapter 19

Hours later, the two of them were finally able to stop on the hillside overlooking the city. Thera flopped onto the dry grass and lay there, panting. Her body was drenched with sweat, and as soon as she quit moving the winter night began to bite with icy needle teeth, threatening to freeze her skin. She'd seen no more demons as they'd escaped the city, though she had seen the sign of their passing: mangled bodies, severed limbs, and great bloody footprints going into and out of houses.

She'd seen none, but Ashok... *Oceans.* She didn't know how many of the evil monsters he'd fought along the way. As they'd run, he'd see or hear something she couldn't, and veer off for a moment. She'd keep running in the same direction, and then he'd rejoin her a short while later, wearing even more demon blood. Somehow each time Ashok had returned to her miraculously uninjured, while another sea demon had been left incapable of killing anyone else that night... or ever again.

Still flat on her back, but after her pulse had slowed enough that she didn't think it was going to give out, Thera asked, "Are we safe?"

"For now." Ashok stood there, silently surveying the destruction below. Great swaths of Kanok were burning, and firelight flickered across the mountainside. "Everyone has fled the city. It appears the Thakoor's mansion is gone entirely, swallowed by the ground. I think the demons have retreated. From the sound of things, they have returned to their holes."

"That's good ... right?"

"I don't know." He went over and sat down next to her. For the first time since they'd been reunited, he actually looked tired, and human. "This is new behavior for them. I'm glad I had Angruvadal again, otherwise it is doubtful we would have survived."

"How *do* you have Angruvadal again?"

"It is a long story."

"And you said you've become more powerful?"

"A longer story ... While I starved in a Fortress prison, the shard changed me in ways I cannot fully understand."

"You went to *Fortress*?"

"Yes. And according to their customs, I may also be their ruler now."

"Oh ..." Thera lay there, too tired to make sense of that. "Alright, then. While you were away, we crippled the Capitol."

"I saw the remains of the aqueduct. Most impressive." Weary, Ashok lay down next to her. Even the unstoppable man could be exhausted. She reached over and took his hand. He held it and didn't let go. "I'm glad I found you."

"Me too, Ashok."

He was silent for a long time, before speaking hesitantly. "Your old husband is dead."

"About damned time."

"Do you wish to take another?"

Thera snorted, then laughed at the absurdity of the moment until she wheezed. She wasn't sure if the moisture in her eyes was from the exertion, the despair, the mirth, or the joy. "Is that a proposal? *Now?* After I've not seen you for a year, when we're fugitives on a plain full of refugees from a burning city menaced by sea demons while we huddle together for warmth to not freeze to death during the night?"

Ashok mulled that over for a moment. "Yes. It is my proposal."

She went through several emotions faster than the spokes of a quickly turning wagon wheel, then giggled like she was a young hopeful girl again.

"You're laughing at me?"

"No. It's just not what I imagined is all. That works for me.

Only there's no arbiter here to draw up a marriage contract—not that either of our families would claim us anyway—and no judge to perform the ceremony."

"I have disregarded the Law over far less important things lately," Ashok pointed out.

"We have no witnesses."

"I have Angruvadal. You have the Voice. Gods and ghosts will suffice."

Thera had expected her day to end in execution, not marriage. This was certainly an odd, but pleasing, turn of events. "I suppose that makes it official enough...husband."

Ashok seemed pleased by this. "Then you are my wife now."

Together they watched the stars through the smoke and said nothing else.

Chapter 20

News traveled slowly in Lok by normal means. It could take weeks or even months for word of great and pivotal events to spread across the continent. On the other hand, magical communication, by which messages were sent from one piece of demon bone to another, was nearly instantaneous. Since the Inquisition held a near monopoly on the legal use of that ability, the timely control of information was a powerful weapon for them.

It was customary for Grand Inquisitor Omand to learn exactly what had transpired long before most of the world would hear even the first vague rumors of something happening. Only this time the news was so staggeringly inconceivable that even devious Omand was too stunned to figure out how to use this knowledge to his advantage.

Kanok had been savaged by a horde of demons. Thousands, maybe tens of thousands, of the Makao were dead. This wasn't some raid, or even the rare coastal massacre a handful of sea demons would sometimes inflict upon those unfortunate enough to live by the sea. No. This attack was entirely unlike anything anyone had ever heard of. Dozens of demons had struck across the city, simultaneously, without warning, appearing from seemingly out of nowhere. Their rampage had lasted throughout the night, and then they had vanished before dawn as suddenly as they'd arrived. His spies had no idea how the demons had gotten in unseen, though Omand suspected it was because the Makao had done such a thorough job of eliminating their casteless that there had been no poor fish-eaters left living near the shore to cry out as they were eaten first during the demons' march inland. Forcing the casteless to live near bodies of water served a similar purpose to tying bells on strings around an estate to alert the owners to the presence of skulking thieves.

Omand stood at the window in his office, near the top of the Tower of Silence, high upon Mount Metoro, and stared down upon his Capitol below, pondering this new evolution in demonic trespass.

It is time, the prisoner had told its fellows before it had died. Was this slaughter what that demon had spoken of? Or was there still more yet to come?

Half a dozen Inquisitors waited nervously around his desk. Dealing with demon incursions was the responsibility of the Protectors, but among the many reports they had received so far was one that declared the Protectors assigned to Kanok had died fighting the monsters. The rest of the Protector Order might not even be aware of the attack yet. For the moment, Omand and his people were Lok's only defense against what quite possibly might be an invasion, the likes of which the world hadn't seen since long before the Age of Law began.

One of his men cleared his throat nervously. "How do you wish us to proceed, Grand Inquisitor?"

With all of Lok descending into war and chaos, the timing of this attack couldn't be worse for him. He needed the great houses fighting rebels or each other while he continued to consolidate his hold over the Capitol. He needed the Raja's army subjugating Vadal, not breaking apart so its warriors could rush back to their demon-threatened homes. He simply needed more time.

If destroying Kanok was all the demons had planned, then he could feign ignorance, warn no one, and weather the storm. However, if there were more attacks of this magnitude coming, and the Inquisition failed to alert the great houses before they too were struck, then his carefully constructed alliance would fall apart—especially after the judges had been tricked into turning over their power to respond quickly to any great and looming menace to a single man. Even Omand couldn't influence his way out of allowing whole cities to be annihilated under the new Raja's watch.

To warn or not to warn... When faced with such a choice a strong leader had to choose. It was rare there was a middle ground. Those who dithered, perished. Except in this case, Omand could see no other choice. Sometimes one had to gamble in order to win the great game.

"Send word by bone to every great house." Omand didn't bother to turn around to face his underlings as he spoke, but instead, continued staring at the great city that was now his. "Inform them only that there has been a demon raid in Kanok and to be on the alert for similar activity, but *do not* tell them the size."

"But, sir, this was unprecedented. Shouldn't we—"

"You will do as you are told. Nothing more. Nothing less." Then he deigned to look upon his men. Even with their masks on, he could tell they were afraid, for they had all heard the panicked reports sent by their brothers in the south. Their weakness irritated him. It made him miss his usual stalwart assistant, but Taraba was busy instigating a war in the north on Omand's behalf. "Bring me the demon bones that are connected to the ones in possession of Inquisitor Taraba, as well as the one for the Inquisitor currently serving in the council of Raja Devedas. I will send those messages myself. You may go."

Underlings dismissed, Omand turned his gaze back to the most important city in the world. He had always enjoyed the view from his office; the Capitol was his plaything now, to do with as he would. Yet the temptation to abandon it all in order to chase after his inheritance buried in the distant jungles was great. Oh, how he yearned to say to hell with these petty insects, and then abandon them to their fate, as Omand went to claim what was rightfully his.

This morning's report had told him the excavation was proceeding ahead of schedule... which was the only good news he'd gotten today. If the demons were truly daring to come back on land, then Omand could use that ancient magic to smite them with the power of a wrathful god. He would boil the ocean with a thousand pillars of fire and leave the demons no place to hide. But Omand had to set those amusing thoughts aside as he realized that one of his Inquisitors had not left as commanded. It was the same one who had interrupted him earlier.

"What is it, Zankrut?"

"Apologies, Grand Inquisitor, but I am unsure about something."

Omand scoffed, for it had been quite a while since one of his Inquisitors had dared to question him. Rather than be offended, he decided to allow the lad to speak. He couldn't afford to make a habit of such generosity, but at times it was interesting to hear the opinions of lesser men. Sometimes, a rat could see things a vulture could not, just from being closer to the ground.

"Why do you say that?"

"I transcribed the Kanok Inquisitor's reports. There was much confusion between them, but there were more anomalies in that city at that time than just the demons."

"An army of demons is insufficient for you, Zankrut?"

"Of course not, sir, but other things were going on in Kanok and I doubt these oddities could be a coincidence. Our informants who were at the great house that night all perished, and the Thakoor and his advisors have retreated to an unknown location. But the day before that, Witch Hunter Nikunja sent us an emergency message about the treachery of Witch Hunter Javed concerning ownership of the magical anomaly—"

"You mean who got to claim the false prophet, Thera? Speak clearly, boy."

The young Inquisitor dipped his mask in shame. "Yes, sir. Thera Vane. It appears she and Javed were being held in the dungeons of the Thakoor's mansion, which has since been destroyed."

Javed Zarger had turned out to be a terrible disappointment for Omand. He'd had such high hopes for that man—a veritable prodigy of deceit and murder—that he had welcomed Javed into his dark council to plot against the judges. Like Omand, Javed had that rare and peculiar mental detachment that enabled him to think of his targets as things rather than people. Such callousness was a valuable trait among their kind. Having Javed fall to fanaticism's seductive call was unexpected, but such was the dangers of being a witch hunter. When your life is nothing but lies, it becomes easy to forget what is true.

"So, what is your theory, Inquisitor? That the demons were in league with this false prophet? Did they break her out of jail?"

Omand chuckled, not because he thought such a deal was outlandish, but rather because he alone had attained the mastery of magic sufficient to communicate with demons. From what he'd heard, Thera's powers were unique, being fueled by an unknown source other than demon or black steel, but her meager tricks were nothing compared to his own. "Did they rescue her and carry my prize off to the sea?"

"My theory is that this woman, this Voice—as the fanatics call her—maybe she was the demon's target. Or if not their target, her presence was an added reason why they attacked when they did. If we were intrigued by her odd magic, might not the forces of hell be curious as well?"

That actually caused Omand to pause. He'd been looking forward to dissecting Thera to find the source of this Voice, until the blasted prideful Makao had deprived him of that opportunity. Perhaps there was something to Zankrut's idea after all.

"I expected silly ideas from an inexperienced man, but I am intrigued by your observation, Zankrut. Well done. Most of your brothers think of demons as simple animals, driven by hunger or anger. Why do you ascribe to them this greater motive?"

"For the last three years, my obligation was to guard the tank and help with the flesh harvesting."

"Ah..." With their demonic prisoner dead, that explained why this one had recently been reassigned to the bone room. There was no purpose in guarding an empty tank. "Then you know demons are far more clever than they look."

"I do, sir. The prisoner would watch us from the water, and there was a cunning to it that you could sense. You get a sense for a creature, when you have to harpoon it and drag it from its home to cut its limbs off over and over again. That demon was intelligent, but it was intelligent in a way foreign to our understanding." Zankrut gave an involuntary shiver as he recalled the unnatural beast. "I know just enough to be frightened of what they're capable of."

"Do you have any other theories why demons would be after Thera in particular, Zankrut?"

"No, sir. We don't even know if she was among the dead, or if she escaped."

Both Sikasso and Javed—before he'd gone mad at least—had been reliable witnesses and had believed that there was actually something to Thera Vane's odd prophetic magic. She wasn't just another typical religious charlatan. Did the demons see in her some kind of threat? "I will consider this idea. You are dismissed."

Zankrut obediently left, and Omand turned back to the city he loved and resented. His man had brought up an interesting thought, but right now Omand had bones to inscribe. He needed his Raja destroying his human enemies rather than worrying about the inhuman ones from the sea.

Chapter 21

Devedas read Omand's message for the third time, trying to grasp the implications. "Is this all?"

"That was all that was upon the bone, Raja," the Inquisitor reported.

Multiple demons appearing on land at once was exceedingly rare. Four or five demons raiding as far inland as Kanok was inconceivable.

"How did no one see them walking all that way from the ocean?" Since they had been traditional rivals to his ancestral house, Devedas had little respect for the Makao, but no one deserved demons. From the sound of things, a couple hundred workers had lost their lives needlessly because the Makao warrior caste hadn't been fulfilling their duty. "Their watchmen must have been asleep in their towers."

"This is surely the case," the Inquisitor agreed.

"There's nothing I can do about it from here. I'm certain the Protectors in that region have it in hand by now. They'll obligate however many warriors they need in order to hunt down the raiders and kill them or drive them back into the sea. Rane, see him out."

"Of course, Raja," his bodyguard said. "This way, Inquisitor."

The messenger bowed and left the command tent. Rane Garo escorted him outside to make sure there weren't any more Inquisitors skulking about outside to eavesdrop. It was well known around the camp that the Raja didn't care to have Inquisitors in his presence. The only reason Devedas tolerated the masks at all was as a courtesy to Omand. They could run the Grand Inquisitor's errands and watch the troops for signs of Law-breaking or fanaticism as the Law required, but those were the only things Devedas allowed them to do. Omand had promised the judges that the Inquisition would play no commanding role in this endeavor, and that was all the excuse Devedas needed to keep their presence to a minimum in his Army of Many Houses.

Unfortunately, he'd recently been informed that more Inquisitors were on their way—led by one of Omand's closest lackeys named Taraba—who would serve as the Grand Inquisitor's voice in any further negotiations with Vadal. The idea of additional masks lurking about annoyed Devedas, as there were whispered insinuations among his troops that they weren't really obligated to the Raja at all, but rather to Omand. In addition to being bad for morale, this sort of backbiting infuriated him...mostly because there was a kernel of truth to it.

Without greater purpose to bond them together, his army was already splintering. They had been obligated to him because their masters had temporarily been more afraid of pillars of fire shooting down from the sky to consume them than they were of their rival houses. Now with the scourge burned and the fires gone out, their old foes remained. Omand believed he could move warriors about as simply as he moved the tokens and banners that represented them on the Chief Judge's map table. Omand could never understand the true nature of the warrior caste. Warriors possessed passion and vigor, were eager to fight, but were loyal only to their family and house. Without an enemy to be unified against, this was no army at all, just a collection of fractious angry men who all held ancestral grudges against the soldiers of every other house.

His warriors had been told they were coming here to save Vadal from demons, only to find by the time they got here, those demons were gone. And though they currently had a truce, Vadal—the very house they'd been sent to save—was now their likely foe? That was joyous news for the men from houses that were Vadal's enemies, but it was an insult to those who were Vadal's traditional allies. While that simmered, every phontho beneath his command secretly worried his house might be the next to be invaded by the combined might of the Capitol.

Yet for now Devedas would set those worries aside, and rejoice, for this was to be a day of celebration, as today he would be reunited with the woman he had decided would be his queen.

The Raja couldn't afford to dwell on personal matters for long, because his station attracted a never-ending line of powerful individuals seeking an audience with him. There were arbiters, phonthos, and bankers, the most connected of each caste, all offering him gifts and favors. There were endless messengers from the Capitol crying for his ear, mostly sent by the heads of various Orders to assure him that they supported the Raja. There were so many obsequious letters sent from the judges smart enough to understand which way the wind was blowing now, and that it was a cold and bitter one from the south.

Those high-status guests always seemed a bit surprised when they entered the Raja's tent, for Devedas kept it as stark and unadorned as the Protector's Hall. Devedas had no use for frivolity. His golden armor was his only emblem of his office, and he didn't bother wearing it unless there was a chance he might get to fight. After he was king, he supposed he would require a crown, and perhaps an extravagant throne to impress the gullible. But for now he would sit on the ground, no more comfortable than the warriors who'd been obligated to serve him. His next guest was shown in—some rich worker of no real importance— and as he went into his endless formalities and praise, Devedas daydreamed of his upcoming reunion instead.

It was illegal for Protectors to court until after their obligation was fulfilled, to prevent any one house from offering up its beautiful daughters to sway the forces of the Law. Despite that, Devedas had known the affections of many women in his life, both professional pleasure women as the Law allowed, and affairs when it didn't, but only one woman had ever actually caught and kept his attention. Rada had been an unexpected oddity, completely unique from all the others. She was beautiful, though she couldn't seem to grasp that fact, but Devedas had known many beautiful girls. That was not it. As a man of great importance, high-status families had kept pushing their most attractive daughters into his path, but those had usually left him annoyed by how sluggish their thoughts were. Unlike those pretty but vapid things, Rada possessed a keen intellect, sharp as the edge on a Protector's sword.

More importantly, though, Rada was just...decent. And unlike the rest of their caste, kind. There had been very little kindness in Devedas' life. Experiencing it had made him yearn for more.

Yet it had been so long since he had last seen her that he worried...He had done things he wasn't proud of during Rada's absence, like secretly betraying the ideals of his Order and consorting with criminals. He'd even killed the man he'd once considered his closest friend. Would Rada sense these things and recognize Devedas was no longer the honorable man she'd first met? Or worse, would she be bitter at him for the many trials she had been forced to endure because of his ambitions?

It seemed odd that a man who had risked his life countless times in hundreds of battles and duels would find himself nervous over receiving the approval of a woman...but such was life.

Rane Garo ducked into the tent, interrupting the latest wealthy worker's tiresome ass kissing. "Your attention is required, sir."

"What now?"

"The Vadal delegation approaches."

"They're early." Relieved, Devedas stood up and addressed the worker who'd been bothering him. "Thank you for these fine gifts. We will speak again in the future. My guards will escort you from the camp." Since he had already forgotten the man's name and what favor he had been asking for, Devedas tried to disguise his eagerness as he left the tent and walked out into the sunlight.

It was a beautiful day in Vadal, as most days were here. Even though it was the end of winter everywhere else, the trees here were perpetually heavy with fruit and giant flocks of songbirds. Devedas was a winter-born child of the south, where survival was a constant battle, hardly any crops grew at all, and if the white bears didn't kill you, the volcanic eruptions might. It was said Vadal water tasted like honey. The ice-choked rivers of Dev tasted like sulfur.

"The Raja is among you!" Rane shouted. The Garo warriors on guard duty immediately slammed their spear butts against the ground as a warning to all. "This way, sir." Rane led, and the rest of the Garo immediately fell in behind them.

Though Devedas was entitled to the Protectors' service, he had declared he wouldn't waste such valuable assets just to watch over him. The real reason was he couldn't risk having men of such perfect integrity inadvertently end up as witnesses to his criminal conspiracy. So instead he had obligated the warriors of Vassal House Garo to serve as his personal guard. They were also from the unforgiving south, hailing from a valley that was either choked with snow, flooding from a demon-infested river, or being consumed by wildfires. The poor but proud Garo had saved him from Ashok, and in exchange Devedas had granted their house freedom from Akershan. That freedom had bought the undying loyalty of their fearsome warriors. So now the Garo enjoyed the prestige and wealth that came from their warriors serving as the Raja's right hand.

The camp was busy, as the officers did their best to keep their idle men occupied, for a bored warrior was a dangerous one. When the soldiers saw Devedas, they immediately presented whatever salute was the tradition of their house. He saw five different kinds as he walked toward where the Vadal delegation would be arriving. It was good to see there was still admiration for him in these warriors' eyes. The factions of his army might not care for their mission, but at least they still respected their commander. His reputation was that of a fighter, not some soft-palmed weakling who'd gotten rank merely by the status of his birth.

Devedas knew something was wrong as soon as he saw how many riders there were in the Vadal contingent. There were a mere five warriors on horseback, wearing their distinctive blue-gray and bronze armor, one in fine robes with the white turban of a diplomat, and a couple of servants. That was an insufficient force to be a proper escort for a woman of Rada's status. He called upon the Heart to sharpen his vision, and confirmed there were no women among them, nor anyone even close to Karno's size.

"This had better be the vanguard to announce that there's a nice carriage following along right behind them," he muttered.

"Spotters say this is all that's on the trade road," Rane responded.

What game is Harta playing at now? Devedas cursed himself for ever mentioning Rada's name to that snake. So much effort had been expended to keep her from being captured and used against him by Omand, only to instead have her delivered into the hands of a different ruler with nearly as much wicked cunning as the Capitol's spider.

The riders drew nearer and the one in the lead shouted, "Great House Vadal comes bearing gifts and invitations for the Raja Devedas!"

He had enough gifts and invitations. They were supposed to be delivering his woman, but he did his best to disguise his anger. "You have permission to approach, Vadal."

They dismounted and were immediately surrounded by scowling Garo, who were a dour and humorless lot on the best of days. When they could sense their master's displeasure, they became downright surly. The drastically outnumbered Vadal warriors remained as polite as could be.

The man in the diplomat's turban was elderly and wore the mark of a senior arbiter on his sash. "I bring greetings from Harta Vadal. I am—"

"I don't care who you are. I was expecting Senior Archivist Radamantha Nems dar Harban and Protector of the Law Karno Uttara. If your answer for their absence is anything other than they've been slightly delayed, I'll be rather annoyed."

The arbiter gave him a very deep bow. "Apologies. You must be Raja Devedas. I was told to look for a man in fine golden armor."

Today, Devedas was attired in a simple, unadorned uniform. Since everyone in this camp knew who he was he didn't even bother with a sash or any mark of office. The infamous scar from Angruvadal that split one side of his face was the only badge he needed for recognition here. "No offense has been taken...yet. Where is she?"

"Radamantha remains in Vadal City, Raja. There has been a delay, but I have been sent to inform you this delay was by her own choosing."

"Doubtful."

"I do not know her myself, but that was what I was told to report." The arbiter was a calm one, Devedas would grant him that. "I have brought you something which I'm told will explain her decision, as well as correspondence from your man Karno." The arbiter signaled for one of the warriors, who took several letters out from a pouch.

Devedas snatched the letters from his hand, broke the seal of Great House Vadal on the first, and began reading... "I am invited to a wedding celebration of some Vadal warrior? What is this foolishness? I don't even know who this man is."

"Phontho Jagdish is one of Vadal's greatest heroes, slayer of illegal wizards and many demons, but most pertinent to you, he is a good friend and ally of Radamantha Nems dar Harban. Jagdish aided her in a time of need, rescuing her from brutal Sarnobat raiders, and then allowed her to recuperate on his estate in the east after her ordeal."

"Hmmm..." Devedas didn't know what manner of game this was, but he didn't like it at all. "Then this... Jagdish has my thanks, but why is Rada not here?"

"As a personal friend to this family—I am told she is considered like unto an aunt to Jagdish's daughter from his first marriage—Rada's presence was requested as an honored guest at their celebration. Having declared a great personal debt for Jagdish's kindness, Rada agreed, and asked that you join her there. It will be a lavish event, attended by Vadal's finest... as well as our honored and respected guests from the Capitol, should you so choose. As you can see, the date is only a few weeks away. Not nearly enough time for a lady of Radamantha's status to come all the way here and still be able to get back in a dignified manner."

Devedas very much doubted that thought had ever entered Rada's mind. "Will Harta Vadal be there as well?"

"Of course. Phontho Jagdish is one of his dearest friends. Our Thakoor looks forward to meeting with you again. When the celebration is over, the librarian can return home with you."

He had no patience for these courtly games. "So Harta thinks he can manipulate me so easily?"

Despite facing the clear and growing frustration of an extremely dangerous man, the arbiter remained perfectly composed. Almost serene. Which was probably why he had been picked for this assignment. "I know nothing about that, Raja."

"If I go to this wedding feast, Sarnobat and Vokkan spies will surely see me there and say, 'Look how the Raja and Thakoor Harta are friends now. Perhaps we should stop our war, to not draw the Raja's fury?'"

"I am sure this is not Lord Harta's intent. Though it is better to be friends with the house of the elephant, than the monkey or the wolf. Elephants step on monkeys and wolves and only notice when they feel the squish between their toes. Our Thakoor respects you greatly, Raja Devedas, and would be honored by your presence, but if you have reasons not to attend this celebration, those reasons will be respected. Harta Vadal does not try to deceive you. The last thing he would ever wish would be to cause offense, but he must honor the wishes of his honored house guest, and I am told Radamantha takes her oaths very seriously."

At least that last part was accurate. It was guilt over breaking one of those oaths that had driven Rada to seek him out to begin with. Even though he was angry right then, the memory of her awkward disguise made him chuckle.

The arbiter took that small bit of mirth as a good sign. "Jagdish's estate is in the east, near Mukesh. It is not too far from Goda and the land that was scorched by the pillar of fire. A journey deeper into Vadal lands—by a reasonably sized contingent of your army, of course—would give you a chance to survey the destruction for yourself, to see that the demonic scourge which brought you here is truly gone with your own eyes."

Harta was clever, laying out paths that seemed so reasonable that even his opponents had no choice but to follow them. In that moment Devedas wanted to snap Harta's neck, but he couldn't fault the man for governing so effectively.

"I will consider this invitation."

The next letter had been sealed with a wax imprint that came from a Protector's ring. The plain and square handwriting was unmistakably Karno's. As expected, the message was direct. Rada was safe. Jagdish had been a loyal friend to them. This was not a trap as far as Karno knew but as usual he trusted no one. Then, the letter went on to tell of their exploits at length.

The pages could have been a clever forgery from someone who understood Karno's nature, but then Devedas noticed there was a Protector cipher hidden among the words. The language was stilted, and words misspelled, not because Karno didn't write well—he'd actually been one of the most literate among their acolytes—but because the letters and words were intended to be rearranged. Only senior members of their order knew this code, and Protectors kept their secrets well.

"Rest from your journey for now, Arbiter. The two of us will speak again later. Garo, take our guests so they may wash and get a warm meal in their bellies. Care for their mounts."

Once the Vadal were guided away, Rane asked him, "So, do you want us to take them as hostages or just kill them outright? That old arbiter must be of sufficient status to be worth something in trade."

The young warrior was the son of his house's only phontho, so he was no stranger to these kinds of diplomatic exchanges. "I thought I concealed my anger better than that."

"I watched you fight Ashok Vadal, so I know you're probably the greatest swordsman still alive. You are doubtlessly very good at many other things as well, but keeping your emotions from your face isn't one of them. It's good you don't join in on the camp's gambling."

Devedas laughed, as he was the sort of commander who appreciated an honest soldier. "I've already gambled more than you can imagine, Rane. Leave them be. They're our guests and will be treated as such. My anger is reserved for their master. Now I have to decide if I ride to war, or a wedding."

As he walked back to his tent, Devedas tried to decipher the hidden meaning in Karno's letter. The message was long, and nearly unbelievable in all it accounted of Rada and Karno's trials—though Devedas didn't know how much of that was real, and how much had been embellished to give Karno more room to hide his secret message. It would probably take longer for Devedas to piece it together than it had Karno to think of how to hide it. Even as a boy, Karno had looked like a gigantic brute who seemed as slow and ponderous as a glacier, but that had always concealed a quick wit and a mind for puzzles. Even clever old Master Mindarin hadn't been able to stump Karno with his logical riddles. Devedas had always been far too impatient for that kind of thing. He needed something to write with.

A brief while later, Devedas had deciphered Karno's real message:

Hidden under Vadal City in tomb of ancient Protectors
There is another Heart
Vadal does not know

Devedas stopped, unbelieving, and read it again. Then he went back and checked his work to be certain this was accurate.

Another heart? There was only one thing Karno could mean by that. The Heart of the Mountain was the source of the Order's power. It was what made Protectors more than men. Stronger, faster, able to withstand poison or disease, capable of heightening their senses, and turning what would be mortal injuries into mere painful inconveniences. All that was due to the power granted to them by that ancient artifact. The Heart wasn't like other black steel devices. It didn't weigh who was worthy or not. It simply granted incredible abilities to anyone who touched it.

The greatest secret of the Order was that the Heart was slowly dying, its magic having been used up over the centuries keeping so many Protectors alive...

This was more valuable than a black steel blade. This could revitalize the Protector Order for centuries more. Or a second Heart could be the foundation of a new Order, equal in abilities to the Protectors... only molded in the image of its creator.

This changed everything.

Chapter 22

It was a time of darkness, yet strangely enough, also a time of jubilation.

Ashok had returned to the Sons of the Black Sword bearing somber witness that an army of demons had just laid waste to one of the great cities of man, yet he had also brought their beloved prophet back. The Sons had hope for their future once more. What were demons compared to that?

Tears had been shed. Proud warriors had shouted thanks to their invisible gods. A triumph of this magnitude was one of the few times even the most stoic of warriors could display their emotions to the world. With General and Voice reunited, the men felt as if there was nothing they could not accomplish. They had defeated the forces of the Capitol before and would do so again. They had saved a multitude of casteless, and now they would save the rest.

They had retreated back toward Gutch's kingdom of industry. The Sons were weary from cutting a path through miles of snow. It would be a long and treacherous journey to reach the relative safety of Akershan and the Cove, but still their small army rejoiced.

All except Ashok.

He'd done the impossible, crossing frozen sea and treacherous underworld, proven he was worthy to bear an ancestor blade once more, and saved his woman from execution. After such effort even a man as grim as he was should have been able to allow himself a few hours of joy, yet as they lost sight of Makao beyond the mountains, it was as if he could still sense a terrible danger beneath their feet as the demons burrowed inexorably toward their next target.

That night Ashok, Thera, and their officers sat around a campfire planning their next move. Morale was so high their ration of dried goat and stale naan might as well have been a feast. With them were Toramana, chieftain of the swamp folk and now leader of their archers; Ongud Khedekar dar Akershan, their cavalry risalder and strategist; Eklavya Kharsawan, infantry risalder; Laxmi, their wizard; Gupta, miner of Jharlang turned gunner commander; and the tattoo-faced killer who was now leader of their skirmishers, Shekar Somsak.

What had begun as tiny group of criminals had swelled into a formidable army. While Ashok had been away, many more secret faithful from several different houses had sought them out. Most of those had been told where to find the Sons by the enigmatic Mother Dawn, who appeared to each group wearing a different face. Their ranks had also swelled with casteless, both those who had already been rebels, but also angry survivors of the Great Extermination who now lived only for revenge.

Ashok remembered when all of the men who took upon themselves the name Sons of the Black Sword had fit on two humble barges. Now their mighty number filled a mountain valley with campfires. This army had been organized by Jagdish, inspired by Thera, and armed by Gutch. Once Ashok had been offended by the sheer criminality of their existence. Now he took pride in their courage. They were fanatics, but honorable ones, willing to die to put things right, and were thus worthy of his respect.

"My scouts think we should be in the clear all the way back to the high desert," Shekar reported. "The checkpoints are unmanned. Every Makao warrior who'd normally be on the border is running toward Kanok trying to save what they can."

"Nobody will spare the time to fight criminals when they've got demons to worry about," Thera agreed. "Fortunate for us."

"But a nightmare for Makao," Eklavya said. "I wouldn't wish demons upon our worst enemies."

There was solemn agreement around the fire at that. Even the most dishonorable foe deserved a better death than being consumed by demons. Then Shekar chuckled, for the Somsak were a brutal raider house, grim of humor. "Well, I wouldn't mind if demons ate the judges..."

That caused the officers to laugh. Even Thera, who had seen the horror that descended upon Kanok, cracked a bit of a smile. The warrior caste tended to find laughter in even the darkest situations.

A few years ago, such disrespectful talk about the Law's most trusted servants would have filled Ashok with anger, but there was almost none of that left in him. He'd given so much to the Law, and it had kept taking, until he had nothing left to give. The Law had proven itself unworthy of his devotion. He made his own law now, and the judges were not part of it. The Capitol was a distant threat, aloof, yet willing to order the death of millions on a thoughtless whim. They were a perversion of justice, not representatives of it.

"To the oceans with the judges," Ashok said. "Let the demons eat their fill."

His words seemed to surprise the officers, because before he had left them to duel Devedas, Ashok would never have so openly spoken ill against the highest among them. None dared note this change, however.

After a moment, Toramana asked, "Do you think there'll be more demons appearing inland, prophet? My tribe knew how to hide and outwit them. The city folk will have no chance."

Thera shrugged. "I don't know, Chief. The Voice hasn't revealed a thing to me since it told us to attack the aqueduct."

"More demons will be coming." Ashok continued staring into the fire as he made his dire prediction. "When I was in Fortress, I learned of an ancient underworld that runs beneath land and sea. I was shown these things by an Order there known as the Collectors, whose obligation it is to delve into this dark land below searching for resources. The ancients cut these paths beneath Lok. Now demons break into the tunnels, and when they flood, they become extensions of hell. They use these paths to move around beneath us now."

Toramana glanced nervously toward the ground, as if expecting a demon claw to suddenly poke through the dirt. "Where do these tunnels lead?"

"The Collectors only access a few now, so I do not know. There are entire cities below, long abandoned, yet haunted by mad gods." Ashok scowled as he recalled his fight against the Dvarapala in its theater of bones. "I fought and killed one of them."

Nobody questioned that claim. If Ashok said he'd killed a god, then it had been done.

"I'm not afraid of demons," Toramana quickly assured the others, as if anyone there could doubt the chieftain's courage by this point, but his tribe didn't like to ever show weakness. "Let them come. My whole life was spent in a swamp between the ocean and the House of Assassins. I'm used to evil lurking nearby, but my people have enjoyed our time in the desert and mountains not having to worry that every puddle hides death."

"Battle is preferable to constant uncertainty," Eklavya agreed. "Better to fight and get it over with."

All the warriors seemed to agree with that sentiment.

"But why now?" Ongud asked, ever the strategist. "If these tunnels were dug by the first men of Lok, that means they've been there since before the demons fell out of the sky. Why would demons wait so long to use them to strike inland?"

"Something has changed," Ashok agreed.

"Everything has changed in these perilous times!" Gupta gestured toward him. "A casteless boy takes up a black sword." Then he pointed at Thera. "A bolt from heaven gives a warrior-caste child the gift of prophecy! The Capitol says to murder all the heirs of the gods' last chosen king, but then fire shoots down from the sky as a warning to the judges to repent of their evil ways. These are all signs the gods have returned! Of course the demons are enraged. Demons are enemies to the gods. They're trying to stop the gods from coming back!"

Perhaps the worker was right. It seemed as sound a theory as any. Ashok barely understood humans. The motivations of demons remained a mystery.

"We shall see soon enough, gunner Gupta," Ongud said. "The question is, what should we do about it? Will these demons spell our doom? Or are the gods allowing this evil, because it's the opportunity for our people to break the Capitol's chains once and for all?"

The officers pondered on that, for faithful or not, they all recognized that as things stood now, no matter how many little victories they stole, their rebellion's defeat was all but inevitable. The best they could do was hit, run, and hide. How could rebels expect to outlast the might of the Capitol and all the great houses combined?

Eklavya snorted. "You really suppose if the first caste is distracted by a greater menace, we could use that chance to carve out a free house of our own?"

"Why not?" Ongud asked. "The gods are wise, seeing far beyond what we can imagine. If we gather up the casteless and all the faithful from every house to a place of our choosing, we can make our stand. It could be like the Cove, but greater. The Law will be more worried about demons than us. By the time they turn their attention back to their vile extermination order, Gutch will have supplied us with too many Fortress rods to ever be conquered. The demons could be our way out!"

"If your gods were as wise as you think they are, they would not send demons to aid us," Ashok said. "No good ever comes from those vile things. Only suffering and death."

"Forgive me, General." Chastised, Ongud dipped his head in acknowledgment. "But we fight a losing battle. What else are we supposed to do?"

Thera was sitting on the ground right next to Ashok, close enough to share their warmth, and Ashok felt it as she gathered a deep breath, as if she was finding the courage to say something difficult. "There has to be a path to victory. As fickle as the Voice can be, I don't think it ever lies. I've trusted everyone here enough to tell you how the Voice really works. Keta keeps the words it speaks, because when it manifests, I'm out of my head. I hate to count on understanding what the Voice really means, but there's been a couple prophecies in the past that I think might help us know what to do next. Keta will have the exact words for us to examine."

During their rushed journey he'd not yet had a chance to tell her about Keta's death. However, he had briefed the men about Bharatas' attack on the Cove before leaving to find her. Their stricken glances at the mention of Keta's name told Thera something was terribly wrong.

"What? What is it?"

Ashok was a stranger to comforting another, but instinct told him to reach out and gently take her hand. This was a different instinct from the one that helped him fight, but in that moment, it was just as powerful. "I am sorry, Thera. Keta died defending the Cove."

"That can't be." Thera began blinking rapidly as she realized this was coming from a man who always spoke the plain truth. "How?"

"Keta showed great courage, even challenging a bearer to a duel to buy time for the people to hide." Ashok was surprised by the sudden feeling that welled up inside him as he recounted this memory. "Because of him, and the bravery of Laxmi's brothers and sisters"—Ashok nodded toward the wizard girl—"the Cove held. The people there are safe. I found Keta, still alive, but barely. I heard his last words. Then I avenged him."

"Ashok told us the Keeper faced a black steel blade with nothing but that little meat cleaver of his," Shekar said, clearly trying to comfort their prophet. "That is a death worthy of respect."

Thera had to let go of Ashok's hand to wipe the sudden moisture from her eyes. "What did Keta say before he died? The man sure loved to talk."

Ashok thought over the last words of his friend. "He denied that there was a great nothing beyond death. He said he saw glory instead."

That caused Thera's face to crack and her sorrow to burst through. In that moment, she was no leader or prophet, merely an exhausted woman who had been put through far too much and could bear no more. Her officers politely looked away. Most of them were warrior caste. They understood.

She didn't allow herself to appear feeble for long. Thera forced her feelings back and composed herself. Ashok knew she would sob for the lost later, but for now she had an army to command. "If Keta said it, then it's true. That settles that debate among the faithful. As Keeper, Keta wrote down the exact words of the Voice, but I can probably remember enough to get us by."

"What of Javed?" asked Ongud. "He was Keta's constant companion. Surely our other priest learned everything as well? We thought he got captured when you were."

"Javed's dead," Thera said, too quickly. "I saw him fall into a hole full of demons inside Makao's Great House."

"Such a tragedy." Eklavya shook his head sadly. "Javed was a good man."

"Especially for a merchant," Shekar said. "I rarely felt the urge to stab him."

"He cared for the people of the Cove," Toramana agreed. "May he reach that same glorious kingdom that Keta saw."

Thera gritted her teeth as the warriors commiserated the tragic loss of their traitorous priest. She'd told Ashok of Javed's true nature, but why she withheld that from her officers, he didn't know. He would trust that she had her reasons.

"We're out of priests, then," Shekar said. "Don't we need one of those?"

"Who'll keep the book of names?" Gupta asked. "Who will teach us the gods' will?"

"Keta preached about how a Voice said a priest would be necessary to fulfill the prophecies," Eklavya pointed out nervously.

The metal writings Guru Dondrub had shown Ashok in Fortress had the same prophecy carved upon them. But the Guru had also claimed those same ancient prophecies declared that the Voice would have to sacrifice herself to defeat the demons once and for all, so Ashok had chosen to disregard those words. If the gods required Thera's death to fulfill their ends, they would have to go through him first.

"It is the belief of the Fortress religion that we will require prophet, priest, and king to be rid of the demons once and for all. Yet even without them ever having an Inquisition to smash their history to dust, the Fortress monks still confuse things. They thought I might be this expected king, but I am not." Ashok looked Thera in the eyes. "My obligation is to you alone, not Lok or its people. You."

His sincerity must have been a little overwhelming, because Thera rarely was at a loss for words. "Thank you, Ashok."

"I know we've been resisting the Law, but the gods want us crowning kings now?" Eklavya asked incredulously. "That seems like we'd be going backward. The Sons fight so we can believe and worship freely, not to trade many little tyrants for one big tyrant."

"This king is not our concern." If that truly was Devedas' role in the Voice's schemes—and the way Angruvadal had gone so far as to give Ashok a heart attack to spare Devedas' life indicated the black steel had some greater purpose for him—then Devedas would rule. He had always been a man of unrelenting ambition, unsatisfied by anything less than greatness. If there was any one man who could bend the Law to his will, it was his former brother.

Gupta spoke wistfully, "If the Capitol got a king, maybe we could convince him to leave the faithful alone, or spare the casteless, or even better, get rid of the castes entirely and just let everyone live as they choose. If one man can change the Law by himself, then let's get him to change it so that we're free. That would be quite the thing."

"You dream big, my friend!" Ongud said. "I'll give you that."

"Maybe it would be easier to sway one man than a hundred, but judges or kings, neither one is here now." Thera had to deal with the world as it was, not as they wanted it to be. "If our rebellion needs more priests, then we'll have to trust the gods will send us some. We can't dwell on what's been lost. We've got to look to the future. For now that means getting out of Makao while they're looking elsewhere, getting back to the Cove, then finding some new fights to pick."

"It's good to see being a prisoner didn't harm your determination," Toramana said.

"Not a bit. Our war isn't over until we break the Capitol's will once and for all."

It was an impossible thing to ask, but these men would try anyway.

Eklavya spoke for all of them as he said, "It is good to have you back, Prophet."

Chapter 23

At dawn, the Sons of the Black Sword set out for Akara. With no patrols to avoid they made excellent time the first day.

Thera had been separated from her army for a season. Ashok had been gone for over a year. Yet the Sons had remained steadfast, loyal to their mission and their gods. It didn't matter that no two of the men could ever agree on what their gods actually wanted from them, and the only ones among them who pretended to understand their doctrine—the priests—were now dead. Regardless of their continual campfire arguments over theology, many of which turned into fist- and even the occasional knife fight, the men shared a common enemy, and faith in their prophet. That was enough. Their morale was high. Their order remarkable. From experienced senior warriors to fish-eaters hastily trained on how to use a Fortress rod, all of them were prepared to die for their cause.

Ashok had once warned her that an army made up of men of different castes and houses would never be as effective as a real army, but from what the Sons had shown her, she'd pit them against the forces of any phontho in Lok.

Thera often missed her father. Now, Andaman Vane had been a truly great phontho! It said something that if her father had still been alive, she'd have been honored to present the Sons of the Black Sword for his inspection. She suspected he would be impressed, and proud of her, because he had often said that an army was nothing but a complex reflection of the character of those who led it.

The downside of all that loyalty was how her religious fanatics kept wanting to pay their respects to the gods' chosen. It was hard being doted on. Ashok could avoid that attention and escape by riding off alone, presumably to scout ahead. And even when he was with the main body, he was too scary to approach. Thera wasn't so lucky. Not being the deadliest combatant in history armed with a sword that could slice an ox in half, none of the new recruits were frightened of her. On the contrary, they saw her as precious and in need of guarding. The Sons had lost her once, and they'd rather die than risk losing her again. Before she'd had Murugan. Now at any moment she had five or six warriors vigilantly watching over her, and all of the new ones who'd joined since she'd been captured were unbearably excited to be in the presence of the legendary Voice for the first time.

So by the time Ashok rejoined the Sons late in the afternoon, Thera was so tired of her watchers and worshippers that she eagerly used needing to plan with her general as an excuse to flee. Even the most protective fanatic couldn't complain about leaving their precious prophet vulnerable when she had Ashok and Angruvadal by her side.

The two of them rode ahead of the column, and once they were far enough away that she felt safe to be herself, Thera gave Ashok a gigantic grin. "I'm free!"

He raised an eyebrow. "From the dungeons of Makao?"

"From that, and my need to act respectable and prophetic. I know this won't last long, but I'll take it." Thera laughed and coaxed her mare into a run. "Yah!"

The sun felt good on her face. She rode so fast her hood bounced off, and with her hair whipping in the wind, it must have revealed the terrible scar left by the bolt from heaven, but Thera didn't care. It was only her and Ashok, and things like marred beauty simply didn't matter to him.

With the mountains to one side and miles of sage to the other, the two of them raced across the high plains. Ashok easily could have overtaken her, since he was riding the fearsome white stallion he'd painstakingly named Horse, but he must have sensed she needed this small bit of freedom.

Once the Sons were out of sight, Thera found a hilltop where the brown grass was entirely clear of snow. It was a chill, yet beautiful day, so she dismounted and walked her steed. Their breath made little clouds.

Ashok rode up behind her and got off Horse. "Why didn't you tell them of Javed's treachery?"

"Back to business already? Can't you just enjoy the day?"

"The Sons trust you because you have always been honest with them."

"Not always. That scum was a secret witch hunter, sent to spy on us. Except he did such a good job pretending to be their priest that he turned into someone all the people loved. What am I supposed to tell them? That they had faith in a lie? What will that teach them? I'm worried that they'll learn they can't trust anyone, especially each other. Javed helped them grow crops. He performed marriages and preached to them when Keta couldn't." Her voice caught as she said Keta's name. "Damn it..."

"I curse myself for not getting there soon enough to save him."

"You told me you walked underneath the ground, all the way from Fortress, fighting horrors in the dark the whole way, then ran across half of Akershan, to battle your way through a siege and hundreds of Akershani warriors, to reach him at all. Save your curses for those who deserve them, Ashok. You did all you could do. We've got enough curses enough on us as it is."

And to think, for a moment there she'd been having a nice day...

"Nonetheless," Ashok muttered, "his death was a waste."

"I think Keta would say most deaths are." Now she couldn't help but cry, as out of nowhere all the emotions she'd been holding back broke through as violently as the demons had through the mansion's floor in Kanok.

Ashok reached over and pulled her cloak tight around her shoulders, probably mistaking her sobs for shivering. It wasn't that Ashok didn't feel things. She knew he did. His emotions had just been muted by the Law. Except every now and then he surprised her.

"It is no crime to weep for the loss of a good man."

"Oceans. I'm an embarrassment."

"There are no witnesses here. No one will think you weak."

"What about you?"

"I already know of your true strength," he assured her. "As did Keta."

"Damn him..." She wiped her runny nose with her sleeve. "I warned him this would all catch up to us eventually, but Keta didn't care. He believed so hard in something bigger than him that dying didn't matter."

"Then being a good priest is like being a good swordsman."

It wasn't like Ashok to be philosophical. "What?"

"It is natural for all living things to desire continuing to live above all else. Only one must disregard that desire to achieve greatness. You must simultaneously want to live but be willing to die in order to defeat any enemy."

"Did Ratul teach you that?"

Ashok nodded.

"Yeah, sounds like that grumpy old bastard."

"On this thing, Ratul was right. And in his way, Keta was a braver man than I."

"Says the man without fear."

"Exactly."

They continued walking through the dead grass. After a while Thera ran out of tears. Keta wouldn't want her moping. Since he wasn't around to see his dream fulfilled, she'd have to do it for him.

"From now on, it isn't enough just to hide and survive. We must win. Keta was the one who talked about the end while I always worried about how we'd get through the day. That's got to change. We have to carve out a place for the faithful to live in peace, where we're either accepted by the Law, or we've defeated it badly enough it learns to leave us be forever. I'm not just talking about another hideout like the Cove, but building a new great house, equal and respected."

Ashok seemed to mull that over. "Houses respect each other because each one is mighty and capable. Houses spill ink or blood. The strong houses grow, the weak are conquered and consumed. They must fear us in order to respect us."

"Then help me figure out how, Ashok. We've got the gods in my head, your black steel, a small army, Gutch's guns, and even wizards now."

"We are few in number, with no allies or resources."

He was giving her the hard truth, but there had to be a way.

"The faithful are many but spread across every house and hiding from the eyes of the Law. There are multitudes of casteless, but that number is getting smaller each day the Great Extermination continues. What of these Fortress people you told me about?"

"I asked." Ashok shrugged. "They are foreigners. I would not count on their help."

The politics of Lok were all about balance. The great houses retained some autonomy from the Law because of the uneasy equilibrium between them. If the Law became too meddlesome, the houses would push back. If any one house became too strong, the others would unite against them. If one of the three castes took too much, the others had ways to punish them. Warriors could make war, but the workers just had to stop tilling the fields to make everyone starve. The first was the smallest in number but used Law as their weapon to pit everyone against each other for the first's benefit. As the old saying went, every man had his place. Except it wasn't really true, because there was no place for her kind, the outsiders, the criminals, and the believers.

Thera just needed a way to carve a place for them. *Simple.*

"I've made my decision, Ashok. We'll never speak of Javed's true nature to the Sons. The people need their heroes, and they can't all be unkillable Protectors or prophets with special gifts from the sky. They have to be regular folks, doing their best. If we're going to build something new, as Keta imagined, then the people need to believe in each other. They love the Sons because they fight for them, but the Sons don't herd the livestock or sew the clothes. From now on, Javed's memory will be honored. He was a merchant who set aside his wealth and status to help the poorest among us. He tended the plague sick in the Cove, and then he gave his life trying to save mine . . . and I'll tell this lie with a smile on my face, as many times as it takes, no matter how angry it makes me inside each time I do."

"Despite being a criminal, deceit does not come naturally to you. I can tell there is more about this treachery you haven't told me."

Thera sighed, for there was no hiding things from Ashok. "Back in the Cove, Javed took on the form of a tiger and murdered one of Toramana's sons and another boy of the swamp people. I'm assuming because they somehow discovered his real identity."

"Ah . . . If Toramana found out, the chieftain's rage would be great."

"Laxmi sensed the magic afterward. I didn't know who to trust. I tried to catch the spy. I failed. Murugan died for it, and I ended up a prisoner. Every day our numbers swell as word spreads and more of the faithful seek us out, but I've got to worry which one of them is the next secret witch hunter, waiting for the opportunity to destroy us."

"If we are building a house, houses have spies." Ashok was quiet for a long time as he considered her concerns. "I was not there when you needed me. From now on I will personally deal with any potential infiltrators."

"You'd be the Forgottten's Inquisition, then?"

"I will be myself."

The way Ashok said that almost made Thera pity any Capitol agents who might be sent against them. "You spent twenty years rooting out criminals for the Law. This can't be too different."

"It is very different. Criminals adapt. Inquisitors cannot. When enough criminals die, the survivors learn and change their behavior. As long as the Law does not give, neither can its servants. The Inquisition will never stop. For us to succeed, the Inquisition must be utterly destroyed." Then Ashok paused, scowling.

Her Protector walked a few steps and knelt, placing one palm against the dirt. He lifted his head and stared in the direction of distant Mount Metoro.

"Pondering what to do about the Capitol?"

"No ... A feeling. That is the direction the demons are tunneling next."

Chapter 24

"Oceans, woman, what have you done?" Jagdish demanded as he barged into Lady Shakti's office.

She was sitting at her desk, writing a letter, and looked up from her correspondence, seemingly baffled by his consternation. "I've done a great deal lately, as I'm the one currently keeping two armies supplied and fed. I also just finished wrestling Vadal City into obligating Father another hundred horsemen and you another hundred archers, so you'll have to narrow it down for me, my betrothed."

He'd ridden from the border to the Mukesh warrior district as fast as he could. Even the many flowers and candles that decorated Shakti's part of the estate couldn't drown out the stink of horse sweat and travel dust. Jagdish's bodyguards caught up and began entering the doorway behind him. "Boys, you do not want to hear this part. Wait in the garden." They were quick to leave, probably happy thinking that they were about to avoid some lovers' spat. He closed the door behind them.

Now Shakti could tell Jagdish was honestly shaken, and she quickly dismissed her attendant scribe as well. Once that woman was gone, Shakti asked, "Is this it? Is Sarnobat's bearer on the way?"

"I wish it were that simple. Fighting an ancestor blade would be less frightening than this. I just got word Harta Vadal accepted your invitation. Our Thakoor is coming to our wedding."

She stared at him for a long time. "Oh..."

"That's it?" Jagdish asked. "'Oh'?"

"I didn't think he would actually accept the invitation. Thakoors are very busy. I don't understand why he'd do us the honor. I especially didn't think a man used to so much comfort would want to risk traveling during the rainy season. This is most unexpected."

"Like getting trampled by a horse is unexpected. I was also just informed that not only is his high and mightiness coming, he's also bringing along Raja Devedas and a horde of his little Capitol minions with him."

Shakti was as much the natural politician as Jagdish was a warrior's warrior, but from the stricken look on her face, his words must have been the equivalent of walking into an ambush and realizing it only because of the sudden volume of arrows suddenly protruding from your body.

"You're normally not the one to be at a loss for words, my dear."

"Two of the most important men in the world are coming to your estate in a matter of weeks! If Harta is there, then so will everyone else who matters." Shakti leapt to her feet and began to pace back and forth. "We've got to change *everything*. No offense, but your estate is far too small. We'll need to move it to my family's here in Mukesh. Even then, nothing's good enough. The east is humble, not like what wealthy Vadal City dwellers are used to. We'll need a bigger feast. More musicians. More dancers. I'll need all of Father's war elephants on parade for the added spectacle."

"Well, they're kind of busy, what with having an actual war on and all." Jagdish sat on the edge of her desk. Her flailing reaction made Jagdish feel guilty for springing this on her so suddenly... but not that guilty. "Maybe we should see if Gotama's got time to teach his elephants to dance for us as well? Kill two birds with one stone that way."

"I'm being serious, Jagdish!"

"Three if we teach the elephants to play an instrument."

That was so outlandish it actually made Shakti laugh, which broke the tension, and that genuine sound made Jagdish smile.

Having a worthy partner made every challenge seem more manageable.

"All right..." She took a deep breath and composed herself. "I'm fine now. I was taken by surprise, that's all. If we are poor hosts this could bring endless shame to both of our families and even Great House Vadal itself. There are a thousand things to be done between now and then... Saltwater, Jagdish! Most brides only have to worry about looking pretty on their wedding day."

"No need to swear." Jagdish reached out and gently took her hand. "Looking pretty won't be an issue for you."

"Now is not the time for flattery."

"Nor is it the time for panic. We're warrior caste. Meeting insurmountable challenges is what we do."

She took another deep breath, then gave him a determined nod. "You're right. Every test brings opportunity... Come to think of it, there is a bright side to this announcement."

"Really?"

"If Harta is bringing such important guests with him—including the former master of the Protectors himself—then surely Harta no longer intends to pin the blame for his war against Sarnobat on you. With Protector eyes upon him, he'd be distancing himself from you, not blessing your home with his presence. You getting executed a season later would stain his honor."

"As long as my blood isn't staining the ground, I'm happy." Jagdish hadn't thought of that angle, though, and it gave him some hope. "But why would he do this? Harta does nothing unless it benefits Vadal somehow. Why bring the Raja here? Devedas is a dangerous man. He'd make for a powerful enemy."

"I know you are familiar with this Devedas, but you've never spoken much about him."

Jagdish shrugged. "I only know what Ashok told me about him, but Devedas was one of the only men in the world Ashok actually respected. Not just as a combatant either. Devedas is easily one of the best swordsmen who has ever lived, even without a black steel blade. When I asked if he thought I could defeat Devedas in a duel, Ashok laughed at me."

"How rude. You're one of the finest swordsmen in Vadal."

It was good Shakti believed in him, but Jagdish was under no illusions. "He didn't even intend offense. His reaction was more like I was a puppy growling at one of the ferocious white bears of the south. Ashok Vadal was the strongest man I've ever known—not just physically and mentally, but possessing a will of steel. No matter the cost, he did what he thought was right, and his nature was so obvious that even proud warriors who'd barely met him were prepared to follow him into the sea. Keep that in mind, because Ashok considered Devedas his equal, and saw Devedas as someone potentially worthy to take up Angruvadal and all that entails. He only ever said that about two men I know of."

"Then we shouldn't underestimate the Raja...but do me a favor. When the important people are here, don't talk about the most infamous rebel criminal in history like he's your esteemed older brother."

Jagdish missed his friend, who had possessed far more honor than any of his detractors could muster, but he was no fool. "I think I can manage."

"Ashok mentioned two he thought would be worthy of Angruvadal..." Shakti put her hands on her hips and gave him an appraising look. "I have my suspicions as to who the second was."

"Idle talk between sparring partners." Jagdish waved that away. "It is nothing."

"Of course...The character to be a proper bearer is surely nothing at all like that of a warrior who was willing to risk it all to raise himself from disgrace to mighty phontho by cleverness alone. Wanting what's best for your family can't possibly be anything like wanting what's best for your house."

Shakti understood him far too well, and they weren't even married yet. "Sure, I'd have tried for that black sword, but fate had other things in mind for me. I've got a different future now, with you. So let us figure out how to make the best of it."

As Shakti adjusted her plans and made a list of the various crises she needed to attend to in order to spare them from eternal embarrassment and dishonor, Jagdish felt a sting of shame, for he hated lying to his woman.

The truth of it was fate had denied him the opportunity to bear one black sword, but when he'd thought that Sarnobat's blade had taken the field, he'd rushed directly toward that danger, hopeful for the opportunity to try again. He could have been killed by a bearer, or worse, the sword could have found him unworthy and made him spill his own guts, and then Shakti would have no husband at all.

But Jagdish was a warrior, and Shakti was to be a warrior's wife, and warriors had to be willing to risk death or they weren't really warriors at all. When a husband died doing his duty, he did so knowing his wife would carry on and raise whatever children he'd left behind to be honorable too, because that's what warrior wives had always done. They were the reason their caste survived. The men did the fighting, but it was the women who kept their legacy alive. If that mad wolf had been armed with black steel, Jagdish might have lost, but he'd die knowing that Shakti would care for Pari, and make sure she grew up to be as capable as a warrior-caste woman should be.

That momentary guilt and reflection did remind Jagdish of a different problem he'd been procrastinating over, though.

"Now that I know the crisis is in capable hands, I must go." He leaned over and kissed Shakti on the cheek. "There's something I must attend to."

Chapter 25

Jagdish had Roik Kutty deliver the mad Sarnobat warrior Najmul to a secluded corner of the estate. This orchard was as good a place for an interrogation as anywhere else, and it was a lovely day. It took four of his men to wrestle and drag Najmul across the grass, and the stubborn bastard fought them every inch of the way. It was only when Najmul saw that it was Jagdish sitting under a plum tree waiting for him, rather than an executioner, that he quit struggling.

"Oh, there my new master is! If you Vadal boys had just told me where we were going, I wouldn't have bit you."

"Shut it," said the warrior with the bleeding hand. "Here's your prisoner as requested, Phontho."

Old Kutty was leaning against a nearby tree, observing the spectacle with mirth. "He's a feisty one."

"That he is," Jagdish agreed.

"I am a man of Sarnobat. Within each of our warriors beats the heart of a savage wolf. You will learn this pain if you keep invading our lands."

Kutty chuckled at the bravado of the wide-eyed madman. "I've been doing this too damned long, boy, so spare us the chest beating. I've got plenty of other prisoners we just took, which proves the rest of your house isn't so tough. Judging by how quick the others surrendered when Daula fell, you're abnormal in both heart and head. The phontho here has got some questions for you. Answer them truthfully and I'll tell your guards to keep the amount of spit in your gruel to a minimum."

"You consider the rations I've been getting bad? You Vadal are too fat. I thought it was a hearty stew, so delicious I licked the bowl."

"Sit down. Get comfortable."

Despite Kutty's command, the religious fanatic remained proudly defiant, even in chains. Jagdish could respect that.

"Leave us," Jagdish told his men.

"He's a dangerous one, Phontho," Zaheer warned. "I'd like to remain close by."

Najmul sneered. "Do not insult my integrity. I've given my word. I'm not dangerous to your master, for he is my sworn master now too. It's the rest of you Vadal worms who are feeble and should fear me."

"Can I get your permission to send this cur to the endless nothing, sir?" Zaheer moved his hand to his sheathed sword.

Najmul held up his shackled wrists and shook his chains. "I'm game. Unlock these and let's give our master a proper duel to watch."

"With great sadness, permission denied, Zaheer." Jagdish just shook his head at the obstinate nature of the prisoner before him and continued eating his lunch. He spoke with his mouth full. "Go on, boys. It'll be fine. If I get murdered by a man in chains, I deserve it. Besides, I beat him once."

"I let you win. The gods would've been upset with me if I'd cut down someone they've got big plans for."

That made Jagdish laugh, which caused him to nearly choke on his curried lamb. Now that would have been a shameful way for a warrior to die! He coughed and took a drink of wine to wash it down. "Alright, Sarnobat, it was a good fight, I'll give you that, but I've heard enough foolishness about your imaginary gods already. Don't make me play pretend that your swordsmanship is all that too."

"We'll be right over here if you need us, Jagdish," Kutty said as he led the other soldiers away.

Jagdish kept on eating, waiting for his men to get out of earshot. "Want some?"

Grudgingly, Najmul sat down a few feet away. "I am starving. Despite what I said to annoy your officer, Vadal obeys the Law on how much to feed prisoners, but no extra."

Jagdish passed over the rest of the bowl, and Najmul began greedily shoveling the food into his mouth with his fingers.

"Alright, Sarnobat. Before we begin, I want you to understand I've known many warriors like you."

Najmul kept chewing even as he boasted. "There are no others like me. I'm the fiercest swordsman in the north. I only told the old man I am normal so your bodyguards would leave us be."

"I meant delusional religious fanatics. I rode with the Sons of the Black Sword."

"Well, in that case, sure. There's more of us hidden among our caste than the Law or the masks realize, but we keep to the old truths in secret. We've just been waiting for our time to rise. I think that time is now."

"I'm no fanatic. I follow the Law."

Najmul openly scoffed. "A friend of the Forgotten's warrior claims to obey the Law?"

Jagdish let that pass. He was used to the same thing being said as an accusation, rather than a compliment. "I don't believe in your silly gods, but I do know there's more to this Mother Dawn creature than meets the eye, because she's sent far too many quality warriors to serve in the Sons for it to be a coincidence."

"She's an unassailable heavenly messenger, who arranges things so those of us who have a part in the gods' great plan cross paths."

"Or she's a crazy wizard with a fine eye for martial talent. I'll keep to the story that doesn't get me beheaded for believing illegal religion . . . What did she say exactly when she sent you?"

"I already told you, before you rudely bashed me over the head. Your life will be in great danger. The gods want me to keep you alive."

"How will I be in danger?"

"I don't know, but I'll know somehow when the time comes. Then I will act, and once I save your life you will be forced to admit the gods are real and can see into the future."

"Better men than you have tried to convince me of that pile of rotting fish already." Jagdish thought of the odd little priest, Keta, and his endless stories of courage and sacrifice, but more importantly, he remembered the Sons he'd led, and their simple faith that had sustained them through challenges that would make even the greatest among their caste quail with fear. "Your god mother creature mentioned a black sword."

"Oh, now the Lawful man is a believer of prophecies?"

"Answer the question or go back in your hole, Sarnobat."

Najmul finished the lamb and licked his filthy fingers. "She wanted you to know that getting a sword isn't the answer to your problems. Helping the gods is what you're supposed to be doing."

"Why me?"

"Ah, that's a question I've been asking myself every waking moment since I met you, Vadal. Mother Dawn didn't share her reasons with me, but I've got an idea. I don't know you, but your men who guard this place do, and they tell stories about you all the time. Congratulations on your wedding. The guards all say she's a beauty enough to make a eunuch blush."

"It's a lovely, peaceful day. Don't ruin it by making me gut you."

Najmul chuckled. "No offense was intended. They say she's pretty. But the stories they tell each other about the great Jagdish all tell me the same thing: You're a leader. A real one, a rare good one whose actions match his words, whose honor is worth more than saltwater and can't be bought with notes. I reason I'm supposed to keep you alive because the gods will need someone like you to lead their army when the time comes. After all, you led them once already."

"Then you're wrong, because according to your own priest, your gods already had somebody else in mind for that obligation. They named Ashok general, and Ashok died anyway. So much for the word of the gods."

Najmul laughed uproariously at that. "You dupe! Ashok isn't dead because Ashok *can't* die." The fanatic reached into his shirt to take hold of a leather necklace. He held it out, to show that there was a tiny metal hook tied to the end of it. "This is the symbol of Ashok undying."

"I was there that day, stupid."

It appeared that Jagdish had finally found something that put the cocky raider in his place, for stunned Najmul whispered, "Then you are more blessed than I thought."

"My caste blessed me with good sense and no patience for

foolishness. I fought by Ashok's side after he lifted himself off Sikasso's meat hook, but it was Protector Devedas who did him in, not some wizard."

"No. He's alive. Word moves quick among the networks of the faithful, Jagdish. I swear to you Ashok is alive. This hook is a symbol of hope, for as long as Ashok lives, we may prevail. He is the Forgotten's warrior. But I think he'll need your help." Najmul wrapped his fingers around the hook and made a fist. "By saving you, I will be aiding him. That is my part in the gods' great plan."

Being reminded of Ashok saddened Jagdish, for he was the best man Jagdish had ever known. However, Najmul was right about one thing, Ashok had certainly needed help being a commander! A leader had to be fallible himself in order to understand fallible men. You needed to have been weak to understand weakness. Warriors followed other warriors. It was hard for a mortal man to follow a force of nature.

"I've had enough of your insanity for one day, Najmul. Be thankful the Sons were the best bunch of soldiers I've ever fought alongside, because their quality has bought you my mercy. I won't turn you over to the Inquisitors as a fanatic. Instead, I'll just have you put with the other hostages to be ransomed back to your house." Jagdish raised his voice so his men would hear. "Put the prisoner back with the others."

"Then I will wait there patiently until you need me."

"That'll be a real long time, Sarnobat."

Najmul stood up and bowed. "As the gods will it."

The soldiers led the fanatic away, this time without all the kicking and biting.

Kutty strolled over. "Learn anything new?"

"Just rumors from a madman." Jagdish held the wine bottle out to his officer.

"Such as?" Kutty grabbed the bottle and took a swig. "Ah, that's good stuff. I knew I should've made phontho."

"He doesn't think my trying to take Sarnobat's sword will solve my problems."

"That maniac may be smarter than he appears, then."

Jagdish gave the grizzled old soldier an incredulous look. "What's that supposed to mean?"

"Black steel is judgmental." Kutty lifted up his uniform shirt to display a massive scar that ran from his belly button to his hip. "When Bhadramunda died, Angruvadal rejected many. Back in those days, I was free of disgrace enough to try myself. Angruvadal didn't find me up to the task, but it was kind enough to not cut *too* deep. Some of my friends weren't so lucky."

"I didn't know that you'd tried."

"It was a long time ago." Kutty let the uniform fall, hiding his old injury.

Then Jagdish wondered if Kutty's blood had been among the puddles young Ashok had scrubbed from the great house's floor before that casteless boy had picked up a sword and put events into motion that would change the whole world. "Even great men fail, Kutty. There's no dishonor in reaching for greatness."

"Some things aren't about honor or failure, Jagdish. Just be careful what you wish for, because fate might give it to you good and hard."

Chapter 26

Despite her odd status in this place, Rada had to admit that Great House Vadal was a rather lovely place to stay. Most importantly, their library was second only to the Capitol's, but it was also a rather luxurious life, with the finest food, and the most gifted of musicians. The Thakoor's garden contained incredible arrangements of plants and flowers that grew nowhere else in Lok.

Rada didn't know why she had been summoned by Thakoor Harta Vadal to accompany him on his evening stroll through those gardens, but tonight it was just the two of them and his usual contingent of Personal Guard. She had asked Karno to remain in the guest quarters, because her Protector's presence hadn't been requested and bringing him along might be taken to mean she thought Vadal's finest couldn't keep her safe, which would be very insulting to their host. Karno did whatever he felt like regardless of her wishes, but luckily he'd acquiesced because her relationship with Great House Vadal was rather delicate right now, and that was all his fault.

Rada was nervous, as any sensible woman would be while trying to deceive a master of propaganda and manipulation. She'd honored Karno's request to keep the black steel artifact they'd found secret, but feared what would happen if Harta found out she was lying to him about it. She didn't believe Harta to be a cruel man by nature, but rather a pragmatic one, because every action he took was calculated for the benefit of Great House Vadal. That made him a fine leader for his people, but a menace to anyone who got in his way.

"Tell me, Librarian, how goes your search for the ancient treasures you swore to me you'd recover?"

"The mirror isn't very forthcoming. There are many gaps for me to fill in. Scholarly matters take time."

"Sadly, time is something the casteless you bargained for are running out of." As usual, Harta appeared calm and utterly in control, even as he threatened to unleash a great and unrelenting murder. "We had a deal, Rada."

"I assure you I'm doing the best I can."

Harta paused to pluck a flower from a vine to smell it. "My wizard Saksham tells me that you've visited more than twenty secluded places around my city now, yet each time, you've found absolutely nothing of value. No ancient weapons, no hidden black steel, as promised." He dropped the flower and crushed it beneath one sandal. "Nothing but dust and ashes."

Dust and ash would soon be all that was left of the casteless if she didn't find a way to placate this man. "You have to keep in mind the information inscribed on the mirror is very old and incomplete. Some of those may have been the incorrect locations, but I can't know until I check. Others, it's possible that there were items stored there originally only they were looted long ago." When she realized how defeatist that sounded, she quickly added, "Except they can't all have been discovered. Vadal City was the biggest settlement in the ancient world and has always been the primary center of trade, especially in magic. I'm still researching other possibilities but I'm sure I'll find something sufficient to satisfy our terms."

"I tire of waiting, Rada. The Capitol wonders why Vadal is still buried in filthy slothful casteless while the other houses have begun eliminating theirs. In fact, as untouchables have fled the other houses which have been obedient to the Law, our caste-less population has actually *grown*. Some among the first have even begun to question my personal adherence to the Law. Now Saksham tells me he believes your promise was nothing but a clever ploy to buy time for your beloved fish-eaters. My advisors think I'd be better off ignoring your claims, and let my wizards have your broken mirror to play with the pieces."

"That would be foolish."

"Oh?" Harta seemed more bemused than offended by that.

"I mean that you're clearly not a foolish man, Thakoor."

"It is more foolish to offend the powerful in exchange for nothing. I've postponed the Great Extermination based on what you said you could provide in exchange. You have failed to hold up your part. Why should I continue to wait?"

"Because you know I'm smarter than your wizards."

Harta chuckled. "A bold claim ... Probably accurate, for what it's worth. Whether you'll admit it or not, your time in my court has been good for you. You actually speak with the confidence of a proper member of the first caste now."

Grudgingly, Rada knew that was true. She'd grown up in a powerful and connected family but had always been far more interested in her obligation to the Library than participating in the vicious first-caste games surrounding it. Harta was a master of such things and seeing him in action—even as a hostage—had been supremely educational. Should she ever find herself back in the Capitol, she would be far better equipped to navigate that wilderness.

"However, there is another valuable lesson you must still learn, Rada ... Our caste never guarantees what is beyond our control. Otherwise, we become no better than the warriors with their hotheaded duels or the workers with their games of dice. The first must be above such things. If we do not honor our vows, then our word becomes meaningless. Our reputations, saltwater." Harta scowled as he spied a lone weed sprouting up from the perfectly level grass. He bent over and plucked it out, root and all. "A member of our caste who gains a reputation of weakness, of ineffectiveness, becomes useless." Then Harta held out the weed to show the leader of his guards. "Have the worker responsible for this part of the garden whipped."

"It'll be done, Thakoor."

Inwardly, Rada cursed her friend. *Damn it, Karno.* He'd asked Rada to trust him, and this was the result. She didn't even know what the strange thing hidden in the crypt did, Karno had sworn he couldn't tell her, and the Mirror held no answers either. What was the cost of this secret? How many casteless had already died across all of Lok because of her cowardice? How many more would have to die in Vadal before she took a stand?

"I beg you, Thakoor, please, grant me just a few more days."

Surely Harta could tell she was a bundle of nerves, as he was as good at reading human emotions as she was at reading books.

"In a week you will be accompanying me to the eastern border for the wedding of Phontho Jagdish. A celebration that I have been informed Raja Devedas will be attending. I'm sure your safe return to him there will be greatly appreciated."

As much as Rada liked Jagdish and Pari, saving innocent lives was the reason she'd volunteered to stay in Vadal lands, but Jagdish was an honorable man who would understand that and take no offense. "It's more important that I continue searching for what I've promised than it is for me to attend some party."

Harta shook his head. "Oh, poor naïve Rada. You've learned so much about the methods of your caste, yet the obvious eludes you. You're profoundly educated yet lacking in instinct about the real nature of things."

That provoked her rage, but she bit her tongue. She wanted to snap that she'd been chased by witch hunters, mercenaries, raiders, an army of tiny demons, and been bombarded with fire from the moon, so who was this perfumed prince to question her experience?

Yet she refrained. "Then educate me further, Lord Harta."

"Very well. The service you've provided my house warrants that much honesty, at least. You have failed me in one way, but that doesn't mean you are without other uses. Ideally, for Vadal's long-term survival, my house requires another sword, or equivalent black steel weapon. Not as important as that, yet still vital, I would prefer the deadly Raja Devedas to become an ally instead of a threat. You can aid me in this. He is in love with you, after all."

"What?" *How did Harta know?* "Not at all! I never—"

Harta held up one hand to silence her. "Please. His scarred face lies worse than your attractive one. Don't insult me with denials about secret affairs. I may not know your history, but it's plain Devedas cares deeply for you. I'm unused to dealing with someone who has power *and* honesty. He was forthright about his damning ambitions, yet tried to lie to me about how some librarian was merely a family friend. Even extremely dangerous men sometimes develop weaknesses of the heart."

That was simultaneously nice—for she'd not seen Devedas in a very long time, and it was good to hear he still loved her—but also terrifying, because Harta wouldn't hesitate to use that information to his advantage. "Devedas is a friend. I will say no more about our relationship."

"It also explains why he dispatched the fearsome Karno Uttara to protect you. Karno is a one-man army, yet that valuable asset watches over a single librarian. Devedas cares for you. You care for the plight of the casteless, oceans know why. I care only about the safety of my house. So if you want the fish-eaters of Vadal to continue breathing, you will whisper into your beloved's ear it is best to not place Vadal into a position where we must do something to those casteless that you'll regret."

"That wasn't our agreement."

"The non-people are already hostages awaiting the ransom you have failed to deliver. I have simply adjusted the terms. If you'd given me what you promised in a timely manner, we wouldn't be having this conversation now. I taught you how to be an advisor." Harta looked her in the eyes, unflinching, and lowered his voice to a dangerous whisper. "Now you will go and advise the man who would be king that *it is too costly to cross Great House Vadal.*" Then he smiled. "Come, let me demonstrate."

The Thakoor continued walking between the artistically trimmed shrubbery. Rada hurried and followed.

Several members of the personal guard were waiting at the rear of the estate, not too far from where the Asura's Mirror had once eaten a witch hunter's arm. Three large wagons were parked near the stable, guarded by many warriors. She had no idea of these warriors' station, but these uniforms were humble compared to the pristine attire of the personal guard that she was used to. As they got closer, a bad smell hit Rada's nostrils. It wasn't from the horses either, but rather it was the scent of human waste and sick, strong enough to overcome the natural perfume of the gardens. That stench was coming from the wagons.

Because she wasn't wearing her glasses, it took her a moment to realize the wagons were basically metal cages, packed tight with people who were too scared to even whimper.

"The Thakoor has arrived," one of the Personal Guard declared. "It's time to unload the cargo."

The other warriors hurried and unlatched the rear doors of a wagon that was so overfilled with bodies that as soon as the bars dropped several terrified casteless spilled out. Those sprawled upon the ground and covered their heads, afraid of further beatings. The warriors immediately grabbed those by their filthy rags and dragged them out of the way so they wouldn't get crushed by the rest who were being goaded out.

"What's going on?" Rada asked, but Harta said nothing. He simply watched as all three wagons vomited out a pile of feeble non-people. Slowly overwhelmed by an increasing dread, Rada realized that the wizard Saksham had arrived, and wore a gloating look on his narrow face. Saksham was accompanied by another, far older, wizard, a tiny man wearing a robe lined with black feathers, who walked with the aid of a cane. The old wizard appeared unmoved by this display. The noble warrior Luthra was among those near the wagons, but he looked ill, and was keeping his gaze averted, unwilling to meet her eyes because of his shame.

It took a while to get so many non-people out of the wagons and herded into a single group in front of the stable. As a child of the first, from the most sheltered of all cities, Rada had never seen so many casteless before. They were a filthy, sickly lot. It wasn't a cool night, but they were all shivering from fear. Her heart cried at their plight, even as she understood they were only here because of her.

"What are you going to do to these non-people, Thakoor?"

"That's entirely up to you, Rada...Saksham, come here."

The wizard approached and bowed. "Yes, my Thakoor."

"Restate your suspicions."

"I believe the librarian is lying to us. Her attitude abruptly changed during our search and her actions have been odd lately. Her Protector has a face of stone, but she does not. I believe she found something out there but chooses not to reveal it to us."

It was like an icy hand grabbed her stomach and twisted. "I would never! How dare you!"

"I thought I'd taught you better than that, Rada." Harta shook his head, accentuating his disappointment. "I was not lying when I said Vadal's fish-eaters have only been spared from the Capitol's wrath because of you. It saddens me that you'd doubt my word." He gestured toward the pathetic group. "Slay these vermin."

The warriors reluctantly drew their swords.

"Wait!"

"Oh, but I *have* been waiting." Harta regarded her with cold animosity. "I've been waiting with incredible patience, far beyond what my station should require. This is a handful. An example. A reminder that actions have consequences. I have hundreds of thousands more untouchables where these came from. This tiny culling is nothing compared to the Great Extermination, but hopefully this taste will be enough to remind you of your promises... *I said kill them.*"

The warriors started toward the mob. The casteless shrieked and cowered.

"I'll give you what you want!"

"I want Vadal safe and free. I'll do whatever I must to make sure it stays that way."

Swords rose.

"It's in the old Protector's tomb!"

Harta lifted one hand. His warriors paused.

"I knew it," Saksham crowed. He turned to the older wizard. "I told you so."

"*What* is in the Protector's tomb?" Harta asked.

Karno would hate her for this betrayal, but so be it. She couldn't bear the weight of one more drop of casteless blood on her conscience. "An intact device of black steel, easily massing as much as ten swords. I don't know what it does. It's well hidden behind a secret door in the back of the tomb near the urns."

Harta studied her, but Rada's spirit was clearly broken and she was doing her best not to weep. He reached out, with surprising gentleness, touched her chin, and made her look him in the eye. "It was foolish to test me, Rada. Why would you try to deceive me?"

"Because I told her to."

All eyes turned to see Karno Uttara striding from the garden. His presence startled and unnerved the Personal Guard, who clearly hadn't realized they'd been followed. Hands tightened upon the hilts of their already drawn swords.

With the war going on there was so much extra security within the walls of the Thakoor's estate that one shout would summon a multitude of reinforcements, both mundane and magical. A Protector could be brought down eventually, but that didn't mean much to those who would die first. Such was the nature of Protectors.

Sensing their nervousness, Karno slowly held out his open hands to show he was unarmed. "Leave her be. It was I who deceived you, Thakoor."

"I have offered you nothing but hospitality and respect, Protector. Why would you insult me like that?"

Karno stopped a polite distance from Harta, so as to not make the wizards too worried for their master's safety. Despite that, both of them had their hands clenched into fists, probably with bits of demon inside, prepared to inflict some manner of magical violence against the Protector if necessary.

Karno studied them, blinking slowly, seemingly not concerned in the least about being set on fire, before he addressed the Thakoor again. "As you'd do anything for the good of your house, I would do the same for my Order. The thing in that tomb is best left to the Protectors. I did not want you to be tempted to use something dangerous beyond your comprehension."

"The Law says that's not your decision to make. It is mine alone. Black steel isn't some meager property your Order can claim on a whim. It is a treasure, precious beyond all others."

"Correct..." Karno seemed to mull that over for a time and didn't like the taste of it. "The judges would most likely rule my attempt to keep it from you the same as robbery. So torment this woman no more. I'm the one who gave you offense."

Rada realized Karno was offering himself up to save her. Harta would be within his legal rights to have Karno killed as a thief. She looked between the two men, each incredibly frightening in their own way, and both too proud to yield. "Lord Harta, please—"

"Quiet," he snapped, never taking his eyes off dangerous Karno. "What does this device do?"

"I cannot tell you."

"Cannot, or will not? It doesn't matter. Whatever this thing is, it's valuable enough you'd risk ruining your name and bringing dishonor to your office to claim it. That means it should be more than sufficient to satisfy Rada's vow to me. I started the evening expecting to send a message by butchering a few score of casteless. Not a Protector...Casteless mean nothing, but a Protector's death would have ramifications I don't feel like dealing with currently. Thus your offense is forgiven, Karno Uttara."

Karno gave Harta a polite bow. Every warrior in the garden breathed a sigh of relief.

"Saksham, go and secure the device. Luthra, get this wretched trash out of my garden." For a moment Rada thought Harta meant her and Karno, but he was talking about the casteless, because next Harta addressed her politely. "I'm disappointed this is how our arrangement ends, but as you can see I am not entirely without mercy. I will do whatever is necessary to keep my house safe, but nothing more. Make sure your Raja understands that for all our sakes."

Then Harta Vadal simply walked away.

"You would've killed all of them, just to frighten me?" Rada shouted after him.

The Thakoor didn't bother to turn around. "You were already afraid. That's why I knew it would work."

Chapter 27

Outside a humble settlement in the desert, Ashok sat beneath the shade of a merchant wagon's canopy. He had given the worker who owned the wagon a few notes for his trouble and ordered him to come back at sundown and when the merchant had realized whom it was he was speaking to, he had taken those notes and fled into the hills to hide.

Horse was tied to the back of the wagon, greedily eating the merchant's oats. Ashok still struggled with the concept of money, and had little idea how much things should cost, but he would leave a few more bank notes in the wagon to pay for Horse's hunger.

This humble waypoint between the Capitol and Akara was called Shabdakosh, and existed for the simple fact it was one of the few places in the central desert with a decent well. Ashok had learned that not too long ago there had been a casteless uprising here, and tremendous bloodshed had been carried out in his name. Once again, Black-Hearted Ashok had inspired rebellion. The well had been poisoned, many workers had been murdered by fist or stone, and the first had been trapped and burned alive in their quarters.

No wonder the merchant had been so quick to run away when Ashok had told him his name.

In the distance, a lone rider approached along the trade road.

With eyes aided by the Heart of the Mountain, Ashok spotted the gleam of silver armor. Despite the heat—and it was always hot here—the Protector came prepared for conflict. Ashok knew from experience that being dressed in metal was miserable beneath this sun, but the Protector was sure to be suspicious. The message was urgent enough it could not be ignored, but its suspiciously dated cipher meant it wouldn't be fully trusted either. The private nature of the anonymous letter made it unlikely the Protector who received it would obligate any local warriors to unnecessarily involve them in private Order business.

Ashok had planned it that way.

He idly wondered which of his former brothers it would be. Hopefully, his letter had been delivered to one of the calmer ones. As loyal servants of the Law, any Protector would be required to try and kill him, but Protectors were valuable assets and weren't expected to throw their lives away pointlessly, either. If it was one of the young hotheads, Ashok would probably be forced to slay him, and then he'd have to try a different tack. This journey had already taken him away from the Sons and Thera for far too long as it was. He should have been accompanying her to the Cove instead of wasting time on this errand. He held no more loyalty to the Law that had used and manipulated him, but honor compelled him to at least give them this warning.

The rider was a large man on a very large horse. At first Ashok thought it might be Blunt Karno, but then he saw that the Protector was a bit thinner than that hulking beast of a man. Then he saw the Protector had a black scarf wrapped around his head in such a way that it draped over one eye, and that told Ashok who it was. Even the Heart couldn't regrow an eye when the fragments of bone around it had been removed entirely.

It was Protector of the Law and ten-year senior Broker Harban. An excellent combatant and very experienced Law enforcer, Broker was an unfortunate choice for this meeting, for he was a man of great passion and fury, and that had been before one of Gupta's gunners had launched a lead ball through his eye socket.

Ashok sighed and prepared himself for the inevitable duel.

A warm wind blew sand across the road. Vultures circled overhead. They must have sensed where Ashok went, death followed, and they would eat well. He still hoped that somehow today he would find a way to disappoint the carrion birds.

Surely Broker was using the Heart himself, searching for signs of ambush, but he would only see a lone man in humble worker attire sitting next to a wagon, face hidden beneath a straw hat. There were only a handful of Protectors who'd been born with the rare gift of sensing the presence of magic, and Broker was not among them.

Fifty feet away he shouted, "Greetings, worker. I am Protector of the Law, Broker Harban. I was told someone would be waiting at these crossroads with information for my Order. If it's you, speak up and collect your reward."

Ashok stood up and walked out of the shade. "I ask for no reward." He took off his hat and threw it into the back of the wagon. "The knowledge I have I give to you as a gift, and all I ask is that you accept it in peace."

To his credit, the Protector hid his surprise extremely well. "You're looking healthy for a corpse...Ashok."

"I come bearing a message for the Protector Order."

Broker reached for the gigantic mace that was secured to his saddle and pulled it free. His horse began to stamp nervously.

"Don't," Ashok warned. "The last time we fought, I was badly outnumbered, but I still prevailed."

"You were the bait in a criminal's trap. Your tricks took the lives of several good men that day."

"And every one of those deaths saddens me. That time you had a chance. Now you're alone."

"So are you," Broker answered.

"No. I'm not." Ashok drew forth Angruvadal and held it out, letting its negative light consume the bright desert sun.

Broker flinched, for there was no mistaking the deadly thing displayed before him. "Impossible!"

Once freed, Angruvadal wanted to know who it was supposed to destroy, but Ashok urged it to be still. "I killed that many of you without an ancestor blade. Imagine what I can do with this."

Ashok was unable to experience fear, but he could recognize when he inflicted it upon others. In that moment Broker must have realized if Ashok wanted to kill him, his life was simply over. A lesser man would have immediately fled, but Protectors were made of sterner stuff than that, and Broker held his ground. It was a good thing he didn't ride off, because Horse was clearly the superior animal, and Ashok would have added the insult of chasing him down.

"Calm yourself, Protector. I did not come all this way to fight, but rather to warn you of danger. A threat looms, far greater than me."

"Is that so?" Despite facing the most feared swordsman in the world, armed with an artifact legendary for its killing power, Broker dismounted anyway. He pulled off his scarf, revealing the ruined remains of his face. The area where his eye had been had healed into a mass of misshapen scar tissue. "Is this threat greater than the foul Fortress magic that your rebels have been spreading across the houses like a pox?"

"Yes. Much worse."

Ashok waited patiently while the Protector put on his helm and gauntlets and took up his shield. The metal rattled because of his shaking hands, but Broker still conducted himself as if he stood a chance. He had to admire his former brother's bravado to face certain death so willingly. The two of them had never been close, but his good friend Ishaan Harban—who Ashok had also been forced to kill—had always spoken highly of Broker's courage.

"Deliver this message quickly before I bash your Law-breaking head in, then."

"It does no good to tell you, only to kill you, because then I will have to repeat my warning to someone else."

"But I might win."

That actually made Ashok smile. "In that case, the Order needs to know what happened in Kanok was no fluke. It was a test. The demons did not walk there from the sea. They dug their way inland beneath the ground. I believe they will attack the Capitol the same way."

Broker stopped walking toward him and shook his head as if trying to clear his mind of this odd trick. "Why do you speak absurd lies?"

"I came here directly from Kanok."

"I heard five demons killed hundreds of workers and our lone Protector who was there."

"Then you have been lied to. It's more like dozens of demons killed thousands. Entire districts burned. I have seen the ancient tunnels the demons used to sneak there, and they are big enough to march armies through. I can sense that the demons are heading north beneath the desert. Where else would they be going, except the Capitol? Prepare your defenses."

"When is this impossible attack supposed to happen?"

"However long it takes the demons to clear the path and gather their forces, I suppose. All I know for certain is they are on the move. Our cities are no longer safe, no matter how far inland they are. You must warn the judges."

"The judges want your kind dead. Why would you tell me this?"

A good question. Ashok had tried and failed to articulate the need for this journey to Thera, and she understood him better than anyone else. He couldn't even really justify it to himself. The Capitol was their enemy, but sea demons were everyone's enemy. The Law would crush their rebellion, but the demons would devour all mankind. Ashok owed the Order this warning, not as a former Protector, but as a human being.

"I've come to despise the Capitol more than you could ever begin to understand, Broker Harban. Only, I hate demons more."

The two of them stood less than twenty feet apart, Broker armed with a mace that had shattered a great many skulls, and Ashok wielding a blade that was a magical slash through the fabric of the real world. The desert wind rose in intensity.

"I don't believe a word you're saying, traitor, but after I end your miserable life, I'll pass your nonsense on to wiser men to decide what to do with it."

"I'd rather not fight you at all, Broker. A living witness gives better testimony. Ancestor blades are not known for their mercy once crossed...though come to think of it, if Angruvadal decides you must die, then I can simply pin a letter to your body, and go home." Ashok nodded, satisfied at this logic. "A dead Protector should be enough to convince the Order of the seriousness of this threat."

The Protector's face was no longer visible because of his helm, but the casual way Ashok had just figured out how to carry out his mission regardless of Broker living or dying must have unnerved him a bit more, because the Protector hesitated. Despite that, Ashok could already tell how this was going to end, because Broker was a man of Law, and as such his pride could never abide letting a criminal as vile as Ashok go. He'd rather die than cower.

There was no announcing of offense. This wasn't a proper duel, as Ashok was not a whole man, worthy of such respect. Broker simply closed and attacked, shockingly quick for a man of such imposing size, but it still seemed ponderously slow to Ashok's profound new understanding of violence. The mace whistled through the air where Ashok's head had just been, then again, as Ashok danced aside. The steel spikes smashed a hole into the side of the merchant's wagon, but Ashok was already long gone by the time it landed. He supposed he would have to leave some bank notes to compensate for that damage as well. What was the cost of wooden planks?

Angruvadal wanted to destroy Broker, but Ashok's will was greater than the sword's desire to kill. The Protector roared and kept swinging as Ashok calmly circled across the packed dirt of the trade road. Broker struck with incredible fury, calling upon the Heart of the Mountain to drive his body ever faster. Not just limited to the mace, Broker also swung the edge of his round shield as a weapon. Ashok ducked beneath the shield, came back up, and slammed one naked fist into Broker's helm, hard enough to leave a deep dent. As the Protector staggered back, Ashok could have killed him ten times over, and they both knew it.

"How are you more skilled now than when we fought by the Akara River? It has to be that sword," Broker spat. "Put down that black steel and fight me, man to man!"

"So *now* a servant of the Law admits a casteless is a whole man?" When Angruvadal felt Ashok's flash of indignant anger it promptly presented him a multitude of options to take Broker's head, but he shoved those instincts back. Instead, he stabbed Angruvadal deep into the road, and left the sword planted there. He'd give the Protector what he asked for.

Broker immediately launched himself at Ashok. He ducked beneath the flashing mace and struck Broker hard in the side. Mail cut into Ashok's knuckles, but ribs cracked beneath the meat. Another strike was blocked by Ashok smacking his palm against Broker's wrist. Ashok caught the shield and twisted so hard that Broker had to let go to keep from losing his arm. Ashok slammed the stolen shield into Broker with enough force to fling him across the road and against a wagon wheel. Ashok would have to buy the merchant a whole new wagon at this rate.

Broker came at him again. Ashok blocked the blow with the stolen shield. The attacks kept coming. The Protector was extremely skilled. No regular man would have had a chance against so many rapid, bone-crushing strikes delivered with such perfect accuracy. Yet Ashok remained untroubled, waited for the right moment, then slammed the edge of the shield against the Protector's helm. Ashok promptly used that brief distraction to grab and toss the much larger man over his hip. Even though Broker was far heavier than Ashok, and clad in an additional seventy pounds of metal, he flung the Protector on his head.

With astonishing grace in so much armor, the Protector rolled right back to his feet. A dagger appeared in Broker's left hand. Westerners loved to fight with two weapons. Ashok dodged two more rapid strikes of the mace and three slashes of the blade. He caught a thrust aimed for his throat, and wrenched it around, snapping Broker's wrist. The Protector roared in pain. The blade landed in the sand with a thump. When Broker tried to bash him over the head with a desperate overhand blow, Ashok drove forward, caught the Protector around the midsection, hoisted him up, and slammed him down hard against the packed ground, flat on his back. Vertebrae popped.

He easily could have finished it then, but Ashok stepped away. "Get up."

Thanks to the fortifying magic of the Heart of the Mountain, Broker promptly did, and Ashok even allowed him time to retrieve the mace. Broker's other hand hung at an award angle, blood dripping down the fingers of his glove from where a wrist bone was sticking through the skin. Broker's breathing went ragged as he was forced to redirect the Heart of the Mountain from strengthening him, to repairing his many sudden injuries.

Ashok waited for the Protector to come at him again.

But his opponent paused, and when he spoke, he sounded truly bewildered. "When I was young, even in training, everyone knew you were the best of us. Whenever we sparred, I learned much, but I still thought you might be beatable. Only, I underestimated you, for in Garo, you were the most skilled fighter I've ever seen. Yet that was *nothing* compared to how you fight today. What are you now? How did you become *this*?"

"I am unsure myself," Ashok said truthfully, for the shard in his heart had changed his body in ways that he couldn't begin to understand. "You will hate me even more for this answer, but the fanatics believe it was their long-forgotten gods who made me this way, to serve as their warrior."

"That can't be real."

"Perhaps. All I do know for certain is that if you choose to continue this duel, I will most likely have to kill you. Then I think I would cut your head off, leave a folded note in your mouth, and order this merchant to deliver it to the Capitol. By the time another Protector decodes the cipher, I'll be a hundred miles away, so your death will be without meaning. My conscience will be troubled by the murder of one more former brother and the Capitol will remain unprepared to face an army of demons for that much longer."

Broker stood there, bleeding and in pain, weighing his options for a time, before saying, "I don't care for that plan."

"Nor I. There are too few honorable men in this world, and I have killed far too many of them as it is. I beg you to spare me from slaying from another. The choice is yours, Protector."

Broker took a deep breath to steady himself. Protectors would happily fight to the death, but they were trained to do so only when it was absolutely necessary. Otherwise they were wasting a valuable asset of the Law. They were too hard to replace to end their lives fruitlessly. Against such an insurmountable threat, the Order's own doctrine demanded that Broker retreat, regroup, and return with overwhelming force.

"There's been rumors out of Akershan that our job wasn't done. Once the Order knows for sure you're still alive, we'll be coming for you."

"I am aware. There is no dishonor in stopping this fight now, though. You are not defeated. You are merely choosing better ground so that you can fight me another day."

"Alright..." Honor satisfied, and with no doubt that Ashok would keep his word, Broker dropped his mace and reached up with his good hand to undo the mask of his helm so he could breathe better. On his mangled face was etched the relief of a man who understood his getting to live one more day was a gift. "I suppose I'll let you off with a warning, criminal."

That actually made Ashok snort. "Noted."

Broker would keep some small measure of his dignity today, but only fools would question the integrity of anyone who failed against unstoppable Ashok. "So Kanok's worse than I've been told and there's demons underground. Is there anything else to this warning?"

Ashok reached into this shirt and pulled out the letter he had written. "All I know is here."

The Protector took it. "You already had that note ready to stick in my decapitated head? You always were the efficient one."

In truth, Ashok hadn't thought of the beheading part until later. "Ride to Devedas. Tell him hell is on the way."

"Devedas is in Vadal."

"Then tell whoever commands the Capitol."

Broker paused, seeming more agonized by what he was about to admit than the bone sticking out of his skin. "Things are different now. The judges are in disarray, so the office of Lord Protector remains unfilled. Many of status have been accused of secretly supporting your rebellion. Hundreds of bodies decorate the Tower of Silence. A few of them might even have been guilty. The Inquisition governs while the Capitol is consumed by this conspiratorial madness."

"Omand..."

"From the Tower of Silence the Grand Inquisitor makes his whims into rules, woe unto any who balk, and the one man who might have the strength to resist them is away in the north." The Protector couldn't hide the disgust he was feeling and Ashok could recognize that for what it was now. This was the guilt a decent man experienced when his obligation put him at odds with what was just. Such a conflict between what was right and what was lawful was something Ashok should have felt decades ago, only he'd been incapable of it back then.

It was no longer Ashok's place, but he couldn't help but ask, "Why doesn't the Order do something about this?"

"It is a *legal* madness. The Order is scattered, occupied dealing with your rebels' Fortress rods turning up in the hands of the surviving fish-eaters in every great house..." Broker shook his head, knowing he'd admitted too much. "I'll say no more about our affairs to a criminal, but I will see to it the Capitol receives your warning."

Protectors didn't make promises, because the simple act of them saying a thing would be done was as powerful as a normal man's greatest vow. Broker would certainly return here with a multitude of obligated warriors to try and track Ashok down, but he would deliver the message first.

The defeated Protector was already walking back to his mount, and in a moment of human clarity Ashok realized that today was just the most recent defeat in a long line of defeats for this Protector. A bullet had taken his eye, the Law had taken his trust, and Ashok had just taken the last of his pride. Just as the Sons of the Black Sword had their dreams of freedom, were they any more naïve than a Protector's ideal vision of order?

"Broker, wait . . . Devedas holds a new office, but could you still get word to him as well?"

He stopped and glanced back over his shoulder, incredulous. "I have to. Devedas assured the world he killed you in a duel. He's going to lose his mind when informed you're still alive."

"Good. Coming from you, he will know I am no imposter. Tell Devedas it does not have to be this way. The casteless only want to live. The rebels simply want to worship their gods. If the Law can change enough to name him its ruler, it can change enough to let my people be free. Tell him . . . Ashok offers peace."

Chapter 28

Sometimes, it was good to be the Raja.

Devedas lay awake in bed as Rada slept next to him. Content, he listened to the heavy night rain against the fine glass windows and Rada's gentle breathing. Their reunion had been as joyous as he'd hoped. His worries had been for nothing. She had wept tears of joy at the sight of him, for Rada's heart had remained true to him the long time they'd been kept apart.

All was well.

The Capitol was cowed. His old enemies were dead. His current enemies feared him so much they sought to be his allies. He was beloved by the people. Soon enough he would be crowned king, and this faithful woman by his side would be his queen. Rada didn't even know about his plans yet, for she was too honest to be corrupted by involving her in his conspiracies. After his ascension he would be free to lead Lok into a glorious new age, unbound by the corrupt traditions of the past.

The finest estate in Mukesh had been given to Devedas and his Capitol delegation to use for as long as he decided to stay here. The judge the estate belonged to had been sent away, because what was the status of a judge compared to a Raja? It gave Devedas a place to rest, satisfied and triumphant, as he contemplated the scope of his achievements and the greatness that was to come.

Except there was one other thing he still had to attend to, and he wouldn't be able to sleep until it was dealt with. So, careful to not disturb Rada's sleep, Devedas got out of bed, grabbed one of the judge's fine silk robes, and slipped out of the room.

Four Garo warriors were in the hall, guarding his door.

"Where is Karno Uttara?"

"Last I saw he was on the courtyard balcony watching the storm, Raja."

He started walking that way and the warriors began following him, but Devedas told them, "See to it Rada is not disturbed. From now on you will guard her life as if it were mine." Then he couldn't help but grin, because soon enough, they *would* be the same life, and that thought brought him joy.

Rain was pounding the courtyard as Devedas made his way through the unfamiliar estate—Vadal properties tended to be outlandishly gigantic compared to all the other houses—until he found Karno. The big Protector was sprawled on some cushions, sitting beneath an awning that was spewing water from the drain spouts on the side. Karno didn't seem to care about the damp or the chill. Having lost his armor and regalia along the way, he was dressed in a simple Vadal uniform with the insignia pulled off. They'd probably had to scramble to find the biggest warrior in the great house and then robbed his closet to properly fit Karno.

As a bolt of lightning crashed across the sky, Karno took a swig from the bottle in his hand. "Lord Protector." He didn't need to turn around to recognize who had quietly approached.

"That office is currently unfilled, but it was good to see you today, brother." Devedas walked out onto the balcony and sat on the pile of pillows across from Karno. Devedas didn't mind the cold either. This was downright pleasant compared to his homeland. "Once again, you have my thanks for keeping Rada safe."

"It was my duty."

"No, truly. She told me much about your adventures today. When I sent her off I never expected so much trouble to find her. I believe if I'd entrusted her to a lesser Protector, she wouldn't be alive to be reunited with me now... Thank you."

Karno nodded but did not reply. He had always been a man of few words.

Earlier, Devedas had listened to Rada's tales about trying to atone for her part in the Great Extermination, and it had made him appreciate her character even more. It was good for a man wielding absolute power over so many to have someone so moral as his wife. Devedas was practical. Rada was charitable. Everyone like him needed someone like her to bring balance to their life. Perhaps if his fellow conspirator Omand wasn't alone he wouldn't have turned into such a vile bastard, but realistically there was probably no woman alive who could have moderated such a malicious creature.

"I'm forever in your debt, old friend, but I sought you out because there is still another matter. My staff includes several wizards and they've assured me they can keep this estate free from magical spies, so we can speak freely now about what you found in Vadal City."

"A second heart." Karno grunted. "Who would have thought such a thing could be? Except Vadal has it now."

"Yes, Rada told me."

"She did nothing wrong."

"I know. The rules of decorum kept Harta from threatening her physically, but he's bastard enough to water the grass with fish-eater blood just to send me a message."

"I should not have put her in a moral predicament."

"Don't worry, Karno. Vadal doesn't understand what they have, and they'll not have it for long enough to figure it out."

Now Karno looked over at him, curious.

"They don't have our Order's secret knowledge. If that heart is anything like ours, it will take their wizards years to puzzle out how to access its power, and they have no way to move it safely in the meantime. This is the Raja's jurisdiction now. I'll not speak of my plans further, but an item of such importance cannot belong to a single great house. Events have been set in motion to make sure it is secured for the Capitol's gain."

"By treaty? Or by sword?"

Devedas shrugged. "Ultimately, they're the same thing."

"And when you claim the artifact will be taken for the Capitol's gain, do you speak of the Law? Or yourself?"

Devedas bristled at that insinuation. "Again, they are one and the same. That second heart will provide the foundation for a new, elite Order, which will force all the castes and houses to heed the will of my new office, ensuring their respect and obedience." It went unsaid that having such an Order loyal to him alone would negate the might of the Inquisition, enabling Devadas to keep dangerous Omand in his place.

"So you're the Law now, are you?" Karno shook his head, chuckled sardonically, and took another drink. "Oceans. It's worse than I feared, then."

Devedas didn't like where this conversation was treading, but there was a reason he'd earned the name *Blunt* Karno. Anyone who expected less than brutal honesty from Blunt Karno was doomed to disappointment. "It's true the Capitol has gone through many changes since you've been away, but all is well now. Speak your concerns."

"I don't think either of us would like that, *Raja*." Karno said his title with obvious distaste.

That was an unexpected sleight. "You're obligated to serve the Law, Karno. The Raja is the supreme arbiter of the Law now. My position is legal and official. That was the judges' decision to make."

"Did the judges make it? Or was that decision made for them? Your own men have confirmed to me the rumors of tyranny in the Capitol are true. It is convenient how the circumstances were perfect for your ascension."

Karno had always been far too clever for his own good, and the best among them at sniffing out criminals. Even isolated far from the conspiracy, Karno was still suspicious about the nature of Devedas' promotion. It should not have surprised Devedas, but it did annoy him. "You have my gratitude for your service, Karno, but do not try my patience with disrespect. The Law evolves. It is written by men, on paper, not carved into stone. Your obligation is not to the Law that was, but the Law that exists today."

"I broke the Law for you," Karno responded with far more bitter emotion than Devedas had ever heard from him before. "I tried to hide the second heart from Vadal, and in doing so I put my charge's honor and maybe even her life at risk. All because I trusted you to do what was right."

"I *am* doing what's right!"

"That's what you tell yourself to justify anything you do, but you've always been cursed by that damnable ambition of yours. That ambition was what made you one of our greatest Protectors, second only to Ashok. Except Ashok's service was one of humility. He had nothing to prove to anyone but his sword, while you had everything to prove to everyone, from untouchable to judge, with a chip on your shoulder the size of a Devakulan glacier. The Law declares *every man has his place,* but that was never enough for you. Your restless pride would accept nothing less than to rule the world."

Devedas was suddenly flushed with anger. "Better me than them! The judges were fools, aloof and distant from the costs of their edicts. So now their time is done. You know it! I know it! Every Protector saw their flaws."

"And we accepted them, Devedas, because our duty is to serve the Law as it is, not the Law as we imagined it should be!"

"Are you accusing me of some crime, Protector Karno? Choose your words carefully."

That warning was unnecessary, because Karno spoke so sparingly that every word that left his mouth was always carefully weighed first. For how long Karno considered his response, each of these words was heavier than lead. "I accuse you of *nothing.* For what good does it do to accuse a man of a crime, when he is the only man left who determines what crime is?"

"This is real life, not one of Master Mindarin's philosophy lessons."

"If only you'd paid more attention to those, perhaps we wouldn't be here now." Karno abruptly stood up. For just a moment, Devedas wondered if Karno would be foolish enough to try and arrest him here, but with one shout of alarm fifty Garo would rush to the courtyard to aid their master. But Karno just bitterly chugged the rest of his wine, then tossed the empty bottle over the edge of the balcony to land with a splash in the puddles below. Devedas had seen Karno frustrated, injured, and exhausted, but never before had he seen him defeated.

"What's done is done, Devedas. The Law has spoken. Lok is your plaything now. Try not to ruin it."

"*How dare you!* I was going to offer you the office of Lord Protector tonight, and instead you spit on my gratitude."

Karno walked out into the rain.

"Where are you going?"

"Back to Uttara, I suppose. My years of obligation to the Order have been met. My service is done. If our Law is meaningless, I will no longer give my life to protect it."

This betrayal wounded Devedas more than he'd ever admit.

"Then run back to your poor country house and be a farmer or herd sheep for the rest of your days! Stay far from my sight, never meddle in my affairs, and I'll allow you to live in peace, but if you challenge my rule, I will destroy you." Karno was getting farther away, so Devedas raised his voice to be heard over the distant thunder. "Because you were right about one thing: *I am the Law now!*"

Karno paused for a moment, looked back at Devedas, and shook his shaggy head in resignation. "You are not worthy of her."

Stung into silence, Devedas watched his old friend walk away.

Sometimes, it was hard to be the Raja.

Chapter 29

⟿⟿⟿⟿

Jagdish's second wedding was nothing at all like his first. That ceremony had been a humble affair between a disgraced warrior and a worker girl to seal a contract supplying bread. The witnesses had consisted of Pakpa's worker family and a handful of Jagdish's warrior comrades. An arbiter had put his seal on the treaty and declared he and Pakpa were now husband and wife according to the Law. Afterward they'd thrown a party, and the only thing special about it had been the incredible variety of sugary treats because Pakpa's family were mostly bakers and very competitive to see who could come up with the most delicious thing. Then he and Pakpa had gone back to the tiny house the warrior caste had issued him and begun their life together.

In stark contrast to that humble beginning, today had been a spectacle of color, music, feasting, and chaos as thousands of guests had invaded the Mukesh warrior district. Jagdish was a beloved hero, his name known by every warrior in Vadal, and as many warriors as could make it arrived to pay their respects. Everyone else in the region who didn't know him or Shakti had still shown up for the free food and dancing. The estate of Phontho Gotama had been turned into a resort for the highest-status guests to stay in comfort, while the parade ground had been made into a festival area full of tents for those of low enough status to be outside, but even then, fate had been kind, and gifted them with clear skies.

Their glorious Thakoor and his contingent had brought with them important diplomatic guests—including the new Raja himself— so Great House Vadal's wealth needed to be accentuated for the outsiders. The local judges had opened the treasury and the notes had rained down harder than the monsoon. Great House Vadal was known for being vibrant and extravagant so it could not disappoint its guests, so the humble border city of Mukesh was visited with a spectacle the likes of which it had not seen in generations.

Jagdish had met many important people in the three days of celebration leading up to the actual ceremony. Most of them wouldn't have considered his life worth saltwater a couple of years ago, but today he was a *very important man*—Harta's presence confirmed that—so they sucked up to Jagdish harder than a junior risalder on his first obligation. There were lunches and dinners and parties and drinking and proposals and promises and a great deal of flattery and carrying on, all of which Jagdish would have avoided if possible. He much preferred being at war to being in the courts. War was far more honest.

As for his war, it was on hold, as the house of the wolf had been quiet since Daula's defeat. Jagdish had been trouncing them so consistently that the Sarnobat were probably happy Vadal's most effective general was taking some time away from the front. Jagdish's honeymoon would give them time to regroup and lick their wounds. If it had been up to him, he'd be married one day and back to raiding the next, except that the presence of their Thakoor and the Capitol delegation had turned his wedding into a lengthy event. Those Sarnobat dogs should have sent him a wedding gift in thanks.

Poor Shakti had run herself to near exhaustion in preparation for this event. Jagdish had it easy in comparison. All he had to do was command an army and win a war. Harta had ordered the local first caste to help her—and they would die of shame if they failed him—but Shakti considered the first lazy and useless so had insisted on handling most of the details herself. She'd been so busy before the wedding—organizing, making deals, and being charming to the various high-status visitors—that he'd barely seen his bride-to-be at all.

Yet that morning when she walked into the Arbiter's Hall, escorted on the arm of her proud father Gotama, Shakti had been so poised and beautiful in her flowing dress of silks and jewels and flowers and precious sparkly things that she had stolen his breath away. If there were no gods, how was he marrying a goddess? Jagdish had been waiting before the judge in his finest uniform, wearing the highest award for valor that Great House Vadal could bestow on his chest, and stars of rank on his turban, yet he had still looked like dirt in comparison to his bride. As was proper!

As the judge had rambled through his speech, he'd gone unheard, because Jagdish had been too busy holding Shakti's hands, and grinning like a fool as he stared adoringly into her loving eyes. Jagdish was happy, and in that moment, had known that life was good, and all was well.

A dozen people had watched Jagdish's first wedding. A thousand watched his second. Both times he'd barely noticed any of them were even there.

At dinner that evening, Jagdish sat on a cushion next to his new bride, at a table with some of the most impressive names in Lok. It was the greatest food he'd ever tasted. He had seen and smelled some truly fancy dishes while serving in the Personal Guard of Great House Vadal, for it was said Bidaya Vadal had the finest chefs in the world, but it hadn't been like a lowly soldier had ever been allowed to actually taste any of it. The Thakoor and immediate family had food tasters to watch out for poison, so even some of their house slaves ate better than their soldiers.

Across the table from him was Thakoor Harta Vadal, who was engaged in an animated conversation with some diplomats from the Capitol, and the Thakoor's wife, Dharinee, who turned out to be a beautiful yet aloof lady who spoke little yet sneered a lot. Even charismatic Shakti had a difficult time making conversation with her, and Jagdish suspected Shakti could charm the bark off a tree.

This party was probably the costliest endeavor that Jagdish had ever been involved in—and he had a legion of troops to feed—yet their Thakoor's wife still looked down upon Mukesh like it was a slum, the warriors as if they were casteless, and the astounding feast before them as if it were pig slop. It was clear she was only here because her husband had commanded it. She'd even examined the cushions with distaste before sitting down, as if the grunge of this poor eastern city might stain her dress. Yet the first caste wasn't all bad, as demonstrated by the lovely lady sitting next to Shakti. If more of the first were like Radamantha Nems dar Harban and less like Dharinee, the warrior caste wouldn't resent them. While most of the first regarded the other castes with nothing but contempt, Jagdish had watched Rada, without hesitation, pitch in to carry buckets of water to fight a fire in his estate, as if she were no better than the lowliest worker. Her mind turned as quickly as the marvelous gears in his pocket watch, and she'd demonstrated that she could remember everything she'd ever read. Odds were she had the sharpest mind of anyone in the room, yet she never acted as if that made her better than anyone else.

Jagdish figured that if the rest of her caste were more like Rada, and less like the Thakoor's wife—who was currently berating one of the slaves for serving her a strawberry that was of perfectly uniform coloring—Lok would be a much better place.

Next to Rada was Devedas, whom Jagdish knew by reputation alone. Despite being a bit shorter than Jagdish—southerners were not known for their height—the Raja was an imposing man. He had that kind of square jaw and handsome face that sculptors liked to imagine all great heroes possessed, but one side was split by a scar so brutal that, rather than making him ugly, instead suggested he had survived things that would've killed any lesser man.

The others around this prestigious table were politicians. Devedas was a fellow soldier, but also something more. He smiled easily and laughed at the jokes and clever banter, yet there was always a dangerous energy about him that suggested capability beyond mortal understanding. Jagdish had felt the same thing around Ashok, and later, Blunt Karno. Jagdish was a warrior, but Protectors were perfect killers, apex predators. There was a difference. One was a job. The other was a calling and a curse.

Devedas caught Jagdish studying him, not as an adoring ass kisser as most of the crowd had been all night, but rather scrutinizing him as a duelist would.

"So, Phontho Jagdish...I've been told you spent a year sparring with Ashok, nearly every day, while he was in Cold Stream Prison."

The mention of that hated name caused everyone seated around their table of luminaries to stop their conversations. All eyes were upon him.

"That's true. I did." Jagdish was too honest for his own good, but the truth was the truth. "Practicing against him made me a far better swordsman."

"Me as well," Devedas agreed. "Fighting Ashok is like fighting a whirlwind that can see into the future."

Harta openly scowled as Devedas so casually named the man who'd been the death of his mother, the breaker of his family's sword, and the blight of his house.

"He spoke highly of sword your skills as well, Raja Devedas." Then Jagdish added sadly, "I suppose in the end, you proved which of you was the better duelist."

Just as Jagdish had sized up Devedas, Devedas was doing the same to him. Protectors possessed incredible physical powers, but also had to develop a keen awareness necessary to recognize threats. Jagdish must have passed muster, because Devedas gave him a nod of respect. Someone like him acknowledging Jagdish as a potential challenge was perhaps the finest compliment he'd gotten this entire celebration. Thankfully, their illustrious guest decided to drop that line of awkward conversation—because Jagdish knew of no way he could continue talking about his dead friend Ashok without offending his Thakoor or the man who'd killed him—and the Raja turned his attention back to Harta.

Rada leaned in toward Shakti and Jagdish. "I'm so happy for you two. I'm leaving with Devedas in the morning to go back to the Capitol, but I was wondering if I could say goodbye to little Pari before I go?"

"Of course," Jagdish said. "She'd love to see you. I thought about having her at the head table with us for this banquet, but it was pointed out to me that she's got a nasty habit of rubbing her food in her hair."

"I assumed some of our guests might not appreciate the table manners of a youngster," Shakti whispered, but didn't dare look in the direction of their Thakoor's snooty wife. "Can you imagine the offense if she started throwing her vegetables at people again?"

A golden-masked and black-robed Inquisitor approached the table, and Jagdish couldn't help but think to himself, *Oh, here we go.* Leave it to that pack of vultures to interrupt one of the two happiest days in his life. Shakti, knowing how much he disliked their kind, reached under the table and gave his hand a squeeze, urging patience.

"Why do you interrupt our meal?" Harta asked. "Inquisitor…"

"Senior Inquisitor Taraba."

"Hold on," Jagdish said. "Taraba… We've met before."

The mask turned his way. From behind it came a young man's voice. "I'm sorry, Phontho. I don't recall that."

"Understandable." Jagdish had been a mere disgraced risalder when this one had danced around accusing him of treason. Oh, the irony that it would be the same bastard interrupting his wedding feast all these years later.

Taraba bowed to the Thakoor. "Please accept my humble apologies for disturbing you. I have an urgent message for Raja Devedas from the Capitol."

"Ah, the Raja's work is never done." Devedas sighed, signaling the Inquisitor to come closer. "What is it?"

"It is of a sensitive nature, Lord Raja, for you only."

"He means no offense, Harta," Devedas assured the Thakoor.

"Do as you must, Devedas. I would hope the Capitol would show such discretion when talking about the affairs of my house in front of others. Their history at such courtesy has been sorely lacking."

The Inquisitor bent down to whisper into the Raja's ear. Devedas listened, displaying no emotion, but then something Taraba said suddenly made him twitch. As the message went on, Devedas' jovial façade continued to slip. Though trying not to show it, it was clear the news both angered and worried him.

"This is certain?"

The Inquisitor stepped back and nodded.

"Saltwater…"

"What's wrong?" Rada asked.

"An issue requires my attention." Devedas threw his napkin on the table and said to Harta, "It appears my long journey back to the Capitol can't be delayed until tomorrow. I must depart immediately."

"A pity." Harta seemed intrigued by this development. "However, I am glad we part as friends."

"As am I." Devedas stood. *"Hear me, Vadal."* And since Devedas spoke with a commander's voice, the entire hall stopped talking so they could listen to what the important man had to say. He held his glass of wine up. "The courage of Jagdish is a testament to the quality of your house's warrior caste. Let us salute the warriors of Vadal, who have so capably defended this blessed land."

Everyone else lifted their glasses in response. "Great are our warriors," Harta heartily agreed, probably because there were many high-ranking officers seated at the nearby tables, and it would make them happy to hear their Thakoor praise them. "Let it be known that Great House Vadal respects all who fulfill their obligations, from the newest nayak to the mighty Raja, who has spent his entire life in service of the Law and every house of Lok."

Devedas accepted the public compliment gracefully. "You honor me, Thakoor." And then demonstrated that Harta wasn't the only one who understood the power of having an audience. "And as your Raja, I am greatly pleased to announce that the demonic threat which caused the judges to send me to these lands has been capably dealt with by your warriors."

"Well, the warriors and one librarian..." Rada muttered, but she did so low enough that only the people immediately nearby heard her.

"And one brave librarian," Devedas immediately added with a smile, which caused many in the audience to laugh. Rada, who never expected public accolades, blushed. "My duties in Vadal have been fulfilled, thus I will be returning to my Army of Many Houses. We will depart Vadal and return to the Capitol, where I will inform the judges that Vadal remains strong, under wise leadership, and utterly devoted to the Law." Devedas bowed toward Harta. "Thank you for your hospitality, Thakoor Vadal." Then toward Jagdish and Shakti. "And congratulations to your family."

As the people cheered him, Devedas put down his glass, untasted. "Alert the men, we leave immediately."

Inquisitor Taraba bowed once more, then walked quickly from the room. Since Devedas had brought a small army with him, and they too must have been enjoying the pleasures of a citywide celebration, that sudden order was going to upset a lot of soldiers. Such was a warrior's life.

"That was abrupt," Harta said, knowing no one beyond the table would hear him over the clapping of the crowd. "You don't strike me as prone to theatrics like so many of our caste, so the situation must truly be dire."

"It might be. I'll know soon enough."

"We've been lucky so far this season, but traveling after dusk this time of year you could get caught in a storm," Jagdish warned.

"Then we will ride in the rain."

"In a Vadal monsoon, it would be more like swimming. At least let me send a few paltans to escort you."

"Do you think I or my men are incapable?"

Jagdish had meant no insult. "I just mean, we're in the borderlands, there could still be Sarnobat raiders lurking about."

"The Sarnobat are your enemies, not mine. Only a foolish house would risk angering the Capitol." Devedas looked suspiciously toward Harta as he said that, then offered Rada his hand. "We must go."

The goodbyes were quick. Rada asked Jagdish to give Pari a hug for her.

Chapter 30

The Raja and his men rode south by torchlight, but upon reaching a crossroads on the trade road, they unexpectedly turned east.

Rada was pleased that she'd learned enough about navigation during her travels with Karno that she could actually tell which way they were going by the stars above. When she'd first left the Capitol she'd spent a lot of time being hopelessly lost, barely able to tell up from down, let alone the points on the compass. Karno had been a patient teacher who had insisted she learn how to survive on her own, rather than counting on others to always do the difficult or uncomfortable things for her, as was common for members of her caste. Rada recognized now that it was far too easy for the first to be carried about, pampered by slaves, and having everything done for them, which kept them ignorant about the world that they were supposed to manage, and insulated from the consequences of their decisions. It was doubtful any of her family or fellow librarians would have realized they were changing direction and heading toward the border with Great House Sarnobat.

Rada urged her mount to a gallop so she could catch up with Devedas at the head of their column. The sullen Garo he'd appointed to be her bodyguards grudgingly followed after her.

The big moon, Canda, was bright and the clouds had parted,

so they had been making excellent time and had already put several miles between them and Mukesh. Devedas was riding alongside his advisors when Rada thundered up next to them. He turned back, annoyed at the interruption, until he saw that it was Rada and smiled.

"No book taught you to ride a horse like that!"

She had in fact read a few books about horsemanship, and Father had once paid for her to take lessons in the Capitol—which had not gone well at all—but it was Karno who had truly taught her how to handle and properly care for a horse to the point that she actually rather enjoyed riding them. Which was why she'd eschewed the offered carriages that were currently carrying the rest of the Raja's diplomats and courtiers. She'd died at the thought of having to sit trapped inside one while listening to their inane courtly gossip all the way to Apura. Oddly enough, Rada felt more kinship with the warrior caste than her own people now.

"I got a lot of practice while we were apart."

"I can see that. Most impressive. When we're settled in at the Capitol, I'll see to it you've got a stable filled with the finest horses from Zarger and Akershan. You can ride around the city whenever you feel like it."

That was rather sweet of him. "This isn't the road to Apura. Why are we crossing into Sarnobat?"

"Ah." Devedas waved his advisors and bodyguards away. "Leave the two of us be."

They obediently fell back, so that Rada's horse could walk side by side with Devedas' steed. "Forgive my hesitancy, my love, but the last time I dealt with the wolves of Sarnobat they set the estate I was staying in ablaze while shooting arrows at me."

"It's the long way around, but it's the path the warriors of Vadal will be most hesitant to chase us across."

"We were just their guests. Why would they be pursuing us?"

"Because my abrupt departure ruined their plans. I was informed the Vadal intended to assassinate me back in Mukesh."

Rada gasped. "That's absurd. Jagdish is my friend."

"He'd serve his house however he's ordered to. He'll do as he was told, as would any warrior."

"No. Jagdish is a man of honor. I've seen it myself. He does what he thinks is just, no matter the risk. If you don't believe me, ask Karno."

"There's no need. If you say it is so, I believe you. I'm sure Karno would agree, but I've sent him off on another secret mission."

"It saddens me that I wasn't even able to tell Karno goodbye."

"I know, but that's the nature of a Protector's duty, and Karno is a tireless defender of the Law. If it comforts you to think Jagdish wouldn't stoop so low, I doubt he'd have any hand in my murder. If he's half as honorable as you insist he is, they probably didn't even tell him of this plot against me. I assume it was Harta who gave the order."

"That's what your Inquisitor told you?"

"Yes. They discovered that a horde of assassins and illegal wizards have gathered in Mukesh, and they were planning to strike tonight, murdering us as we slept in the beds Vadal gave us."

Rada looked around, to make sure no one was close enough to eavesdrop on them. "And you believe an Inquisitor? The very same lying Order that's repeatedly tried to capture me, to bake upon their dome while vultures pick out my eyes?"

"I am deeply ashamed that my actions ever placed you in danger. It will not happen again," Devedas assured her with great solemnity. "The Inquisition are never to be trusted fully, but I've made it so they are no longer our enemies. It's complicated. I'll explain everything when we have time and there aren't so many of them around. Don't worry, I'm not foolish enough to take anything at face value from men who refuse to show their faces. What Taraba told me at dinner matches too well what my own spies had already discovered. I accepted this invitation, suspecting it was a trap, and you were the bait."

"You came for me anyway."

"Of course, but I did so warily. It's like when I was a boy, when you venture out to hunt the white bears, you know they're hunting you back. This was the same. I had my men watching for danger, and they found signs of strangers skulking about the city, foreigners who were not of Vadal, some with the stink of magic on them, always lurking in the shadows watching the estates the Capitol delegates were staying in... During this, the Inquisition was doing its own hunt. Taraba claims they grabbed one of these lurkers off the street and tortured him until he confessed that they were being paid by Vadal to kill me, tonight. And here I'd thought Harta and I had come to an understanding. I can only assume he must have discovered I was plotting to seize the black steel heart you found in Vadal City from him."

Rada was appalled by all this subterfuge. "Harta gave me his word that giving him that artifact would spare Vadal's casteless!"

"When last we met, you much preferred the company of your books to any people. Now you've appointed yourself guardian of the untouchables, who aren't even people at all."

"It's my fault they're in danger to begin with."

Devedas smiled. "I don't mean offense. I admire you for trying to make things right. It's what caught my attention about you to begin with. Well, that and being stunning and formidably intelligent."

Damn Devedas for being so charming. Now was not the time. "If you take the black steel from Harta, what's to stop him from—"

"He's a Thakoor, Rada. His words are worth saltwater the instant any promise he's made becomes inconvenient to his house. There's nothing to stop him from doing anything he feels like except by force or the threat of it."

None of this made any sense to her. Why would Harta try to convince her to persuade Devedas into respecting Vadal, if he only intended to assassinate him a few days after they were reunited? "If you were murdered while a guest of Vadal, all suspicion would fall upon them. They'd certainly be blamed. The Capitol would be furious."

"Vadal would surely deny responsibility and blame it on Sarnobat. Mukesh is a border city and they're at war. I assume those assassins were probably ordered to kill as many notable Vadal citizens as necessary to sell this story to the world. That's what I would do."

That's what I would do? Rada didn't like that at all. The Devedas she had known had been determined, but not conniving. Rada prided herself on being more analytical than emotional. In fact, in her youth she'd often been teased for being too much of a brain and not enough of a heart. Her affair with Devedas had been the first time in her life her heart had won over her brain. She loved him, yet something had changed while they'd been apart, and that difference between him then and him now nagged at the edge of her mind.

"So innocent people are going to be murdered tonight and we just leave them to it?"

"If I was the main target, there should be no attack now. By retreating unexpectedly, I upset their plans, and Harta will call off his assassins . . . Though it says much about your kind nature that you'd still care what happens to any of the Vadal, even after they kept you as a hostage and confiscated your black steel mirror."

That theft galled her still. Historian Vikram Akershan had obligated her to carry the Asura's Mirror, so losing it was a stain on her and the Library's honor. "I understand much better now that politics are cruel, Devedas. The last few years of my life have consisted of getting kicked back and forth like a child's ball in some kind of game I don't even understand. Yet that doesn't mean I approve of the slaughter of those who had nothing to do with those decisions."

"Again, I'm sorry you've been through so much." Devedas reached over and touched her arm to assure her. "There're great events upon us, but I'll see us through. This isn't the place to speak of my plans, but you must trust me, Rada."

Of course she trusted him . . . or at least that's what she told herself at the time, and her heart was rather convincing. They continued riding together in silence, with Rada afraid to ask exactly what had transpired while she'd been away, and Devedas seemingly hesitant to explain. They passed through a border checkpoint that had recently been burned to the ground. The Vadal soldiers guarding the place seemed confused by the presence of so many Capitol soldiers, but once they realized who they were dealing with, let Devedas pass without issue.

An hour later, their column rounded a bend and Rada was shocked to discover that an entire legion of Sarnobat raiders was camped in the farmland ahead of them. There had to be thousands of them.

Rather than being alarmed, Devedas seemed relieved to see all those soldiers waiting there. "Perfect. Right where they're supposed to be."

These men must have been assembled here days ago, long before Devedas had been warned of the assassination plot against him. When he saw her surprise, he said, "The Raja commands an Army of Many Houses, Rada. Sarnobat is one of them. Now I will use them to teach Vadal a lesson about the value of loyalty, and the dangers of treachery."

Chapter 31

Shakti's scream woke Jagdish.

A shadow loomed over his bed. There was a glint of steel as a curved blade rose. By reflex, Jagdish reflexively kicked, planting his heel hard into a man's belly. He was rewarded with a pained grunt, and the sword slashed feathers from the pillow next to Jagdish's ear.

Even with senses dulled by wine and slumber, Jagdish still possessed a border scout's instincts and had come awake instantly, ready to fight. The sliver of moonlight coming through the curtains showed him an attacker, dressed all in black, with a Sarnobat scimitar in hand.

"Guards!" Shakti cried out. "Guards!"

Jagdish grabbed hold of their sheet and hurled it at the assassin, who promptly slashed it from the air. Jagdish was already moving directly behind the obscuring silks to leap over the descending blade. He tackled the assassin, and they crashed to the floor, rolling. Unusable so close, the long blade was discarded, and the assassin desperately reached for a dagger at his waist. Jagdish caught his wrist and squeezed as hard as he could, trying to control the weapon hand as he leveraged his way into a superior position.

Vadal warriors prided themselves on being good grapplers.

Whatever house this intruder was from clearly did not, for Jagdish easily maneuvered him onto his back, then promptly used his knee to pin one arm. As soon as the intruder was trapped, Jagdish began pummeling him, fists raining down, striking him in the face again and again.

The attacker's head was wrapped in a scarf to obscure his features, but that didn't matter, because Jagdish hit him so many times, so hard, that he'd be unrecognizable to his own mother anyway. Driven by an incredible fury that someone had invaded the sanctity of his bedchamber to threaten his wife's life on the very night of their wedding, Jagdish broke nose, cheek, teeth, and jaw, and once the assassin's clawing hand dropped away, unconscious, Jagdish grabbed him on each side of the head and slammed his skull against the wooden floor until it broke open and a puddle of blood began to spread.

Hands throbbing, Jagdish got to his feet, and turned back to Shakti to gasp, "Are you alright?"

She answered by tossing him his sheathed sword. He caught it.

He had no idea what time it was, but it felt like the quiet hour right before dawn, when sleep was the deepest and a raider's victims were the most vulnerable. Shakti had called for help, but no one had come running. His guards should have been here by now.

Jagdish crept to the door, opened it a crack, and peered down the dimly lit hall.

There were bodies sprawled on the rugs, lying with the stillness of death. Cloaked and hooded figures were creeping up the stairs from the courtyard below. Someone had heard Shakti's cries, but these weren't his warriors who were coming to help.

Closing the door, Jagdish whispered, "The guards are dead. Assassins are upon us."

A warrior-caste child of the border, Shakti had grown up with the constant threat of raiders. This was truly a daughter of mighty Gotama, for she didn't hesitate, or dither, or lock up with fear. Instead, with urgent calm, she took up her own sword before she bothered with a robe. And Jagdish knew that though the blade of that delicate talwar was very pretty, it wasn't just for decoration.

"I've got to get Pari. Lock the door behind me."

Knowing Shakti would listen, he crept into the hall. Pari's

room was nearby. He stepped over a dead guard. It appeared he'd been silenced quickly, his throat slashed. Jagdish could only hope that the assassin had skulked into his room first rather than his daughter's. He tried the door, but it was locked.

"Raveena. It's me."

"Master Jagdish?" the maid asked fearfully from the other side of the thick door. She sounded afraid and must have woken up at Shatki's alarm too. If Raveena was alive, that meant little Pari was still unharmed. "Master Jagdish, is that you?"

"Yes," he hissed as he looked back, and saw that more killers had reached the top of the stairs and were coming down the hall, at least five of them, and from the sounds of muffled violence, there were more of them continuing their dirty work below. There'd been a moment of relief to find out his daughter was alive, but now he needed to keep her that way. A great and terrible rage washed over him, the likes of which he'd not felt since raiders had tried to burn his home with his baby inside.

The time for whispering was over. "Barricade this door, Raveena. Don't open it for any voice you don't recognize."

Then he turned to meet the oncoming assassins, drawing his sword and tossing away the scabbard. That Vadal blade wouldn't be sheathed again until every trespasser who'd dared invade his home had been sent to the great nothing, blood-soaked and screaming in agony.

They rushed him, armed with short blades and katars. Those were concealable weapons, best used on unsuspecting victims, not against a skilled warrior armed with nearly three feet of sharpened steel. The hall was wide enough the attackers moved shoulder to shoulder. He was so angry he cleaved through the first rank with a single blow and still planted the tip of his sword deep into the wooden wall. Two bodies hit the floor, gushing blood.

"I am Jagdish the warrior, and you dare come into *my* house?" he roared as he jerked the sword out of the wall and started toward the rest of them.

The next assassin in line responded with contempt. "Fair is fair. You once invaded my home."

Then it was as if a hurricane swept through the estate. Jagdish was struck with a terrible wind, so mighty it lifted him from his feet and flung him down the hall. He hit the wall hard and hung there, suspended, as the wind pummeled him. It was pushing against him so hard he couldn't even lift his arms against its power. His chest felt like it might burst as the pressure crushed the very air from his lungs.

The evil wind died as suddenly as it had arrived, and Jagdish dropped to the floor, gasping for breath.

Wizard.

Even though he was also dressed entirely in black with a scarf over his face, this was clearly their leader. "Don't speak to me of offense, warrior. You and your gang, your so-called Sons of the Black Sword, trespassed into the House of Assassins, where you cut down my brethren, stole our slaves, let demons pollute the place, and then blew it to pieces and burned it to the ground."

Oceans, not these scum again. Jagdish rose, grimacing and trying to breathe. He hated fighting wizards. All they did was cheat.

The wizard seemed as angry as Jagdish was. "Now I hear tales that you're a big hero for invading us, whose Thakoor brags about all the treasure you brought him—treasure you robbed from us. They're paying us survivors a fortune to kill both you and Harta tonight. Don't tell anyone, but I would've done this job for free." He pointed a sword at Jagdish's chest, and unlike the others, he was armed with a proper fighting weapon, capable of taking heads.

Another burst of wind hit, throwing Jagdish farther down the hall. This time the wizard gestured with his demon-clutching hand, guiding the wind in a slightly different direction, to smash Jagish against one of the windows. The fine glass shattered behind his back, and Jagdish was barely able to catch hold of the edge with his free hand to keep from getting hurled into the courtyard. Splinters filled his palm before the wind died again.

The wizard addressed the other masked men. "Break down these doors. Massacre everyone he loves."

No! But the wind had robbed Jagdish of the air to scream.

The wizard aimed his treacherous magic at Jagdish again. "Know before you die that it is Yuval of Lost House Charsadda who kills you. Now, I will take my revenge."

Jagdish turned his sword sideways, so the hilt and the point caught wood before the next wind blast hit. With muscles straining he held on, until Yuval moved his hands a bit, directing the magical hurricane to pick up the dead bodies to launch them toward Jagdish. The window frame broke around him when all that meat struck, and Jagdish and the dead men were thrown, spiraling, into the courtyard.

It was over a twelve-foot drop, but luckily Jagdish hit soft wet grass. He heard the *clang* of his sword hitting the stone walkway. If that had been his body instead of his sword, he'd surely have broken bones.

Yuval leapt out after him. Jagdish didn't watch him land because he was scrambling after his sword. He grabbed it and rolled to his knees, narrowly blocking an incoming thrust.

Yuval's form suddenly seemed to blur. Wizards had a trick where they could burn demon to fuel their bodies to move faster than humanly possible. Jagdish had seen that trick before and knew what was coming next. He got to his feet and had his sword up just in time to meet the incoming flurry of attacks. The wizard's blade darted in, high, then low, thrusting and swinging, back and forth, and it took everything Jagdish had ever learned to keep from getting sliced to pieces. It was simply too fast for a mortal warrior to keep up with, and he'd surely die trying.

Instead, he did as Ashok had taught him. When your opponent is faster, don't try to keep up. Get ahead of them. Control the pace. Control the battle.

Yuval had surely thought Jagdish would be easily overwhelmed. That's what would normally happen whenever a mortal warrior was faced by such a supernatural threat. He hadn't expected Jagdish to suddenly attack him like a frenzied wild man.

The sword sang. The wizard had to retreat.

Magically augmented, Yuval was fast enough to doge, block, and parry, but his mind couldn't keep up with the fury of Jagdish's continual assault. Reacting rather than acting, Yuval's magical speed meant nothing.

Jagdish managed to tag him once, but the wizard retreated before Jagdish could cut him deep. Jagdish followed, furious at this distraction that was keeping him from his wife and child. He could hear the pounding on their doors. Or was that the pounding of his heartbeat in his ears? It didn't matter. Jagdish just kept on striking, over and over. Arms burning. Muscles straining. Chips of steel being taken from both their blades as sweat ran into his eyes.

The wizard had thought he'd have an easy revenge. He'd been wrong. And now he was growing afraid.

"Aid me!" Yuval shouted. "Aid your master!"

Coward. And that thought just made Jagdish even madder.

Black-clad assassins ran into the courtyard with blood dripping from their blades. Many honored guests of Great House Vadal had surely perished tonight. Jagdish would avenge them all.

The murderers dashed toward Jagdish, eager to appease their wizard.

There was a whistle as something metallic spun through the air, and the head of one of the killers suddenly snapped back, spraying red. A filthy man, clad in nothing but a loincloth, rushed from the darkness between the fruit trees, spinning a length of steel chain. He whipped another assassin across the arms, and as that one screamed, he looped the chain around his neck, and yanked the killer off his feet, then promptly stomped on his throat with one bare foot.

It was the Sarnobat prisoner, Najmul.

"Do you believe the gods have sent me now, Phontho?" Najmul shouted as he whipped the assassin's minions with the chains that had so recently bound him to one of Jagdish's walls.

He did, but he couldn't answer the religious fanatic right then, because he had a wizard to kill and a family to save.

Their fight continued across the courtyard. Najmul picked up a dropped sword and laid into the other killers, keeping them away from Jagdish. Luckily, Yuval must have been the only wizard among this contingent because the rest seemed to fight and die with the skill of mere bandits. But even then, from the effortless way Najmul was slaying the mob, the fanatic truly had been holding back when he'd fought Jagdish before.

If he'd had leisure to observe him, compared to the unrelenting fury Jagdish was unleashing upon this wizard now, the fanatic must have thought that Jagdish had been holding back as well.

Yuval must have used up all the magic in the fragment of demon in his hand, because the maddening burst of speed abruptly ended. His mask had slipped during the fight, displaying his face, and he was staring at Jagdish, wide-eyed at the terror he had set free. "You can't—"

Jagdish planted his sword deep into Yuval's shoulder, shearing through his collarbone and severing the great artery that ran across the top of the chest. He ripped it out in a fountain of blood, and as the wizard·spun away, Jagdish hit him again in the back, slicing through the kidney and into his lower spine.

The wizard landed on his face, throwing blood everywhere.

Jagdish didn't have the luxury of watching this foe die, and instead ran for the nearest stairs. *"Shakti! Pari!"* he roared as he went. "Hang on!" He ran as fast as he could, taking the stairs three at a time. At the top, he snatched one of the decorative lanterns from the wall. As he rushed around the corner and into the hall he saw...

His wife, injured, pressing one red hand against the side of her bloody face. The two assassins were down. The last had Shakti's talwar sticking out of the back of his head as he lay there twitching.

Jagdish rushed to her side. "Are you hurt?"

"Yes." Wincing, she moved her hand, to show that she'd been cut across the cheek. "Ah! That hurts."

This was his beloved in pain, but being a trained and experienced warrior, one part of his mind remained detached enough from the righteous anger to recognize that such a wound—though requiring many stitches—wouldn't be life threatening as long as it didn't get infected. "You're going to be alright."

He led her to Pari's door and pounded on it with his fist. "Raveena! It's Jagdish. Let me in."

The maid knew that voice, and there was a great deal of crashing as she hurried to move furniture out of the way, which must have woken up Pari, who began to cry. While Raveena worked, Jagdish cut a strip from Shakti's robe, balled up the silk, and gently pressed it against her cheek. She winced.

"Hold this here. Firmly."

"I would've stayed inside like you said, but I heard them breaking down Pari's door, so I rushed them. Got one by surprise. The other, not so much."

Shakti had risked her life for the daughter that wasn't even hers, and despite the carnage all around them, in that instant Jagdish loved her even more than when the judge had pronounced them married.

Someone else ran up the stairs, but this time it was one of his loyal men, Zaheer. "Phontho! The estate's under attack!" Then he saw Jagdish and Shakti, half naked, splattered with blood, and surrounded by corpses. "Oceans."

Raveena opened the door. Jagdish wasted no time. He plucked Shakti's sword from the dead man's skull and held it out to his wife. "Stay with them. I'll return as swiftly as I can."

"Do what you must, husband."

"Zaheer, guard them with your life."

"I will, Jagdish." And since Zaheer had not quailed before the demon scourge, Jagdish knew he would fight an army of assassins to protect his phontho's family. That certainty would enable Jagdish to concentrate on his duty, rather than worrying about his loved ones.

Jagdish kissed Shakti on the forehead, then rushed back downstairs to fight for his surviving guests.

Chapter 32

It was a grim morning.

At Jagdish's estate alone, ten of his guards, five of his guests, and two servants had been killed, and he had just received word that there had been several other attacks in and around Mukesh. Officers and arbiters, killed. One messenger told them that the city's Chief Judge had returned to his estate after the Raja's forces had vacated it, only to be murdered in his sleep. The next and final messenger Jagdish had heard from had been uncertain if what he'd been told was the truth, or if the tale had been conjured from the fog of war, but if it was real then this was a very dark day for Great House Vadal.

"Is there word from my father yet?" Shakti asked Jagdish.

"Not yet."

"Please, Lady Shakti," the surgeon begged, needle and thread in hand. "Try not to move your head as I stitch. I'm almost done."

"It's going to leave a hideous scar anyway," she snapped at the poor worker who was just trying to fulfill his obligation.

"It'll be a worse one if you keep wiggling."

"Fine." As much as it pained her, for the woman was rarely not in motion, Shakti sat still.

They were in Jagdish's dining room, but instead of a breakfast, the table held the surgeon's kit and discarded bloody bandages.

"We're secure for now. My men have checked everywhere. The intruders are all dead, but I don't know if any escaped. I sent a runner to the warrior district to find Gotama. He should be back soon." Seeing Shakti suffering with worry for her father stoked Jagdish's anger even further, but now was not the time for rage. It was the time for cold, calculated vengeance. "There were no survivors here to question, but hopefully there will be some from one of the other estates they attacked."

Shakti waited patiently until the surgeon tied off a knot and cut the excess string with a pair of scissors before speaking again. "Thank you. Give me your mirror."

"It looks bad now, but the swelling will go down," the surgeon warned. "It should heal well. Barely a scratch."

"Your mirror."

The surgeon gave her the small square of glass, and Shakti displayed no emotion and said absolutely nothing as she examined his work, thirteen fat stitches holding together her once smooth cheek.

"Leave us be for now," Jagdish ordered, and the surgeon seemed glad to gather up his kit and escape the dining room. There were plenty of other people here who needed his help.

Shakti waited until after the worker was gone before speaking, because warriors would rather die than show weakness before another caste. "A man of your status deserves better. I'm going to be ugly from now on."

"No. You're not." He knelt next to his new wife and gently took hold of her hand. "The story of our caste has always been told in scars. Your willingness to defend your family makes you even more beautiful to me than you were before." He could only hope that she could hear the earnestness in his words, because he truly meant it. "I don't deserve better, because there is no better! I'm the one who doesn't deserve you. I lucked into you, because you love a challenge, and that sure hasn't changed!"

Shakti wiped her moist eyes. "You are a good man, Jagdish."

He did try. "I need you now more than ever. I need your wisdom about what this will mean for our house." It would be good to change the subject to something she loved. Better for her to dwell on courtly strategy than her beauty being marred. "There's another rumor I heard this morning that I didn't dare say in front of any other witnesses. There's whispers the assassins struck at our Thakoor last night as well. Harta may have even been wounded."

"No." She stared at him in disbelief. "They wouldn't dare try such a thing."

"Who is 'they'? Who would do this?"

"I don't know. Sarnobat's the obvious culprit. It could just as easily be crafty Vokkan, though. It has to be outsiders. There's no faction within Vadal so disloyal to do this, and even if there were usurpers, targeting so many other high-status people would ensure their coup to be a failure..." She trailed off. "There's one other possibility."

"Devedas left the celebration rather quickly."

"That he did, husband. That he did." She scowled, which must have made the stiches pull, because she winced right after. "Sorry. It hurts to talk." But then she did anyway. "Devedas doing this makes no political sense. The Raja has the might of the Capitol backing him. He leads an army, and many of the warriors obligated to him hold their honor nearly as valuable as we do. Using such underhanded treachery makes Devedas look weak and cowardly. I can imagine him invading us brazenly, not slitting our throats in our beds."

"I can fight, but I need to know who." There was a shout from the courtyard. Someone was calling his name. "I must go."

"I'll see what I can find out. Be sure, husband, whoever did this evil to us, we're going to find out, and make them suffer for it."

He grinned at her, for he'd set out to reassure her that everything would be alright, and here she was turning the tables on him once again, by giving him hope of inflicting a righteous retribution on the deserving party.

The raider Najmul was waiting for him by the stairs. He'd been following Jagdish nearly as close as his shadow since the attack, and Jagdish still really didn't know what to do with the fanatic.

"Why must I wear the colors of cowards?" Najmul whined, picking at the humble nayak's uniform Jagdish had given him to wear. "Do the gods require I suffer this indignity? Have I not done enough to prove my loyalty yet?"

"You'll wear the blue-gray to keep from getting killed as an invader. I'll tell my people you are a mercenary I hired, and you'll keep your mouth shut."

"That's right. Because the Law-abiding can't stand the testimony of a gods-fearing man."

"More like your accent marks you as Sarnobat, and your kind are about as popular as plague around here right now. But that too. You start spouting off about gods in your raspy barbarian tongue and it'll be a race to see who guts you first, warriors or Inquisitors."

"As you've seen, I could defeat either."

That was no lie. Najmul had fought like a demon, and the way things were going, it might not hurt to have someone so capable by his side. Jagdish began walking down the stairs. "How'd you get loose anyway?"

"When I saw assassins killing the guards, I prayed desperately to the gods to grant me the strength of two Sarnobat men—so that would be about five of you soft Vadal—and they granted it, and I ripped my chains from the wall!"

Lunatics could be freakishly strong at times. "You would pledge your loyalty to me over your house? What if these assassins came from Sarnobat?"

"They didn't. This is not our way. But even if these fools did, my loyalty isn't to you or any house of man. It's to the gods and the commandments they gave me through Mother Dawn. You're just lucky she wants me to keep you alive no matter what. The gods must have big things in store for you, Phontho."

"Then shut up, keep your head down, and follow me."

Najmul went with him into the courtyard. There were two sets of bodies arranged here, warriors and honored guests, in a neat row, with their faces covered, waiting to be taken to the crematorium. And the assassins, thrown into a haphazard pile to be searched for clues and then taken outside to be burned in a ditch.

The man who had been calling his name was no mere messenger, but rather sat atop a warhorse, wearing the fine armor that marked him as an officer of the Personal Guard of Great House Vadal.

"Girish, my old friend."

The experienced warrior gave him a solemn nod. "It's good to see you again, Jagdish, though I wish our meeting was in happier days."

"I was having a fantastic time until these scum showed up."

Jagdish paused to kick one of the corpses. The impact stirred up a cloud of flies. "What's going on?"

"You alone must come with me immediately to the government house in Mukesh."

Girish didn't elaborate why in front of Jagdish's men, which confirmed his greatest fears, for this was one of Harta Vadal's elite bodyguards.

"Saddle my horse."

Jagdish was escorted into the chamber where Thakoor Harta Vadal lay dying.

Girish had told him the sad tale as they rode. Dozens of assassins, many of them magically gifted, had attacked the mansion where their Thakoor had been staying. They must have used a fortune in demon to get past so many defenses so quickly. The Personal Guard had still slaughtered them, but one had slipped past them somehow, to strike their master with a single poisoned dart.

Harta had the most skilled wizards and surgeons in Vadal on his staff, but they had been unable to stop the poison's spread as it was some vile concoction that none of them had ever seen before. Girish had openly wept as he had told Jagdish how Harta had been growing steadily weaker all morning, all because the Personal Guard had failed in their duties. The surgeons said Harta's organs were failing. It was only wine and poppy that was keeping him from being entirely consumed by agony. Soon, their beloved Thakoor would embark on the last journey into the great nothing beyond.

Even as the hour of death rapidly approached, Harta remained focused on the good of his house. His deathbed was surrounded, not by family and loved ones, but by scribes, writing down Harta's final commands, and officers to receive their final orders. They had to lean in close, as all that remained of his famed orator's voice was a ragged whisper. Harta was tying up loose ends.

Jagdish could only assume that he was one of those loose ends, and with no further benefit to carrying on their charade, Harta would finally be able to have Jagdish executed, as he had wanted to for so very long. The Thakoor would at least have that satisfaction before death.

Jagdish was relieved to see his father-in-law hadn't been one of those felled during the night, for Gotama had been summoned there as well. When the old phontho saw Jagdish, he gave him a determined nod. They were family now. If Harta was about to condemn him, Jagdish would accept it with dignity. That way Gotama could tell Shakti that her husband had been a respectable warrior to the end.

"As you requested, Phontho Jagdish has arrived."

"Good. Come here, Jagdish." Their Thakoor was bleeding from his eyes, and from the way he was staring into the distance, had lost the ability to see. The Thakoor had been a fit and healthy man, of medium age. To see him perish like this was an insult to their house.

"I'm here, sir."

"Closer."

Jagdish had to kneel next to the bed and turn his ear toward Harta's mouth to hear his words.

"I sent you east to fail. At most, I expected you to take the blame for my ambitions, to pay the Capitol's blood price . . . only you didn't fail. Instead you surprised me, and proved yourself to be the best commander in all of Vadal . . . the best warrior I have. My other phonthos are too old, and the younger ones only care about glory and wealth, while you go from victory to victory, triumphing even when you shouldn't. That is the kind of commander this house needs now."

Jagdish was confused and humbled. "What would you have me do?"

Harta spoke to one of his wizards. "Tell him, Kule."

The smallest and oldest of the wizards nodded. "We have just received emergency messages by magic. This morning the *entire* army of Vokkan has attacked in the west, and all the armies of Sarnobat are on the way here now. In the south, the Raja's Army of Many Houses has begun marching north."

"It's as if all of Lok has gone to war against us at once," Gotama said. "They knew we'd not suspect they'd risk moving such large forces during the monsoon season. Such a brash assault must have been planned long in advance."

Jagdish's mind was spinning. Vadal was mighty, but there was no way they could survive an invasion from three sides. Give him the manpower, and he could crush any one of those threats. Three at once? They'd surely be laying siege to Vadal City by summer.

"You are my witnesses as I appoint Jagdish to lead all the warrior caste of Great House Vadal. Defend our house. Protect my heirs. Avenge my death."

Jagdish struggled to find the words, and all that came out was the response that had been beaten into him since he was a lowly nayak. "I will serve."

"I know." Harta beckoned for Jagdish to come even closer, so he alone would hear what was whispered next. "It angers me that my best hope for my house lies with a friend of Ashok... but if I die believing you will punish our enemies as harshly as he would have, that gives me peace. The other houses are pawns. The Capitol is a shadow. It is Omand who killed me. In his greed to rule the world, he would destroy it. Go and defend Vadal, warrior."

Jagdish drew himself to attention and gave his Thakoor one final salute.

All the high-status men were staring at him in silence. He wouldn't linger here awkwardly. "Gotama, come with me." Jagdish walked from the room. Girish was guarding the door. "You too."

"I can't. The Thakoor's life is the Personal Guard's responsibility. I failed in my duties, Jagdish. I'll wait here until our Thakoor expires, then I'll kill myself in shame."

"The hell you will. Permission denied." Jagdish put one hand on the proud warrior's shoulder and looked him in the eye. "I've been where you are now."

Girish exhaled slowly. "Yeah... I suppose you have."

"That's why I know there's nothing more lethal on land than a good soldier searching for redemption." He turned back to the important men. "I'm claiming every warrior, wizard, and worker who can swing a hammer in Mukesh and the surrounding region, regardless of their obligation, right now."

There was no time to spare. Jagdish had a great house to save.

Chapter 33

Grand Inquisitor Omand Vokkan stood before the Chief Judge's marvelous map table, admiring the gigantic yet intricate three-dimensional representation of Lok. The murdered Chief Judge hadn't yet been replaced. The way things were going, that replacement would never need to happen. So this map was basically Omand's property now. As was the rest of the government.

Taraba had done well in the north. It had been two months since Harta Vadal had died of the poison from one of the assassins Taraba had directed. With that strong leader gone and Vadal in peril, the last political resistance to Omand's coup had crumbled. The remaining judges licked Omand's feet. The other great houses didn't dare protest the goings-on of the Capitol, scared to risk the same suffering that was currently being inflicted on Vadal.

The conflict in the north was summarized upon the table by the many colorful flags representing the various armies rampaging and burning their way across Vadal. Only slaves who had been chosen for their slim weight and dainty feet were allowed upon the map to move those many flags around as the daily updates poured in. In normal times many judges and commanders would have come to this room every day to keep up on the events of the world, but Omand practically had it to himself now, as those great men cowered in their estates.

Yet somehow the blue-gray and bronze flags of Vadal still stood. Despite being pressed on three sides in a house war the likes of which the continent had rarely seen before, Vadal had not yet surrendered. With Harta dead, Omand had expected his young heir to be pressured into giving up within days, a week or two at most; but Vadal held, resolute. Omand was not a warrior. He didn't understand the ways of that prideful caste, but he knew sheer numbers, money, and politics made Vadal's defeat inevitable. Surely Vadal's first caste did as well.

But what did that delay matter? Let the wounded animal linger so the other great houses could witness its suffering. Let the struggle continue long enough that it made their eventual defeat even more tragic, and the lesson to the other houses about disobeying the will of the Capitol more valuable.

Omand walked around to the opposite side of the table, to study the south, and to be annoyed to find that the black flags of treason and rebellion had grown in number since his last visit to the map, spreading like a cancer. Word of the devastation in Kanok had gotten out, and with it, an already uneasy population had been moved to terror. The Akershani were unable or unwilling to stomp on the rebels hiding in their mountains, and it seemed even the leadership of the once reliable Makao were allowing criminals to flourish and flaunt the Law in their lands. The loss of their greatest city must have driven their boy Thakoor mad.

He had secretly encouraged this rebellion before, but now it was no longer of use to him. To cut out this rot Omand had recently obligated more armies and sent them south. Leaders who were too weak to enforce the Law would be removed, and replaced by members of their family who would. Chaos had been useful to him once, but now that Omand was in charge, the time for order had returned.

His long walk around the table continued, up the western coast, noting as he went that there were far more black flags here now as well. Then he stepped back to take it all in and realized that there were a shocking number of small criminal uprisings scattered across the entirety of Lok.

The danger of playing with fire was that if you lost control of it you or something you cherished could be consumed in the flames. It was a lesson from his childhood, as he had enjoyed setting fires around the family mansion, and for a brief moment Omand wondered if he should have remembered that better before unleashing Ashok onto the world.

Recently, a Protector had entered the Capitol, telling anyone in authority who would listen that he had fought Black-Hearted Ashok in the desert, and that Ashok had spared his life so that he could bring them a message. *The demons were coming from below.* Omand had assumed this was simply another rebel ploy to spread fear among the first, like when they had destroyed one of the precious aqueducts. He'd promptly had that Protector arrested and imprisoned at the Tower of Silence before his mad tale could spread too far.

But what if it was not a trick? What if Kanok hadn't been an anomaly, but rather the beginning of a new kind of demonic offensive? Most of the Capitol's defenders were away at war, either in Vadal, or gone to chase rebels. To summon them back now would make Omand's new government appear weak. He couldn't just interrupt a necessary war because of one criminal's lies.

Still, Omand knew that Ashok was a creature of peculiar integrity, and his demonic prisoner had gloated about some manner of revenge.

It is time.

Regardless, the path was committed. There was no turning back now. Omand would not dwell on the unknown.

Finally, he stopped at the northwest corner of the table, looking down at the Gujaran peninsula, at a desolate jungle where there were no flags at all, for the Inquisition mission there was a well-kept secret. That jungle was where Omand truly yearned to be. The source of all magic beckoned him. His inheritance was so close he could taste it. He had worked so hard to take over this city, but now he wanted nothing more than to be rid of it. It wasn't that Omand was fickle, he simply hungered for a new challenge. The glory of man was fleeting. The power of the ancients was eternal.

There was a knock on the door.

"You may enter."

It was Inquisitor Zankrut, and he was carrying a wooden box. Impressed by his willingness to speak his mind, even when his observations might be unpopular, Omand had obligated Zankrut to his personal staff. He was no Taraba, and lacked his second's cunning, but he would have to do in the meantime.

The box made Omand curious. "Did someone send me a gift?"

"It is no gift, sir, but a warning." Zankrut's face was hidden behind his mask, so Omand had not realized until he spoke just how upset the man was. "This was delivered to the Tower of Silence this morning."

Zankrut set the box on the edge of the map table so that it cast a rectangular shadow over Vadal.

Omand opened the lid to find a severed human head inside. "Curious."

From the decay, he had been dead for several weeks. Unmoved by such things, Omand reached into the box, took hold of a handful of hair, and lifted it free to get a better look. The head had been packed in salt to keep it from rotting too much, and Omand had to brush the face off to see who exactly it was that he was dealing with.

It was Inquisitor Taraba.

"Most curious, indeed."

"His face was battered, some of his teeth were broken, and one of his eyes had been put out. From the look of it, I'd guess with an iron spike, heated red-hot."

Omand's brief view agreed with Zankrut's professional assessment. He too had been a torturer once.

Still inside the box were Taraba's golden mask, which had been snapped in half, and a folded letter. Omand retrieved the paper, then unceremoniously dropped his assistant's head back into the box.

The Raja's seal was embedded in the wax. Omand broke it open and read. The message was very short.

I will not be manipulated.

Perhaps Taraba's schemes in the north had not been as successful as his optimistic reports had suggested.

"What does it say, Grand Inquisitor?"

"It is not what it says, but rather what it suggests." It was difficult for Omand to keep the disappointment from his voice. "I suppose when Devedas returns to the Capitol he will most certainly try to kill me. Which means that I should kill him first ... but that is such a waste." Omand handed the letter to Zankrut. "Burn this immediately."

From his hurry, Zankrut seemed relieved to escape the map room.

Taraba was still facing straight up, staring into the great nothing with his one remaining eye, gone the color of sour milk. Omand addressed his dead subordinate coldly. "I wonder what else you revealed to Devedas before he removed your head?"

This was troubling, for Taraba had known many of the Inquisition's darkest secrets, and everyone talked eventually. In fact, it was by Taraba's own hand that the Chief Judge who had commissioned this splendid map was no longer with them. Worse, if Devedas had not been tricked into attacking Vadal by Taraba's fake assassination plot as Omand had believed, that meant that even as Devedas had been befriending Harta he must have been planning to besiege Vadal City the whole time regardless, for reasons that were his own.

It appeared Omand had underestimated his puppet king. At the beginning of their conspiracy, Devedas had been a skilled tactician, but inexperienced at the great game, and thus manageable. But he learned too quickly. His popularity with the regular people of every caste would make him too difficult to replace now. By sending Taraba north, Omand had inadvertently given Devedas an incredible source of intelligence that could be used against him. Taraba had known who among Omand's allies was strong, who was weak, and who could be swayed with what leverage. Taraba had understood where Omand was vulnerable in the Capitol, which meant that he had to assume that now Devedas did as well...

Despite Taraba being the closest thing Omand had ever had to a son, he experienced no significant emotion as he spoke with the dead. "I have lived my entire life trying to win the great game. I learned more about magic than anyone else has in the last few centuries. I have lied and murdered and consorted with demons. Finally, after all that the work is done and the Capitol is mine. Yet, I feel no triumph from this, Taraba. Only a yearning for *more*. The time for petty maneuvers is over. I do not care to defend my kingdom from the king I made for it." He knocked over the flag representing the Raja, carelessly breaking some of the painstakingly handcrafted tiny buildings around Vadal City. Then he looked disdainfully at the black flags festering across the map. "Nor do I want to waste my precious time dealing with the repercussions of a criminal warlord I unleashed simply so that he could terrify the first caste into bending their knee to me."

His eyes turned back to the green-painted jungle of Gujara and lingered there.

"No, there is something more important than this city, more important even than the great game. As my closest confidant I told you many of my secrets, but not all of them. I kept the greatest for myself. You see, Taraba, as a young witch hunter I discovered forbidden texts, guides to how the ancients ascended to realms of might beyond comprehension. The demon showed me the source of their power, a forge from which was created all magic, the very source which turned the men of old into pretend gods. I will leave the Capitol, so as to not endanger my creation. Let Devedas have this city for now. Let Ashok and the demons fight over the scraps of the old world as I go to make a new one. Then I will return as a wrathful god to destroy them all, and rule forever."

Decision made, he left Taraba and went to make arrangements for his banishment.

That night, on wings made of demon magic, Omand Vokkan flew toward his destiny.

Chapter 34

In the south of Lok, summer was the season for war.

Many months had passed since Ashok had seized their ancestor blade, but the army of Akershan had continued to honor the demands he had made of them for its eventual return. Any casteless seeking refuge in the rebels' mountains was granted safe passage.

It was the bordering houses, the ones whose ancestor blades Ashok did not hold hostage, who remained a threat. Thousands fleeing the Great Extermination had found sanctuary in these rebellious lands, but it was unknown how many others had perished trying to get here. Worse, they had recently received word that the Capitol was sending more troops south to hound them. If the Akershani wouldn't enforce the Law in their mountains, then the Capitol would.

As their prophet had commanded, the Sons had rained fury against any who tried to put the casteless to the sword. That morning, fifty raiders of Devakula had been sent to the lands beyond death, and a hundred more had been taken prisoner to be ransomed back to their house. The casteless those warriors had been pursuing had been saved, and now they would be guided to one of the many new settlements that had been established near the Cove.

Before Ashok had executed the most vicious among the captured warriors, they had begged for their lives and claimed they
were only trying to obey the Law, and that Law demanded casteless
blood. Ashok understood, but he could not forgive. The merciless
and cruel among his captives gave their necks to Angruvadal. The
warriors who had been reluctant to massacre untouchables were
spared. Hopefully, those survivors would understand the cost of
obedience to the Capitol's commands, so after they were returned
to their house they would spread the word that it was Black-Hearted
Ashok who determined what was law in these lands now. Hopefully,
the next time refugees passed through their house the warriors
would be wise enough to look the other way.

There were hundreds of new casteless arrivals today, walking
in ragged lines across the grasslands, carrying their thin children
and their meager belongings upon their backs. They had been
coming like this for months, a seemingly never-ending stream
of desperation and hunger.

Thera had exhausted herself trying to find a place for all of
them. The best thing the Sons could do was try to figure out
which ones had valuable skills and then herd them in the right
direction. Unfortunately, they'd discovered many of these fanatics
had very strong opinions on where their gods wanted them to
go. Too many of them claimed to be called as gurus or leaders,
and not enough of them thought the gods wanted them chopping
wood or foraging for roots.

Ashok spotted Risalder Eklavya having a heated argument
with a group of refugees and rode in that direction. He had
no patience for disorder and had found that his presence had
a way of silencing even the most obstinate among the fanatics.
They could never seem to agree on the nature of their illegal
gods, but it seemed every secret fanatic in the world had heard
of Fall-turned-Ashok enough to fear him.

"I was told there was plenty of housing at the Cove. I know
most of the mansions the ancients carved there still stand empty!
I will require one of those to establish my church."

"It's not for lack of room." Eklavya put one hand on the
man's shoulder and gently tried to keep him moving in the
right direction. "We need laborers on the western slope clearing
ground, so that's where this group is going."

"How dare you lay your hands upon me, warrior! I'm no

mere laborer! I'm of the holy priesthood of Ramrowan, come to preach and organize this people."

The one arguing with Eklavya was dressed no different from the rest of the casteless dregs, in frayed, dirty clothing, with a bulging sack thrown over one shoulder, and rags wrapped around his feet instead of shoes, but he certainly didn't talk like a common fish-eater. But for that matter, neither had Keta.

"What's going on, Risalder?"

Eklavya turned, saw Ashok, and immediately saluted. "Some disagreements with the new arrivals over their destination, General. I'm handling it."

The defiant one looked up at Ashok and squinted. He was surprisingly portly for a casteless and must have been nearly blind to not realize who the tall man in black armor was. "Who're you supposed to be?"

"I am Ashok Vadal."

"Oceans!" He immediately dropped to one knee and dipped his balding head. "It is an honor! I didn't realize the Forgotten's Warrior was among us."

"Among you and wondering why a refugee is disrespecting one of my officers. Eklavya of Kharsawan has shown great courage in repeatedly risking his life to save your often ungrateful kind. You're fortunate he hasn't cut your wagging tongue out, beggar. I think his version of the Forgotten is one of the more merciful ones."

"Thank you, sir," Eklavya said. "Just doing my duty, same as all the Sons."

"Stand up, newcomer," Ashok commanded, and Horse snorted for emphasis. He didn't know which of his companions was more bloodthirsty when they sensed his annoyance—his ancestor blade, or his steed. "Explain yourself."

The man did. "Apologies for my insolence. It's just that my obligation requires me to go to the Cove immediately. I cannot delay."

"You are not casteless."

"How could you tell?"

"You talk too much and are too fat."

The truth seemed to hurt his feelings. "This attempt at deceit was for my own safety. The robes of my office and my carriage were stolen by bandits on the very first day of my journey here.

I have been following these untouchables and they were kind enough to give me clothing and share their food."

"Name, caste, and status?"

"Johar, who is free of castes because they are an abomination before the gods."

Ashok didn't have time for fanaticism right now. "What were you born into?"

"The first of Great House Makao. By obligation I was a seventeen-year senior, Arbiter of the Law, of the Order of Census and Taxation, stationed in Kanok."

It was rare to find such a high-status man slumming it among the rebel dregs. The last member of the first caste Ashok had encountered among the rebels had turned out to be a lunatic who had appointed himself god-king of a conquered city. He wouldn't hold much hope this one would prove any better.

"There were secret faithful hidden even among those godless people?" Eklavya was incredulous.

"There were none before! Until a few months ago I believed only in the Law. I spit on the criminals with their illegal superstitions." Johar spat on the ground as if they needed the demonstration. "It wasn't until the night the demons came that changed everything, and I realized the gods were real. For I was there and saw the gods' might manifest when Javed, the Keeper of Names, took up all-powerful Maktalvar, and used our ancestor blade to slay many demons, then willingly forsook that mighty sword so that someone else could be the bearer in his stead so that he could remain a priest."

Ashok frowned at that outlandish tale. "Impossible."

"That's what our Thakoor said! Yet if something is impossible, but happens anyway, it must be a miracle. No man has ever before denied himself such an incredible honor of being a bearer, but Keeper Javed declared that serving the gods mattered more than that. I saw that even black steel answers to the gods, for it respected his wishes and chose another bearer that very night. But we all saw that an ancestor blade found an open worshipper of the Forgotten worthy! This cannot be reconciled with the Law, so the Law must be mistaken concerning the faithful."

Ashok couldn't believe his ears. Anyone who was found lacking by the swords' inscrutable judgment were always injured or killed in the attempt to bear it. The unworthy never escaped punishment, and most were deemed unworthy. Only the greatest among men could wield an ancestor blade and live. To pick one up meant risking all. And to be chosen? One did not simply walk away from such an honor.

"Javed? Javed Zarger?"

"Yes. The Keeper of Names! He said he knows you. After such a demonstration of righteousness and because the Keeper had saved his life, Thakoor Venketesh Makao declared that Javed was free to preach of the Forgotten amid the ruins of Kanok. And in those dark days when all seemed lost in our city that had seen so much wickedness and bloodshed, many of the people heeded Javed's message of hope. I was among them."

Eklavya had a joyous laugh. "Praise to the gods! A Thakoor flouts the Law to let the gods' truth be openly taught in his lands? I never thought I'd hear of such a thing."

Neither had the Capitol, so Ashok had no doubt the child Thakoor would be dealt with harshly once word got out of such flagrant disobedience. It was one thing to have criminals believing in illegal religion. It was something else entirely to have the highest among them openly defying one of the Law's most important decrees. "The Inquisition's response to this will be bloody."

"Oh, it truly was at first. The Inquisitors even tried to remove our Thakoor by force. Which is why Venketesh ordered every Inquisitor in Kanok to be slain and their corpses hurled into the watery pit where Venketesh's mansion once stood. The city is much happier now with all its Inquisitors dead."

It was difficult for Ashok to imagine that the callow youth he had challenged for Thera's life was now openly confronting the Capitol's most dangerous Order over *religion*.

"The Keeper of Names has continued his work spreading the truth to all the people of Lok, but he sent me to bring these gifts to the Forgotten's chosen to demonstrate his eternal devotion. Though bandits stole the rest of my belongings, I protected these with my life." Johar carefully placed his sack on the ground and untied the cord holding it shut. When he opened the bag, Ashok saw that it was filled with papers.

"What's all this?" Eklavya asked as Johar proudly shoved a few bundles into his hands. The warrior began to flip through the pages. Being trained among the engineers of Kharsawan, Eklavya was one of the Sons who could read well. "'The Testimony of Ratul'? 'The Tenth Sermon of Keta'? 'The Tale of King Ramrowan'?"

"Let me see that." Ashok's saddle creaked as he extended one hand downward. Johar happily gave another stack of papers over. Luckily, Horse refrained from biting the arbiter.

The pages had been mass-produced on a printing press. Such expensive devices were rare and heavily regulated, used mostly for distributing official pronouncements from various Capitol Orders. The one in Ashok's hands was titled *The Collected Prophecies of the Forgotten's Voice*.

"These are the sacred texts, as compiled by the Keeper of Names, to be circulated to all the world. I apologize there was not time to bind them properly. I have brought a few samples of each, as well as examples of each of our single-page pamphlets. Those are far easier to smuggle to the believers since they can be folded to hide in a pocket."

"How many of these have you made?" Eklavya asked.

"The press of Kanok has run nonstop for months. Hundreds of books. Tens of thousands of pamphlets. Javed works with a fervor that must be seen to be believed. They say he no longer sleeps but is sustained by the gods. Many of us converts volunteered to help. Some were trained on the press, others—like me—were given authority to spread the word. These papers have gone out to all the world, sent far and wide by merchant and with caravan folk, with the faithful carrying them from town to town and across the borders of every great house. Javed kept the language plain, so it is easier to understand than the Law! The few who are literate can read them aloud to those who can't. Javed told me the blessed free people of the Cove were devout, but unlearned, and needed a priest to guide and care for them. He worries without a priest the Cove will fall to wickedness and lies. So it is my obligation to read these to them, and preach, so the truth will never be forgotten again. Soon the teachings of the gods will be available to all!"

Ashok was rarely stunned into silence. This was one of those times.

"The gods have truly blessed us!" Eklavya held the unbound books to the sky, and the young warrior seemed so happy he might swoon. "What should we do, General?"

Thankfully, that wasn't his decision to make. "Take this man directly to Thera. Get these papers into her hands. She will decide how to proceed."

"Come, priest. I will introduce you to our prophet!"

This time Johar didn't protest Eklavya's putting hands on his arm to guide him. "Thank you. And those scriptures are yours to keep, Immortal Ashok. Javed told me you would need a copy of the Voice's prophecies since you didn't have a Keeper nearby to remember them for you."

As Eklavya rushed off with their new priest, Ashok stared at the book in his hands. The old Law-abiding part of him was aghast, for this was the mass-production of crime, like unto Gutch's avalanche of guns. Only, bullets merely affected the body. These words were aimed at the minds and hearts of all. Protectors and Inquisitors had spent centuries destroying religious texts as soon as they were found to prevent such a contagion. Javed had reversed all their labor in a season.

When the Grand Inquisitor learned of this, an incredible wrath would be unleashed...

Or would it?

Was this record—this *scripture*—the work of an honest priest or a deceitful witch hunter?

Was this Omand's plan? Or the gods'?

Oddly enough, the same question could be asked about Ashok's continued existence. He did not care for this parallel.

Those ominous thoughts were interrupted as a rider appeared over the crest of a nearby hill. It was Shekar Somsak, and his horse was in a lather from the exertion. "General! Come and see!"

Ashok took the time to carefully secure Javed's papers in his pack before riding toward Shekar. "What is it?"

"Gunners, sir, marching across the plains. Half a paltan's worth, and they aren't none of ours."

Gutch's illegal weaponry had been showing up in ever-increasing numbers among the casteless, but the only force with that many rods around here should have been the Sons. "Are you certain?"

"Saw them through the spyglass myself, Ashok, and those sure aren't spears they're carrying. My boys have been hanging back, keeping an eye on them since we saw them about an hour ago. They're crossing the tall grass valley to the south of us right now. I got to you fast as I could."

"Are they casteless?"

"I don't think so. They're dressed funny." And when his commander scowled at the vagueness of that report, Shekar tried to explain. "Not scabby or haggard enough to be fish-eaters. They're uniformed like warriors, but not no uniform of any house I've ever seen. They're in short cloaks of white or gray, and aprons full of pouches. There's one among them in colorful robes, but I didn't want to risk getting too close to see what else was different."

"You were correct not to engage them, Risalder." There was only one possible source for so many gunners, and Collector Moyo had told Ashok there were several exits from the underground world scattered across the plains. Those cloaks would be made of seal, the strange barking creatures who lived along the coastline of Fortress, those aprons would be heavy with lead and powder, and the brightly clad figure would be from one of their priestly sects, which had seemed to be the only users of dyes in that drab land. "What color were the robes?"

"Orange."

That was a good sign. Of their odd sects, Dondrub's had been the most welcoming. If Shekar's answer had been yellow, Ashok would have ordered the Sons to prepare for battle, because the followers of Ram Sahib had been forced to flee the peoples' retribution after Ashok had slain their master. "You are certain?"

"I can tell my colors apart, General Ashok. They're dusty from travel but those robes were orange as the flowers of Apura."

"Then these might be allies. I asked for their aid, but I doubted they would give it. The foreigners of Fortress are a peculiar lot. Their ways can be confusing to civilized men such as ourselves."

Shekar's tattooed face scrunched in confusion, as it was not often that Somsak got lumped in with the civilized very often. "You really think these are Fortress folk who've crossed the sea?"

"Beneath it. Gather your skirmishers but hold back. I will handle this."

Chapter 35

Ashok approached slowly, so as to not startle the Fortress gunners. One wouldn't think that a lead ball would be able to punch through steel plate, but it was surprising how destructive those things could be when driven fast enough. Ashok had seen these bullets—as they were called—shatter skulls or tear right through a man's torso. Since Fortress was where this alchemy originated, and they had an entire Order dedicated to using such weapons, they weren't likely to miss either.

Once they saw him sitting atop Horse, they stopped marching, spread out, and took cover in the tall grass. Their illegal weapons were hidden. Only a few of them remained standing in the open, waiting. Ashok rode within speaking distance and stopped.

The orange-robed one was very thin, his head shaved except for a topknot of hair, and so weathered it was hard to guess his age. Standing next to him was someone who, from the rough worker-style clothing and pack of tools, had to be of the Collectors Guild, like poor dead Moyo. And the last was clearly a gunner of the Weapons Guild, though Ashok had not seen a woman serving in that obligation before.

It was the female gunner who addressed him. "Hello. We are travelers passing through these lands."

With that strange accent it was a good thing they had come

across his people, and not a patrol of Akershani warriors. "You are of Fortress."

She said nothing in reply.

Ashok removed his helm.

"That's him!" the collector shouted. "I saw his face when he revealed the head of the Dvarapala and burned Ram Sahib and threw him from his tower." He immediately went to his knees. "This is the Avatara!"

The monk gasped and bowed as well. That was two very different priests bowing to him in one day, and Ashok didn't know how to feel about that. The gunner, however, remained standing and wary. After speaking with their master, that particular guild had not struck Ashok as given to fits of fanaticism or theatrics. Working with alchemy that had a tendency to violently explode must have kept them levelheaded.

"Are you sure it's him?" she asked the collector.

"It is! It is!"

"The collector speaks true. I am Ashok Vadal."

"Prove it," she said suspiciously.

"Do you think there are many on this continent who know the people of your secluded island? Your guild master is Sachin Chatterjee." Then he nodded toward the priest. "And your leader of the orange monks is Guru Dondrub." Then the collector. "And I do not know what rank Moyo held among you, but he taught me to survive the dark lands below, and I was honored to call him my friend."

"You may know some of our names, but it's said that the mainland's Inquisition spies on everything and speaks with the forked tongues of snakes."

"That's true. You are wise to be so untrusting." Ashok reached into one of the small bags on his belt and pulled out an object. "Catch, Collector."

The man looked up from his bowing, cupped his hands, and Ashok threw the thing to him. The collector studied the reliable fire-starting tool that Moyo had given Ashok, then pronounced, "This is one of ours."

"It was a gift."

The monk was convinced. "Across these vast and featureless plains, it must be the will of the gods to put us in the path of the Avatara himself."

"Or the Master of Guns was wise enough to tell us to send out ten patrols in ten different directions from the exit of the underground, three days out and three days back, and one of us was bound to get lucky in this strange land." But the gunner woman seemed satisfied. She made clicking noises with her tongue and twenty gunners rose from where they'd been hiding in the grass, prepared to shoot him. "We were trying to find any rebels at all. I didn't expect to find the alleged god-king reborn himself. It's an honor to meet you, Ram Ashok. I am Praseeda Jaehnig, designated Envoy of the Guilds."

So it was *Ram* Ashok now? "The only other Ram I knew was your ruler. Do I rule Fortress, then?"

"Well..." The woman seemed at a loss for words.

"It's more complicated than that, Avatara," said the monk. "The treasure you promised us in the down below proved true, a city worth of resources untapped. Thus the prophecy was fulfilled, but some factions still protest—"

"It does not matter. I am not there." Fortress wasn't his land to claim, and he had no time for its strange politics when he had his own people to protect. "When I left, I requested aid against the Capitol. Does Fortress offer it?"

"We do."

"How many soldiers?"

"We brought a thousand gunners."

Oceans.

Chapter 36

The Creator's Cove was far from the isolated island of Fortress, and from how Ashok had described it to Thera, most of that journey had to be made deep underground, in the pitch-black darkness, beneath the demon-infested sea, through crumbling tunnels dug by the mysterious ancients, now plagued by odd creatures and mad gods.

These strangers had come a long and dangerous way to meet her, so she would do her best to make sure it was worth it to them.

"I am Thera Vane, rebel, prophet, and Voice of the Forgotten." As someone who really preferred to remain unnoticed, she really hated saying that part out loud, but such was life. "Welcome to the Creator's Cove, honored guests and friends."

Thera and Ashok sat on one side of the plain stone room, while the leaders of the Fortress delegation sat on the other. They didn't even have cushions enough for so many important visitors to sit upon, as such things were luxuries here, but Ashok had assured her that the people of Fortress were not frivolous and their land was harsh, so they would not be offended over the lack of comfort. He claimed their monks even starved themselves on purpose, because for some inexplicable reason they believed hunger would make them wiser. Foreigners were very strange.

"It is an incredible honor to meet the gods' chosen. Your arrival has long been prophesied among the faithful of Ram-rowan's workshop. I am Praseeda Jaehnig, guild envoy. This is Lama Taksha, who represents Guru Dondrub's sect of the monks of the holy island."

"My master apologizes that his arthritic bones make it impossible for him to make such a difficult journey through the underworld." The orange-robed one saluted Thera by pressing his palms together. Thera thought he looked too skinny, and the necklace of gigantic beads he wore made his head look too big for his body.

"And this is Yajic Kapoor, of the Collectors Guild." Who, as far as Thera could tell, was the only one who might fit in as being from Lok, as he appeared to be a stocky little worker, balding and bearded.

"Guilds are like their castes," Ashok explained. "Then they sort themselves into houses based upon what their obligation is."

"It is more complicated but that's accurate enough," the hard-eyed woman acknowledged. She was stern of face and manner, and nearly old enough to be Thera's mother, but there didn't seem to be a bit of motherliness about her. "After the revelation of Ram Ashok, the guilds gathered in a council to consider his words and challenge to us. Enough of our people believe he is truly Ramrowan reborn that they decided to send a thousand men to help you in your fight for independence. The first few hundred gunners have crossed the underworld and now camp under the stars. The remainder are still making their way below and should arrive over the next few days."

"The underground is narrow, treacherous, and we can only move so many resources at a time. It is a long line of soldiers. This is the most feet to tread the dark path since the days before the demons fell," the collector said. "But I assure you, Avatara, we'll get them through safely to you."

"We do this expedition at great cost to our island," the woman said. "This represents a significant number of our defenders."

"We gladly accept this aid and will put them to good use. Thank you." Thera was still astounded by this development, as their tiny handful of guns had already wreaked havoc against the Law. What could she accomplish with a thousand? The Capitol would tremble.

"There are...caveats," Praseeda said. "This aid is not free."

Thera had been expecting this. Guild or house, nobody was going to risk an army unless there was a benefit to it. "Of course."

"I must choose my words carefully, so there is no misunderstanding between us. It is the duty of our people to prepare for Ramrowan's return. Many believe Ashok is Ramrowan reborn, rightful master of both the mainland and the Workshop, but not all believe this. Many believe Ram Ashok's claim that the gods have chosen another Voice, but not all. Those skeptics withhold their support. The Master of Guns says my expedition will fight by your side for a time, and if you are truly who Guru Dondrub says you are—"

"He is," the priest insisted. "The Guru is never wrong."

Ashok grunted in amusement. "Your Guru thought I was the same person as Devedas, who would be king, and he was surprised to learn the Voice was a woman, rather than a man."

"That was simply a matter of misinterpretation. The language of the forbearers is complex."

"I wonder, though, is this why the emissary your guilds sent us is a woman?" Ashok asked. "It seems odd, as I saw no women among your leaders and few who spoke at all while I was there."

The monk seemed pleased by how perceptive his reincarnated hero was. "Yes! Tradition of the Workshop is that our women mostly work in the fields and raise the babies, but this one is empowered by the guilds to speak for them."

"You talk too much about our private councils, Lama." Praseeda scowled at the monk until he bowed his head and remained silent. "As I was saying, Master Chatterjee believes that if you are truly the Avatara, then you will see to it his gunners are used well in battle, so that we can return proud and triumphant. But steel and powder do not come cheap. After a season he will expect our collectors to start sending back great treasure, taken from your enemies. If we do not, the skeptics will change their votes, and you will have no more help from the Workshop."

"What kind of treasure do you seek?" Thera asked.

"Everything, anything, all the things," the collector said gleefully. "Your lands are lard-fat with treasure—silks, gems, spices, tools, art, rare metals, paper, glass. The collectors will collect."

"I have seen their finest city, and it is poor," Ashok said. "Their island has few resources. The collectors risk the wrath of demons to comb their seashore searching our discarded trash that washes up there for valuables. Their need is an honest one."

"So this arrangement is a test, then," Thera said.

"It is," Praseeda admitted. "And it is a test given by very impatient men, some of whom root for us to fail."

"The yellow robes?" Ashok asked.

"That sect remains bitter at how you burned their false Ramrowan," the monk said. "There are many different interpretations of the prophecies. Your arrival caused great upheaval. Those faithful to the wiser sects volunteered to fight here for you no matter what, but for the rest of the guilds to continue supporting this mission, they will expect a return on their investment, and quickly."

That actually made Thera feel better, because the motivations of mercenaries were simpler for her to grasp than the motivations of religious fanatics. It appeared Fortress was an odd combination of both. If it meant saving her people, Thera would happily let these foreigners loot the Capitol and carry off all the contents of the great museum and all the judges' mansions brick by brick.

"Treasure can be arranged, but if this is a test, then let it test both sides. Ashok has told me something about how your island works, how you quarrel among yourselves, and your weapons are certainly fearsome from behind your mighty walls, but your people haven't fought a real war in generations. You'll receive your treasure, Fortress, but it will be earned through battle. My people just want to be left alone. You will help me convince the Law that they have no choice but to do that. I have a target in mind, only a week's travel from here. We will leave immediately to destroy it."

Praseeda seemed a little surprised at Thera's eagerness. Of course Fortress would be hesitant at the thought of serious bloodshed. That was to be expected from a people who didn't have a real warrior caste. "We will serve, but...this is a strange land. Our expedition will need support, food and shelter, guides to lead us."

"You will have all of that," Ashok said. "The Sons of the Black Sword will accompany you."

"We will need the rest of our men to leave the underground before we go, so we have access to all our weapons and powder."

"The rest of your men will be guided to rally here, to await our return," Thera said. "We already have plenty of powder."

"All Fortress powder is not equal," Praseeda insisted.

"Ours comes from the same formula as yours."

"How? Our alchemy is a secret unknown to the mainland."

"Take that up with the gods who shared it," Thera laughed. "Be truthful with me, Envoy. Fighting my enemies is what you were sent here to do, so why do you balk at doing it now?"

Praseeda paused, as if trying to decide just how honest she could be among barbarians. "I was told to push first, to get as many concessions from you as I could. I did not expect you to agree so quickly to our demands. The guildsmen move cautiously. I'm unused to such . . . enthusiasm. You are a bit more confident than the council expected you to be."

"I've been praying for a miracle. I'd be a fool not to take advantage of a miracle when it comes along. Of course I'm excited to use Fortress soldiers. A thousand guns could thwart the Law once and for all . . . So, did your guilds really choose to send a female ambassador to the Voice because they thought I would be *soft*?"

Ashok snorted at that.

"I don't claim to know our Guru's thoughts, but creating an appeal to sisterhood might have been his intent. Luckily for you when the Guru requested that it be a lady to speak on behalf of the Weapons Guild, my master picked someone who could still kill a man from two hundred paces away. Aim me at your target, Sister Prophet, and I will be happy to demonstrate."

Chapter 37

The Capitol had foolishly sent these warriors to a pointless death.

Most of the poor unlucky fools were men of Thao, but the force also had a paltan of Zarger horsemen, and another of Harban infantry, probably drawn from their comfortable duties guarding their houses' holdings in the Capitol. Proud Harban and cunning Zarger held great animosity toward each other, and both of them looked down on the impoverished Thao as their inferiors, so Ashok suspected whoever had ordered this mission of casteless murder had been a fool incapable of understanding that soldiers were men of opinions and passions, not interchangeable bricks that could be stacked into an orderly wall.

Protectors were drawn from every house, but they were reforged in their brutal training program to be brothers, perfectly unified in their goal of enforcing the Law. The Sons of the Black Sword hailed from many different houses and even castes, but they were united by their faith, and since that faith made them outcasts, they had made for themselves a new family to be loyal to.

The Protectors and the Sons were examples of how warriors of different backgrounds could be made into a powerful unified army. The hastily thrown-together army arrayed before them had been the opposite, and this had been proven the instant the first volley of bullets had been buried in flesh. Order had failed.

Panic had sunk its cruel talons into their hearts. Ashok watched in stony silence as hundreds of Law-abiding men died horribly, and the survivors broke in terror, running for their lives. The Zarger horsemen galloped away, abandoning the men on foot to their fate. The warriors of Thao and Harban dropped their shields and spears so they could run faster as they scattered in every direction across the poppy fields. The Fortress gunners chased them with murderous lead, no longer firing in volleys, but rather individually picking off fleeing warriors and putting holes in their backs. And the foreigners did this with a precise regularity that was disturbing to observe.

"Should the cavalry pursue and run them down, General?" Ongud asked eagerly.

Ashok breathed the acrid stench of the white smoke into his nostrils, stinging his senses with the knowledge that the illegal rods had brought them another easy victory. Even as he hated those cursed weapons for being without honor or dignity, he had to respect their effectiveness. All his men still lived. The Capitol's did not. Should he spare any? These warriors had been sent to kill the refugees who had been fleeing to the safety Ashok had purchased for the casteless in Akershan. There was no pride to be taken from running down defenseless starving wretches, so what did it matter if these warriors died by close sword or distant impersonal gun? They'd already been robbed of their honor by their masters, long before this fight had ever started.

Ashok could not experience fear, but he could feel pity.

"This is enough slaughter for one day, Risalder Ongud. Let them run back to their Thakoors, crying about the unbeatable Sons of the Black Sword." He directed Horse to move him closer to the gunners. "That is sufficient, Envoy."

Praseeda had been waiting midway between Ashok's officers and the gunners. As soon as she heard his command she began shouting, *"Cease your firing! Cease your firing!"*

The men of Fortress repeated her command so that it could be heard between the near constant ear-splitting *boom*s, and then they did as they were told. A last few shots went off before the order sank in across the entire line. The hillside fell eerily quiet, a stark contrast from across the field, where men cried in agony and wounded horses screamed. A great many eyes moved toward Ashok, eagerly seeking his approval.

He inclined his helm toward Praseeda. "That was acceptable."

"Thank you, Avatara."

The Fortress folk seemed exceedingly pleased at that, but the first of them who'd volunteered to cross the dangerous underworld to make war in a strange land had been the most devout believers among their guild. From childhood, their religion had taught them that their island's purpose was to serve Ramrowan reincarnate, and now their priests were telling them that Ashok was that hero returned. And compared to the last greedy oppressor who'd claimed that mantle, Ashok actually acted the part, slaying legendary monsters and toppling tyrants while surviving tests that should have killed a normal man ten times over. These foreigners had marched here, ready to fight anyone, because of that faith.

Ashok took no pride in this undeserved adoration. He was not the legendary king they longed for, but they shared a mission—to save the bloodline of Ramrowan—and that cause was just. So Ashok would employ their faith as a weapon.

"Well done, men of Fortress!" he shouted, and they cheered.

Then he addressed their envoy, because Thera had requested that he be as respectful of the foreigners' odd ways as possible. "The enemy camp is abandoned. Your collectors may take whatever they want from it as payment." Then he thought better of that, because his experience in Fortress had shown him that their reliance on alchemy had robbed them of their ability to fight up close like proper warriors. The last thing he needed was his deadly new force to get surprised and murdered while they were distracted looting. "Wait until my scouts confirm their horsemen are truly gone rather than circling back to strike us unawares."

"As you wish. The collectors will be happy at that, but the Weapons Guild hangs on your word, Avatara. For the first time in centuries, we have struck a blow on behalf of the gods on the continent the Law forced us to abandon. Today is a good day. Let there be many more."

"There will be." Ashok rode back to where his officers had been observing the lopsided battle. Being aware of his own bias, he required their honest assessment about the performance of their new allies. His men were in the saddle, their mounts nervous and dancing because of the recent thunder and the smell of blood and smoke in the air.

"How do you think they did?"

Eklavya shook his head in wonder. "For the first time I truly understand why the Law forbid Fortress magic to begin with. I thought I understood after our victories in Garo or the canyonlands, but that was nothing compared to this. Their gunners are so much more dangerous than ours."

"Drown me in saltwater," Gupta wailed. "They are incredible! And the number of hits...from such a distance! They carry their powder not in a horn, but as individual charges wrapped in paper that they bite the ends off of, and then they ram the paper in around the ball to make it tighter. That must be how they are so accurate, but even then they still reload and shoot twice as fast as my paltan. There is no wasted movement! I swear I didn't know any better, General. Forgive my incompetence. I will resign my obligation in shame and go back to digging in the mines where I belong."

"Don't be a fool, Risalder of Guns," Toramana snapped. "You puzzled out a new thing while your only lesson was some notes left by Keeper Ratul. With no teaching to you, you still taught others, and won us many battles since. You got months to practice. These island men have had their whole lives to learn and stand on the shoulders of generations before them."

There was a reason Toramana had been a wise leader to his swamp tribe. "The chief is right, Gupta. If anything, seeing the masters of their craft at work shows me the limit of their art, and how remarkably well your gunners have done in comparison."

Gupta swallowed hard. "Your praise humbles me, General."

That humility brought to Ashok's mind that time in the woods outside Neeramphorn, where Keta had convinced him to treat the workers of Jharlang as equals to the Somsak warriors and given them an opportunity to train against him as well. Even back then their clumsy tenacity had impressed him. It had been illegal for men of such low status to possess weapons at all. Now the rebellion was arming hundreds of them with illegal rods.

Oh, how far they had come.

"Yeah, don't cry, Gupta!" Shekar crowed. "That'd be like me feeling sad Ashok could beat me in a sword fight! Or that all the girls think Eklavya is prettier than the rest of us. Some things in life just aren't fair!"

His officers laughed at that, and even Ashok smiled a bit, but he had no time for frivolity. "Gupta, your duty now is to compare the technique you developed to the one employed by the Fortress folk. Observe and learn from them, improve our methods so as we integrate more of Gutch's guns and grow our numbers, and the Sons will become even more capable."

"I swear it'll get done!"

"Good. They are our allies now, but we cannot count on the continued goodwill of outsiders forever. If we are to forge a new house, a free house, as Thera has envisioned, we must stand on our own. Understood?"

"Yes, General!" all his officers said in unison.

As they parted to return to their responsibilities, Ashok noted that the orange-robed monk had wandered across the field to go among the wounded on the other side, alone and unprotected, where he could easily be taken hostage or worse.

"Foolish foreigner," Ashok muttered as he thumped Horse and let him run.

By calling off the fire and holding back his cavalry, Ashok had given the Capitol troops the opportunity to carry off some of their injured, but there had been many more left behind in the rush to escape. Some, it was obvious why, as there would clearly be no saving them.

Horse slowed as they approached the killing grounds. As savage as his beast was, Horse didn't like to get blood on his white hide unnecessarily, and there was plenty dripping from the leaves. During a charge, Horse simply did not care, and rejoiced in the fight, but the rest of the time Horse seemed too prideful to dirty himself.

Ashok dismounted and demanded, "What are you doing?"

"I don't know." The Lama had the look of a man in shock. "It is commanded that the monks of our temple always try to aid the injured, but I've never seen so many before!"

That was an admirable but—from the looks of things—futile goal. The lead balls deformed and tore gaping holes in bodies when they exited. Anyone with a limb hit had already run or been carried away. Whether they'd keep that arm or leg or not would depend on the skill of the Thao surgeons. Of those left behind, most of the crying had already ceased as the men succumbed to blood loss.

The monk was clearly distraught by the carnage and confused by the resulting emotions. "There is always violence in our lands but rarely on this scale."

"There are more of us than you, thus our battles are bigger. That is math. By our standards this was a small one. Worse are coming."

"Is all this truly necessary, Avatara?"

"Yes."

"You say it. The Voice willed it. But why do I struggle to believe when I see it? I have seen killing before, but not like this. I came here because of prophecy...but...I...This is..."

"Your faith in what you have always believed has been shaken. I understand what that feels like more than you can imagine, Lama." There was a Harban warrior a few feet away who'd been pierced through the stomach, and he was rolling about, delirious with pain. There was no treating such a wound, and the rot of sepsis was an agonizing way to die, so Ashok drew Angruvadal and put that warrior out of his misery.

The monk flinched. "If you declare this is good, I will believe you."

"War is not good, but it is required when the alternative is worse." Life had been simpler when the Law had simply told him when that was, but the Law had been wrong too often, so now he had to decide for himself. "These soldiers were sent here to block casteless from escaping the Great Extermination. Your guns killed hundreds to save thousands."

The monk turned in a slow circle, still overwhelmed by the spectacle. "As it is proclaimed, one alone must die to save millions."

Ashok stabbed another dying man in the heart. "You speak of your people's prophecy, the one engraved on the metal walls across your island, where the Voice must be sacrificed to stop the demons when they return."

"I do," he quavered.

"Why are you scared to speak now?"

"Because Guru Dondrub said when he told you about that part, you were overcome with a terrible rage, picked him up by the neck, and threatened to throw him down the mountainside."

Ashok looked down at the unnatural blade in hand that he was using to nonchalantly dispatch men who were past hope. No wonder the monk was afraid. The rest of the fallen appeared to be dead or at least unconscious, so Ashok sheathed Angruvadal. "The Guru exaggerates, but it is true I was displeased. Tell me more of this prophecy, including what is on the other walls of metal, and any interpretations of your other sects which disagree with Dondrub's."

"You search for a way that this one death is not required?"

"I do."

"Why?"

"Because I love her."

The monk was silent for a very long time. "There is no argument about that part that I know of. All the sects are in agreement. We don't know how or when, but the great army of demons will return, and only the blood of Ramrowan will have the power to stop them from consuming all of us. How? It is a mystery. But to unlock this power, the Voice must be sacrificed. Now there is a Voice called once more, while the descendants of Ramrowan are being persecuted to extinction, and from what I heard from your men on our walk here, one of your great cities was recently torn apart by demons. There can be no doubt the end of this age is upon us."

Ashok had seen too many things fall into place to deny that. "What else is said must happen in those last days?"

"A new king will rise."

"I know him. What else?"

"There will be a pillar of fire that splits the sky."

"We just had that."

"Oh . . . There are also a few references to the ascension of a new god, to assume the mantle of one of the old dead gods."

Ashok scowled, as that one had not been among Keta's many stories. "Who is that?"

"No one knows. The oracles of old called him *the Masked One*. And he was always shown as a figure of darkness and secrecy. Some call him the Night Father, as he is the enemy of Mother Dawn."

"I have met her."

"I have not had that honor."

"I am unsure if it is an honor, as she is a creature of riddles. Who is she?"

The poor monk shrugged, indicating his relative ignorance. "Another mystery. She is the Unassailable. She builds. Her enemy destroys. She reveals the truth. He hides and distorts it. She is from the old world. He is from the new."

"Is this Masked One my enemy as well?"

"Yes. But also no. It is said there is no lasting creation without balance. Good cannot exist without evil. In the prophecies of the end times, on one side there is always the Forgotten's Warrior, Voice, and Priest, while on the other there is the Demon, the King, and the Mask." The monk knelt down and used his finger to draw a circle in the dirt, then he divided it with a curving line. When he was done, they two halves were somehow equal. "These are oppositional yet interconnected forces. Pressure is applied in both directions to achieve reaction. It is said all must play their part to bring about the world the gods wish their children to inherit."

This was the abstract, symbolic wishful thinking part of religion that always made Ashok's head ache, and he had liked Keta far more than this foreigner. Talking about the gods' will in a blood-soaked field somehow made it even worse. "Enough. The only masks I know are Inquisitors', and if there is a god appointed for that vile Order, then we would surely have hell on land as well as sea. How do I defeat these forces while also saving the Voice?"

Lama Taksha stared at him for a long time. "You don't. She will choose to sacrifice herself, or we will all perish. The gods say—"

"If they declare Thera must die to stop the demons, I will prove them wrong."

"That is hubris."

Perhaps it was, but he knew Thera's true nature. If the choice was her life or the lives of her followers, she wouldn't hesitate. When they had met she had been trying to act the hardened criminal, selfish, jaded, aloof . . . but that wasn't who she really was. That was what she'd become to survive. When given the smallest freedom, the tiniest bit of hope, Thera had turned out to actually give a damn about what happened to everyone she declared to be her people, which was a large and ever-growing mob. Her health had cursed her to be barren, but she had become the mother to a legion. She was an outcast who had become a symbol of hope to all who'd been forsaken by the Law.

But most importantly, she was the only woman Ashok had ever loved, and he would stubbornly fight the whole world to protect her.

"You believe I am your Avatara, the ghost of Ramrowan born into a new body?"

The monk nodded vigorously. "Yes, of course."

"And your sect believes in a life after this one?"

"Also yes."

"Then if you ever tell the Voice about this prophecy, I will see to it you are condemned to suffer in both of them. When you return to our base camp, you will leave Thera in peace. Do not tell her of this supposed sacrifice—or else."

The monk put his palms together and bowed deeply, which Ashok recognized as a sign of subservience in their lands. "I will do as you command, Avatara. But will the gods? They speak directly to her! When the time comes, surely they will make their will known to her. You cannot threaten the gods!"

"I have before..."

Ashok sensed the thunder of hooves approaching, and at first he thought some of the Zarger had returned to challenge him, but then he spotted Ongud riding this direction fast.

"Ashok, come quickly!"

"Continue your work here if you wish, monk, but don't be surprised if one of them is only pretending to be dead and stabs you." Ashok vaulted into the saddle. "Run, Horse."

He met Ongud halfway across the field, as the cavalry risalder's mount wheeled about. "The prophet has fallen ill!"

"What manner of sickness?"

"The runner said it was a mad shaking and then she fell down and won't wake up."

A terrible ache formed in the pit of Ashok's stomach. Ever since Thera had been struck by the bolt from the heavens, she'd been afflicted with rare but unpredictable seizures that rendered her temporarily helpless, and then weak for days afterward. She thought it was a side effect of the Voice inhabiting her head and did her best to keep this frailty a secret.

The two of them rode hard back through the ranks of the Sons, toward where the support troops and supply train had been waiting. Thera had been among them to deal with the many continual issues that plagued a rebellion that collected refugees like a girl collected flowers, and their one-sided battle had been over so quickly that she'd not even had time to come forward to watch.

When they reached the camp, Ashok knew immediately where Thera had fallen because a great crowd of nervous onlookers was gathered. "Make room for your general!" Ongud roared, and the workers and casteless who managed the Sons' baggage train rushed to get out of the way. Fortunate for them, because in that moment, Ashok might have let Horse trample them to get to Thera faster.

She was lying on her back, clearly delirious, but someone had been wise enough to move her beneath the shade of a tree and place a moist cloth on her forehead. Ashok jumped from the saddle and ran to her side.

The wizard Laxmi was kneeling next to Thera. Having been Thera's maid, she too knew of the terrible shaking sickness that Thera had suffered from since childhood. "We were going to the front when she swooned and collapsed. She foamed at the mouth and began to choke, but she's breathing alright now."

Ashok knelt and took hold of her hands. Thera's scarred palms were cold to the touch, but her face was flushed and drenched in sweat. The mob pushed in behind him, whispering fearfully about how they'd be lost without their beloved prophet, and their selfishness infuriated Ashok.

"Damn the Voice which plagues her." When some of the frightened crowd heard Ashok's bitter curse, they gasped, but Ashok snapped, "You can't begin to understand the price she has paid for all of you. *Back away.*"

It was a good thing they immediately did so, for it spared them not just from Ashok's wrath, but the Forgotten's as well.

The Voice manifested in the form of a giant made of fog and light, forming around Thera's body. An invisible force slammed into them. Laxmi was hurled back across the grass, but Ashok took the hit, and leaned into it, gritting his teeth and refusing to budge. It was as if the air around Thera turned to iron, hitting him like a shield slam to the face, and on the other side of that shield was a warrior twice as strong as Blunt Karno. Ashok's boots dug furrows into the dirt, but he refused to abandon his woman.

It was as if the gods' strange magic was designed to keep everything away from their Voice as their message was delivered, but the gods must have recognized the futility of trying to bend Ashok to their will and relented. Pressure gone, Ashok fell next to her, both of them huddled in the shadow of a belligerent deity.

The words of the gods were heard, not by the ear, but by

the whole body, banging around inside his head like a drum, so overpowering it made his bones ache.

The invasion has begun. The demons are upon you.

The fate of man will be decided by the blood of Ramrowan.

"We know! What manner of imbecile god expects meek casteless to prevail against demons? Speak plain for once!" Ashok roared. "Tell us what we must do to end this curse!"

Rally all your forces for the final battle looms. The Voice must lead them. Make haste, for soon the master of the next age will be determined in the great city of man.

Everyone else there was cowering in fear, but Ashok stood up and shook his fist at the giant. "If it means an end to Thera's suffering, Forgotten, then I will destroy the Capitol for you."

You go not to destroy, but to protect. Save the city of man or all will perish.

Chapter 38

The Capitol was a changed place.

The last time Devedas had paraded through this city it had been to celebrate killing Ashok. Back then the streets had been filled with jubilant crowds. There had been genuine joy upon the faces of the people as they hailed their returning champion to this oasis of green in the otherwise lifeless desert. This parade was very different. The streets were far less crowded, nearly deserted in fact. The people who did turn out seemed weary and worried. All the verdant plant life had withered since the rebels had destroyed one of the aqueducts. A few of the great mansions of the first caste had even burned down while he'd been away, and it was a strange feeling to see blackened rubble taking up space in a city where every inch of ground was so valuable.

"What has been done to my home?" Rada whispered.

A hundred warriors rode before them, and a hundred behind, representing every great house but one, while the two of them sat side by side in an opulent carriage pulled by eight of the finest Zarger steeds. A roof shaded their heads from the brutal desert sun, but the rest of their compartment was open, so the people could see their returning Raja and rejoice. That had been the plan at least, but it was clear there was no joy to be found in this city now.

"This is the aftermath of Omand's overzealous actions. The

315

Grand Inquisitor used the crisis in the north as an excuse to crack down on anyone who might threaten our new order." Devedas had finally confided in Rada what had transpired while she'd been away, though he had managed to leave out the details of his many crimes. If she was to be his queen, she needed to be his confidante as well, but there were some things in his past best left unexamined.

"I never paid much attention to the outside world while I was here. I was content to stay in the Library. But this difference is plain, even to me. It's appalling. The people are..."

"Broken," Devedas muttered. It was worse than Rada knew, because she couldn't smell that there were corpses of *hundreds* of prisoners baking in the sun atop the Inquisitor's Dome like he could, nor could her frail eyes spy the mighty cloud of buzzards that circled that dread Tower of Silence, fat and heavy from their feasting. "Most of the first have been pampered and sheltered for so long that a few months of terrorizing them was all it took to destroy their spirits. You must believe me, I wanted to rule, but not by fear. Not like this."

"There's a tale in a book of political speeches I read once, about a Thakoor whose pride blinded him to the disloyalty of his advisors, so that he squandered his house's wealth trusting liars and charlatans. When I return to the Library I will have to see if I can find that tome for you, assuming your new friends in the Inquisition didn't burn *all* the books."

With most of the Vadal warrior caste trapped and Vadal City under siege—and who knew how long that might take—Devedas had thought it prudent to return to the Capitol to confront Omand about his vile manipulations. He was glad that he had, for he had found the Grand Inquisitor missing, the judges cowering, and the city in decline. This presented an opportunity, so Devedas had taken immediate and decisive action. Today would see his plan fulfilled.

"I will correct this," he promised.

"You should. You're responsible for breaking it."

Rada hadn't taken well to the revelation of his conspiracies. She was too honest for such matters. "I have already called for a stop to the Great Extermination."

"For what good that will do those already massacred."

"That was not my doing."

"Nor was it your stopping it," Rada snapped, but then she realized that though the crowd watching them was a depressing one, it was still a crowd, and she was still a representative of their caste. She forced a smile for the witnesses' benefit and waved to them. "I don't know if I'll ever be able to forgive you for that, husband."

There had been no time for ceremony, but the arrangement had been essential for his plan, so they'd found a judge along the way and had him fill out the papers to make their union official. Devedas would give her a proper celebration after this mess was cleaned up, one that would improve the morale of the common folk. In the meantime, however, he needed a union in place for political and legal reasons.

"You may not forgive me in your heart for a long time, but your mind thrives on logic. We both know it would be so much worse if it had been anyone other than me who'd dared to claim the crown Omand forged. The plan for the Great Extermination was in place long before we met, long before they coerced you into lying about it. The fate of the non-people was determined before either of us knew of any plot against them. They used us, so I used them, and now I will right their wrongs and make Lok a better place for all."

"I understand that," she grudgingly admitted. "When you told me of this scheme to be king, I didn't scoff. And when you proposed to me and said you didn't want just a wife, but a queen to stand by your side, I agreed, but with that obligation comes the truth as I see it. I'll not lie to you, Devedas. Both of us have things we must atone for. I've become a willing accomplice in your plan, because repairing the harm we've done will be easier to do as rulers than as nobodies."

She only knew the half of what he'd done, but that would suffice. The carriage ride was uncomfortable enough already. "The powerless can make amends for nothing. A king can change the world. Speak your mind. I didn't ask for just a queen, but an advisor as well. I'll listen to the truth, even when it is an uncomfortable one."

"Whatever is necessary for the success of your house, is it? You know, I suspect you and Harta Vadal were rather more alike than either of you would guess."

"Maybe." Devedas' hatred for that man had turned to grudging respect. Diplomacy had made them temporary allies and Omand's lies had turned them into enemies once more. "Except Harta had but one house to worry about and is dead, while I'm here alive to claim them all. Today we'll rid ourselves of the liars and charlatans you despise so that I'll never have to appease them again."

"If we are successful today, then end the war in the north, I beg you. Omand desired that war. Not you."

Rada didn't know how he'd had his Garo torture the truth from Inquisitor Taraba, so her appeal wasn't based on Vadal's innocence, but rather on what spared the most lives. That perspective was a fine example of why he needed her around to provide balance. Devedas had already been preparing to attack Vadal to try and secure the second Heart long before Omand had forced the issue with his assassins. "Once Vadal surrenders completely and bows to me, I will."

"To do that will ruin them."

"To accept anything less than that now will ruin my rule before it even begins."

"There is more to war than just the war itself, Devedas. While Vadal City is under siege, they pay no taxes and their crops don't get exported. It's the most vital hub of commerce in all of Lok. The entire continent depends on trading with them."

He didn't know if she'd gotten those ideas from spending time as Harta's advisor, or from one of the many books of figures and statistics she'd read. "It seems I don't need to go to the Chamber of Argument today, because I'm getting plenty during my parade. I said I'd listen. I didn't say I would always agree with your conclusions."

They continued in a stony silence of fake smiles and forced waves at a people who were likely only watching because to not turn out would be to invite the suspicion of Inquisitors. His last parade they'd had several elephants, but all great beasts which had once lumbered about the Capitol had been sent away or butchered for meat as they no longer had the excess supply of water sufficient for such big animals to drink.

Rane Garo rode up alongside the carriage and matched their leisurely speed. All of the Raja's bodyguards were dressed for battle, and that wasn't just to add to the splendor of the parade. "Your men have returned from the Tower of Silence."

"Report."

"The rumors are true. Omand has been gone for weeks, having made some excuses about business elsewhere, but none of his men know or will admit where he is. In their master's absence the Inquisitors there were hesitant to provoke us and gave in quickly to our demands."

"That's excellent news. Hopefully there won't be a legion of them waiting for us at the chamber." Devedas hoped to avoid civil war if possible. The Capitol had been shamed enough already with that kind of bloody spectacle. The young warrior seemed hesitant. "I can tell there's more. Spit it out, Rane."

"As you feared, among the prisoners condemned to suffer on their roof were some Protectors of the Law. Five of them had been arrested for treason for standing against Omand's excesses." A shadow of wrath must have crossed Devedas' face as Rane spoke, because the Garo warrior looked down to study his saddle, afraid for a moment to meet that terrible gaze. "It must be because of the Protectors' legendary strength, but three of them were somehow still alive."

"You freed them?"

"We did. They're being cared for now, but I doubt they will live, as their skin was charred black by the sun and buzzards had picked at their flesh. I couldn't even get their names since none of them were able to speak."

"Did their hearts still beat?"

"Yes."

"Then they'll live." Devedas knew those who had touched the Heart of the Mountain could heal from nearly anything. With Protectors, it was kill them fast, or not at all. "Give them water and let them rest."

"It'll be done. There is one other matter..." Rane glanced toward Rada. "There were also several prisoners taken from the Capitol Library, their alleged crimes unknown. They didn't survive. I don't know their names either. With the specter of Omand gone, the Inquisitors were trying to be even more frightening to compensate. They were in such a hurry rounding people up they didn't write them all down. Not just Archivists, but Historians, and Astronomers, and Tax Collectors. The Inquisition culled every Order."

Rada fretted nervously during Rane's report, as there had been no word from her family yet. Their estate had been abandoned, and the neighbors had said Lord Archivist Durmad had told them he was going on a trip to his ancestral home in Nems, far to the west. During Omand's brief reign, many high-status families who hadn't left the Capitol for years had experienced a sudden and pressing need to visit relatives in their distant homelands.

"We're almost to the chamber. Tell the men to be ready for anything." Rane saluted him and broke off. Devedas waited until he was away before telling Rada, "The Library has many obligations. I'm sure it's not your family."

"They're all my family. I feel for them the same as you do your Protectors... Is there a chance Karno is among those prisoners?"

"Not at all. I sent him on a mission far away," he lied. For his sake, it would be best if Karno was back in Uttara enjoying his retirement or plowing some field.

"I hate that this is happening, Devedas. I hate that I had a part in starting it, but I know now that all this pointless suffering was willed into existence by one man. Omand is a spider and spiders must be stepped on."

"Then today let us tear down his web."

Their procession reached the Chamber of Argument, the symbolic home of the judges, and thus the Law itself. A band was present and they began to play a triumphant song as Devedas stepped from the carriage in his gleaming golden armor. He offered his hand to Rada to help her down, and then the two of them went up the steps, past the very spot where the Chief Judge had been assassinated by an Inquisitor pretending to be a lowly fish-eater. The Raja's warriors fell in all around him, eyeing their surroundings for threats. They would not be dishonored by an assassin like the Chief Judge's guards had.

Strangely enough as he climbed those steps, Devedas experienced the familiar sensation of anticipation, nerves, and determination that he often felt before going into battle. He supposed in a way, he was. This was simply a different kind of battle.

The parade route had been relatively empty, but news of his arrival had drawn a crowd around the chamber. He did take some heart from that moment, because now that he was walking among the people, he saw that they weren't all completely despondent. Many still believed the stories of Devedas' greatness, and after suffering for months under a tyrant's heel they were searching for someone who could save them. Those gathered outside were overwhelmingly lower status members of the first caste. Even bereft of rank sufficient to get a seat inside, these people would still tend to be jaded political realists. Their looking to Devedas for guidance was a good sign. The masses made up of the lower castes who just wanted to feed their families and live their lives would be even more willing to accept a single strong leader who would be able to return things to normal.

The crowd began to chant his name. When he stopped at the top of the stairs to turn back and raise his hands in greeting, the mob cheered. Thankfully, it appeared being isolated in the north had kept his reputation from getting smeared by the brush of Omand's bloodthirsty corruption.

The people were desperate. The people desired a king.

"This might actually work," Rada admitted.

Once through the doors, they walked purposefully toward the stand in the center of the auditorium. His return had been an unexpected surprise, but that was insufficient to explain how the judges' section was only half full. The rest had run back to their houses or perished chained atop the Tower of Silence. The remainder of the seats in the gigantic space were set aside for representatives of various Orders and the highest-status members of other castes. Those seats were completely filled by hundreds of curious onlookers who'd come to listen to their Raja, despite his speech having just been announced that morning.

There had been a place prepared for Devedas and Rada among the first row of judges. They walked right past those.

There was still no Chief Judge appointed, but holding the staff and presiding over the chamber was someone Devedas recognized. Artya Zati dar Zarger was a cunning woman who possessed an icy charm and a quick wit, but more importantly, she was a loyal conspirator in Omand's dark councils, and had served her part as the public architect of the Great Extermination. It came as no surprise to see one of the Grand Inquisitor's mouthpieces serving in this capacity.

"I see the Raja is among us," she announced, before banging the end of the staff against the stone floor. "This session of address will commence. Interim Judge Artya Zati dar Zarger presiding. As per the Law, the first order will be the required reading of minutes, followed by—"

Devedas went up to the podium and roughly grabbed hold of the presiding staff. It was her delicate hand versus his golden gauntlet, and Artya had the sense to let go before Devedas had to take it from her forcefully.

"Sit down." His tone left no question about the seriousness of his command.

Artya did as she was told.

The judges murmured at this brazen display of disrespect for one of their kind. He allowed them to get that out of the way early, because it was going to get so much worse for them before this was over. Rada took her place behind him, as groups of Garo warriors moved to cover every exit. The masked Inquisitors who regularly guarded those doors must have felt a sickening realization that they no longer controlled the chamber, for the Raja's men—who were still marching in—were more numerous, better armed, and wearing armor. Devedas hoped none of the Inquisitors would be foolish enough to try anything stupid, but then part of him thought about some of his Protectors being chained to a roof, slowly burning to death in the sun, and thought, *Let them.*

"Hear me, people of the Capitol. I am Raja Devedas, and I have returned, greatly displeased by what has transpired here while I was away. The last time I stood before you in this chamber, the judges obligated me to tend to a crisis in the north because they'd been shaken by a pillar of fire that stretched across the sky. I fulfilled that obligation, only to discover that during my absence many of those same judges shirked their responsibility by allowing Omand Vokkan to subvert a Capitol Order for his own gain, perverting the Law and abusing his authority."

The audience hadn't been expecting this. The judges began shouting about this terrible outrage. Omand's allies—who had so recently been Devedas' allies as well—took great offense and began wailing about their imaginary honor.

Devedas raised the ceremonial staff high, called upon the Heart of the Mountain to give him incredible strength, and swung it with all his might against the stone. The staff, and a big chunk of the floor, shattered violently.

That sudden noise silenced them.

He waited for the splinters to rain down before continuing. "You will not speak again unless I will it." Devedas pointed the jagged end of the remaining half of the ceremonial staff at the judges. "All who were quiet as Omand flaunted the Law gave up their right to speak in this chamber. Test my will again and I will have your tongues cut out, here and now."

None did. *Good.* He hadn't wanted to interrupt his speech.

Devedas made a point of walking away from the traditional speaker's position at the podium, so that he was clearly no longer addressing the judges, but rather the Orders and castes who actually kept the country running. "The office of Raja was created because the judges had become too weak and corrupt to see to the safety of the people. They delegated the responsibility of caring for the Law to me, and as soon as I was gone to fight a scourge of demons, in their apathy and greed they let a criminal take over the Capitol to harass you and make you afraid. When Law-abiding men burn upon the dome, the judges have failed you."

There were many nods of agreement from those galleries. These were the people who had suffered the most during the Grand Inquisitor's purges. That was who he had to sway.

"Lok is consumed by war. Houses are in rebellion. Demons attacked Kanok!" It had taken a hot poker to the eye before Taraba had admitted to him just how bad that had actually been. "As the world has gone mad around us, the judges' response was to let the Grand Inquisitor torment *you*. Not criminals, not fanatics, but the noble backbone of this city. To such evil, I say *no more*! If the Law will not defend you, I will. As of now, order will be restored. By the authority I hold, I declare Omand Vokkan to be a criminal, and removed from his obligation. The Order of Inquisition will stand down immediately. All those who have been recently taken into Inquisition custody will be released. Additions to the Law passed only because of Omand's trickery—such as the wasteful Great Extermination—are void. The brave judges who had no choice but to retreat from the evil which consumed this city will be allowed to return to their estates with dignity. Let the dome be reserved for real criminals, not righteous men."

Though he'd threatened to cut out the tongues of any who interrupted him, he'd allow the cheering, for these people had had enough. Devedas let them make their joyous noise for a moment, savoring it, because he had dreamed of this day for a very long time.

"As for the members of the first caste who shirked their duties and aided the tyrant Omand..." Many of the judges shared frightened looks as Devedas said this, certainly expecting to die. "For you, I will be merciful. I will not punish you. Keep your lives—but you will be required to step down from your obligations because you have failed your caste, your house, and your people. Failure cannot be rewarded, or allowed to continue endlessly, as has been our tradition in recent years. For too long, our Law has failed us. No more."

Calling upon the Heart again, Devedas took the remains of the heavy staff and broke it in half over his knee. Then he tossed both pieces down to roll across the floor with a clatter, his disgust obvious.

"*I* will not fail you."

The people were shocked. The vast chamber fell eerily quiet as the audacity of what Devedas had just said sank in.

"The purpose of the Capitol must be fulfilled. Ultimately, someone must judge. Having already been delegated this emergency authority, I will fulfill the duty of these removed or absent judges in creating and administering the Law. This chamber is abolished. The Capitol Orders will continue their regular duties but will answer only to me. From the loyal judges and Capitol leaders I will appoint other Rajas as I see fit. They will report only to the first Raja. Such an office has existed in our people's history before, long ago, when it was known as the *Maharaja*."

Rada had suggested the name, having read it in an old book once. Devedas found the progression from Raja to greater Raja appealing, and it would help sooth those who would balk at the name *king*. In reality, they were the same thing, but such was politics.

"As Maharaja, I will lead the Capitol, and the Capitol will ensure that every great house has the opportunity to prosper as all are protected by my Law. Maharaja is a hereditary title, for just as a new Thakoor must be raised from among the previous Thakoor's heirs in order to see to the continuation of their house, so must the Maharaja to ensure the continuation of the Capitol. Never again must we allow the center of Law to be consumed by bickering and petty rivalries between vain and useless cowards. One man will command the Capitol. One man will decide what is Law . . . *One* man will rule."

Devedas surveyed the quiet chamber for a long time, waiting to see if anyone would oppose his claims. No one dared.

"*I am he*."

That very same day, as word spread across the Capitol that Devedas had claimed a new title and hope soared that the recent mad excesses of the Inquisition would be quelled, a minor earthquake rumbled through the city.

The Law-abiding claimed to not believe in superstitious nonsense like signs or portents, yet many still found the timing of this event to be ominous nonetheless.

In the nearby desert village of Shabdakosh, the well turned to saltwater.

Chapter 39

Buried in the jungles of distant Gujara was a ruin of the old world unlike anything that Omand had seen before. He had traveled across all of Lok and gleaned more of the ancients' secrets than anyone else alive. In the darkest corners of the continent he had learned forbidden knowledge and conversed with beings that should not exist. Those experiences paled compared to this, for it had once been a castle, not of land, but of sky.

Before Omand lay a door, beckoning him toward his destiny.

It had taken teams of workers weeks to divert the river and excavate the mud to reveal this entrance, and for weeks more his Inquisitors had tried in vain to breach it. Even rotted by a thousand years of corrosion, the ancients' material had remained resilient against their best tools and magic.

Omand summoned to his mind a complex pattern he had seen once, long ago, and willed that impenetrable barrier to be undone for him. The door slid open.

"Amazing," said one of the many Inquisitors guarding him.

"I will proceed alone."

Twenty Inquisitors hesitated, for they stood at the entrance of what appeared to be a great temple that had sunk sideways into the mud. Even covered in centuries' worth of plant life, it was obvious that this was a vast structure, probably the biggest thing the Inquisition had discovered in ten generations. There were sure to be incredible riches inside, caches of black steel, and an untold number of religious artifacts that would need destroying. Despite its age, there still might be incredible dangers inside, as some of the ancients' pets and servants tended to linger in a state between life and death, somehow asleep, yet lethal once awakened. By this point every Inquisitor had heard about how their unfortunate expedition in Vadal had released an all-consuming demonic horde. What ancient terrors might this ruin hold?

This was the sort of adventure that members of their Order dreamed of...yet the Grand Inquisitor was telling them to leave him be, so that he might face unknown peril alone? How could this be?

"Remain here. No one enters this place except me. No matter how long I remain inside, do not follow. Anyone who tries to interrupt my work, kill them. If any of you interrupts my work, I will kill you myself. Are my orders clear?"

Twenty masks bowed in unison.

Good. This close to his goals, Omand had no patience for the impertinence of lesser minds. He was gambling much by abandoning the Capitol while there were so many political games afoot. His entire life's work came down to this moment. He had risked everything based upon the promises of a demon.

Omand entered the forge of the gods.

The barrier automatically closed behind him. For being buried in a swamp since before the Age of Kings, it was remarkably clean inside. He had known it would be sealed somehow, since the witch hunter he had put in charge of this expedition had reported that he'd been unable to use magic to walk through the walls. The ancients' odd metal they built their structures out of was too dense to be passed through, even in the space between.

The air tasted old and lifeless, not unlike the various tombs Omand had invaded in order to smash their religious iconography, yet somehow this was even more sterile than those. Not so much as an insect stirred in this place. A few feet from the entrance everything was lost to shadow, but Omand had been prepared for the absence of light. He wore a very fine coat of mail armor, which was light and comfortable enough to be near useless against any heavy blade, but the Grand Inquisitor's uniform wasn't designed for combat, but rather to strategically carry ten pounds of demon and an entire pound of irreplaceable black steel about his person, ready for instantaneous use. His bracers were demon arm bones, his breast plate was decorated with ribs. Even the teeth of the mask he was wearing were made from real demon fangs, and with a mere thought Omand caused the magic infused through the armor to give off a faint glow, just enough to see by, but not enough to waste much precious demon.

It had been sweltering outside, as Gujara always was. A few steps into the interior and the air became dry and cool. The sudden difference made Omand shiver.

The castle had sunk into the mud at a strange angle, far enough to one side that he had to walk with one hand upon the wall so as to not stumble on the uneven floor, and crouch to avoid hitting his head each time he went through a nearly sideways doorway. From the shape of things, these particular gods who had run the forge had been the size of regular men. Having met ancient giants, Omand had not been sure what kind to expect.

The interior was very plain, just smooth and white, with gently rounded corners. In Omand's experience the ancients liked to engrave everything they touched with scenes of beauty or valor, but these walls were smooth and unadorned. This castle had never been used for artistic creation, but rather the creation of life itself.

He continued toward what instinct told him was the center of the structure. Now there began to be some decoration upon the walls, but they were simple metallic signs, and written upon each in the old language that only Archivists, Historians, and Omand himself could read were warnings. Only the select were worthy to enter the forge. Only those authorized by specifically named gods, such as (Vyavastha Adhisa) or (Jalakam Yantrakara) could pass through the final barrier into the chamber of creation.

In the center of the castle was a floating glass orb filled with roiling smoke, the tendrils of which were dark as black steel. The dark vapor surged toward the light from his armor, alive and hungry, as if this was the first time it had seen a visitor in a very long time. It reminded Omand somewhat of when he'd visit his old friend the demon and it would swim up the glass window of its tank to greet him.

Inside that orb was where magic had first been created, and

where the knowledge of every magical pattern to ever exist was stored. The black steel that Ramrowan had brought with him to Lok was nothing compared to this, for this was the source.

Unafraid, he placed his hands against the orb, only to discover that it wasn't glass at all, but some manner of invisible barrier, which hummed with strange energy. The things Omand had interrogated in the dark places below had told him much, but this last part remained a mystery, even to him. Perhaps he would die? Maybe it would transform him in ways horrific beyond imagining?

Or perhaps he would inherit all the power of the gods and rule the world forever with an iron fist.

Grand Inquisitor Omand Vokkan spoke the secret words he'd been entrusted with by a dying god he'd once met beneath the desert sands. "Soham nava vyavastha adhisa chanakya."

The forge asked him a question directly into his mind. It was similar to, but far less painful than, the way demons communicated.

Kuncika padam?

That old god had been trapped for centuries, driven mad with grief and loneliness. An architect, unable to fulfill the ultimate purpose of his creation, and bereft of heirs. So Omand had tricked that old god, telling him that he would be honored to finish the great work that the gods had started, and he had promised that if he was entrusted with this sacred knowledge, he would only use that incredible might for good.

Omand, of course, had lied.

He supplied the answer that the dying god, so desperate to finish his work, had whispered in Omand's ear. "Loka-kshaya-krit."

The forge pondered his answer.

The barrier opened and Omand received his inheritance.

An unknown amount of time later, Omand removed the barrier and left the forge, to step back into the sticky heat of the jungle...and find that all of his Inquisitors had been slaughtered, their bodies roughly torn to pieces and thrown about the work site. The scene was so brutal it looked to be the work of demons, or at least something roughly their equivalent in ferocity. Time had ceased to have any meaning while he had been immersed in the ancients' glory, but flesh decayed quickly in this humidity, so from the state of their bodies his men had been killed about a week ago...Had he really been immersed in the forge so long? It was odd that none of the many scavengers that lived in the Gujaran jungle had touched these corpses, as if nature understood they had been left as trophies, and thus were off-limits.

His curiosity didn't have to wait for long to discover what manner of beast had caused such carnage, as it appeared the perpetrator was still there, patiently waiting for him, sitting upon a moss-covered boulder.

"I'd say it is a pleasure to finally meet you in person, Omand Vokkan," the woman said, "but that would be a lie."

She was small of stature and cruel of face. Oddly enough, she was dressed in the rough black uniform of an Inquisition torturer, complete with the leather apron with its many pockets to hold various tools designed to inflict pain. Her clothing was strangely out of place in this colorful shrieking jungle.

Omand smiled behind his mask, because he had been waiting for this day for a very long time. "A strange woman who appears in the guise of someone who her target will feel sympathetic relation toward. Marvelous. Oh, I know who you are."

"Do you, now?"

"You must be *the* Witch, the original reason why the witch hunters were formed. It is truly an honor to meet a creature deemed so threatening that an entire obligation was created simply to combat her influence. In training, I thought the great witch was a myth, a frightening remnant of a tale from the old world. It was not until later that I began to see your handiwork in so many seemingly unrelated events that I realized you had to be real. You are the Mother of Dawn. The Unassailable."

"So I won't need to introduce myself after all."

"You are a fortune teller, a shape-shifter, and a manipulative puppeteer."

Now she turned into an old casteless crone, dressed in rags, with a shock of wild white hair. "You know something of that last role yourself, o spider at the center of the web."

"That I do." He nodded at the well-deserved compliment. "We are alike in that respect. Only I accomplished my goals as a mortal man, armed only with whatever powers I had the courage to seize for myself, while you are an unchanging creation, designed for one singular purpose, and capable of nothing more. Is that why you never claimed the inheritance for yourself?" He gestured at the ruin behind him. "Surely you knew the forge was here all along. Did the old gods look upon their insignificant creation and deem you unworthy?"

"They may have. It wasn't my place to ask." In the form of a warrior-caste girl of Harban, she jumped off the boulder and strode toward him. "Unlike you, I never felt a compulsion to take what wasn't mine. I was sent to aid these people, not turn them into my slaves."

"They get what they deserve. Have you come here to try and thwart me, then?"

"I have," answered the Uttaran farm wife, her round face smudged with dirt.

"You can see the future. Surely you know that you are too late. The power of the gods is mine now." He reached up and tapped the side of his head with two fingers, for inside his mind swirled so many patterns, and so much potential. "I can alter all matter and control life itself, and this power is ready to be bent to my will with merely a thought. It is truly breathtaking."

"I imagine it is. The ancients never paused to wonder if they should do something, only if they could. In their hubris they nearly destroyed us all."

"Regardless, their power is mine. Before? You might have had a chance against me. Now? You cannot stop me."

The girl in flowing caravan robes gave him a patronizing smile. "You still have much to learn, Omand. If the gods could see *all* that may happen, then they wouldn't have let themselves be cast down by their jealous rivals to begin with. I can see somewhat into the future, but there are always entanglements which pull the threads from side to side. The more those of us with vision meddle, the more variables we introduce, the more the pattern veers from the course the gods hoped for. I love my children, but I can only nudge them so far in the right direction. I can coax, not command. To do more is to invite dangerous unpredictability. Now that I have done all I can, the rest is up to them, my purpose is fulfilled."

Omand considered her words, but even with his newfound understanding, could not understand her actions. "What kept you from stopping me before I found this place?"

She was a beautiful pleasure woman, wearing the finest silks, and a brand on her wrist that marked her a slave of a brothel

he'd frequented in Sudorat. "There are three and three, oppositional yet entwined forces at work, representing degrees of
freedom and control, creation or destruction, each necessary to
bring us to the end of the predictions. Even my architect didn't
know the ultimate purpose of every part, only that they must
all be present in the final days."

"Who chose these parts?"

"They represent various plans. The gods were never united.
They were a quarrelsome lot, each desiring a different outcome for
this world. Yet the one thing there was unified agreement upon
was that the demons must not be allowed to win, for demons are
beings of pure hate, and in their nihilistic rage they would eventually destroy everything, forever. The demons are a dying race,
but a sliver of what they once were, and this is their final desperate
chance. Believing the blood of Ramrowan to be gone, this is their
only chance. If the demons claim this fallen world then they will
rise to become greater than ever before. *If* this remnant of demons
is defeated—and that outcome is very much in doubt—the human
survivors will be able to forge a new path of their choosing. Of the
remaining five, I know which of them I root for."

"Who are they, so I may remove my final obstacles?"

The matriarch wore the white robes of a senior arbiter.
"You'll know soon enough. Of those with important parts in
the plan, you alone were ambitious enough to learn the demon
tongue and consort with their foul kind, cruel enough to begin
the Great Extermination the demons had been longing for, and
then treacherous enough to deceive the demons into invading the
land before the bloodline of Ramrowan was fully extinguished.
As to why I was required to allow you to claim your reward...
I would guess it is because a new religion will require its devil."

That pleased Omand, for a devil must be far greater than
any king. "You were required to let me come this far, and now
that we have moved past that point into the unknown, you are
no longer bound. Thus you have decided to try and stop me...
even knowing you will surely fail."

"I'm aware this battle will be futile. I'll surely be destroyed.
But I must try because *I hate you.* I despise all that you are
and all that you stand for, Omand Vokkan. I knew what you
would turn out to be long before you were born. For centuries
I have seen all that mankind can offer, from its noblest to its

most despicable wretches. Of them, you represent the worst, most dangerous type of all."

"What is that?"

She was a plain, ordinary woman, unmarked by anything that denoted house, status, or caste, only her face was etched with the profound sadness of a mother mourning a lost child. "The kind who truly believes if only he could deprive everyone else of their will, he could control the outcome of everything. The universe does not work that way, Omand, but you will never stop trying to force it to, no matter how many lives you must ruin in the process. I believe my creators' predictions were wrong. I think you might ultimately prove to be more dangerous than the demons."

Omand chuckled. "Oh, you naïve creature, I guarantee that is the case."

Mother Dawn grew into a fearsome being of gleaming silver, towering over him, her six arms extended, and in each of her many hands was a differently shaped blade. She wore a necklace of skulls. Her voice boomed with a thunder that flushed thousands of birds from the nearby trees. *"For my children."*

"For myself."

Mother Dawn attacked. Omand hit her with the entire world.

The stones of the riverbed rose and flew at her with the speed of Fortress bullets, putting hundreds of dents into metal skin. Then with merely a thought and a slight draw of magic, Omand ripped two mighty boulders from the ground beneath her and slammed them together with the Mother trapped between. Tons of rock exploded and Omand whipped the remains into a violent tearing whirlwind with his enemy still inside. Then he filled that whirlwind with fire.

The ancient creature came out of that onslaught, wounded, but swinging. Omand simply extended one palm and slammed her back into the jungle. Tree trunks were blown into splinters on impact. She slid for hundreds of yards before coming to a stop, buried in the dirt.

Omand crossed that great distance instantly to appear before her. He had to take a moment to compose himself, as the man who rarely felt anything was nearly overcome with joy. "There are so many patterns to choose from...I could incinerate you into ash instantly, or peel you apart, strand by strand, for an eternity. The suffering I could inflict is beyond imagining. The potential, endless. Oh how I look forward to exploring the limitations of godhood."

She rose from the ground, bleeding silver dust from a multitude of cuts upon her many-armed form, and struck, faster than mortal comprehension. Yet such fury still seemed sluggish to the perception of a god. Omand moved, and moved again, letting the silver blades pass by, and then curious, he let one hit him, just to see how it would feel.

The silver blade pierced his chest and tore out his side. He simply desired that terrible wound to be made whole, and it was.

Even as she did her best to slash him to pieces, Omand called upon various patterns the ancients had developed. He restored his body to the prime of his youth, and then bestowed upon himself incredible physical might, easily twice that of what even what the mightiest Protectors could achieve using their little black steel particles in their blood parlor trick. With that new might, he caught one of the Mother's arms, snapped it at the elbow, snatched away her curved sword, and slashed her across the belly with it, engulfing them both in a cloud of silver dust.

Flesh was but clay to be sculpted by him now, yet it was interesting to discover that even the most efficient fire still required fuel, and his actions were rapidly depleting the demon bones lashed to his armor. The forge had the capability to create new black steel, and even more interestingly, renew the power within the already existent material. He had commanded that process of revitalization to begin, though Omand could not yet comprehend the details, and was unsure how long that might take. It turned out knowing everything was a very different thing from *understanding* everything.

Omand needed to finish this distraction and then resupply his demon, for there were many pressing matters that required his attention, so he ripped one of the demon ribs from his armor and willed that magically infused matter to reform into a molten spear of pure destruction, deadly enough to slay a god.

Mother Dawn surely recognized that pattern, as she moved to intercept him with her swords, but he smote off three of her arms, and then plunged the glowing blade into her chest.

She fell. Omand's hand was on fire. He let it burn, feeling nothing.

Strangely enough, even as she lay dying, Mother Dawn laughed, mocking him.

"Why do you laugh?"

She coughed up silver dust. "The trickster has been tricked. You may be a god, but it shall be a stunted, crippled one, forever envious of what might have been, because in your pride you have cursed yourself forever."

"Explain yourself."

Only Mother Dawn was already gone, her true form sprawled there, lifeless.

A curse? What was her ploy? In the first minutes of ascension Omand had already made himself functionally immortal, easily defeated a legendary enemy, and he had only begun to toy with his newfound power.

He reached for one of the multitude of ancient magical patterns the forge had burned into his mind...and was denied.

"No."

He tried another. And another. The knowledge was there, tantalizingly close, but his access to it had been stripped from him. *"What have you done?"*

The *Unassailable* Mother Dawn had been the appointed custodian of the ancients' knowledge. By killing her, Omand must have broken their protocols.

As a result, his inheritance had been revoked.

When a god screams in rage and despair, the whole world shakes.

Omand turned back to the forge, just as the hasty dam the workers had constructed to divert the river away from the dig site burst. A mighty wave of rushing water crashed over the forge and swept the devil away.

Chapter 40

Thera woke from a nightmare, screaming.

Ashok was instantly kneeling over her in the dark, hand already upon Angruvadal, prepared to kill whatever had startled her.

But even mighty Ashok couldn't kill her fears.

"What's wrong?"

His inhuman senses could detect any physical danger, but he couldn't read her mind. He hadn't seen the confusing images of a silver woman with extra arms being brutally killed in a distant jungle. "It was just a bad dream, Ashok."

There were footsteps outside their tent as one of the camp's sentries approached. "Are you alright, Prophet?"

"I'm fine," Thera said. "It's nothing."

"Return to your post," Ashok ordered. He waited, probably to make sure that particular Son of the Black Sword was doing as he was told, before asking quietly, "Troubled sleep, or something more?"

"I don't know. All my sleep's troubled now, but the god who picked me likes to shout rather than whisper."

Ashok lay back down next to her. The two of them were naked in her tent, in the middle of an armed camp, at the eastern edge of the central desert. From the quiet feel of things, it was the middle of the night. Hopefully her cries hadn't woken too many of her warriors. Their rushed journey had been hard. They needed the rest, as they would surely be spotted by the Capitol's patrols soon.

"We will reach the city in a matter of days." Ashok reached out and took her by the wrist. It was difficult for hands so strong and callused to be gentle, yet somehow he managed, but only with her. "Your heart is pounding. There's no shame in worry. I would be more concerned if you were not worried at all."

She lay back, trembling, trying to find a sense of calm. "The Voice makes it sound like we're supposed to be the Capitol's saviors, but just as likely they'll see us as invaders."

"We might yet be."

"The gods sent us here to fight demons, Ashok, not the Law."

"That will be up to Devedas. If he is wise, he will parley with us. If he is unwise, then we will settle matters once and for all."

This time the rebels had formed an army of criminals and outcasts the likes of which the Law had never encountered before. She had a legion of warriors, Fortress gunners, and even her own cadre of wizards, each with a saddlebag full of demon bone. All of her forces had been gathered for this supposed final battle. The Sons were marching far from home, into the center of the Law's power. If they failed here, the rebellion would be over. All the casteless left in the world would die. All their work—all of Keta and Ratul's work—would have been for nothing.

"So it's either save the Capitol or burn it to the ground, then?"

"I see no other way."

They were quiet for a long time, but there would be no falling back to sleep for her. There was no wind or chirping of bugs. The only sound was the distant crackle of watch fires. Her nerves were always raw for a month after one of her shaking fits. Lights were too bright. Sounds were too loud. Even the quiet was too quiet.

"There's something else bothering you," Ashok stated.

"Is risking everything on the vague commands of a being made of fog and noise that hides inside my skull not enough?" She tried to laugh it off, but he was right. It was hard to hide things from a man who'd spent most of his life rooting out criminals. "I've got a lot on my mind."

"And you have had more put upon you since we departed the Cove."

He had her there, and he was the only person she could actually confide in. She'd wanted to bring it up for days, but there had been so little time during their hasty march, that in the quiet times when the opportunity had presented itself, Thera had hesitated. "It's just ... it might not be clear what the Voice means at the time it speaks, though this latest one seems pretty straightforward by its standards, but its proclamations *always* shake out to be true somehow. There're some older prophecies that we haven't got to yet, but I think we may be there soon."

The comforting hand on her wrist stiffened. "Which do you speak of?"

This was surprisingly difficult to say. "There's a prophecy that the Voice will have to be sacrificed to save everyone from the demons."

"I told Dondrub's man to keep his mouth shut." Ashok sat up. "If you will excuse me, I have a monk to kill."

"Wait, wait." Thera grabbed hold of him. "I didn't get that from the Fortress Lama. He's been scared to talk to me. At least now I know why. You can't go around threatening to kill our allies."

"I would not have you fretting over the superstitions of foreigners. They cannot read their own plaques without disagreeing over what each word means. Do not let the words of fools trouble your sleep."

It was sweet that he would protect her, even from prophecy. "No, this one came from the Voice, a long time ago, back after I first met Ratul. Oh, how I hated him back then, but he saved my life and kept me safe. Ratul's the one who wrote it down, but Keta kept his record, and it's in the pages printed by Javed too. But the Fortress people believe that the Voice must be sacrificed too?"

"They do not know what they have." Ashok lay back down, sullen.

"That corroborates it, though."

"If the gods want you to die, they must go through me first."

She didn't doubt him on that at all. "It said the survival of man will require the willing sacrifice of the Voice at the final battle, but the prophecies are rarely clear. Keta didn't know when that battle would be, so he was constantly fretting I was about to die. My father listened to the Voice, and then started the wrong rebellion. Angruvadal was the servant who perished in Jharlang, not you or Keta. This is no different. I'm not giving up hope, so neither should you. I'm *not* the Voice. I'm Thera Vane. The Voice is just a passenger. I'm happy to carry it to its destination and then be rid of the thing forever."

She couldn't see Ashok's face in the dark, but just from his angry breathing she could tell he was unconvinced.

"I kind of pushed all that to the back of my mind until I saw it in Javed's book. It's easy to not think about some distant prophesied end to everyone's trouble when you're on the run and it'll be a miracle if you're still alive in a week. But now it looks like this is it, so I have to face the fear and uncertainty. I choose to go into this battle thinking the best, that this means the end of the Voice, not the end of me. And especially not the end of me and you. I have to go toward the end thinking there will be a reward, not a punishment."

"What of anything you've seen from these gods suggests they would show us such kindness?" Ashok snapped. "All they have done is demand and take. You've said this yourself."

"I know . . . but I can't turn back now. Don't insult me by asking me to. If this hope of mine is a lie, then it's a lie I'll gladly tell myself until I reach the end."

"You say the people need you and the gods need you . . . but so do I, Thera. When my purpose was taken away, you gave me a new one. If it is the Voice that must go, so be it. Good riddance. If it is you to be sacrificed, then no one, whether they be god, demon, or man, will take you from me without a fight the likes of which this world has ever seen."

Ashok's promises were never empty.

They made love that night, so as to not alert the guards. Afterward, Thera had forgotten her worries long enough to drift into a restful sleep blessedly free from nightmares.

Thera rose just before dawn, and found herself alone in her tent, with Ashok nowhere to be seen. She dressed and went looking for him, only to have one of the Sons tell her that General Ashok had left camp a few hours before. He had not told anyone where he was going, but he had taken his armor, four of their fastest horses to rotate between, and a few days' worth of food.

Oh, you stubborn man.

Half her force was on foot and their supply chain was dependent upon slow ox-drawn wagons. Traveling in that restless, unsleeping manner that only Protectors could, he would reach the city long before she and the Sons of the Black Sword could.

She knew what Ashok was thinking. Prophecies be damned. What were the words of the gods compared to one man's love? There would be no sacrifice necessary for her if Ashok could defeat the combined might of the Law and an army of demons *alone*.

Chapter 41

~~~~~~

The sun rose over the central desert.

In the distance a massive army—unlike any seen in living human memory—moved across the sand. There were hundreds of misshapen, hulking forms, each one a shadow blacker than night.

The warrior atop the watchtower lowered his spyglass, unable to fathom what he had just seen, for such a horror was inconceivable. Sometimes the sun could bake a warrior's head stupid, or the heat mirage could trick the eyes into seeing things that weren't there, but it was still cool in the morning.

Raising the glass to look again, the warrior watched the approaching horde, and with growing terror, realized death was coming.

"*Warn the Capitol!*" he screamed. "*Demons! Demons are upon us!*"

As a child of the frozen south, the mornings were when Devedas could truly appreciate the beauty of the Capitol. While the malicious sun was still low in the sky, it allowed them a merciful few hours before everyone had to retreat into the shade. During the summer, the Capitol became a nocturnal place, as no one sane wanted to conduct business during the brutal heat of the day here. As Lord Protector he had spent many a morning atop the roof of the Protectors' compound looking out over the great marketplace as its bustling crowds and constant activity slowly drifted into peace and silence. Oddly enough, he felt a bit of nostalgia as he stood in that same spot as a visitor.

"Maharaja Devedas." Protector Broker Harban went to one knee and bowed before Lok's singular ruler. "Thank you for agreeing to meet with me."

"The show of respect is appreciated, Broker, but unnecessary here." It was only the two of them present for this private meeting, so there was no need to keep up the air of aloof invincibility he had to maintain everywhere else. He and Broker had fought and bled together to become brothers in that way that only soldiers of a common cause could understand. His small army of body-guards waited downstairs, because if the supreme arbiter of the Law couldn't be safe with a Protector of the Law, then where could he be? Devedas extended one hand. "I may hold a new title now, but the program made us equals, and we will always remain so. Stand up, brother."

Broker took that offered hand and Devedas helped him to get up. Even with the healing magic provided by the Heart of the Mountain, Broker was still recovering from his ordeal atop the Tower of Silence. Most of his skin had been charred to a blackened crisp when the Garo had found him, and even now it looked to be a red, painful mess. The Heart could heal even the most terrible of injuries, but it still hurt the whole damned time.

Curse the Inquisition. If Devedas hadn't needed them to do his dirty work, he'd have every last one of them condemned to the same fate they had so gleefully dispensed to others.

The Protector met the Maharaja's gaze with his one remaining eye. Broker wasted no time on cordiality. "I've been trying to speak with you for weeks."

"I've been busy. Turning the entire government on its head and then making it somehow work again takes time...but I was told of your encounter."

"Then you know of Ashok's warning about the demons. Do you believe it?"

"That demons can burrow through hundreds of miles of rock and then pop out beneath their prey like a trapdoor spider?" Devedas shrugged. "It sounds outlandish, but they attacked Kanok from seemingly out of nowhere and wrecked a large part of it.

Out of caution I have recalled all the warriors that the Grand Inquisitor dispatched to chase rebels and casteless. They should be returning over the next month."

"Yet you've failed to recall the Capitol's greatest military asset."

That was because his Army of Many Houses was busy choking the life out of Great House Vadal. Devedas scowled, as he didn't care to have his methods questioned. "You were never a tactician, Broker. Do you play at being one now?"

"This is the most undefended the Capitol has been in centuries. These walls are currently guarded by a fraction of the men necessary. Of the warriors traditionally obligated to serve here, you took the majority north, and then Omand sent most of the remainder away so they wouldn't be here to get offended and take up arms against the Inquisition when the masks humbled their houses and whipped their masters in the streets."

"I have put an end to those excesses. Those responsible have been executed and Omand is in hiding."

Broker nodded respectfully. "Yes, and the people celebrate you for it. The whole city sings your praises."

"And what do you think about it?"

Broker had never been counted among the Order's diplomatic sorts, but his response was measured. "Protectors of the Law think whatever the Law tells us to think. When the judges decided the Law, we did as the judges commanded. Now the Maharaja decides the Law, so the Protectors will do as you command."

That was the kind of trite response Protectors gave to ignorant first casters, and to have it used on him now, like he was some kind of outsider, and not a man he'd stood shoulder to shoulder in battle with, made Devedas grit his teeth. "Don't pour honey on your words. What do the Protectors really think?"

"Very well... Some celebrate the fact that one of our kind is finally in charge of this mess. No more soft-palmed hypocrites and perfumed peacocks sending us off to die on foolish errands. Others... well, you know we're a suspicious lot. I'll just say some are unconvinced this sudden change will be for the better."

Devedas didn't like that, but that did not make the response any less honest. "Then I'll have to convince them through my actions, won't I? Enough of that. You believe this man you fought in the desert really was Ashok."

"Absolutely."

"Impossible. Ashok's dead. I killed him."

"It was him. I'm only alive because he felt like my dying would complicate things. He even had a black sword."

"I don't believe you."

Broker snarled at that insult to his honor. "I'm more certain that was the real Ashok than I am that I'm talking to the real Devedas now."

He was taken aback. "What's that supposed to mean?"

"Forgive me, mighty Maharaja, lord of all he surveys. I thought I knew Protector of the Law Devedas." Broker gestured at the scarf that hung over his missing eye. "I lost half my face loyally following him into battle on the banks of the Akara, so I believed I knew him well."

The idea that Ashok somehow survived was outrageous, but reason prevailed over offense, so Devedas decided to hear him out. "Speak your mind, Broker Harban."

"This man in golden armor I stand before now shares Devedas' name and face yet seems to many Protectors to be a distant stranger who would risk the safety of the Law itself over what appears to be a war of conquest against a house which gave us no offense."

"If any are confused why I don't recall all my troops based only on the mad claims of a criminal who was probably trying to trick the Capitol into sparing his rebels, then they prove why I was chosen to lead, and they weren't. Vadal City is surrounded. Its supply lines cut. They only hold out because of the strategic genius of a single phontho, and Jagdish's luck will run out eventually. To call off that campaign now without achieving a clear victory will invite defiance from the other houses. With defiance comes chaos and lawlessness."

"And what if it's the criminals who are the ones proposing peace?"

Devedas had no idea what Broker was talking about.

"They didn't tell you...From the confusion on your face, that unseemly part of my report wasn't passed on to Your Highness. Ashok offers peace. He says if we let them alone to believe in their superstitions, the rebels will stop fighting us."

"That's madness!"

"Is it any madder than Inquisitors burning judges in their mansions? Or warriors dying to Fortress rods in every great house because our betters decided we needed to throw out generations of tradition and suddenly slaughter a million fish-eaters?"

Devedas scoffed, yet Broker seemed earnest about what he was saying. "Ashok wants me to just let them *go*?"

"That was what he asked me to convey."

"All is forgiven. Live in peace, criminals! As if that could ever be. Surely as a Protector you're disgusted by this insult to the Law."

"Of course I am, Devedas! My honor was wounded by the very suggestion of such evil. That was my initial reaction at least, except being slowly sunburned, lingering near unto death for weeks gives a man plenty of time to contemplate everything he's ever done. How many of our brothers have already died fighting Ashok and his rebels? How many more will we lose before we defeat the seeds of dissent he planted? And for what? A Law that can change the instant you alone say it does?"

"It's not that simple!" A bell began ringing toward the south. Anger interrupted, Devedas turned that direction.

"That's the alarm for fires," Broker said.

Devedas used the Heart to refine his sense of smell. "There's no more smoke in the air than usual." They thought of that sound as the fire bell because that was the only thing it ever got used for here. The Capitol didn't have different kinds of alarm bells for different sorts of emergencies like some common border city, because the Capitol was supposed to be above such mundane events. "I wonder what they're ringing that for?"

There was a commotion across the market. A rider was crashing down the lane, whipping his horse furiously, heedless about running over merchants or customers. That warrior was shouting something over and over as he neared the Protector compound.

He and Broker both called upon the Heart to heighten their hearing, and then they looked at each other in shock as the words registered.

The demons are coming.

Chapter 42

By the time Devedas and his bodyguard reached the southern wall, fear had spread through the populace. This district was filled with the homes of workers of middling status but great wealth, such as master craftsmen and successful merchants, the sorts who had mostly been spared from Omand's purges because they had not been interesting enough to attract his contempt. Now those workers were rushing about, either gathering their children and their most precious belongings in a vain attempt to evacuate, or rushing home to hide inside their estates. The people of the Capitol had never had to deal with demons before and this fact was demonstrated by their panicked demeanor. To never have to worry about demonic raiders was the entire point of building a great city in the middle of the continent far from the clawing grasp of hell. The Capitol residents who had grown up in coastal houses took the news better. They were still frightened, because if anything they were even more aware of the danger a demon represented, but they also understood that the warrior caste would most likely be able to protect them, even if the cost to the warriors was great.

If there was only one demon, as in a normal rampage, they would be correct.

When Devedas reached the top of the wall he saw *hundreds* of the things approaching.

This section of the wall had been obligated to Uttara to man, and one of their officers was standing there, quaking in his boots as Devedas arrived. "Maharaja!" he squeaked and then managed to salute.

"Report, Roik."

"We spied them coming up the trade road from Shabdakosh. I don't know why any of the outer patrols didn't spot them sooner."

"Those patrols probably did but got run down and eaten. Fast demons can outrun a horse." Broker Harban had accompanied Devedas, and he swore when he sharpened his vision to take in the details of the approaching horde. "*Oceans!* That's a bloody lot of demons."

The spectacle before them was horror beyond imagination, and as Devedas watched, it got worse. The demonic army was lurching their way, stirring up a cloud of dust, but they were moving at different rates of speed for it to be called a march. Some ran, others lumbered. Most appeared to be roughly the size of men, but in various unnatural shapes. Some were big around as cattle. A few had to be large as elephants, and then there were shapes in the dust somehow even bigger than that. The way the small ones darted back and forth around the imposing giants brought to mind turning over a rotting log and seeing the multitude of insects beneath scurry away from the light. Except these were no bugs. Even the weakest demon out there could still rip a man's head off with ease.

It was generally accepted that a paltan of fifty warriors could be traded for a single raider from the sea, but better two paltans to be make certain that demon wouldn't live to trespass again. Throw a hundred regular warriors at a lone demon at once and half of them might survive. Even if his Army of Many Houses had been here, he didn't know if that would be enough to fight a force like this.

"Who has command over this section?"

"I do, Maharaja." The Uttaran roik was young and had the chubby face of a boy who had never once set foot on a real battlefield.

"I command now. Stay close by to relay my orders to your men." There were defensive plans in place. They weren't prepared for anything this outlandish, but the fundamentals remained the same. "Have runners been dispatched to every garrison in the city?"

"Yes, Maharaja. They've already been sent."

Supposedly those garrisons would then contact every Order and every important household, commanding them to rally their bodyguards and wizards for the city's defense. Even the merchant caravans' mercenary guards would be obligated to fight. Physically capable workers would be drafted as sepoys and given weapons that were normally kept locked in armories. Every man had his place. Or at least that was the plan should this city ever be threatened. But Devedas knew those plans had been ignored and neglected for years, for who would ever be foolish enough to test the mighty Capitol? Any great house that tried, their offensive would be known about long in advance, and then they'd be crushed beneath the weight of politics forever.

Demons did not care about politics.

The army of hell began to fan out from the trade road. The terrain immediately around the Capitol was flat sand, empty of barriers. The faster demons began to run, not toward the walls, but rather parallel to them. The giants followed.

"They intend to encircle us."

"They're cutting off every avenue of retreat," Broker said.

Too late for it to make any difference, Devedas had finally been given accurate reports from Kanok. This was at least ten times as many demons as had appeared in the southern city, and these were acting in a much different, seemingly more methodical manner. He had never heard of sea demons behaving like this before.

"No, Broker. They are surrounding us to make sure no one escapes the slaughter."

Never before in his life had Devedas been jealous of Ashok's inability to feel fear.

There were now dozens of warriors standing atop the southern gate, staring at the approaching menace, yet it was eerily silent except for the banners flapping in the breeze. There was always a phontho obligated to coordinate the city's defenses, but Devedas held no hope that man wouldn't be a political appointment, and thus completely useless.

"How many Protectors do you have in the city?" he asked Broker.

"Seven seniors, fifteen acolytes."

That was nothing compared to this demonic menace, but

those were likely the only men in the city who had experience, or at least serious training, on how to fight demons. "Split them up, send them to different walls, and have them take command of the warriors stationed there. Let nothing through."

"It'll be done." Broker rushed off.

He looked for his trusted guards, and as usual, Rane Garo was only a few steps away, ready to serve. "My wife is at the Library. Send some of your best to warn her bodyguards." He knew Rada would surely fight demons to protect her precious books. "And don't let her dally worrying about anyone else. Order them to move her someplace safe and keep her there."

Except there was no place safe in this city. Not against a threat like this.

Every minute, more warriors rushed into place. The city's armories were opened to the workers, and if the commander with the key hadn't turned up yet, those locks were smashed open. The Capitol's fashion and culture kept their warriors lightly armed most of the time, as the first found wearing implements of war in such a cultured place to be barbaric, which was a fact Omand had surely found most useful when he'd been terrorizing them. Now those men would be hurrying to get dressed in armor that would be nearly useless against demon strength, and handing out spears and polearms that would all but surely bounce off demon hide.

The horde was picking up speed.

"Surely the walls will stop them," said one of the Uttarans, who had clearly never dealt with demons before.

The Capitol's walls were low and flimsy soft. They existed as a symbol more than an impediment. On one side was order and wealth, on the other was barbarity and poverty. These feeble sandstone blocks had never been meant to withstand a real attack because who would ever dare to attack the sacred home of the Law?

The Capitol was about to pay for that assumption.

"We'll hold!" the young roik told his men. "They've not got any siege engines!"

That poor fool. Demons didn't need siege engines. Demons *were* siege engines.

"Warriors!" Devedas shouted. "Hear me!"

"*Attention!*" Rane roared. "Your Maharaja speaks!"

"Risalders, I want half your men stationed on the battlements, half your men waiting below. The demons who climb the walls, strike at their hands. Demon bone is like iron, but fingers break easier than skulls. The ones who smash their way through the walls, stand back far enough you don't get crushed by the falling stones, and then try to pin them at the breach. Do not give them room to maneuver. Keep hitting them! When all seems lost, when your blows seem to do nothing, *keep hitting them!* All it takes is one sword to pierce a heart, one mace to break a bone. Demons can die. I have killed them. Today you will too."

Some of the men cheered. Most were too scared. It would have to do. Perhaps if there'd been thousands more soldiers here as intended, they wouldn't have been so afraid, but alas, those men were in the north. Devedas could curse himself as a fool for not calling them home, but he would have to survive long enough to do it.

The demons were closing.

There were always caravans and traders coming and going, especially in the mornings, and there were hundreds of wagons stuck outside the walls. Those were mostly unfortunates who couldn't pay the entrance taxes, who'd set up shop along the road until they sold enough goods to buy their way into the grand market. As those merchants realized what was coming, they ran for the still open gates. Some would make it inside. The ones who did not would die.

"Close all the gates," Devedas ordered.

"They'll be cut off!" the roik cried. "I sent some of my men out there to warn the caravans. We still have time."

Except Devedas had seen how deceptively fast demons could move and knew their time was up. *"Close the gates!"*

Chains were pulled and steel portcullises dropped. Poor workers screamed as they were caught beneath. The ones trapped on the other side begged for mercy. The wooden doors were heavy enough that it took three warriors on each to swing them shut, even on well-oiled hinges. Once they were closed, the wood muffled the sound of the cries.

As cruel as that had been, it proved to be the right decision, for as the demons closed within the last half a mile, they began to *run,* and they were incredibly fast. It was a sight that would haunt anyone who survived for the rest of their lives.

"You should go, sir," Rane whispered to him. "The warrior leadership will gather at the chamber, and it's a fort on its own. The demons might tire themselves out before they reach the city center."

"Or maybe I'll get lucky and they'll eat their fill and be too stuffed to eat me last?" His bodyguard meant no insult to his courage. Rane was simply doing his best to keep his charge safe. The Garo lived by the sea. They knew demons as well as any man could. "Don't tempt me with safety, Rane. The Capitol is my responsibility." It appeared this gate was where the largest number of demons were massed, so this was where Devedas would stand. He put his golden helmet on and began walking along the battlements. "I didn't replace cowards to become one."

"No, you clearly did not." Rane took one of the long spears offered by an Uttaran. "It's been an honor serving you, sir."

"We're not dead yet, boy...*Roik!* Tell your archers to let fly when they're in range and to not stop until they run out of arrows or demons." The soldiers of hell had no ranks to disrupt, so there was no point to organized volleys. All they could do was send thousands of missiles in the hopes that a few might pierce demon hide.

The Capitol had a handful of powerful ballistae upon the walls, but those were mostly used for decoration. They had been gifts from the Kharsawan, who took great pride in the artistry of such complicated devices. Made of steel, brass, and wood, they launched large bolts by the power of mighty springs. Warriors who had never practiced with such weapons were struggling to use them now. If he'd not been so busy trying to rebuild an entire government himself, he really should have taken the time to inspect the defenses of his own city, because seeing their incompetence under pressure was infuriating.

"Hurry those up and aim them at the big ones." It stood to reason it would be easier for the inexperienced to hit something the size of an elephant rather than something the size of a horse.

Arrows flew. These Uttarans did not appear to be good archers. Devedas wished that it were a different, more warlike house that had been obligated to this section of the wall today, but it was what it was. Uttara was a quiet, rural house, rarely embroiled in any notable conflict. Karno had been an anomaly among his people...Oh, what he would give to have Blunt Karno and his war hammer here now. He was no stranger to fighting demons.

The fastest of the creatures had reached the caravans trapped outside and pounced upon the people, biting and tearing. Wagons were flipped over, wheels still turning. The demons couldn't seem to tell the difference between man or livestock and killed either with equal bloodthirst. Arrowheads bounced off ebony hide as the monsters feasted.

Demons leapt onto the wall and immediately began to climb. Their black claws sank into the soft sandstone, and they seemed agile as monkeys. Featureless heads turned upward, and the fact they had no eyes somehow made their staring even worse.

The warriors watched the horrific things get closer, their fear growing. There was an aura about demons that made strong men piss themselves, and the weak-willed shake until they could no longer stand. Warriors sank to the floor and waited there quivering for death.

"Stand and fight! Don't even think of running. There's nowhere to run to!" Devedas reached down and grabbed one of the cowards by the neck, hoisted him up, and set him back on his feet. Then he gave that warrior's helmet a smack that was surely hard enough to knock some sense into the man. "If you won't fight for yourself, fight for your brothers. *Spears over the edge!*"

Most of the men managed to do as they were told. They went to the side, spears clutched in white-knuckled hands, and got to stabbing as soon as the demons were in range. Steel struck downward and glanced off hide. The creatures made no noise, but the warriors did, bellowing in rage or screaming in terror. For each demon that lost its claw hold and fell, five more kept climbing. Those that dropped landed on their feet as if the distance was nothing and immediately started climbing again. To a distant observer, the tan-and-yellow walls would appear to be covered in black dots, like ants swarming a rock.

The powerful spring of a ballista released with a *thwack*. The thick bolt whistled through the air and somehow struck true. The missile slammed into a big demon's chest and broke through, unleashing a shower of white blood upon the smaller demons between its feet.

The men who saw that strike took heart from it. *Demons could be hurt!* And they went back to fighting even harder, few of them realizing that singular blow from their strongest weapon had been one among the thousands so far delivered that had accomplished nothing.

Warriors hurled stones over the edge. More demons were dislodged. More replaced them. Devedas wished they'd had time to boil cauldrons of oil. Not that he knew if hot oil could even scald a demon, but it might have helped.

Devedas took up a spear, called upon the Heart of the Mountain to lend strength to his arms, and went to the edge. He picked out a demon and thrust, striking it clean in the head. *Nothing.* Then he hit one of its hands. Then the other. And when than one slipped in a shower of broken stones, and the demon dangled briefly from one claw, Devedas stabbed it the top of the chest with all his might. He was rewarded with a spray of white blood and the creature slid down the wall.

No one else present was as strong as a Protector, but the rest of them saw that feat. They didn't have the Heart of the Mountain, but they could draw strength from the heart of their king. For every foot a demon gained it was struck a dozen times. By some miracle, more white blood flew and another monster lost its hand to a glaive.

A demon made it over the top. The warriors there stumbled back as it began swinging its long apelike arms. A man was hit, armor crumpled, ribs shattered, and he was sent flailing back over the edge to die on the Capitol's cobblestones below.

Devedas slammed the end of his spear into that demon's chest. It didn't pierce the armored hide, but he shoved as hard as he could. The wooden shaft flexed, and the off-balance creature was pushed off its perch to plummet to the ground below.

Demons were quick, and spears were lost as they were snatched from the warriors' hands. Those who refused to let go were promptly yanked over the edge to fall screaming into the enemy's teeth. Those poor bastards got ripped apart like a pack of dogs fighting over the body of a single rat.

The wall shook. Warriors slipped. Then it shook again, so hard that men were sent flailing over the edge and even Devedas staggered. Mortar split. Rocks broke free. One of the giants had rammed into the wall below hard enough to crack the foundation. "On your feet. Keep fighting!"

Arrows, bolts, and spears struck the big demon as it backed up to charge again. Devedas noted that there were wizards upon the wall now, men of various houses and Orders. With no idea of their abilities, he shouted, "Wizards, pitch in as best you can!"

Demons were engulfed in fire or knocked from the walls by powerful gusts of wind or magically hurled stones.

They kept coming.

Arms were weakening. Hearts were faltering. Some warriors fled. More died. Devedas refused to budge. His spear broke against a demon's head, so he drew his sword and launched himself at every obsidian claw that reached over the top, hacking furiously. The forward-curving Dev blade was made for chopping, but even driven by Protector might, he only managed to remove a few fingers. Demons fell. More appeared.

The biggest demon of all was a mere hundred yards from the wall now. It was the largest living thing Devedas had ever seen. It launched itself forward like a charging bull. Each footfall of its tree-trunk-thick legs shook the world. Its head was nothing but a lump with a mouth on it, but by some miracle a ballista bolt hit it right in that gaping maw. The thing tripped over its own feet, momentum still carrying it forward. A few smaller demons were caught unaware and crushed between its bulk and the stone wall. Even that stunted impact still knocked twenty warriors off their feet.

Another giant demon was right behind that one, and it was heading straight for the gate.

Devedas shouted down at the warriors waiting on the other side. "Prepare for breach!"

Bolts hit. They did nothing. The monster lowered its shoulder.

That blow echoed through the entire Capitol.

Beams shattered. Steel bars bent. Men fell to their deaths.

Built from the sturdiest trees of the eastern forests, somehow that door didn't break, and the warriors rushed to reinforce it. Hastily conscripted workers were sent to gather anything that could be piled against the splintered wood. Only that big demon didn't retreat to try again. It simply kept pushing.

Devedas fought and fought. Demons made it over other parts of the wall, but not his. Never his. Any demon that clambered up to his level, he struck it from its hold. Claws scored his armor and dented his helm. His sword snapped off when he planted it into a demon's shoulder, so he kicked that one in the face until it fell. Then he snatched another sword from a dead Garo's sheath.

Men were dying all around him. The sun was getting higher. The heat was building. Soon he would be baking inside his armor.

Devedas could only hope that the creatures who lived beneath the dark ocean were even more uncomfortable under the burning sun than he was.

"Maharaja!" A warrior ran up the stairs. "They've climbed up the aqueduct and over a section of the eastern wall! Demons flood into the Ivory district, killing everyone!"

That was where the Capitol Library was located.

Before Devedas could speak, the great demon below pushed over a portion of the Capitol's feeble wall. Pillars broke. The stones beneath his boots buckled as the battlements collapsed, and the Maharaja of Lok fell into a storm of swirling dust, falling rocks, and sea demons.

Chapter 43

—◄◄◄◦►►►—

"We must hurry, Maharani!"

Rada was surrounded by an escort of nervous warriors as they rushed her across the main floor of the Capitol Library. As they passed by a bank of lattice windows she heard hundreds of people screaming outside. A couple of junior Archivists were at the window, eyes wide, hands pressed over their mouths, as they watched the carnage.

There was a flash of black as something big clambered past the window. The Archivists screamed. The warriors drew their swords. Ther was a sick *click-click* of claws on the other side of the wall, but that demon kept going.

When they passed the window, Rada was greeted with the most unsettling thing she'd ever seen, and she'd survived the scourge and being buried beneath Upagraha's cleansing pillar of fire. This was worse, for that terror had been greeted upon her and a band of stalwart warriors, men trained and hardened for violence. These were the regular citizens of her caste—average men, women, and children who were being devoured. Demons were clambering up the walls of various government buildings or chasing innocents through the streets. The people of the Capitol were dying in droves.

As they ran down the stairs, Rada was so scared she could hardly breathe. "Where's my husband?"

"The Maharaja defends one of the gates." They rounded the corner into the Library's grand entryway. "We must get you to the—"

The great room was filled with blood. There were puddles of it on the floor. It dripped from the ceiling and walls. The mangled bodies of patrons were sprawled across shelves or limp upon the floor. In the middle of the room a hideous thing crouched, its sleek back to them, as it hungrily gnawed on the corpse of a Librarian.

"Fall back. Fall back," the lead warrior whispered.

The demon heard and spun around, dropping the dead woman and rising to its full height, a head taller than the largest warrior there. Scarecrow thin, it spread its incredibly long arms wide, and immediately started toward them.

The first warrior shouted, "Get her out of here!" and then charged the monstrosity. He would die bravely for a woman he didn't know. Rada had never even gotten his name.

The rest of them ran back toward the stairs. "Not up," Rada insisted. They didn't know this place like she did. She'd grown up here. "Down!" There was only one way into the restricted selection, and it had thicker walls and heavier doors.

Behind them, the demon picked up the warrior and slammed his body against the stone over and over. Bones snapped. Organs ruptured and splattered. The sound was sickening.

They went down a level, across a hall, and then down another set of older, steeper stairs. Rada had to hoist up her fancy silks to keep from tripping. With her luck she'd roll all the way to the bottom and break her neck and then be paralyzed as the demon ate her. The four of them reached the bottom and Rada led them directly to a door that was worthy of a border fort. It would take a battering ram—or even an angry demon—a bit of time to break this down. Unfortunately, it was also locked. She took out her father's old key ring—it had been the first thing she'd claimed upon her return to the Library—and began looking for the key to this area.

There was a whisper of demon hide sliding against the stone above. It was pursuing them.

The three Garo readied their forward-curved blades. "We'll stop it here, Maharani."

"Your husband gave our house its dignity back. It is an honor to die for his family," proclaimed the next.

Her father had owned *so many keys.* "Quit distracting me and we can all hide on the other side together." She glanced back just in time to see one of the demon's clawed feet land upon the topmost visible step. *Saltwater!*

The tips of the swords were shaking as the Garo awaited certain death, but the demon paused its descent. Surely, it knew it had them trapped here, but slowly, that one foot shifted as if the demon sensed something coming up behind it.

Thud.

The demon rolled the rest of the way down the stairs.

A hammer slid across the floor to stop near Rada's sandals.

The monster had landed on its belly, but with incredible swiftness its limbs splayed outward, and it twitched itself back upright, nothing but a jerking shadow in the flickering lantern light. The unnatural movement reminded Rada of a centipede running. It was back up so fast the Garo hadn't even had time to react. Long claws balled into fists, the demon faced the stairs, clearly more threatened by what was above than the mere humans behind it.

A giant of a man walked down to them. Clutched in his meaty fists was a mighty war hammer that made the hammer he'd thrown at the demon look like a toy. He was dressed as a humble caravan guard and had shaved off his notorious mane of hair and beard so as to not be easily recognized, but there was no mistaking her Protector.

"Karno!"

"Rada." Karno nodded her direction but never took his eyes off the demon as he reached the bottom of the steps.

The demon and the Protector circled. It had been casually ripping people apart mere moments ago, but it recognized this man was not prey like the others. The Garo kept their bodies between her and the demon as she continued fumbling to find the right key.

The demon struck. Karno hit it in the knuckles with the head of his hammer. It swung with the other hand, but Karno leapt back, far too quick for a man of his size. Claws ripped into the wall where Karno had just been standing, as he swept around and slammed the hammer's back spike into the monster's ribs.

"Do not watch me, Rada. Focus on your task," Karno ordered with eerie calm.

Having a demon fight a Protector while hovering seconds from certain bloody death was rather distracting, but Rada managed to find the correct key and the lock clicked. She yanked the heavy door open. "This way, hurry!"

But when she turned back she found two more of the Garo rushing into the fray, while the last bodyguard rudely shoved her through the entrance. "Hide, Maharani!" Then he slammed the door behind her.

Rada stood there in the dark, heart pounding, breathing hard, listening to three strangers and one friend fight a demon to the death on her behalf.

Then she realized this was the room that had started it all.

It was among these shelves of ancient books that a wizard had threatened her life and coerced her into silence. This was where her fear had made her an accomplice to a terrible evil that had cost an untold number of lives and spawned rebellion. All the memories came rushing back. The smell of the wizard's breath in her face. The terrible pressure of his hand on her throat. The sound of her glasses being crushed.

On the other side of that door was the noise of desperate battle against something so much worse.

When that wizard had threatened a girl, she had cried, and then sought out a Protector. Now that a demon threatened a woman and her entire city, she wouldn't cry, nor would she abandon her Protector. If she were going to die, she wouldn't do it cowering in the dark. The dagger at her waist had been a gift from one of the city's artisans trying to gain her husband's favor, but it had a very fine point. Enough to wound a demon? Probably not, but she would find out!

Rada drew her dagger and flung open the door.

Two of the Garo were already down, with jagged ends of bones sticking out of their broken limbs. As she watched in horror, the last bodyguard was thrown against the wall, but before the demon could slash his throat out, Karno blocked its claws with the shaft of his hammer, then kicked it in the chest. The Protector must have had a kick like a mule because the demon actually lurched a few steps back.

Directly toward Rada.

Lifting her dagger high overhead she screamed, *"Get out of my library!"* and stabbed.

The fine tip bounced harmlessly off the demon's hide and the collision was so jarring it knocked the weapon from her grasp.

The demon turned its malevolent eyeless attention toward her. Karno brained it.

The demon stumbled. Karno lifted the hammer overhead with both hands and hit in the head again. It went to one knee, and Karno swung the hammer from the side. That impact was so great it launched the demon's head against the wall, where it hit so hard it left droplets of milky white blood and a crack in the stone. Its head drooped downward, momentarily shaken, so with a roar Karno brought the hammer up in a flashing arc from below. That impact deformed its blank face and black fangs flew out. If the thing had a human neck that hit surely would've turned vertebrae into powder, but as it was the incredible power of the hit still knocked the demon on its back.

Karno slammed one boot onto its chest as he lifted the hammer high, then he proceeded to slam that block of steel into its skull with methodical repetition, like a worker breaking a boulder. Karno beat it until the demon's head popped open, and he kept beating it until the contents of its skull were stuck to the ceiling.

Chest heaving, Karno stopped, letting the hammerhead rest against the floor.

Rada rushed over and engulfed him in a hug.

"It's good to see you too." He patted her on the back with his free hand, before turning to the last Garo standing. "I've got more demons to kill. Get your wounded into that room and barricade the door. If she tries to escape in some vain attempt to save any people or books, tie her up."

She let go of him. "I'm not stupid, Karno."

"No. You are noble. That is worse." Then he thought of something and reached into his cloak to pull out a leather bag that he held out to her. "Before I left Vadal, I reclaimed this from their wizards. I believe it belongs to you. Perhaps it can help again, as it did against the Scourge."

Rada took the bag, and just from the familiar weight and shape, she knew that it was the Asura's Mirror. "The mirror was my obligation."

"As your safety is mine. Neither should be abandoned."

Chapter 44

~~~~~~~~~~~~~~~~~~

Blinded by blood and choking dust, Devedas lay in the ruins of the south gate, letting the Heart of the Mountain repair his many wounds. His helmet had been badly smashed by falling stones, but it had saved him from getting his skull crushed. Deprived of sight, the only thing he could hear over the ringing in his ears was the screaming of his subjects being torn apart by demons. He managed to pull off one gauntlet, and then used that hand to remove his helm, so he could rub the grit from his eyes.

The south gate had collapsed entirely. Everyone who'd been defending it was dead or currently out of sight. He was partially encased in rubble, suspended twenty feet from the ground. There were demons *everywhere*. He had not been out for long, but they'd moved far beyond the hole they'd punched in the wall and were rampaging throughout the district. With the Capitol's defenses pierced the unified demonic army had fragmented into hundreds of individual raiders, each one spreading out into the city to inflict the maximum amount of butchery possible.

Once his internal bleeding stopped, he tried to move, but discovered his leg was pinned beneath a great beam. That was the only thing that had kept him from falling all the way and being eaten by the first wave of demons through. When he tried to push it, the beam barely budged. So Devedas redirected the

Heart from its healing work to providing strength to his arms, and with a roar he pushed with all his might. The beam moved just enough for his leg to slip free.

Devedas tumbled down the rubble pile to land in a clanking heap of battered armor and bruised muscle. With back wrenched, pain radiated up and down his spine with every movement.

Unfortunately, a nearby demon must have heard his fall, because it looked up from the Uttaran soldier it had been pulling the guts out of. It was a small demon, barely man-sized, and its odd lump of a head twisted to the side like a curious dog's, studying him. Blood dripped from its claws as it pondered what manner of treat Devedas would be. It rose and began stalking toward the fallen human in the once-golden armor.

Devedas stood up and searched for a weapon, but the nearest dropped sword was on the other side of the demon, so he snatched up a length of board in one hand, and a chunk of sandstone in the other. "Come at me, sea spawn."

It obliged.

The flung stone cracked off the demon's blank face an instant before Devedas shattered the board over its head. The monster hit him in the chest and Devedas found himself sliding on his back down the trade road, with a dent in his breastplate, a new crack in his sternum, and no air left in his lungs.

The demon followed him out of the city.

Devedas cursed his weakness as he wheezed and tried to rise. His people needed him to protect them, and here he was about to die to a single monster, disarmed and alone, the first and last king of a new, very short, era.

The demon clawed at his face. Devedas ducked and struck the monster with his gauntlet. It tried to hit him again, but Devedas lowered his shoulder and rammed it in the chest, shoving it back. Before it could recover, he wrapped his arms around the creature's midsection and hoisted it off the ground. Dense with magical muscle, it was far heavier than it looked and the only thing that kept him from getting eviscerated immediately was surprise. Devedas rolled it over his body and slammed the demon's head against the road.

The demon thrashed madly, and each wild hit was like a blow from a mace. Devedas was hurled off and sent rolling away. It sprang up unnaturally, and immediately leapt on top of him.

He tried to shove it away. Claws pierced his arms, forcing them down, and its head opened, revealing a mouth full of snapping teeth, heading straight for his throat.

There was a black flash, lightning quick.

Maw open, the demon froze... and then slowly, ever so slowly, the top half of its head slid off, to fall in the dust next to Devedas with a *splat*. The demon went limp, and he grunted as he shoved the dead weight off of his chest.

"What kind of fool tries to grapple a demon?"

Devedas coughed. "A desperate one who lost his sword."

"Then let us find you another."

He knew that voice. It was the voice of a dead man.

Impossible.

A figure in black armor stood over him, wielding a blade made of pure darkness.

"But you're dead. I killed you."

"You came closer than most."

Devedas lay there, unable to comprehend what he was seeing. Was this real? Had the demon struck a mortal blow and Devedas was bleeding out in the sand, hallucinating through his final moments?

No. It really was Ashok.

"Has my brother's ghost come for revenge? To slay me and gloat over the destruction of the Capitol?"

"Many think I should... but I will not." In that moment, Ashok could have easily killed him, but he didn't. Instead he extended his open hand to help Devedas stand up. "Set aside our war for now and rise, King. There is work to do."

Devedas accepted that hand and went to fight for his city.

Chapter 45

The Capitol was being torn apart before Ashok's eyes. Hundreds were dying by the minute. This was far worse than what had been done in Kanok. His rebel army was still days away. Regardless of the gods' wishes, there would be no saving this place. The Capitol would fall. Even if the demons quit now the city would never recover, for surely they had already inflicted a mortal wound.

Ashok would still kill as many demons as he could before he died.

With Devedas by his side they entered the southern district. His former brother had been soaked in blood and covered in dust. Even the finest golden armor looked no different from anyone else's once coated in the mud-filth stink of death.

"Why are you here? These aren't your people anymore."

"No, Devedas, they are not. That doesn't mean they deserve to be slaughtered. If you survive today, remember that concept."

"We killed yours. You aid mine." Devedas spit out a gob of blood and looked him in the eye. "I won't forget this."

"It's your city. What's your plan?"

Devedas took up a sword and shield from a dead man. "Push toward the Ivory District. Kill demons and gather fighters as we go."

Ashok didn't know why that particular district was their destination, but it seemed there were demons in every direction, so that way would serve as well as any for him. "You distract and divert their limbs. I'll deliver the killing strike with Angruvadal."

"Just like we did on the Makao slope." That battle had been against men wearing steel plates rather than demons in impenetrable hide, but the principle remained the same.

"Or the battle of Tunka River," Devedas agreed. Or a dozen others they could name, since the two of them had fought together many times. It was unexpected that they would be doing so once again, but for now their animosity would be set aside, and together they would do what Protectors had been trained to do. Despite having become enemies, there was no one else Ashok would rather have at his side in a fight than Devedas.

Ashok spied a blood-covered demon crashing through the doorway of a home a hundred yards ahead. "That one."

"Go." Devedas broke into a sprint.

Ashok was right behind him.

The demon was a lean one, but it still carried a man's severed leg in one hand. Devedas went left, slashing at the monster's back. It immediately swung the leg like a club, but Devedas let the shield take the hit, then he danced back, taunting. The demon followed.

Angruvadal ran it through. Black steel erupted from between its ribs, an instant before Ashok wrenched the blade from the demon's back so violently it sprayed milk blood in a ten-foot arc.

"Keep moving!" Devedas shouted. "Cripple them and leave them to bleed!"

There was a fight ahead of them. Warriors who had survived the collapse of the gate had been joined by desperate workers and they were fighting against a muscular slab of a heavyset demon, big as either of the pair Ashok had once fought in Gujara. The humans seemed insignificant in the monster's shadow. With each swing of one of its mighty arms, men were sent flying.

Devedas charged, striking over the top of the shield. The demon lifted one massive fist and brought it down, smashing a hole in the cobblestones where Devedas had been standing, but he had already jumped out of the way.

Ashok hit that demon so hard that even though the hide didn't split, Angruvadal broke the bones beneath. Any regular blade would have shattered. Angruvadal hungered for more. The demon flailed back to crash against the wall of a mansion house.

Desperate men fell upon it, hacking away, only to be knocked aside as the demon rolled over onto its hands and knees.

Leaping high, Ashok landed on the demon's back, driving the ancestor blade deep between its shoulder blades. It heaved itself violently upward, but Ashok held onto his sword as the black steel cruelly sizzled its way through a foot of demon flesh.

The beast collapsed.

"Warriors! Sepoys! Rally to me!" Devedas roared. "This way!"

The men who weren't too overcome by terror to do anything coherent fell in line behind their Maharaja. Ashok doubted they'd be of much use against the host of hell, and they probably wouldn't be able to keep up to a Protector's pace for long, but in the meantime their numbers would provide more distractions for him to take advantage of. If a demon was busy killing a normal warrior, it would be less likely to see black steel death coming.

They collided with another smaller demon at the next intersection. Devedas and Ashok both went at it with unrelenting fury. Green sparks flew as Angruvadal struck aside demonic claws before they could hit Devedas, and Devedas' shield blocked the demon's blow meant for Ashok's head. When Ashok's draw cut opened its belly, Devedas thrust his sword deep into the wound, and then twisted it upward to stab through the demon's heart. They left it there twitching for the workers to club and kept running through the city.

Despite the destruction all around him, Ashok had never felt stronger. Angruvadal didn't need to whisper to him the suggestions of its prior bearers, for in that moment he was the culmination of a millennia worth of warrior evolution recorded onto two ancestors blades. His body and mind, perfectly united in pursuit of destruction, Ashok became a demon-slaughtering terror.

The fanatics called him the Forgotten's Warrior. On this day he would prove them right.

"Watch out. Demon on the left."

That one was a squat, but powerfully built creature, twitching about with an incredible quickness. Though demons had no faces, if it had possessed one it surely would have displayed murderous glee. It was chasing down fleeing workers, bowling them over, savagely biting them, but then leaving them there wounded in order to quickly chase after its next victim. It had left a trail of injured and dying behind it, as if it was in a hurry to taste as many different flavors of human flesh as possible.

As Ashok rushed the creature, a strange thought came over him. This particular demon was biting as many people as possible, not out of spite, but rather because it was *searching for a certain kind of blood.*

The earliest instincts imprinted on Angruvadal confirmed this suspicion. This particular demon's strange obligation was to see if the bloodline of Ramrowan was present here. Of course its sampling had been futile, as the Capitol had killed all its casteless, just as its search must have been equally futile in Kanok, where the Makao had done the same to theirs.

There was only *one* casteless present today, and this demon would not have to look far to find him. Filled with disgust, Ashok caught up with the sample taker. That demon whirled about, mouth wide, black fangs dripping. It raised one arm, surely expecting to effortlessly block the descending Angruvadal as it had so many other blades today.

It seemed taken aback when its hand flew off.

The demon turned to run, but Devedas crashed into it with his shield, knocking it off-balance. Ashok struck it again, slicing through its lower spine and leaving it there on dead unmoving legs. It would run down no more prey today. The mortal warriors rushed in to beat the foul thing to death behind them.

They continued on through the city toward the Ivory District. It was difficult even for Black-Hearted Ashok to comprehend the carnage before him. Everywhere he looked was death. There seemed to be no end to the bodies in the streets. The gutters ran over with blood. Endless screams echoed between the great buildings. It was a slaughter the likes of which the world hadn't seen since the Rain of Demons.

Anguished over the fate of his subjects, Devedas continued fighting so viciously it would have made even Sword Master Ratul proud. They had nearly two paltans' worth of men following them now. If the demons had concentrated their efforts against this paltry force, then surely they would have been wiped out, but the demons seemed too fixated on their rampage, ignoring capable fighters, while desiring to kill as many innocents as possible instead. So Ashok and Devedas kept picking monsters off one by one, crippling them, leaving them vulnerable, and then abandoning them to the less capable warriors to finish off.

Half a mile and half a dozen demons later, they were joined by another Protector.

Broker Harban's mace had bits of demon skull stuck to it, and when he saw who was at the head of the force coming to save the intersection he and his men were defending, he bellowed at Devedas, "I *told* you Ashok lived!"

"Mock my doubt later, Broker. Right now I'm just thankful to have him as an ally."

Broker looked Ashok over suspiciously. "So ally it is, then?"

"Against demons, yes," Ashok said. "Afterward, should we live, we shall see."

"I'm alright with that," the one-eyed Protector responded. "Let's send these fish-reeking bastards back to their ocean in pieces."

They fought on. Three men who had touched the Heart of the Mountain proved far deadlier than two.

Four would become a demon's nightmare.

They found Protector Bundit Vokkan near the entrance to the Ivory District. He stood upon the steps of the Order of Agriculture and Irrigation, holding off a nine-foot demon with mighty swings of his polearm. Bundit was a master of the reclining moon blade, as Ashok knew from experience, having faced that deadly thing himself once in a construction site in distant Neeramphorn. He was glad to see that the solemn Protector had survived that last encounter, but it didn't appear Bundit would be alive for much longer, as his silver armor was slick with his own blood running from a laceration on his neck. Bundit was near defeat and needed to give the Heart a chance to mend his wounds, but the demon he was fighting wouldn't relent, not even for an instant.

Ashok fell upon the creature, striking it furiously from behind. Devedas hit it from the side. Broker smashed it in the shin with his mace. This demon was particularly fearsome, and it immediately kicked Broker down the stairs and flung Devedas into a pillar. It swung its claws at Ashok, but he moved aside faster than even a demon could comprehend and stabbed it through the pelvis. Near-invincible hide split like paper before Angruvadal's wrath.

With hip shattered, now it was the demon's turn to roll down the stairs.

Its head was promptly met at the bottom by Broker's mace . . . twenty times.

Bundit reflexively turned his reclining moon blade Ashok's way, for the last time they'd met, Ashok had cracked his skull and left him in a coma.

"I would not advise that," Ashok warned.

"Easy, Bundit, he's on our side today!" Broker shouted as he finished rendering the demon's head into mush. "I don't think I've ever been so glad to see a criminal."

It wasn't often a man got his life saved by a vengeful ghost, but Bundit lowered his weapon and gave Ashok a respectful nod. By that Protector's notoriously reserved standards, that was a positively warm greeting to someone who had once been his foe.

They pushed onward. Bundit brought up the rear, pinching his jugular back together with his fingertips until the Heart could mend it.

They picked off more lone demons. The soldiers of hell were unprepared to meet humans of such tenacity. And with each one Angruvadal slew, Ashok felt even stronger. The shard in his chest burned with a holy fire that no amount of demon blood would be sufficient to quench.

The heat was stifling, but then they were running through the rain. They were in the shadow of the aqueduct, and it appeared to be damaged and leaking. Ashok realized that those were gigantic claw marks that had scored the stone above. Where the demon that had made those marks had leapt down, its weight had been so great that the street had broken in a wide circle. Ahead of them, buildings had been damaged and carvings had been scraped from stone, as high as twenty feet up, from shoulders that had been wider than the road. It had stepped on a carriage and flattened the entire thing. They were following the trail of something *gigantic*.

The oldest memories buried in his sword suggested to Ashok new perspective, which he promptly conveyed to the others. "The biggest demons are their controllers. They serve a purpose similar to human leaders. Their orders and desires are conveyed to the lesser demons by thought. The one ahead of us is one of these."

"Then let's take its head," Devedas snarled. "Forward!"

It was two men in silver, one in gold, and one in criminal black who fought their way into the Ivory District. The city's last hope hung upon two former Protectors, two current, and a hundred poor fools who'd been swept along in their wake.

Then there was a fifth champion.

In the courtyard of the Capitol Library, a giant of a man fought a giant of a demon.

Surely this vast beast had to be a mighty prince of hell. It must have been the biggest living creature in the world. Its footfalls shook the city. Its limbs were mighty oaks, each tooth a sword. The great demon Ashok had fought at the House of Assassins would only come up to this titan's shoulder. It wasn't just big, but he could tell it was ancient as well. It had scars on its hide, inflicted by black steel weapons centuries ago. This thing was older than the Law. It had been created when the gods had still sailed the sky. It was the living avatar of demonic might.

Yet the one man standing against it didn't quail before such a horror. He wore no armor at all, but rather the shredded remains of a humble caravan guard's uniform. Despite that, there was no mistaking that this was someone who had touched the Heart of the Mountain, for when he swung his war hammer it struck that demon's leg so hard that everyone in the district felt it vibrate their bones.

Even that great strength would be insufficient to save Karno Uttara from a demon big as two elephants.

The demon quickly recovered from the mighty hit Karno had inflicted and it swung its arm in a great arc. There was no dodging an attack that spanned half a courtyard. Karno was sent flying, crashing through the dry fountain and sliding across the ground on his back.

With each step covering many yards, the demon soon loomed over fallen Karno, cocking back its other arm, giant claws curling into a fist, to punch Karno through the street.

It struck.

Angruvadal split the giant's hand in half.

Ashok stood over Karno, sword extended in a torrent of white blood. He'd hit the descending fist directly between the center knuckles. It had been a perfect cut. Two fingers were embedded in the stone on one side of Karno, and two on the other.

"Ashok." Karno gave a simple greeting, as if he'd not been a sworn enemy of the Law for several years.

"Karno."

The monster was so huge that it must have taken time for the sensation of pain to travel such a great distance to its brain.

As the wounded arm rose in surprise, Ashok jumped atop and held on. He rode it upward, high into the air, and before the beast realized it had a passenger, Ashok slashed it across the face.

It stumbled back, striking at itself in a desperate flailing attempt to remove the vicious little attacker from its body, like a man panicked he'd found a stinging scorpion in his robes. Ashok vaulted over one of its shoulders, slid down its back, and landed on the ground. He immediately struck the back of the giant's knee. In the second it took that mighty limb to buckle, Ashok rolled between its legs, rose, and stabbed it in the belly. The demon crashed into the Library's façade, destroying centuries of delicate artwork as Ashok walked away, unharmed.

Devedas stared at him in stunned disbelief, for though they'd fought together many times—and against each other a few—he had never seen Ashok—or anyone—accomplish *anything* like that.

Of course he hadn't. For not since the days of ancient Ramrowan had there been a warrior capable of such a feat. The shard of Angruvadal had changed him into a force beyond even Protector comprehension. At this terrible reckoning the black steel in his chest burned with a molten fury like never before. Ashok and black steel were one, equally deadly. There was no difference between him and the sword in his hand.

Ashok spoke no words, but he gave the Maharaja a knowing nod, as if to say *That's right, brother. Things have changed.* If they lived through the day, hopefully Devedas would recall this moment before restarting their war.

Behind him, the great demon pushed itself off the Library wall, furious.

They were only beginning, for it would take many wounds to kill such a mighty demon.

The five champions spread out across the courtyard. Their warrior-and-sepoy escort hung back, terrified, and utterly useless against such a titanic threat. The demon raised itself to its full height, its dome of a head rising over the second-floor windows of the Capitol Library. While it studied them, the men who had touched the Heart of the Mountain used that time to mend their wounds, as they mentally prepared themselves for what was next.

The great demon's blank gaze lingered on Ashok and his sword. From the scars, today was not the first time it had felt the sting of black steel. Slowly, it reached up, took hold of its two dangling fingers that were just getting in the way, and ripped them off. The demon threw that discarded part of itself on the ground. It would grow new fingers after every living thing in the Capitol had been slain.

Devedas spoke for them all. "Offense has been taken."

Both sides charged.

Bundit's polearm cleaved into one hip. Devedas and Broker immediately attacked its other leg. Ashok inflicted another deep gouge into its abdomen, and then Karno was by Ashok's side, bludgeoning it in the damaged knee.

The demon kicked Broker across the courtyard. Bundit was flung into the air when tons of demon stomped on the stone he'd been standing on. Ashok had to dive to avoid a scooping claw. The demon missed, but the blow uprooted one of the Capitol's precious few large trees, and a few seconds later it fell onto the Library's roof.

Each time a Protector was thrown away, they came sprinting right back.

Incredible amounts of magic were drawn from the distant Heart of the Mountain. They were no longer all brothers, yet they still fought as one. Each of the demon's attacks were intercepted. Blows meant for one man were redirected by another. When one was knocked down, another took his place. The great demon thrashed, but it had blundered into a patch of endless steel thorns. White blood sprayed across the Library as the five of them took it apart, piece by piece.

The demon seemed too big to be felled with a single killing strike, so they had to outlast it. While Karno and Broker battered joints and bones, Bundit and Devedas kept stabbing and slashing. It took dozens of solid hits to inflict a single cut, so they sent a hundred more. And each instant the demon gave him a chance, Ashok demonstrated Angruvadal's power by taking another piece out of its obsidian hide. Chunks of meat the size of hams went flying.

When Ashok inflicted one of those wounds on the monster's thigh, exposing a slab of white muscle, Bundit swept past him and stabbed with his polearm, driving the entire length of metal and even some of the shaft into its leg. With a violent twist, the Vokkan broke his weapon and left it lodged in the demon's leg.

When it tried to move, its leg began to buckle. Karno's hammer hit it in that knee.

The silent creature stumbled.

The Protectors sensed weakness.

Ashok dove beneath the swing of its injured hand and came up behind the sea demon. Before it could locate its greatest threat, Ashok had bounded up the broken bricks of the Library wall to gain elevation, then he jumped onto the monster's back. Using the many cuts they'd inflicted as hand holds, the great demon was just another mountain to be climbed. The black hide was smooth one way, but rubbed the other it was so abrasive that it took the paint off his armor.

Understanding now that the most dangerous human of all was on its vulnerable back, the demon threw itself against the Library, trying to scrape Ashok off. The impact was excruciating as Ashok was smashed between stone and demon. He should have died. The shard wouldn't let him. Stone broke before Ashok's body did.

The demon moved away from the wall in a shower of dust, not realizing that Ashok still clung to it like a tick, until he reversed Angruvadal in his grip and plunged it downward with all his might.

It went to the hilt.

When Angruvadal pierced the giant demon's heart, that great pump ruptured, releasing a torrent of hot white blood in such a vast quantity that it flooded the courtyard sufficient to sweep the distant warriors from their feet.

Ashok rode the dying beast to the ground.

It landed face-first in one of the Library's beautiful fountains. That basin had been deprived of water by the rebellion's destruction of the aqueduct, but it quickly filled with white blood.

The exhausted Protectors stepped back to watch it expire.

In Ashok's experience, demons rarely made any sounds, only this one did now. Its vast mouth opened, black tongue lolling out, as it let out a long *hiss*. Yet, there seemed to be words in the hiss, in a language beyond hearing.

Angruvadal warned him that dying sound was for Ashok and the other humans, because demons spoke to each other not with voices like men, but rather mind to mind. While it cursed the humans who had felled it, the prince of hell was also sending a message to its army.

The Capitol was still filled with the sounds of pain and fear and dying, yet somehow it was as if an eerie silence fell over them. The cacophony of terror faded into the background until it was barely perceptible, replaced by an uncanny stillness.

They were being watched.

"Oceans..." Broker muttered, as he slowly turned in a circle. "That's a bloody lot of demons."

They were surrounded by dozens of demons. They were perched high upon rooftops, clinging to walls, or waiting down distant streets. So focused upon this battle, none of them had seen the rest of the monsters approach.

The dying beast had summoned them to come and witness its end.

Ashok limped toward the great demon, ancestor blade clutched in both shaking hands. "I warned you not to trespass."

He thrust Angruvadal deep into its brain.

The hiss died off.

Black hide gleamed beneath the hot desert sun as the soldiers of hell watched them for a long time. It was odd that beings without eyes could *stare*, yet there was no other way to describe it. Such a large number of demons would easily overwhelm the meager force Devedas had assembled at the Library... but that must have not been the great demon's final command to them, because rather than attack, the demons gradually pulled away and slunk off, not to continue their slaughter, but rather to fall back. In eerie silence they jumped from rooftop to rooftop or ducked around corners and out of sight. All of the demons were moving south, from whence they'd first came.

The samples had been taken. The killing was done for now.

Some of the warriors cheered when they realized the demons were leaving. They were fools. This was no retreat. The demons had accomplished everything they'd come here to do.

The Capitol was defeated.

Chapter 46

Thera looked upon the desolation of the Capitol and wept. They'd come so far, for nothing.

Long before the city had come into view, her scouts had found bodies lost on the sand. Those had all been recent deaths from what appeared to be exhaustion, dehydration, or heat stroke. Even a hardy warrior couldn't run across the desert for long without water. Pampered members of the first caste had no chance at all ... but what had forced these poor fools out here so desperately unprepared?

Then they'd found some still alive, but they'd been driven mad with terror, telling tales of demons rampaging and the streets of the Capitol drowning in blood.

As they'd gotten closer to the city, the Sons had discovered the trade road was packed with once-proud citizens of the Capitol, thousands upon thousands of them marching dejectedly back toward their distant houses. There were carriages, wagons, horses, camels, and a multitude on foot. Great families of wealth and status were reduced to refugees. None of those fleeing even had the energy to be afraid of her mighty criminal army. Family treasures and works of art deemed important enough to carry off had been abandoned on the side of the road only a few miles later because they were too heavy. The Fortress collectors picked through those things with great joy.

Now the great city lay before her. Gates had been torn down, entire sections of wall were gone, great edifices had fallen, and swaths of ashen debris still smoldered from fires that had consumed entire neighborhoods mere days before. Even from her vantage point outside the walls, she could see an unthinkable number of corpses, stacked into haphazard piles. The sky was filled with wheeling vultures. It seemed as if every carrion bird in Lok must have flown here to feast.

Even though the Capitol was her sworn enemy, she'd never wished anything like this upon them. This was beyond cruelty. The most vengeful and fanatical of the Sons were somber at the sight of this travesty. Even Shekar Somsak had no rude quip to make, seeing the high and mighty brought this low. The Sons were shaken, for this wasn't just a defeat. This was a failure of prophecy.

She heard their fearful whispers... *Woe unto man for surely the age of demons begins.*

What of the Voice? This was what they'd been commanded to prevent. The rebels had come here as fast as they could. *Oh, Forgotten, why didn't you warn me sooner?* What more could she have done? This was a shell of a city now. What would happen to a land deprived of Law? What would this mean to her rebellion? Was this victory? If so, it would be a hollow one, because if the Voice was right the demons would be coming for the rest of them soon enough. City after city would fall as the demons struck with impunity from beneath the ground. They'd all be dead soon enough.

Waiting on the road, a quarter mile from the gate, was a lone figure in black armor sitting upon a majestic white horse.

Ashok lived.

That was a small bit of relief on such a dark day. As much as Thera despaired, as long as indomitable Ashok survived, she'd retain some hope.

Ashok hailed her and the forlorn Sons. "Apologies for my abrupt departure."

His attempt to thwart prophecy was the least of her worries. "We're too late."

Ashok nodded his head in resigned acknowledgment. "I was here. I did the best I could."

She didn't doubt that. "We came as fast as we could."

"It wouldn't have mattered. There were far too many of them. Even if all of the Sons and our Fortress guns had been here, it wouldn't have been enough."

She stopped by his side and together they looked toward the fallen gatehouse. "I long dreamed of conquering this place, Ashok. Of forcing the Law to bend enough to let us live. But this... Did we fail the gods so now we can rule over rubble?"

"There's still some rule here. Devedas does not sulk in defeat. He organizes, calls for reinforcements, and prepares to fight again. What remains of his army awaits us on the other side of those walls."

"Could we take them?"

"In their current state? Easily. The demons ruined them. Devedas understands this, so he has agreed to parley with you."

"Do you trust him to keep his word?"

"Yes, but this is your decision to make. I told him he would know your answer if I returned with just you, or with a thousand rods."

Thera sighed, for as tempting as it was to crush the Law once and for all, the gods had sent them to protect, not to destroy. The Voice was a fickle, cruel being, but it had always been ultimately proven right. She would just have to trust it. "You'll be at my side, but if they're foolish enough to cross me just because they think I'm some common rebel, they'll pay a price." She turned toward where her officers were waiting a respectful distance back. "Eklavya, take up a defensive position here. If the first caste betrays us, make what the demons did to this place seem merciful in comparison."

The young officer appeared to be in shock at the destruction before them, yet he heard her command and understood. "It'll be done, Prophet."

Chapter 47

Thera was still reeling from her ride through the ruination of the Capitol when her group reached a grandiose building near the center of the city.

In all her life, she had never seen so much death. She had been through a house war, years of rebellion, and an attempted genocide, but nothing had prepared her for the horrors that an army of demons could inflict in a single morning. This was far worse than what had befallen Kanok. That city had been wounded. This one had its guts torn out and been left to die. She struggled to comprehend the aftermath of hell's rampage, but her mind refused to take it all in. There were so many dead that the living who remained couldn't even begin to move them all. Proud government buildings had been converted to field hospitals, filled with the injured. Soon this place would be consumed with the stench of rot, followed inevitably by disease. Oceans, the demons had even slaughtered the exotic animals in the famous Capitol zoo! Their malice didn't even discriminate between species. If it lived on land, they were driven to kill it.

There were many soldiers assembled at the illustrious palace to guard the notables gathered here today. Surely most of the warriors who had been obligated to the Capitol had died trying to defend it, and many of the survivors were now escorting their prestigious refugees back to their homelands. Those who remained seemed drained of life, vacantly staring into the distance, trying to forget the unforgettable. She'd been worried about them attacking her as a wanted criminal, but these warriors no longer cared about such minor things as rebellion. What was the presence of a mortal witch to those who'd just experienced the cruelty of the sea?

She had brought a small cadre with her in case she needed advisors or messengers, but only she and Ashok went up to where she would be meeting with the new king. Ashok led her up many stairs to a large room that had a vast map table in the center. She couldn't help but gasp when she saw that. It was such a beautiful rendition of the continent that even surrounded by despair, she had to marvel at the artistry of the thing. It was as if the whole world had been laid out before her in perfect miniature.

There were over fifty people standing or sitting around that table, and they all looked in her direction as she entered. There were phonthos, judges, and wizards, Protectors in their silver armor, Inquisitors in their golden masks, and representatives of various Orders and workers' groups she didn't even recognize. Then all those eyes turned toward Ashok, and they were nervous eyes, for he had long been considered the greatest threat to their precious Law.

Oh, how wrong they had been.

Ashok served as her herald, but they were paying such rapt attention that he didn't even have to raise his voice. "This is Thera Vane. Prophet leader of the rebellion, Voice of the Forgotten." There was some muttering and angry glances at those titles, but Ashok continued, unperturbed. "Most importantly to you, she is my commander and the master of the army which is currently waiting outside your fallen gates. Respect her accordingly or else."

A handsome man with a jagged scar on one side of his face listened to Ashok's introduction, and then gave Thera a reserved nod of greeting. "Greetings, Thera Vane. I am Maharaja Devedas. Welcome to the Capitol . . . or at least what remains of it."

This was the living embodiment of the Law, yet Thera did not bow.

Her defiance angered some of the important men. "To allow a criminal in this hallowed place is an insult to the Chief Judge's legacy." Despite being in a ruined city, that judge was wearing necklaces of rubies, and enough perfume to stave off the stink of the dead outside. Everyone else here was dirty or stained somehow, including the king himself. All who remained in this city had done something to help it. This one was entirely clean. "This is an outrage! *An outrage!*"

"How can anyone's robes be so tidy in a place wallowing in filth and death?" Thera mused aloud. She hadn't even meant it as an offense, but the judge certainly took it that way.

Devedas had no time for petty distractions. "This council is not here to discuss anyone's legal standing, Faril Akershan. It is to address how man can prevail in a war against hell." Then Devedas looked toward a young warrior in a uniform that might once have been purple and white but was now the color of blood dried in sand. "Rane, if this one interrupts me again, toss him out that window."

"I will do so with great delight, sir."

The upstart judge bowed his head and stepped back, which was wise considering they were several stories up.

"The judge is not wrong, but these are strange times, and I'm not a man bound by tradition. My obligation is to keep the people of Lok safe, whatever that entails. Ashok Vadal has told us that your rebels are willing to set aside your quarrel with the Law in order to help us against the demons."

"Oh, we've been having a *quarrel* now, is it?" Thera laughed. "You make it sound as if it's such a small thing, the killing of so very many of my friends."

Devedas shrugged. "I'm too weary to play games with words. Call it what you will. I watched noble Protectors struck down by illegal alchemy you put in the hands of lowly fish-eaters. I saw firsthand the brutal atrocities your kind inflicted upon the cities you captured in Akershan."

"That madness was not my doing."

"Yet it was done in your name. As I'm sure a great many terrible things have and will be done in mine. War between whole men and non-people proved to be a futile, bloody waste. I'm willing to put that in the past because we can agree the demons are far worse."

It was odd, being able to finally put a face to someone she'd heard so much about. This was one of the only men in the world Ashok respected. That was not a thing easily earned, so it would be best not to trifle with him. She would be direct. "I'm sure you've had eyes on my force since we've gotten close to the Capitol, so you know I'm not boasting when I say it's a potent one. I have the fearsome Sons of the Black Sword at my command, as well as an army of gunners straight from Fortress itself."

There were nervous mutterings at that. These illustrious men knew how vulnerable they were. Had they survived demons only to be destroyed by rebels? Would their deaths not be from sea creatures with armored hides, but rather a delusional criminal in humble desert garb?

"Calm yourselves, first caste. My army came here to aid the Capitol, not occupy it."

"That same army destroyed the Capitol's aqueduct. Why would we believe you?" asked a one-eyed Protector.

Devedas did not threaten to have that one thrown out the window for interrupting. Surely attempting to do so would prove fatal to the Maharaja's poor bodyguard, but more likely, Devedas allowed the question because it raised a valid point.

"You spilled casteless blood long before we spilled the Capitol's water."

"Yet now you offer help. What changed your mind?" Devedas asked.

"Simple. The gods told us we needed to protect the Capitol, otherwise the demons would win, and all mankind would fall."

While the other high-status types were obviously aghast at her brazen illegal religious talk, Devedas gave her a sardonic chuckle. "Ashok told me the same thing. He's many things but liar is not among them. It sounds to me that these so-called gods of yours are some manner of magical construct that manifests in the form of a glowing giant who dispenses vague proclamations which have a troubling tendency to come true. Sadly, it appears your gods also have terrible timing. This warning came too late."

Thera spread her hands in mock apology. "They speak when they want, but they're never, ever wrong. They said the fate of the world would be decided here. We marched this way quick as we could, and set a pace that would make any army in Lok envious, so my assumption is that the demons must be coming back to finish the job."

"That's probable. Demons don't occupy. They kill until they're sated, return to the water, then strike again when they feel like it.

This is just the beginning." As a Protector, Devedas understood the methods of hell far better than most. "After what we saw there can be no doubt a new war is upon us."

She had to remind herself that this was no sheltered politician like most Capitol inhabitants. "Your army is hurt. It'll take time for you to gather more soldiers from the houses . . . if they bother to send any at all. My army is fresh and ready to fight, but our service does not come cheap."

"Name the price for your offered aid, witch."

As she was the one here claiming to speak for gods, she took no offense at that title. "The price is an immediate end to the Great Extermination." As Thera said that she noticed that a young lady who had been sitting off to the side was suddenly very interested in what she had to say. She was a rather pretty, yet simultaneously mousy, little thing, with lenses of glass perched upon the top of her head. Thera hadn't noticed her before because while the other high-status types had been posturing, she had been quietly reading a fat old book.

"That's already been done," Devedas said.

"Is this true?" She looked toward Ashok, who nodded in the affirmative. "You've officially called off the genocide?"

"I can present whatever evidence you require to prove that was one of the first things I ordered when I took this office. The Great Extermination is over. Its architect is a fugitive in hiding. The few who balked in public at this reversal, I had hung. The command to leave the remaining fish-eaters alone was sent to every Great House the day of my ascension. Is that all?"

That was a lot, but it would not be nearly enough. If such a terrible thing had been ordered once before, surely it could be ordered again. "There must be a change of status. There will no longer be a division between non-people and whole men, but *all* will be considered whole men under the Law."

Despite Devedas' earlier threats about silence, the reactions of the high-status types to that outlandish demand was noisy outrage. "She wishes to do away with the castes?" one woman wailed. "That's the very basis of society!"

"Your precious society will not survive more demons," Ashok snapped.

The Maharaja held up one hand, and his underlings obediently shut their mouths before Ashok had to kill anyone to protect

Thera's honor. Devedas licked his teeth, considering her request. "It is said every man has his place. Where would you put all of these casteless? Would you make them workers? Warriors? Surely they don't belong in the first."

"Let the people figure it out for themselves. Let them make their own place," Thera said. "As you did yourself, Maharaja. When the Law left you nothing, you carved for yourself a throne. If you could accomplish so much, why not let them make the best of their little lives? You may think they're beneath your contempt, but the casteless dream and yearn the same as you or I. Let them."

"You ask for much."

"I'm not done."

Devedas laughed. "Ah, Ashok. I see now why this is the one who finally caught your attention...Name your next ludicrous demand, woman. I've got a continent to protect, with or without you."

"Allow the practice of religion."

There were gasps. She might as well have screamed her offense to the sky and challenged the entire Capitol to a duel. The Inquisitor reflexively reached for the hilt of his sword. Ashok stepped in front of Thera, ready to slaughter the entire room on her behalf.

"Stand down, imbecile," Devedas told the Inquisitor. "Oceans, you damnable idiots, be still or I'll kill you myself." Then, he addressed Thera politely. "What you ask...is madness. It is the end of order. It goes against everything the Capitol has ever stood for."

"The Capitol doesn't look to be standing very well right now at all. To me, it looks like one strong breeze away from being blown over."

"These things you ask for would never be accepted by the first caste."

"I don't need to convince them anymore, though, do I, Maharaja? I only need to convince you."

The woman who had been reading the book stood suddenly. From her manner of dress she was obviously of the first, but her finery was torn and stained with blood, as if she'd been laboring among the wounded, which was a very un-firster thing to do. "I would offer counsel."

"Please do," he said. Thera didn't know who this was, but

Devedas seemed to care a lot more about her opinion than the rest of these fools combined.

"Both the casteless and the religious have existed among us for centuries. When the fanatics worship in secret, no one knows of their internal disobedience, because outwardly they live compliant, orderly lives. It's not until the Inquisition backs them into a corner that they fight with the desperation of trapped animals. It isn't until the casteless are treated too harshly, or threatened with slaughter, that they rebel against us."

"What do you think of her demands, then, Rada?"

"Though what the rebel woman asks for sounds outlandish, I do not think it would be that great a change in practice. I believe the Law is best used to punish individuals who do harm, not to punish whole groups for believing wrongly, or being born too low. If a fanatic hurts others or steals their property because his false gods told him to, then punish him as we would any other murderer or thief, but if he harms no one, then leave him be to believe what he wants." She gave the masked Inquisitor a look of pure contempt as she walked over and put her hand on the Maharaja's shoulder. "We've been so afraid of what these fanatics *might* do that we created an Order so meddlesome and tyrannical that they became far more dangerous to us than the thing they were supposed to protect us from."

"This woman speaks wisdom," Thera said. "Leaving us alone is a small price to pay for the service of the only army that's available to defend this place. We were told the demons were invading, and the future of man would be decided here. It was our duty to protect this city or else all would be lost. Accept my terms, or don't. I'm long past caring about the feigned offense of the Law-abiding."

Devedas scoffed. "And if I fail to agree to your mad terms, instead of helping us, you could just as easily attack us. You've seen the state of this place. You must understand how far away help is. The Law would be trapped between rebels and demons."

"Your words, Maharaja, not mine. I didn't ride all this way to bark empty threats."

"No, I'm supposed to believe you did so because some magical creature ordered you to, and thinks only the untouchables can save us."

"That might not be as mad as it sounds." The woman, Rada,

showed the book she'd been reading to Devedas. "I've been going over everything there is in the restricted collection about the rain of demons, because if we stopped them before, then surely there must be a way to do so again. I've found one consistent thread throughout all the ancient's tomes. Even long into the Age of Kings all were in agreement that the bloodline we now know as the casteless will be necessary to defeat the demons when they come again."

"Which is clearly now," Devedas said.

"Undeniably so," Rada agreed. "But if descendants of this Ramrowan—whom the Law later made into non-people because of their crimes—are essential for our survival now, as all the old scholars believed, then you should grant them the protection of the Law. There are far fewer of them now than there were a few years ago. Elevate the survivors to the status of whole men. Then if the bloodline of Ramrowan does somehow help repel the demons as the ancients hoped, my husband will forever be known as Devedas the Wise."

"And if the casteless don't?"

"Then we're probably all going to get eaten by demons anyway so there won't be any generations after us to remember our names at all. Worry about the politics and details later, my love. Protect your people now. All of them."

Rada spoke with such great and seemingly heartfelt sincerity that even Thera believed her, and the only person in this room she trusted was Ashok. The Maharaja pondered on her plea for quite some time. The judges standing around the table seemed poised to faint under the stress of waiting for his decision. In a small way, Thera felt sympathy for the plight he was in as a leader. Whatever path he chose, someone would be upset. But her people had a thousand guns, so to the ocean with what the rest of them thought.

After a nervous minute, Devedas stood up and walked around the map table toward Thera. For a moment, she worried that he might be coming over there to murder her with his implausible Protector speed, but Ashok was standing right beside her, and as long as he wasn't worried, neither would she be.

Devedas extended his right arm in the southern style of agreement. "Your terms are acceptable, Thera Vane."

Thera clasped arms with the Maharaja.

And just like that, a rebellion ended.

"This cannot be!" the perfumed judge shrieked. "This is barbaric! This is—"

The young bodyguard wasted no time. He immediately struck the judge in the mouth with his fist, then grabbed hold of his neck and dragged the thrashing man to the window, the glass of which had been broken at some point during the attack, so he didn't even need to open it in order to hurl the judge headfirst through it.

He screamed all the way to the bottom.

Devedas didn't bother to look back. "Thank you, Rane."

"My pleasure, sir. I tired of the stink of him."

Thera let go of Devedas' arm. "Then it's settled, Maharaja. The castes and the casteless will share the same fate, whatever that turns out to be. We no longer fight each other, only demons."

"One can hope. As you just saw, some of the first caste will not agree with such a controversial decision. I'll deal with them later. For now, let's figure out how to stop the army of hell."

"First, please allow me to send a note to my army that the two of us are now on good terms," Thera suggested. "I'd hate for them to get nervous waiting outside. They can get rather agitated when they're nervous."

"That's wise. I'll send a few water wagons out to them as well. That's a thirsty journey."

She looked to Ashok, who said, "That would be appreciated." Apparently, treacherous as he was, Devedas wasn't the poisoning type.

It was odd to Thera that so much in her world had changed so very abruptly, but she supposed that was just the nature of things. Devedas was not a good man, but he was a powerful man. Yet in this dire moment she had used that cruel and ambitious man to accomplish a miraculous good. At any other time in history, such momentous changes would have been impossible, but right now everyone was far more worried about a demonic invasion than upsetting their society...Would the great houses refuse to obey Devedas? Would his new decree be gutted by the long knives of politics? Would all of Thera's efforts be for nothing?

She supposed they'd just have to survive the demons long enough to find out.

Runners had been summoned and Ashok had written a brief

note in a simple code that he had taught to his officers. Ashok whispered a few things in that messenger's ear, and then sent him to Eklavya. He told Devedas, "I have asked for one of the Fortress men to be brought here. His customs will seem odd, but his knowledge may be valuable."

"Do the Fortress folk even speak our language?" Devedas asked.

"It is close enough. He knows about how the demons are traveling."

Devedas gestured toward the great map. "We're using black stones to mark demon sightings. The Chief Judge surely would have hired a sculptor and a painter to create tiny demons, but the city's artisans are a bit indisposed right now. Inquisitor Zankrut, has the Tower received any new messages by magic?"

The mask who'd placed his hand on his sword against Thera's words earlier stepped forward, obsequious since the Maharaja had made his decision to deprive that Order of their greatest purpose. His compliant nature was no surprise. If the Inquisition expected to survive, they had best make themselves useful to their king somehow. "There have been new demon raids in many places along the coast, and several miles up every major river, but all of them involve only one or two demons at a time, and most of those areas have been depopulated since all the casteless went into hiding. However, there's been no sign of the great demonic army since it left the Capitol. They were last seen entering a hole in the ground where the village of Shabdakosh once was."

There was a pile of black stones there on the map.

"We can't watch the demons after they go beneath water or dirt, so we don't know where they'll strike next," muttered one of the phonthos who was standing next to Kharsawan on the map. "Forgive me. May your advisors speak freely now, Maharaja?"

"That's what you're here for. Proceed."

That phontho took a nervous glance at the window the judge had been tossed from before continuing. "The Capitol still commands your great army in the north, but as the people learn what has befallen us here, that army will surely fragment. Soldiers will want to rush back to defend their own great houses from the demon threat. No great house possesses an army sufficient on its own to stop the force we saw here. The demons will be able to destroy any city they wish with impunity, one by one, leaving us weaker and weaker as they go."

A woman of the first, who wore an insignia of a plow on her sash, spoke up. "It's not only the direct attacks we have to worry about, Maharaja, but their effects. As trade and agriculture are interrupted, starvation will surely follow. The granary stores across most of Lok are already at dangerous levels because of the disruption caused by the Great Extermination and the war in the north."

Devedas paid a great deal of attention as the woman—who must have been from whatever Order kept track of important things like crops and famine—continued her dire predictions. Though their outlook was grim, it did make Thera feel a bit better about her new arrangement to see that the Maharaja actually seemed to care what happened to his people. That was a small comfort, considering she had no idea how her army was supposed to keep demons from razing this place to the ground. What good was commanding an army of guns, if the bullets simply bounced off the enemy?

They were silently joined by the Fortress collector, Yajic, whom she'd left waiting downstairs. The poor little man seemed very overwhelmed to be here, but then he was as awestruck and fascinated by the map as she'd been, only Thera had hidden it better. It appeared to take all of his self-control to keep from stealing any of the tiny buildings and sticking them in his pockets.

"What's his purpose?" Devedas asked when he spied the foreigner.

"His obligation is called Collector," Ashok explained. "His kind knows about the ancient tunnels the demons are using to move their army beneath Lok. That's why the things came out in Shabdakosh instead of directly under your feet as they did in Kanok."

"Can you show us, Fortress man?"

Yajic did the odd salute of his people. "Sure, I can. Many of the dark paths are collapsed and others flooded so only demons can go down them, but every collector has seen the old maps written in metal on the walls. I'm honored to remember these paths for you, o great king who has long been prophesied."

Devedas seemed unsure if that was a compliment or an insult.

"Fortress has been expecting us." Ashok did not elaborate on that further. "Knowing where the tunnels lead will help us predict the demons' other targets and adjust accordingly."

"I beg you, great king, give me a moment. I will figure out where the path the ancients called the main line runs, and from there I will get the forks in the path." Yajic eagerly scurried around the outside edge of the map, trying to reconcile his Collector teachings with the geography of a continent he'd never been allowed to see until recently. "Your land is very pretty. In the short time I've been here I've seen grasslands and plains, tall mountains, and hot deserts. My land is all gray and rocks." Being unaware of the status of the various important people clustered around the table, Yajic simply shoved them away, until he stopped at the south end of the table, near the representation of Kanok, and pulled a ball of string from his belt. He looked around, then handed one end of the string to a phontho with four stars on this turban. "Hold this."

That illustrious officer did as he was told, and then Yajic climbed up onto the table. From the gasps, that was a terrible violation of protocol. Yet no one claimed offense because Ashok would surely serve as the strange little foreigner's chosen duelist. The collector walked toward the Capitol, unfurling his string. He tried not to crush too many carvings and was mostly successful.

"The demon army is probably going to heal up, and then come back to finish us off," the one-eyed Protector mused.

"They won't even need to," Devedas said. "A city of this size shouldn't exist in this trackless waste to begin with. The Capitol is a monument to hubris. It was only built here to be as far from the sea as possible, but the sea came for us anyway. The Capitol survives on caravans, and those will turn back as soon as they encounter the fleeing hordes. We must face the ugly truth. The Capitol must be abandoned for now."

Thera couldn't accept that. "The Voice was clear. If this city falls, we're all doomed."

"I can't wage war according to the dictates of your imaginary god."

Ashok scowled. "I do not know what the Voice is, but it is not *imaginary*."

"Your faith doesn't outweigh my logistics, Ashok."

Collector Yajic paused in the middle of the map and looked around. The string now made a line from Kanok to Mount Metoro. "It is said the rock was too hard here, even for the ancient diggers." Yajic looked around, then looped the string around the representation of the Tower of Silence to hold it in place, so that he could veer a bit to the east, then he continued walking, leaving sandy boot tracks on the paint.

It seemed backward to Thera that she had to plea on behalf of the Capitol to the man who ruled it. "The Voice sent us to defend the city of man."

"Wait..." Rada turned to Thera and asked with utmost earnestness, "What exactly did this being tell you?"

For a first caster and supposedly Law-abiding woman, the lady who was apparently married to the Maharaja seemed remarkably nonchalant about the existence of gods. "The Voice isn't exactly known for its clarity, but it said we need to rally all our forces and I need to lead my army in a great battle."

"I mean specifically, as pertaining to the location."

Thera had no memories of when the Voice took over, but she'd heard this one repeated so many times by the witnesses that she had no issue getting it right. "The Voice declared: *Soon the master of the next age will be determined in the great city of man.*"

"Ah! Then your army might not be too late after all."

"What do you mean?" Devedas asked.

"Assuming this Voice creature is a remnant of the prior age, *the Great City of Man* is a term the ancients used long before the Capitol was settled. This is its sign." Rada opened her book and quickly flipped to a page in the middle, to point out a peculiar symbol. "Up until when the demons fell from the sky and destroyed everything, this signified what was the largest city in the world at the time. It was a place of splendor and the center of magical research and governance. This symbol is used often by the Asura's Mirror." Thera didn't know what that was, but Rada looked excitedly toward her husband. "I know this symbol well because I saw it many times as I searched the city's tombs to fulfill my promise to Thakoor Harta."

Yajic reached the opposite end of the map and hopped off the north coast. Arbiters moved out of the way as he pulled the string tight. That action knocked over many of the colorful flags representing several different armies surrounding the second biggest cluster of buildings on the map.

"Behold the path of the main line, partially collapsed and all flooded now, tragically lost to us collectors, now pathway of demons."

The string cut through the heart of Vadal.

"All is not lost yet, because the Great City of Man was never the Capitol," Rada explained. "It's Vadal City."

Chapter 48

The sun set over the Capitol.

Ashok Vadal stood upon a balcony high atop the Chamber of Argument, looking out over the husk of the place that had administered the Law he had so faithfully served for so many years.

Even so late in the day, the desert wind was hot.

Karno Uttara joined him at the balcony. His arrival was surprisingly quiet for a man of such imposing strength.

"Protector Karno."

"It's just Karno now, Ashok. I'm a Protector no longer. My obligation has ended."

"Was that by choice? Or by command?"

"A bit of both, I suppose."

Ashok grunted in acknowledgment.

The two old friends hadn't had a chance to speak since the battle. There had been wounded to help and fires to fight. There was no weariness, of both body and spirit, quite like what came after a defeat.

Karno looked out over the silent ruin. It belonged to the vultures now. "In the end, what did we protect? It feels as if the Law is collapsing. Was all our service for nothing?"

That was a question that Ashok didn't know if he possessed

wisdom sufficient to answer. "We did good on the Law's behalf. We also did evil, unquestioningly...Most of those we hurt deserved it. Some did not."

"The Law said they did. That was all I needed at the time."

"Save lives. Take lives...We did what we were told, what was expected of us. We burned villages together. We were taught to never doubt the rightness of the Law, Karno, but a man who does not question his actions will inevitably go too far..."

"Yet here we are."

"Here we are..." Ashok agreed. "When I was in Fortress, one of their monks would yap incessantly about their beliefs. About how all deeds have consequences."

"That is obvious."

"The Guru did not speak just of the cause and effect in the real world, but beyond as well. They believe in more than endless nothing. Their monks say there will always be good and evil in the world, right and wrong, just and unjust. Our intent and actions, both good and bad, are recorded upon us, and that determines our status in what comes next. Our deeds will be weighed at the end of our lives, and we will be tested to see if our good outweighs our evil."

"Like on a scale?" Karno asked.

"I think so." Guru Dondrub had blathered for hours about such things. Ashok had not paid attention to most of it, but watching a city die made one contemplative.

"There's not a big enough scale in the world to measure what you've done," Karno mused.

"That is likely true." Ashok mulled that over, but not for long, as he was not given to philosophy.

"We're not dead yet, though. As long as we live, we can stack more weight on that scale." Karno glanced toward the north. "The armies march tomorrow morning for Vadal. Criminal and Capitol united in vision...We live in strange days."

Ashok had just returned from a scouting mission into the desert. The new senses granted to him by the shard had confirmed that the underground path suggested by the collector was accurate, and the demons had moved on. Far beneath them the army of hell was slowly making its way toward Vadal. The combined armies of man would be waiting for them there.

"Will you ride with one of those forces, Karno?"

"I have not decided yet."

"The Sons of the Black Sword would be honored to serve with a man of your courage."

"Hmmm..." Karno thought about that. "Can you imagine Karno Uttara fighting alongside religious fanatics?"

"Did you not hear? That's legal now."

Karno actually laughed, which was a rare sound indeed. "*Very strange days.*"

The two of them watched the city together for a long time.

"May I ask you something, Karno?"

"Of course."

"Your obligation was over, so why were you here? You wear the uniform of a caravan guard, an obligation for disgraced warriors trying not to starve. You never struck me as a man who would lower himself to mercenary work. I always thought in the off chance you did not die as a Protector, you would return to the green fields of your homeland, request a plump wife, and find a quiet place to grow crops."

"That sounds pleasant. I would have several children and die a long time from now, a content grandfather, tending my garden. I do not think these hands are meant for war alone. I would like to grow something with them before I'm through."

Ashok had never held such illusions about himself. "Yet, you were here, pretending to be something you are not, in a place I know you have always despised for its dishonorable ways. Why?"

The big man sighed. "My obligation was officially over, yet it didn't feel complete to me. So I went where I thought I might be needed."

"You followed Devedas all this way in secret?"

"No...I followed his wife."

Ashok raised an eyebrow.

"It's not like that. Devedas usurped the Law. He surely broke it to do so. What's done is done. He may yet prove to be a good king, or he may become a tyrant. We've both known him at his best and his worst. We both know either outcome is possible."

The last time Ashok and Devedas had met before the Battle of the Capitol, Ashok had ended up in the sea with his throat cut. Yet during that duel Angruvadal had stopped Ashok's heart in order to spare Devedas' life, and yesterday, Devedas had made concessions to Thera's rebellion that had shown incredible mercy to millions. Had correcting that terrible injustice been why Angruvadal had stopped Ashok from slaying his former brother? How much would that single bold declaration weigh on the Fortress gods' judgment scale?

"As you say, what's done is done. Now we can only hope for the best."

"Hope is for fools, Ashok. Devedas is a great man, but he is an irreparably flawed one. As are you, just in different ways."

Ashok took no offense at that, because the truth was the truth.

"No. Devedas *might* become a great king someday, but I know Radamantha *will* be a good queen. I have watched them both under circumstances where one's true character is demonstrated. Where he is consumed by pride, she is guided by compassion. When he is overcome with anger, she seeks knowledge. He is ruled by passion while she is ruled by reason. For this new Law to govern with wisdom, it will require her to temper him."

Karno had always been an astute observer of humanity. It was what had made him such an effective investigator of crimes. "So should we survive the demons, Lok's best chance to not descend into endless house war and criminal madness is the odd Library girl who needs panes of glass over her eyes to see?"

"Yes," Karno stated, without any doubt whatsoever. "That conclusion is what drove me to steal an artifact from a Vadal wizard to return to her, and why I have been watching her from a distance ever since."

"And that's the only reason?" Ashok had always respected the straightforward assessments that had earned his former brother the nickname Blunt Karno, but Karno was still a man. Not nearly as flawed as Devedas or Ashok, but still human nonetheless. Not all Protectors possessed black hearts. "It sounds to me as if you have become infatuated with her kindness and intellect."

"Then your ears are broken."

Ashok had been designed to be a creature of pure devotion to the Law, yet Karno had nearly equaled him in accomplishment, simply by always trying to do the right thing as he saw it. Even if he was in love with another man's wife, a man this honorable would go to his grave before allowing even the idea of impropriety to creep into his mind. Ashok suspected Karno had no scale, because he doubted there was a god worthy to sit in judgment of Karno's morals.

"Devedas is going north to take command of his army there. Only a minimal number of the first will remain in the Capitol to manage it. The Maharani Rada, the remaining judges, and the leadership of the various Orders are being taken to the Astronomers' holdings on the other side of Mount Metoro—where the collector says even demons cannot burrow—to govern in exile. She will be extremely well guarded there. Do you feel your obligation has been seen to for now?"

Karno grunted in acknowledgment.

"Then you are more needed in the north. Come fight demons with me . . . brother."

Karno looked out over the Capitol one last time as he pondered which path to take. It took a while because he did nothing without great consideration. "If criminals are to be our last chance against demons, then I suppose I must ride with criminals."

"They could use a good example of what a Protector should be. So far they have only had me."

"I will join you in the morning, brother." Karno walked away.

Though he had much to do in preparation for tomorrow's journey, Ashok remained upon the balcony, for his meeting with Karno had been happenstance. The appointment that had brought him to this secluded place to begin with was late, but that was to be expected when dealing with someone of such importance.

Maharaja Devedas arrived long after the last of the sun had vanished over the mountains. He joined Ashok and leaned upon the edge of the balcony, clearly exhausted.

"It's odd, Ashok. Normally this city would be filled with lights by now. The bands would just be beginning to play as the bitter sun went away. The theaters would be opening. The sports games starting. Tens of thousands would come out to watch and make merry. Families . . ." Devedas trailed off. "So many of those are dead now. The rest are running away. This is supposed to be a place of excitement and prosperity. I find this quiet unnerving. It's an insult."

"You wished to speak with me?"

The most powerful man in the world looked over at the most dangerous man in the world. "The Law has made peace with the rebellion. You and I have not."

"I did not choose our war, Devedas."

"Grand Inquisitor Omand chose your war for you . . . Did you know he used you, and the threat of you, to destabilize the judges? They held plays about you in that very amphitheater below us. The shows were trite, but effective, propaganda. The secret casteless Black-Hearted Ashok and his undefeatable sword are coming to murder the judges and overthrow the Law! The first hugged their children tight, frightened that Ashok would come to slaughter them in the night. You were his ultimate implement of terror until he gained control."

"I reasoned that out eventually." Being chained to the wall, starving in a Fortress dungeon, had granted Ashok the time and clarity to understand how much he had been used. "I will kill Omand for this if given the opportunity."

"Get in line."

"I have thought about killing you as well, Devedas."

"Of course you did. If you didn't, then you wouldn't be you."

"You must have committed many crimes to claim your title. Even now I wonder if our alliance is a mistake."

"Omand may have planted the seeds, but I harvested the crop. Be happy your rebels get to eat the fruit." Devedas took a deep breath, and then exhaled. "I had to hunt you down, Ashok. Omand turned you loose on the world, but he didn't understand what he'd done. How could he? He's not like us. He thought you were merely some weapon to be wielded against his political enemies, and then thrown away once you'd outlived your usefulness. But I knew what you really are."

"What is that?"

"A spark that would refuse to go out, hot enough to ignite a flame sufficient to burn the whole thing down. And it turns out I was right…What I don't know, is what are you now?" Devedas looked to him, earnestly seeking wisdom, too resigned and weary to be bitter about it. "I saw how you fought those demons. You were the best swordsman in the Order, maybe the whole world, maybe even who has ever lived! But *that*? That was far beyond the capability of any bearer or wizard. If we were to repeat our duel…"

"It would be over before it began," Ashok stated without exaggeration. "You would perish."

"You know how much it pains me to admit that, but even I can't deny it. But how?"

Having repeatedly survived trauma that would have killed even the mightiest Protectors, Ashok had given it much thought. "When demon magic is fused with human flesh, it creates a hybrid creature, possessing elements of each species, far more dangerous than either of its progenitors."

"You're clearly not tainted by demon like those freaks."

"Not demon, but the other form of magic." Ashok put his palm to his chest. "Black steel. There has been a shard buried in my heart since the first Angruvadal was destroyed."

"Impossible. That was years ago. No mortal body has ever withstood that much exposure to pure concentrated magic for so long. The Heart of the Mountain is the maximum extent that a man can be changed by magic, and that's barely a drop in all our blood. Trying to use the Heart a second time always results in agonizing death."

"I'm unsure if I'm capable of dying anymore."

Devedas was incredulous. "Then throw yourself over this edge to test that theory."

He had nothing to prove. "I prefer to test it against the demons."

Devedas shook his head and laughed. "So the only casteless bearer ever, who showed up the rest of us Protectors, who then went and became the most infamous criminal in the world, is now the first hybrid of man and black steel... Oceans, Ashok, you always had to be the special one, didn't you?"

"You know I asked for none of those things."

"I know! That's what makes it even worse. You give all and ask for nothing for yourself in return. You're the effortless living paragon of duty and justice and honor and bravery every other thing a man is supposed to aspire to be. Everyone always said Ashok Vadal was born to great purpose! No wonder these glowing god-thing creatures picked you to be their champion. Who wouldn't?"

"Be careful what you mock. It appears the gods chose you as well."

Devedas scoffed at the absurdity of that. "Oh, really?"

"These beings called me to be their warrior, to protect their Voice. Only they predicted a new king would rise as well, long before either of us were born. It is obvious now they spoke of you."

"Sure they did."

"It is the truth. It was written in metal a thousand years ago in Fortress. Probably here as well, but the Inquisition destroyed those records whenever they could find them. I could have killed you in Garo. In that instant I wanted you to die more than you can imagine. Only Angruvadal gave me a heart attack to stay my hand. My oldest friend stopped my heart to spare your life."

"Your oldest friend also gave me this." Devedas touched the mighty scar on his cheek.

"And yet you still failed to learn your lesson. Jealousy is your greatest weakness, Devedas. I am not the only one born to greater purpose. So are you, but you must accept it is a different purpose than mine."

Devedas considered this for a time. "You never lie."

"I'm not incapable. I simply prefer not to. I speak no lies now. The gods, whatever they really are, gave us black steel, and black steel still serves their mysterious will. Angruvadal has spared your life twice for a reason. Maybe it was for you to give the fanatics and casteless the protection of the Law? Few others would dare to make such a tremendous change. Maybe your part is done, or maybe it is just beginning. I do not know. All I do know for certain is that all black steel is intertwined and of one will. That will is for you to be here now."

Something Ashok said there seemed to shake Devedas to his core. He frowned, deep in thought. "All black steel is one? Explain this."

"This is the second ancestor blade I have carried, yet it is also Angruvadal. Black steel is matter forged to share the same ultimate purpose, united across distance and time in a way we cannot comprehend. The will of the swords is the same, and everything they have done is to fulfill the designs of their original creator."

"They're all the same, pushing our lives in different directions." Devedas remained leaning against the railing, deep in thought for a long time, but then suddenly he shuddered, as if overcome by a tragic memory. He even had to reach up and wipe moisture from his eyes. "Oceans."

Surprised, Ashok scowled, for he had rarely seen such weakness from Devedas, and they had been children in the Order's brutal program together. "Why do you weep?"

"Something from my past suddenly makes more sense . . . My father was a bearer."

"I'm well aware. Your prideful entitlement over that broken sword is how you earned that scar."

"Except I never told you what my father confided to me alone after his sword broke. It was the last thing he ever said to me before he leapt off a cliff in his despair. I never told anyone else what he said—not family, not our instructors, not even you."

Having lost an ancestor blade himself, Ashok understood all too well what that felt like to a forsaken bearer. The connection was so great, that having it snatched away was like losing a vital part of yourself. If he'd not been assigned the greater purpose of protecting Thera, he might have followed the example of Devedas' father and hurled himself into the sea.

"People wondered what he did wrong to displease it. Only my father told me he knew our house's ancestor blade didn't shatter because of him or anything he did." Devedas looked to Ashok, stricken. "The sword revealed to him that it shattered because of *me*. Because I was his heir, I was everything expected of me and more, but I wasn't ever meant to bear that sword. Our ancestor blade destroyed itself, and ruined our house and our name, rather than let me have the chance to wield it."

Ashok was taken aback, because suddenly the pieces fit. So this was why Devedas had always been so inhumanly driven to achieve, to test and prove himself beyond reason. He thought the sword had found him unworthy and because of that unworthiness everything he had ever loved had been destroyed.

"You blame yourself for the fall of your family and the end of your house. Even your father's suicide. Your entire life has been spent trying to prove a broken sword was wrong about you."

"I was only a boy, Ashok."

The gods could not allow their intended king to have an ancestor blade. Then he would have been able to rely on the instincts of the generations that had come before him. They could not give him that crutch. For this darkest time, the gods required a strong leader, a man of singular will and focus, who would do whatever it took to prove himself, regardless of Law or cost. A man who, once wronged, would never be content, ever restless, and always striving for more.

So they had built that man.

Just as Ashok was the son of the black sword, Devedas was its orphan.

As Devedas came to this profound understanding of his own nature, Ashok felt pity for a king. He reached out and rested one hand on his former brother's shoulder.

"We are no longer enemies, Devedas. Our war is over."

Devedas wiped the last of the tears from his eyes and composed himself. It was doubtful he would ever show weakness again. "Agreed. Our feud is in the past."

"Be a good ruler, and it will remain there."

"And if I'm a poor one?"

"I have been a rebel before. I would not hesitate to be one again."

Devedas smiled. "So you're my conscience now, Black-Hearted Ashok?"

"I always have been."